Praise for Iris Johansen's previous bestsellers

SIGHT UNSEEN

"The stellar team of Johansen and Johansen is back with the next installment of this clever and terrifying suspense series . . . Filled with frightening twists and terrifying turns, the book ends on a cliffhanger. The reader's heart will be racing the entire time, so waiting for the next book is going to be difficult!" —*RT Book Reviews* (4½ stars)

"The Johansens do a page-turning job of tying up all the loose ends in this complex cat-and-mouse game, but they always manage to leave one thread dangling: just the kind of ploy designed to keep loyal series fans eagerly anticipating the next installment." —*Booklist*

"A thrill-a-minute, chill-a-minute thriller that keeps reader[s] on the edge of their seats. Each character is minutely defined and believable; the good guys, the victims, and the executioner. Iris Johansen and her son Roy Johansen are true masters of page-turning terror guaranteed to shock and awe you." —*Reader to Reader*

CLOSE YOUR EYES

"Gripping . . . The authors combine idiosyncratic yet fully realized characters with dry wit and well-controlled suspense that builds to a satisfying conclusion." —*Publishers Weekly*

"Mind-blowing . . . The scenes with Adam and Kendra ooze sexual tension, making this thriller a titillating delight." —*Booklist*

"Intrigue at its best!" —*Reader to Reader*

"Gripping."   —*Booklist*

"[In *Silent Thunder*] . . . you'll be rewarded with a bumpy roller-coaster ride as you try to separate the good guys from the bad."   —*Rocky Mountain News*

"Talent obviously runs in the Johansen family . . . The duo has no difficulty weaving in fascinating technical details with the explosive action of this nonstop stunner."
                                                   —*RT Book Reviews*

"*Silent Thunder* [is] another grab-you-by-the-throat dash that pulled me along on a frantic chase for a deadly puzzle piece."   —*BlogCritics* magazine

"[A] smart and exciting thriller."   —*Ellenville Journal*

"[An] action-packed book about the search for a hidden treasure."   —*Treasure Coast Newspaper*

"Ms. Johansen and Mr. Johansen have put together a captivating tale of thrilling suspense . . . It was a real edge-of-your-seat page-turner."   —*Night Owl Romance*

"*Silent Thunder* is an intelligent and riveting espionage thriller, peopled with mysterious characters, and a first-class narrative."   —*Reader to Reader*

"*Silent Thunder* is very much a suspense-filled, exciting thriller."   —*Romance Reviews Today*

ALSO BY IRIS JOHANSEN

THE PERFECT WITNESS

IRIS JOHANSEN

St. Martin's Paperbacks

This is a work of fiction. All of the characters, organizations, and events portrayed in this novel are either products of the author's imagination or are used fictitiously.

THE PERFECT WITNESS

For information address St. Martin's Press, 175 Fifth Avenue, New York, NY 10010.

ISBN: 978-1-250-06724-1

Printed in the United States of America

St. Martin's Press hardcover edition / October 2014
St. Martin's Paperbacks edition / June 2015

St. Martin's Paperbacks are published by St. Martin's Press, 175 Fifth Avenue, New York, NY 10010.

10 9 8 7 6 5 4 3 2 1

CHAPTER ONE

SHE WAS BLEEDING . . .

The pain in her side was almost overwhelming.

Teresa could hear the three men behind her in the forest, crashing through the underbrush.

Run.

No time to try to stop the bleeding. If she didn't get away from them, there would be another bullet, another wound.

Or death.

She had been lucky to have seen them coming up the road toward the cabin and guessed that they had been sent to kill her. She had slipped out of the cabin, but they had caught sight of her running into the woods. She had heard Mick Judaro shout to Tantona when he saw her. He's been surprised, they'd thought she'd be easy game. But she'd been waiting for them for the last three days.

Waiting for death.

No, she wouldn't let them kill her. She could feel the anger tearing through her, smothering the fear.

"Stop, Teresa. We didn't mean to hurt you. That was only supposed to be a warning shot." It was Hank Tantona calling out to her. "We were just sent to bring you back. You know me. I've watched you grow up. I was at your sixteenth birthday party last month."

She had not wanted to have that party, but Mother had insisted. She had said it would look strange if she didn't throw a party for her. And she had been aware of Tantona leaning against the wall while she blew out the candles. Smiling, joking with her father. She hadn't been able to look at him.

His memories were too dark, too ugly, swirling around, pushing into every corner of his mind. He didn't try to keep that ugliness tucked away. He was proud of it.

Like her father.

But she had learned to shut herself away from her father's memories. She wouldn't have been able to survive living with him if she hadn't.

She ran faster.

"I know you're scared," Tantona shouted. "But Rico Camano doesn't want to hurt you either. He only wants to talk to you. He was a good friend to your father. He wants to find out who murdered him. He thinks you can help."

Liar. Liar. Liar.

"But you have to obey Camano just like you did your father. After all, he's our boss now, Teresa. He's the Don. And your father would like him to be in charge now that he's gone. Camano will treat you well if you just do what he says."

Camano would kill her. She had seen it in his face at her father's funeral. He had smiled at her and patted her shoulder, but she could still feel the coldness of him.

Then he had smiled at her mother, Gina, and she had smiled back.

And Teresa had known that she was alone.

"But if you don't stop, we may have to take you down, Teresa," Tantona called. "We'll try not to hurt you again, but I can't promise. Just give up and let us talk to you."

Her breath was coming in gasps, and the pain was getting worse. "Blood," she muttered. She had to do something about that blood . . .

"Yes, you do."

She paused, startled at the words that had come out of nowhere. Her gaze flew to the path in front of her.

A man stood on the path a few yards away. Tall, dark-haired, gleaming, light blue eyes. Dressed in dark jeans and sweatshirt. She didn't recognize him. He was a stranger. But everyone was the enemy.

Her hand tightened on the branch in her hand, then she crouched and swung the branch at him like a club.

He grabbed it and wrenched her arm until the branch dropped to the ground. "You don't have time for this. I'm no threat to you, Teresa."

She punched him in the stomach.

He muttered a curse and swung her around and shoved her up the path. "I told you I was no threat. Get out of here. You have only a few minutes. I'll take care of Tantona and the others. Wait for me on the hill, and I'll look at that wound."

She hesitated only for a second, then took off running again. She didn't know what was going on, but it couldn't be worse than what she was facing now. He was a stranger, but strangers couldn't be any more dangerous than those people with whom she'd spent her entire life.

Mother . . .

Don't think of her. It hurt too much.

Keep running.

She heard a scream behind her. Then a curse, then another sound that was like a grunt.

Had Tantona killed him?

The wet shrubs were striking her face as she ran up the hill.

Get away. He had told her to wait, but he was probably a dead man.

If he wasn't, he could be just as much a danger to her as the men who had shot her. She couldn't trust him. She couldn't trust anyone.

"Dammit, stop." The stranger's voice behind her. "You're okay now. No one's chasing you. Correction. No one but me. Stop."

She kept running.

Two minutes later, he tackled her from behind and took her down.

She rolled over, and her fist struck out and hit his mouth. Then she butted her head up and struck his chest as hard as she could.

Dizzy. Her head was spinning.

But she tried to do it again.

He muttered a curse as he straddled her and pinned her shoulders to the ground. "I'm not going to hurt you, you little tarantula."

"No, you're not," she said fiercely, and moved her head, so that she could sink her teeth into his hand on her shoulder.

He didn't move but said through clenched teeth, "Get your fangs out of me, or I'll knock you out and explain later. Do you want me to prove that I'm not one of Camano's errand boys? I will. No problem. Let's go down the hill, and I'll show you their bodies."

She stiffened and removed her teeth from his hand. "That doesn't prove you're not just as bad." She was silent, looking up at him. "Did you really kill them?"

He shrugged. "It was the only way to stop them. Camano had given them orders. He would have taken you alive, but he'd be relieved if you were dead."

"How do you know what Camano wants or doesn't want?"

"Not because I belong to his fine organization. He's as dirty a gangster as your father was before him. I don't give a damn about him." He met her eyes. "But I do give a damn about you. I want to help you."

"Bullshit. I don't know you. Get off me."

"Then let me introduce myself. My name is Andre Mandak. And I'll get off you if you promise you won't kick me in the nuts or run away. And if you'll let me take a look at that wound and stop the bleeding."

"Why would you want to do anything to help me? I don't know you."

"You've said that before. Maybe I'm just a good Samaritan."

"Bullshit."

"You've said that before, too. I know you're scared, but think. I saved your life. Why would I want to take it now?"

"I don't trust you."

"You don't trust anyone. Deal with it. I'm the only game in town."

She stared up at him, then slowly nodded. "Get off me."

He swung off her and helped her to her feet. "I'll take you to my car on the road and see if I can stop that bleeding and—"

"I'm not getting into any car," she said flatly. "And

how do I know that you really did kill those men who were after me? Maybe it's a lie to trick me." She started back down the hill. "I want to see them for myself."

"Really?" He followed her. "Are you sure? Corpses aren't a pleasant sight."

"I have to know if you lied to me." Her hand was holding the wound in her side. It was wet with blood. Pain . . . She had to keep on going. "If you work for Camano, too, I don't think you'd kill his men. It wouldn't make sense. So I might be able to trust you to— No, but maybe I could—" She stopped again. She wasn't thinking clearly. She whirled to face him. "But you took away that club I had. If you really want to help me, give me your gun or something else to protect myself if you've lied to me."

"What?" He shook his head. "I didn't expect that." He hesitated an instant. "No gun, that would be too easy to turn against me." He reached in his jacket pocket and took out a long, slender dagger. "That's not enough to prove I'm on your side?" He gave the dagger to her. "No, I guess not."

"I have to know that they're dead. Then I might be able to listen to you and decide what you want from me."

"And someone is always wanting something from you, aren't they, Teresa?" he asked quietly. "You're only sixteen. How long has it been going on?"

"None of your business," she said jerkily. Don't give in to the weakness. Put one foot in front of the other. "Where are Tantona and the others?"

"You're my business, or I wouldn't be here," he said roughly. "And part of that business is keeping you alive. Will you give this up and let me stop that bleeding?"

"Where are they?"

"Behind those trees up ahead. You're running a big risk just to see if I'm lying to you."

"I know. How else can I find out? You could be tricking me. But you could have killed me back there. I don't know why you didn't. Either way it's a risk. I can't trust anyone. But I have to find out for sure who I have to fight."

"By all means, go check them out. Considering the fact that your dirtbag father raised you as a Mafia princess, I'm sure you shouldn't be shocked at a few dead bodies."

He was angry, she realized. Were those words supposed to hurt her? It didn't matter. Nothing mattered but finding a way to get away from Camano.

She faded to the left when she reached the trees and tried to creep quietly forward in case there was someone in wait for her. Her hand tightened on the dagger. She stopped and listened.

No sound.

Her gaze searched the darkness.

She went a few steps deeper into the trees.

The first body she saw was that of Georgie Sohler. He was lying crumpled beside an oak tree. His head was twisted at an odd angle.

Shock. She stopped short, then forced herself to keep on walking.

A few yards later she saw Mick Judaro lying with eyes wide open staring at the sky.

"Seen enough?" Mandak asked, behind her.

She shook her head, moving forward.

Tantona's throat had been cut, and there was a pool of blood on the ground around him.

Dead. All dead.

"Satisfied?" Andre Mandak asked.

"Satisfied I'm safe from them." She couldn't take her eyes from the wound in Tantona's throat. "Not satisfied that I'm safe from you. You're a murderer like them. You killed them all in just a matter of minutes." She was dizzy, and it was hard to form the words. "Maybe you're . . . worse than they were."

"Or better. It depends on how you look at it." He took a step closer to her. "But I'm not going to hurt you, dammit. Now let me—"

Her knees were buckling. She was falling . . .

He caught her before she reached the ground. He took the dagger from her hand. Then he lifted her and was carrying her through the trees.

"Let me . . . down."

"No way. I've wasted enough time already. I can't be sure that Tantona didn't phone a location to Camano while he was chasing you."

"Camano already . . . knew I was at the cabin. That's why he sent them."

"How did he know?"

"She . . . told him."

"Who?"

"My mother." It hurt to say the words. "She . . . told him."

He was silent. "You're sure?"

"I'm . . . sure."

"Son of a *bitch*."

He was angry again. She didn't think that it was with her this time . . . "What are you going to do to me?" She moistened her lips, then said fiercely, "I won't let you kill me. I'm not going to die. Do you hear me? I'll fight you."

"I know you will. You're ready to fight the whole damn world." He was looking straight ahead. "But you don't listen. I'm not going to hurt you. I'm your best hope to stay alive."

"Why?" she whispered. "If you help me, Camano will kill you."

He didn't answer.

And she didn't care. She was getting dizzy again. It might be okay to hope that he didn't want to hurt her or kill her and just let go . . .

"You were wrong about me," she whispered. "I've only seen one man who had been murdered before tonight. But he was shot in the head. Hideous . . ."

"Your father did it?"

Jokman's skull exploding and blood and brains blowing in all directions.

Guilt. Terrible guilt.

Scream. She had screamed . . .

"No, I did it. It was me . . ."

Darkness.

GLITTERING STARS. TALL TREES. Wisps of smoke.

A crackling fire only a few feet away.

And Andre Mandak was kneeling beside her, his gaze focused intently on the bandage he was applying to the wound in her side. He looked up as he felt her stiffen. "Back with me? I was beginning to worry. You lost quite a bit of blood. The wound isn't all that bad, just a flesh wound. But you probably suffered shock."

"Where are we?"

"After I stopped the blood, I drove twenty or thirty miles down the road and set up camp to finish the job." He was buttoning up her shirt. "You need blood, but it's not urgent. I'll get you to someone I trust to check my first aid within the next twelve hours or so." He smiled. "But I don't anticipate any complaints. I'm pretty damn good."

She shook her head. "You're crazy. I'm not going to take that chance. I don't know or trust you. Why should I trust your friend?"

"No reason. Except that from now on I'm going to run the show."

"Bullshit."

"That's the way it has to be," he said as he moved a few yards away from her. "Unless you particularly want Camano to kill you or get his hands on you. Neither would be pleasant. I understand that he has certain ambitions in which he thinks you might be a help or hindrance."

"I can run. I can hide. I don't need you."

"The hell you don't. If I help you, you'll survive. If I don't, you may last six months." He smiled and coaxed, "Come on, Teresa. Use me. People have been using you for most of your life. It's your turn now."

She stared at him. He had suddenly turned from brutal frankness to a charisma that was almost mesmerizing. She had only been vaguely aware of him as a man since he had appeared in her life tonight. He had only been a threat and a puzzle and the faint stirring of hope.

Close-cut dark hair, blue eyes beneath slashing dark brows, high cheekbones, and a beautifully shaped sensual mouth. How old? Late twenties? Early thirties? He was dressed in dark jeans and a sweatshirt that revealed he was lean but muscular and very strong in spite of his slimness. He had carried her with no problem at all. "Who are you? Not your name, Mandak. Who are you to me?"

"Who am I?" He thought about it. "Your savior? Your teacher? Anything else will have to be worked out between us."

"Savior?"

"I killed three men for you tonight. Doesn't that qualify?"

"How did you even know I was in those woods tonight?"

"I've been waiting . . . and watching. I knew it was going to happen soon."

"What? How?"

"Because it wasn't reasonable that they'd let you go peacefully. It would have been too dangerous for Camano." He paused. "I didn't know that your mother was involved."

"I don't want to talk about her," she said shakily. "She didn't mean for anyone to hurt me. She loves me."

"Very well. But I had to know if she's a threat."

"Why? Why do you have to know anything? Who the hell are you? How do I know that you won't try to sell me to Camano? I don't *know* you."

"But I know you. I've been watching you for a long time." He held up his hand as she opened her lips to speak. "I'll tell you as much as I can. I've been keeping an eye on your father and his relationship with you for the last few years after it came to my attention."

She stiffened. "What came to your attention?"

He only stared at her.

"What?" she said through clenched teeth. "You're bluffing. You don't know anything about me. You couldn't."

"I know your father discovered what he thought was a treasure trove in you and exploited it for at least two years. I know Camano probably killed him and is wavering between trying to use you the way your father did or killing you to be sure you don't reveal that he was the one who ordered the kill." He paused. "Tell me, do you know for certain that it was Camano?"

"How could I?" she asked cautiously. "Even the police weren't sure that he killed my father." Her lips twisted. "Not that they cared. They were just glad to get rid of one more gangster. When Camano became Don, they just refocused their attention and forgot about my father." She had a sudden thought. "Or maybe they didn't. Are you with the police? Is that how you know so much about me?"

He shook his head. "God, no. But it's refreshing of you to jump to that connection. At least, you're not still thinking I'm going to sell you to Camano."

"I'm not sure that you're not. You know too much about me." She defiantly met his eyes. "Or do you? Just what do you know, Mandak?"

"You want it all? I know that you're the only child of Antonio Casali and his wife, Gina. Casali was pretty much a scumbag and involved in murder, vice, and longshore racketeering. He was so dirty he managed to climb up to head the New Jersey Mafia. Three weeks ago, he was gunned down in the streets in Trenton." He paused. "You went to the funeral, but then you disappeared from view. I assumed that it was your mother's doing to get you away from Camano, who had just taken power. Is that right?"

She nodded jerkily. "I thought that it was going to be okay. I prayed that she wouldn't do it."

"Do what? Betray you?"

She didn't answer.

He was studying her face. "Too late," he said softly.

"You've already slipped and told me too much. You're her daughter. Why would she do that to you, Teresa?"

"Why should I tell you?" she asked bitterly. "You believe you know it all. But all that stuff you rattled off doesn't mean anything. Guesswork. Or you could have read it in the newspaper."

"Then should I go a step farther? Your parents were far too busy to take care of you. Your father was a mob boss who had ambitions to take over the entire Northeast territory. Your mother liked being married to Casali and acting the queen bee. She had no time to be a mother. You were sent away to boarding school from the time you were six. You didn't seem to mind. You did extraordinarily well at school. You're exceptionally bright, and very early on, the teachers found that you had a special talent. You have a photographic memory."

She stiffened. She didn't like where this was going. "No big deal. It's not common, but photographic memory isn't really that special."

"Special enough. The school principal advised your parents, and they were curious enough to bring you home and show you off for amusement value. Your mother particularly liked to be the center of attention. The glow didn't last long, and they sent you back to school about six months later." He grimaced. "I'd bet you were relieved. You liked your books and your teachers and had no desire to be a star."

But those months had held their own magic, she wanted to tell him. For the first time, she had felt important to her mother. Her father was always cold and had never paid any attention to her. But her mother had been a beautiful butterfly who fluttered and smiled, and occasionally lingered in Teresa's world for brief instants. "Are you nuts? I was no star. I told you, a photographic memory isn't all that rare."

"But you were relieved to go back to school?"

"Maybe."

"But it didn't last long, did it? Two years later, the school expelled you and sent you home. They couldn't deal with you." He paused. "Would you like to tell me why?"

Her hands clenched into fists. She couldn't breathe. He *knew*.

"Shall I tell you?" he asked softly. "It wasn't the photographic memory. They could have handled that in a student. But that talent had changed, metamorphosed, in those two years. The teachers and students were regarding you as a freak. They felt insecure and afraid of you."

Nightmare time. Loneliness. Oh, the aching loneliness. It was all rushing back to her.

"They were idiots. I didn't want to hurt anyone."

"I'm sure you didn't," he said gently. "But even the teachers weren't prepared for what you were able to do."

"I didn't want to do it. I'd just look at them, and it was there before me."

"What?"

She didn't answer.

"What, Teresa?"

"Why are you asking me? I don't know who told you. But you *know,* damn you."

"Tell me."

"The memories," she said unevenly. "I could read their memories. Whenever they remembered anything, it was clear as glass to me."

"You couldn't read minds but you could read past thoughts, past actions, memories. Intimidating."

"I didn't want to do it. I didn't know what was happening to me. At first I thought I was actually reading their minds. But it was blank for me unless they were remembering something. But one was as bad as the other. No one would believe me. They thought I was lying." She moistened her lips. "But it was worse when they did begin to believe me."

"They kicked you out and sent you back to your parents."

"I was glad to go. I didn't think it could get any worse."

"But it did."

"Yes," she whispered. "My father . . . was interested. It wasn't like before when I was just a curiosity. He thought that I might be . . . He wanted to see if he could use me."

"Your mother?"

"She said I should do whatever my father said. She said this time we had to keep it a big secret just between the two of them and me. She made me go to this fancy Dr. Kramer on Fifth Avenue. He was a psychiatrist. He told my mother and father that he didn't believe in what the school was telling him, but he'd investigate and let them know." She said hoarsely, "I hated it. He kept asking me questions. Over and over. He wanted to know how I knew when I was making contact with someone's memory. I told him that it was like being sucked into a dark tunnel, and I was suddenly just there. He told me to stop making up stories. He'd use big words like 'hippocampus' and 'frontal cortex'. He'd tape wires and stuff on my head. He'd bring in strangers and try to trick me

into saying the wrong things about what they were remembering. It went on and on . . ."

"But then he found out you weren't making up the
stories."

"Yes, all those tests showed that my brain appeared
to make contact with the amygdala segment of the brain
of anyone with whom I came in close contact. Those are
the cells that harbor memory. He told mother that there
was evidence of stimulation in both brains. He said that
my sensation of being pulled into a tunnel was my mind
focusing, making adjustments."

"That tunnel signal interests me," Mandak said. "It
may indicate you're struggling for control."

"Control? Are you crazy? I have no control. I just have
to accept. My mother was excited. But she told me that I
wasn't to go back to see Dr. Kramer. He wanted to write
an article for some medical journal, and that was making my father angry. He didn't want anyone to know
about what I could do."

"Exit Dr. Kramer. What happened to him?"

"I don't know. My mother said that he was going to
Europe to study for some degree."

"How convenient."

Though she had accepted what her mother said at the
time, that's what Teresa had thought in the years that
followed. People who displeased her father often just
went away never to be seen again. "I was glad at the time.
I hated going to his office."

"But you hated more what happened when your father
and mother believed his report."

"Yes," she said jerkily.

"And what did your father make you do?"

She didn't answer for a moment. She didn't know why

she had already told him as much as she had. Secrets . . .
Her mother had told her that she mustn't tell anyone,
that it was a secret. But she was alone now, and this
man might have saved her life. And just telling someone
about those years made her feel less vulnerable.

"They'd sit me down in the library with my father and
whoever he chose to bring home with him," she said
haltingly. "Sometimes it was one of his men, sometimes
a politician, sometimes it was someone from another
mob. He'd ignore me, but he'd laugh and joke with them.
I guess that they thought it was a little weird to have me
there, but maybe they felt safer and more at ease having
a kid in the room. After they'd left, I had to tell my father
what memories had surfaced in their minds during the
visit." She closed her eyes. "So ugly. Mean and cruel
and ugly. Memories are never anything like what's on
the surface. They're almost always selfish, and the reasons why anyone does something are usually based on
what they remember as being good or pleasant for them
in the past. But often what those men thought pleasant
was cruel and bloody and—" Her eyes opened, and
she stopped as those memories began to come alive for
her again. "Sometimes I wanted to throw up. I begged
my father not to make me do it. He wouldn't listen. My
mother said that it was my duty and that I mustn't say
anything that might upset him."

"Did it continue until he was killed?"

"No." She drew a shaky breath. "Until about six months
ago. I knew what my father was by that time. At first, I
was numb and scared and just did what he told me to do.
Then I began to wonder what effect my telling my father
about those memories was having on those people he
had me read. One night Ned Jokman came to see my

father. He had worked with him for years. His memories were . . . bad. Death. Cheating. Bribes . . . After I gave my father the report, he seemed angry. He stormed out of the house. I followed him. He went to the guesthouse, where Jokman was staying. My father's men dragged Jokman out into the woods and made him kneel." She shuddered. "My father shot him in the head."

Blood and bits of skull and brains flying everywhere.

"I screamed. I kept on screaming. My father hit me and hit me again. I deserved it. It was my fault." She swallowed. "My fault. My fault."

"No, it wasn't."

"Don't tell me that," she said fiercely. "I told my father what Jokman remembered doing, and he dragged him out into the woods and killed him. It wouldn't have happened if I hadn't told him. It wouldn't have happened if I'd shut away those memories and blocked them."

His eyes narrowed on her face. "Can you do that?"

She was silent. "Sometimes."

"Not often."

"But I can pretend," she said quickly. "I can make people think I'm not able to do it any longer."

"Is that how you kept your father from forcing you to tap into anyone's memories after he killed Jokman?"

She was silent.

"It would be the only way to do it," he said. "He wouldn't give up such a prize advantage, and he obviously didn't give a damn about you. Did he make it rough on you?"

"Yes."

"How?"

The regular beatings with the belt. The ropes. Isolation, verbal and physical abuse.

"It doesn't matter. It's over."

"Your mother didn't interfere?"

He didn't understand about Gina. Nothing bad ever touched her. Beautiful butterflies never interfered in anything ugly. But she had come to Teresa after every punishment and held her in her arms and dried her tears.

"I know, baby," Gina had whispered as she held her close and stroked her hair. "I grew up with beatings, too. You just have to do whatever you have to do to survive. Give him what he wants, if you can. Just remember that I'm always here for you."

"Teresa?"

She didn't answer.

"You fooled him?"

"I had to make him believe me," she said jerkily. "I couldn't do what he wanted any longer. It helped that I couldn't stop crying for days after it happened. He thought maybe I was going crazy."

"Yes, I can see how that would help convince the son of a bitch," Mandak said harshly. "A raving maniac wouldn't be of much use to him." He was silent. "Did you try to get away from him?"

"Once. He caught me and locked me up. Then, two weeks later, he was killed, and I thought that I'd be free."

"But you weren't free. It's difficult keeping a secret as valuable and intriguing as your father was trying to do. Just the fact that you, a child, were present at certain crucial meetings was unusual. There had to be leaks. Camano knew about you and wanted to take over the action." He paused. "Or to get rid of you before you could read some of his own memories that might prove fatal for him."

"No!" she said sharply. "That wouldn't happen. I'm never going to do that again."

"But you can't help yourself, can you? You wouldn't do it intentionally, but if you leave yourself open, don't the memories come flooding?"

Her eyes widened in shock. "How do you know that?"

"Don't they?"

Panic was suddenly racing through her. Why was she even talking to him? Why had the answers to his questions tumbled out helter-skelter? Perhaps because he had already seemed to know so much already. But those facts could have been learned by diligent research.

But not the way the memories worked. That was what was scaring her to death. There wasn't any way he could know how that worked. No one could know how people's memories flowed gently to her at times and at others came and went like wind and thunder. Or how impossible it was to stop them when they wanted to be heard.

"I've frightened you." His gaze was searching her face. "You're such a tough kid, I keep forgetting that I'm supposed to deal gently with you. It's not my modus operandi."

"You didn't frighten me." Then she said hoarsely, "Yes, you did. You know too much. Things you shouldn't know. But it's nothing I can't get over. I just have to find out if it's going to hurt me."

"It might. But not right away. You'll have a chance to recover and develop good defenses. That's all I can promise you."

"Are you being honest with me?"

He smiled faintly. "Yes. Can't you tell? Why don't you see what kind of horrendous memories I'm storing away? It might help."

"I told you that I won't do that again. It's not what—"
But she could feel the familiar darkness of the tunnel
pulling her, his memories flowing toward her, overwhelming her.

And she could feel herself reaching out, searching . . .

Nothing.

Blank.

Reflecting like a mirrored golden wall.

She was stunned.

"You've never run across a block?"

"You can do that?"

"Yes, and so can you if you let me help you. Accept it.
Isn't it really a relief not to be able to read me?"

Relief? It was weird and terrifying. There was nothing comforting about this blankness. It was like looking
at the edge of a machete that could turn and cut in a
heartbeat. "Who are you? You said you weren't the
police."

"And I'm not. That doesn't mean that I can't offer you
a certain amount of protection." He opened a bottle of
water and handed it to her. "And that I may eventually
be able to give you a gift that you'll find priceless."

"What gift?" she asked warily.

"You have a talent that's wild and erratic. I can teach
you to block and control. Wouldn't that be wonderful?"
he asked softly. "I can give that to you, Teresa."

"I don't want to control it. I want to get rid of it."

He shook his head. "That's not one of the options."

"Then just let me go, and I'll work it out for myself."
She took a drink of water, then asked, "Why can't I read
your memories?"

"Control and blocking. Which makes me stronger
than you. You've been surrounded by people who have

made you a victim. Aren't you tempted to make sure it doesn't happen again?"

"All I want is to get away from here and stay alive."

"That's part of the package."

"It is?" She was trying to think, trying to work it out. "You know what's happening in my head. Or at least some of it. Is it because you're a freak like me?"

"You're not a freak. You're very special." He shook his head. "People call me special, too, but I don't possess your gift. You're not unique, but your ability is very rare. I don't share it."

"Be grateful," she said bitterly.

"Oh, I am. I have enough on my plate without that. But it's not as if I couldn't deal with it. It's a tricky path, and you've just been dealing with the wrong guides." He smiled. "For instance, I'm a guide without equal."

"You think well of yourself."

He nodded. "Confidence is a valuable weapon."

"But even if you aren't like me, that doesn't mean you're not a freak. Special is only a pretty word for it. People use you, and when they're through with you, they push you away because you're different."

"Then you learn to wear a mask and push back when it becomes necessary."

"Like you pushed back tonight? You killed those men."

"It was necessary. If they'd caught you, they would probably have killed you. Wouldn't you have fought back?" He stared her in the eye. "Didn't you intend to kill if you had to do it?"

"That's different."

He chuckled. "It's always different in the first person."

"But you had no reason to do it. You had no quarrel with them. You could have walked away."

"No, I couldn't have walked away." He paused. "And I had a very good reason."

"What?"

"I had to pay in advance for services rendered."

"What services?"

"Future services."

"What future—" She stopped as he shook his head. "Services. That means you want to use me, too."

"I won't deny it," he said quietly. "But you'll find I always pay for what I want. But you're not ready for me to offer you a deal yet. We'll discuss it later."

He was being annoyingly deceptive. She changed the subject. "How do you know what goes on in my head? Are you some kind of slimy egotist like Dr. Kramer?"

He shook his head again.

"Stop *doing* that." She wanted to hit him. She was brimming with frustration. "I want to know who you are and what you have to do with me."

"I'm sure you do, but that's not an option, either. You'll find out in time, but you need that time. You're only sixteen, Teresa."

"You say you want to help me, but that's not true, is it? You're like everyone else. You said you wanted to use me."

"Yes, I do." He reached out and gently tucked a strand of hair behind her ear. "In the end, we all use each other. I'll take what I want from you. But I'm giving you a chance to grow and strengthen and fight me. I consider that very generous. Don't you?"

She didn't know what she thought. His hand was exquisitely gentle against her temple, and his light eyes were mesmerizing. She was tired and frightened and desperate, and she had to ignore the physical appeal of Mandak. It had nothing to do with who he really was. Her father had been sleek and handsome, too, but inside he was ugly or he'd never have had those chilling, callous memories. And she couldn't know what memories Mandak was hiding, and that was scary in itself. "It's all double-talk. How do you expect me to make sense of you?" She went on in a rush, "That doesn't mean I'm going to let you fool me. What . . . How would you keep Camano away from me?"

"Have you disappear. Create a new identity. You've heard of the Witness Protection Program? Something similar to that."

"It wouldn't work. They'd find me. My father had the police in his pocket. Camano took over and kept the bribes going."

"We wouldn't deal with local authorities. I have someone high up in the U.S. Marshals Service who would make sure that all information was strictly confidential. Josh Dantlow would handle the details of your resettlement himself, and any communication would only be through him . . . or me."

She gazed at him skeptically.

"You doubt it would work? Dantlow would answer to me. There's no question that he would betray me."

"You killed three men tonight. If he's government, are you saying that he'd turn a blind eye to murder?"

"I'm saying that I have him under control." He shrugged. "And that he'd probably regard that scum as unimportant in the scheme of things. They all had records a mile long. I did the police a favor by removing them."

"Your opinion."

"And yours. You weren't crying when you saw those bodies. You were shocked. You were a little sick. But all you could think about was that men who were trying to kill you had been taken out. They were the enemy." He paused. "Like your father, like Rico Camano."

He was right, she thought wearily. Why was she arguing when she might have been dead except for his lethal intervention? He had been there when she needed him most. She could never trust him. She could never trust anyone. But by that single act of violence, he had formed a chain it would be hard for her to break. "But you're like Camano. You're like my father. You said yourself that you were going to use me." She glared at him. "How? I won't do it if there's any way I can get out of it. Would you beat me? Would you kill me if I learn too much?"

"A beautiful young girl like you? What a waste that would be."

"You didn't answer me."

"No, but I've told you that I'm giving you your chance to save yourself." He added, "And I'll promise to make sure that you'll be safe until you're ready for me. That will probably be at least a few years." He smiled. "After all, it would be to my advantage to keep Camano at bay and you alive. As you pointed out, you're no good to me if I can't use you."

"Promises? I can't trust your word. I don't know anything about you."

"You'll have the opportunity to learn more. Once I have you settled, I'll be visiting you frequently."

"No! I want you to leave me alone."

He didn't answer.

No, of course, he wouldn't. He had told her he was in control of the situation, and he was manipulating her into a position where he'd remain in control. "What . . . would you do with me?"

"Find you a safe place, surround you with safe people, let you grow and learn."

"It sounds too . . . good," she said doubtfully. "Where do you fit in?"

"Oh, I'm a very important part of the picture. I guard your body, and I give you gifts that only I can provide." He smiled. "Because I can teach you how to block those memories assaulting you and push them away to some extent. It's one of my more freakish talents. In some cases, I can also create a complete barrier and make you unable to read some of the people surrounding you so that you can have a few normal relationships."

Her eyes widened. "You could do that?"

He nodded. "My pleasure. I thought you'd like that."

Like? It would seem like a miracle to her. To reach out and touch and not have the poison of being thought strange or having everyone afraid of her. "It's been . . . a long time. Not since everything went wrong when I was a kid."

And he had probed and studied her and decided that this was an offer she couldn't refuse. The idea that he was right and that she desperately wanted what he said he could give her made her suddenly angry. "You're probably lying."

"I'm not lying," he said. "I promise you."

"How do I know that? You're setting all of this up and expecting me to go along with it. You can go to hell," she said defiantly. "I'll do what I please."

He smiled faintly. "And you'll be pleased to go along

with the plan at least in the beginning. The Witness Protection Program is eminently respectable and will give you the opportunity to take it on the lam if you begin to feel threatened. I'll have Dantlow give you impeccable references to verify his identity. On the other hand, it may be the only sure way to save your life. True?"

So true that it was filling her with desperation and panic. She had no money and no friends. She wasn't afraid to go out on her own, but she knew that the odds would be against her. And she would *not* let Camano kill her.

"It . . . might be true," she said reluctantly.

He nodded. "Then you agree."

She was silent, considering if she had any other choices. "Temporarily. Don't expect it to last."

He chuckled. "God, you're stubborn. And what a firecracker. Stubborn and full of anger and fire." His smile faded. "But who could blame you? Defense mechanisms all the way."

"You're talking like one of those doctors again. Are you sure that you're—"

"Very sure." He was putting out the campfire. "And now that we're on the same page, let's get the hell out of here. I had to take the time to bind that wound and come to terms with you. But I want to be over the Kentucky border by dawn."

"What's in Kentucky?"

"An airport at Louisville and a meeting with Josh Dantlow."

She stiffened. "You made an appointment with him before you talked to me?"

"Yes, and save the complaints. Time was important. You'll have a lot more to be pissed off about before this is over." He reached down and half pulled, half lifted her to her feet. "Can you walk?"

"Yes." Her knees were shaking. She took a tentative step forward. "Give me a minute."

"Screw it. Time's still important." He lifted her in his arms and headed for his car, parked by the road. "There's one other thing that I have to tell you." He was looking straight ahead. "Dantlow will ask you if you want to include any other family members in the Witness Protection Program. He'll ask about your mother. I didn't tell him that she wouldn't be acceptable." He smiled crookedly. "I didn't know myself. But you'll have to do it now."

Pain. Sadness. Not acceptable? Who would ever believe that beautiful Gina wouldn't be welcomed anywhere . . .

"Teresa?" He was looking down at her. "It has to be done. If it's true that she betrayed you to Camano. Are you certain?"

She didn't answer.

"Teresa."

"I'm certain." She cleared her throat. "I didn't want to believe it, but no one else knew I was here. I know she didn't want to do it. He probably lied to her. My mother knows she has to do what Camano wants her to do. She was always saying that we were both weak and had to obey if we were going to survive." She could feel the tears sting her eyes. "And I knew it was coming. At my father's funeral I could see it . . ."

"See what?"

"My mother. Camano. They were smiling at each other. She was remembering how much she liked being the queen that my father had made her. The fancy resorts, the designer clothes, the respect and fear she could sense in all the people around her when she was with my father. It was her whole life, and I could see that I wasn't important in comparison. It was only the power and the glamour she'd had as his wife. Now Camano has the power." She closed her eyes. "And I knew that she'd reach out and take Camano if she could get him. It would be her way to survive. I prayed she wouldn't." She whispered, "How I prayed . . ."

"She's his mistress now?"

"I guess so. Anyone would want her. She's so beautiful. I always thought she was like a wonderful butterfly."

"And evidently with a soul that was not at all beautiful. And certainly not wonderful to you."

"She never hurt me. Not like my father. She'd smile whenever she saw me. She even brought me presents sometimes." She opened her eyes. "She dazzled me. She dazzled everyone. So beautiful . . ."

"You'll be more beautiful in a few years. All her glamour and with character, too."

She shook her head. "You're crazy."

"And you have a softness toward your mother that could be fatal." He had reached the car and was putting her down on the passenger side. "You can't have any contact with her."

"I know. I'm not stupid, Mandak. Camano might force her to tell him where I am." She reached out to steady herself as he opened the car door. "I knew when Tantona and the others came for me that I couldn't trust her to save me. I have to look out for myself."

"Right. And you may see a beautiful butterfly, but I'm seeing a prime bitch." He settled her in the seat and fastened her seat belt. "Good riddance to her, Allie."

She frowned, puzzled. "Allie?"

He reached out and touched her hair. "Such pretty dark curls. It shines in the moonlight. It's a shame we'll have to tint it, but it's too eye-catching."

"Allie?" she repeated.

He nodded. "Get used to it. No more Teresa Casali. She's gone forever. You're Allie Girard."

Before she could answer, he'd slammed the car door and was running around to the driver's seat.

Gone forever. No more Teresa Casali.

The words repeated over and over in her mind as he started the car and drove onto the road.

Loneliness . . . and relief.

"I was wondering how you'd take it." Mandak's gaze was on her face. "First shock and then . . . ?"

"I can start over. No one will know I'm . . . weird. Fresh start. I can make my life what I choose." She grimaced. "If I can keep from getting killed."

"Not quite a fresh start. I'll still be in the picture."

"For the time being."

He smiled. "And I can see you're already plotting on how to rid yourself of me."

"It's possible." She lifted her chin and stared at him challengingly. "If I don't find a reason to use you as you say you're going to use me."

He chuckled. "I look forward to watching you make the attempt, Allie."

"Allie," she repeated, trying to get used to the sound of it. "What was the last name?"

"Girard."

She leaned back in the seat, her gaze on the darkness beyond the windshield. She could rid her life of that darkness. She could turn her back on all the ugliness. She could pretend to—no, she could teach herself to not let herself see what she should not see. If she was strong enough, determined enough, she'd be able to do it. She might even take Mandak up on his offer to help her conquer that helplessness that had made those years a nightmare. Why not? He'd made no secret that she was only a means to some complex, shadowy end to him. He had said use him, and she should have no compunction about doing it. Not if it meant that life could be different for her.

Teresa Casali was gone, never to return. Only this new, strange person was left to reach out and take hold and shape the world to suit herself.

A person named Allie Girard . . .

CHAPTER TWO

"SHE GOT AWAY." CAMANO muttered a curse as he hung up the phone. "And Tantona and the others are dead."

"What?" Gina raised herself on one elbow in bed. "That's not possible. How did it happen?"

"How the hell do I know? Navarro was driving the car. The last he heard from Tantona was that Teresa was running through the woods, and they were going after her. He tried to contact Tantona later, and there was no answer, so he went looking. He found the three of them in the woods. Whoever did the job knew what he was doing." He got out of bed and strode naked over to the bar and poured himself a drink. "Maybe you should tell me what happened, Gina? You told me your freak of a daughter has no friends. There was no way she could have taken down Tantona and the others herself. Not given the skill Navarro said the kills were done with."

"Of course she couldn't do it." Gina got out of bed and slipped on her cream-colored satin robe. "You don't understand. She's just a kid. Teresa is only interested in her books and music." She moved across the room to the bar. "And I don't appreciate your talking to me like that, Rico. Why would you think I'd know anything about how she got away? Haven't I done everything you asked me to do? I took her to the cabin, didn't I?" Her smile was dazzling. "Naturally, I know that you only meant to take Teresa somewhere more private than the compound and question her about a few things that are worrying you. I realize you would never harm her." She reached out and brushed her fingertips against his hand. "Now, may I have a drink, too?"

Camano felt a jolt of pure lust at her touch. Long, shining, dark hair, breasts and buttocks that made him get hard just looking at her. What a magnificent bitch. How many times had he had her tonight? He couldn't get enough of screwing her. He'd had a king-size craving for Gina since Casali had acquired her when she was only in her teens. She'd only gotten more sexy and alluring as the years passed. But then he'd had a craving for everything that belonged to Casali. It had been difficult to wait until the time was ripe to reach out and gather it into his hands.

But he hadn't realized that Casali's brat, Teresa, was something he was going to have to deal with. Not until he saw her looking at him at her father's funeral. Freak. All he'd heard might or might not be true, but he wasn't going to give up all he'd snatched on the chance that big-eyed kid could be a threat to him.

"I didn't say that you had anything to do with this." He poured Gina a glass of wine. "But I have to find out what happened. As long as Teresa is running around out there without you to guide her, she could be a danger to me."

"Then find her and bring her back to me." She sipped her wine. "I have no problem making her do whatever I wish. Antonio always relied on me to handle her."

"I'm trying to find her," he said through set teeth. "I've got men out there combing those woods to find answers. But she knows too much, dammit. I'm scared shitless that someone from the Vice Squad or the District Attorney's Office has heard about your freak of a kid and wants to question her. I've put an alert out to all our informants to see if there's any chat about her being snatched by the cops."

She shook her head. "The police wouldn't kill Tantona and the others, would they? Wouldn't they get in trouble or something?"

"Yes." Occasionally Gina came up with logic though that wasn't her forte. She preferred to twist reality to suit herself. "But Teresa might be valuable enough for them to run the risk."

"Because you're so important," she said. "And so smart." She took his hand and slipped it beneath the silk of her robe to cover her breast. "Too smart for any of them. But you shouldn't worry about Teresa's being a witness against you or the family. Even if the police have her, she wouldn't say anything if I didn't want her to do it."

His hand slowly tightened on her breast until he knew it must hurt.

She didn't flinch, and her smile never left her lips. "Do you want it that way? I know you're upset. You know I'll never say no to you. I'll love every minute of what you do to me." She opened her robe, took his other hand, and put it on her other breast. "Do whatever you want with me."

"Oh, I will." Gina was better than any professional

whore he'd ever paid. She never disappointed. He found her acceptance of any erotic play he chose to be mind-blowing. "You'll scream for me." He bent down, and his teeth closed on her nipple.

She inhaled sharply at the pain. "Good. And when it's over, I know you'll forget all about blaming me for Teresa. After all, none of it is my fault. She shouldn't have run when you only wanted to talk to her."

No, nothing was ever Gina's fault. But could she really be lying to herself to this extent? Yes, probably. It didn't matter. She could control her daughter. And he could control Gina Casali. "Yes, it's all Teresa's fault." He lifted his head and smiled into Gina's eyes. "We both know that's all I wanted to do. Don't we?"

FLAGSTAFF, ARIZONA

"What is this place?" Allie's gaze wandered over the snowcapped mountains in the distance as she went down the steps of the private plane. "Where are you taking me?"

"I thought you'd never ask. You haven't said a word since we got on the plane." Mandak followed her down the steps and took her elbow and nudged her toward the small terminal. "It's just a small private airport near the campus of Northern Arizona University. You'll be attending classes there in a few months."

"If I'd asked you anything, I'd have had to count on you to tell me the truth." She shrugged. "I'd already committed to doing what you asked. I knew I'd find out eventually."

His brows rose. "No curiosity?"

She'd been curious. But the entire situation was intimidating her, and she hadn't wanted to plead with him to tell her what she wanted to know. Not until she gained a little more confidence. "Maybe." She watched him as he signed out a tan Camry rental car at the curb. "Maybe not."

"Well, that's definitive." He opened the passenger door for her. "How is the wound in your side?"

"Hurts." She'd received a blood transfusion before they'd left Kentucky, and the weakness had almost disappeared. "But it's okay." She got into the car. "You made me rest on the plane. That probably helped."

"I had to make sure you were in top-notch shape." He went around and got in the driver's seat. "Perish the thought that I had even an ounce of humanity."

"I believe you're very human." She didn't look at him. "I can feel you . . . seething."

"Oh, can you?" He started the car. "That's interesting." He glanced at her. "Anger?"

"No. You're like one of those lava streams from a volcano. It would sear you to touch, but there's no malice present right now."

"You seem sure." His gaze turned speculative. "Perhaps you have another talent beside your gift for reading memory?"

"No. Heaven forbid." She grimaced. "I just sometimes feel things. It's not all that unusual for someone to be able to guess what others are feeling. It doesn't have to be freak-oriented."

"There's that word again. No, it's not that unusual. Quite common for anyone studying human psychology. You just appeared to be more certain than I would have thought." He chuckled. "Though I believe you've been studying and probing me since I wandered under your radar. I had the idea you were giving Josh Dantlow the same attention when you met him. What did you think of him?"

"Smart. Very nice." She looked out the window. "What you wanted me to think."

"And?"

"Did I let his memories flow to me? Yes, I had to be sure that he was what you said he was. He was relatively clean. A little tortured about putting his mother in a nursing home before she died. And he's a little afraid of you because of something you did last year. It kept floating and interfering." She looked back at him. "But I couldn't see anything that would make me think that he would hand me over to Camano."

"And that's all that's important?"

"I can handle anything else." She paused. "Where are you taking me?"

"I've rented a lodge in the mountains a few miles from the university campus. We have some work to do before I can turn you loose on your own."

"What kind of work?" she asked warily.

"Blocking, principally. You said that you couldn't be sure of its working every time. Sometimes not at all. You couldn't trust it. In crowds, you became overwhelmed."

"I didn't tell you all that."

"No, let's just say I had a 'feeling' that was your problem."

"Because you've known other freaks like me."

He flinched. "I'm going to have to insist that you refrain from using that word. It offends me. It should offend you. We're going to have to work on your self-esteem."

"There's nothing wrong with my self-esteem. I just don't lie to myself. I am what I am."

"Because people told you that you're a freak doesn't mean it's true."

"It doesn't mean that it's untrue. It's all a matter of perspective. In most people's eyes, I'm a freak." She looked him in the eye. "Right?"

He nodded slowly. "If you want to believe that other people have the right to judge. Personally, I think that's crap. Don't you?"

"That's a defense to keep you from admitting that—" She stopped. That sounded like something Dr. Kramer would say. "Yes, it's pure crap. No one should judge someone else if they're not harming anyone."

"Then we have an agreement. I'd better enjoy it. I have an idea they'll come rarely."

She changed the subject. "What else are you going to teach me?"

"Oh, a few other things. We can discuss it later."

"Why not now?"

"Because we've arrived." He pulled into the driveway of a small, rustic, one-story chalet. "You don't have to know everything right away. No curiosity, remember?"

"I didn't say that. I said maybe." She jumped out of the car as soon as it stopped. "Is anybody else here?"

"No, we have maid service every three days. Other than that, we're on our own."

"For how long?"

"Until you're ready for me to let you go." He got out of the car. "Come on. And try to relax. Didn't you say Dantlow vetted me when you were probing?"

She made a rude sound. "I told you, he's afraid of you. What happened last year?"

He sighed. "You're impossible." He unlocked the front door and entered into a large, high-ceilinged living room dominated by a huge stone fireplace and comfortable, brown leather furniture. "Your room is the second door on the right. Shower and change. Be careful about that wound and don't get your bandage wet. I'll make us something to eat."

She stood gazing at him uncertainly as he headed across the great room toward the open kitchen beyond it. She was suddenly feeling very vulnerable.

He looked back at her. "What's wrong? Do you need help? Say the word." He smiled. "I became fairly familiar with that body of yours while I was dealing with that wound. I've no problem with taking care of it for another night or two."

"No." She felt a flush heat her cheeks. She didn't know what he was thinking. His smile was slightly sensual though his words held no hint of intimacy. "I'm just catching my breath." She turned in the direction he'd indicated. "I can take care of myself."

"Pity." He turned back and headed for the kitchen again. "I'll give you forty minutes, then I'll check to make sure you're all right."

"I'll be fine," she said firmly. "Forty minutes."

"RIGHT ON TIME." HE TURNED as Allie came toward him across the great room. "You even washed your hair."

"Very clumsily." She made a face. "But it was filthy from the woods. I had to do it."

"And exhausted yourself." He held her chair for her.

"Sit down. Drink some water. I'll get the potpies out of the oven."

She picked up the water goblet beside the plate and took a drink as she watched him. It was strange sitting here. She felt awkward and uneasy. He was treating her as if she were grown-up and his equal. All her life she had been the victim, the child, the puppet. Her only importance had been the gift that was more a curse. No one had been interested in talking to her or asking opinions or wanting to be with her. Mandak might not want to be with her, but he was treating her as if she had value. It felt . . . odd.

"Here we go." He turned away from the oven and moved toward the table. "It's hot. Don't eat it yet." He slid the potpie onto her plate. He hesitated, looking down at her. "What are you thinking?" he asked softly.

She stiffened. "Why do you want to know?"

"Not to use it against you." He slid his own pie onto his plate and moved across the room toward the counter. "You just had a peculiar expression, and I wanted to know what was going on in that head of yours. I was simply interested. Unlike you, I admit to curiosity. I find you . . . extraordinary." He held up his hand as she opened her lips to speak. "And not in the way you think. That part of you is just something we have to work with. The other aspects of your psychological makeup are fascinating."

"Why?"

"You're a complex combination of child and mature woman. I'm wondering which side you're going to show me next." He sat down and spread his napkin on his lap. "And firecrackers are always interesting." He picked up his fork and repeated, "What were you thinking?"

She was silent. "I was thinking that no one but you

has ever treated me like this. Everyone else has always had a reason to . . ." She rushed ahead. "Not that you don't have a reason, but you're not looking at me the same way."

"You mean like a human being? Normal?"

"I don't know if—" She picked up her fork and started to cut the pastry on her potpie. "You confuse me. I have to figure you out."

"You bewilder me a bit, too. But I'm looking forward to exploring the unknown." He smiled. "Tell me, how are you used to having people look at you, Allie? Was I right?"

"I was weird. No one wants to be around people who are weird."

"On occasion, evidently your father did. What about your mother?"

"What do you want me to say? My mother wasn't bad to me. She was just busy."

"Too busy for you?"

"I didn't need her. I was busy, too."

"Doing what?"

"Reading, studying. I swam a lot."

"Yes, you could do all those alone. That would keep you away from everyone."

"I asked my mother if I could have my bedroom in one of the guest cabins. It's what I wanted."

"Was it?"

"Yes." She glared at him. "Don't be stupid. Why would you think I'd want to be near anyone? It . . . hurt. Sometimes it made me sick. If I stayed away, most of the time it would be okay."

"How far away? How close do you have to be to a person to risk being attacked by their memories?"

"Fifteen, twenty, thirty feet. It depends. Some people are stronger than others. But when I was in my father's office, it was always close enough to be clear." She swallowed. "Too clear."

"I imagine that's true." His lips tightened grimly. "He would want to make certain that you were superefficient when he needed you. Being alone might have been a good defensive attack, but loneliness isn't healthy for a kid. Didn't you have any friends?"

She shrugged. "When I was little, I used to play with kids at school. But that was before everything changed, and they didn't like me anymore. At first, they thought it was kind of cool that I knew stuff that only they should know. It was like I was some kind of circus act. But then it began to make them uncomfortable, and they didn't want to be around me anymore."

"They just didn't understand."

"Same thing."

"Not at all."

"Same result."

"Now I can't quarrel with you there."

"Because I'm right. People don't like what they don't understand." She looked up from her plate. "Why are you asking all these questions?"

"I told you, I'm interested. And curious. We're going to have to interact very closely. I want to be able to gauge your reactions."

"So you can try to manipulate me."

"You've accused me of that before. It's rather a mature charge for someone of your age to level at anyone. What do you know about manipulation, Allie?"

"I told you, I read. I study. In books, everyone is always trying to manipulate everyone else." She paused.

"And as soon as I realized what it was and how it worked, I recognized it. I watched for it. Like I'm watching you, Mandak."

"Intelligent. I'm not above trying to manipulate you to get my own way." He added, "But it's not purely a desire to manipulate, I'm genuinely interested in how you think."

"Why?"

"Because you're a rare find, and I'm beginning to discover that I want to see how you tick." He was silent a moment. "Though that may be very dangerous for me."

She was feeling uncomfortable. He was looking at her with an expression that was almost . . . sympathetic. She had become accustomed to his hardness, to that sharpness and sophisticated dry humor. She didn't know what to think of—

Pity, he was pitying her.

And she didn't like it. She didn't need his pity.

"I'm tired of answering your questions." She stared him in the eye. "Now I want you to answer mine. I don't really know anything about you. You know I have to go along with you because I'm scared of Camano, and you're dangling a way out for me. But I don't like it, and I want to know why I shouldn't bolt as soon as I get the chance."

"I'll give you a hint." He said quietly, "You can trust me to do the best for you until we're on level ground. Then you'll have to look out for me, Allie."

"I'm looking out for you now, Mandak." She took another bite. "And why do you think we're not on level ground?" She stared at him challengingly. "Prove it."

He threw back his head and laughed. "Oh, I intend to do that." He put a little catsup on his beef potpie. "But not now, eat your dinner and relax. Is there anything I can do to help you?"

"Talk to me. Tell me about who you are and why you think you can make me do what you want me to do."

"So that you can use it against me?"

"If I have to."

He shook his head. "Sorry. Not now. It's not the time."

"Okay, then tell me how you managed to kill Camano's men as if you were swatting flies?"

He smiled. "I'm very fast, and I've been trained by experts. Also, I spent several years as a mercenary in the Congo."

She studied him critically. "You seem pretty young for all that."

"You seem to be pretty young for all you've gone through, too. I have no intention of telling you tales of my bloody past, Allie."

"Okay, but who trained you?"

"I had a sort of mentor from the time I was a child. I had potential, and they wanted to make sure the potential was realized."

"Potential for killing?"

"No, the lethal training was to ensure that I was able to defend myself so that I'd be able to accomplish what I needed to accomplish." He shrugged. "Scenarios like the one with Camano's men aren't that unusual in my life."

"But it happened because you interfered with what they wanted to do to me. I don't think you make a habit of going around and swooping down to do stuff like that. That would be nuts. It would be stupid."

He chuckled. "Yes. And I try to avoid being stupid at all costs. But sometimes necessity dictates that I swoop.

You're very special, Allie. I couldn't take a chance. You're at a very crucial stage in your development. You could go either way."

"I don't know what you're talking about. I'm just trying to survive." She nibbled at her lower lip. "You said you could help me with blocking those memories. How do I know that you can do what you claim? Are you just telling me what I want to hear? All I've seen so far is that you can kill people. Anyone can kill people. I grew up with scum who could do that."

"I realize that," he said quietly. "But I thought I'd wait to demonstrate anything out of the sphere with which you're familiar. You'd be less intimidated by violence than intrusion."

"Intrusion?"

"You see, you're already prickling."

"What do you mean, intrusion?"

"I can't straighten you out without going inside."

Inside. He meant going inside her mind? Panic jolted through her. "I told you about that Dr. Kramer, who kept at me and wouldn't leave me alone. I won't go through that again. I don't need to be straightened out."

He tilted his head and looked at her.

"I don't!"

"You know better. It wouldn't be like what you went through with that doctor. He wanted to explore. I just want to clear the way."

"And what kind of magic do you think you can pull out of your hat?"

"No magic. But I have a talent for clarifying and unwinding all the twists. Once we get rid of all the debris, then I can lead you toward building protective walls."

"I don't believe you can do that. It's weird. It would make you more of a freak than I am."

"Certain talents exist. Accept it. Make the most of it." His smile faded. "Q and A is over, Allie. I've told you all I'm prepared to tell about myself. None of that is important. You're the one who has to talk to me. Your mind is closed, and I have to open it."

"Bullshit."

"You say that because you're afraid that if you open your mind, you'll be bombarded." He shrugged. "And it could work that way if it was anyone but me that you let come calling." He met her gaze. "But I have to come in and clear out all the debris and ugliness that have built up so that you can start building walls. And, yes, you'll be vulnerable."

"No, I won't," she said violently. "Because I won't let you near me."

"I could force it, but I won't do that. You've had too much force already in your life." He said gently, "But you will let me come in. I can be very persuasive."

"No. This is all crazy. I don't believe anything you're saying." She jumped to her feet. "And I don't have to stay here. I'll call that Dantlow and tell him I want him to come and get me. The only thing he cares about is getting Camano anyway. He'd do it . . ." She turned her back and stalked across the room toward her bedroom. "Stay *away* from me, Mandak."

"I can't do that."

"No choice." She slammed the door behind her. Her breath was coming in gasps, and she felt dizzy with panic. He had been so damn certain, so confident. He had made her believe that he could actually mess with her mind. Not that he would call it "messing." He would say it was all for her good, a cleansing.

As if she'd believe him. As if she'd let anyone close enough to hurt her.

Run away or call Dantlow?

She'd decide in the morning. She was too weak, and her wound was aching. She'd get a good night's sleep, then make the decision.

No, she wouldn't. Mandak had been too sure of himself and it was frightening her. She couldn't risk staying with him one more hour, much less a night. She had to get away from him.

She headed for the window.

Screw you, Mandak.

SHE HIT THE GROUND RUNNING as soon as she jumped the four feet from the window.

"Allie!"

She glanced back as she heard Mandak's voice. He was standing on the front porch, watching her. "I expected this." He started toward her. "Let's talk. Don't do this."

"Go to hell."

Running.

Darkness.

Trees.

Forest.

Familiar. So familiar.

Running from Camano.

Now running from Mandak.

"Allie!"

He was behind her, his feet pounding the earth.

Close.

Very close.

"Stop." He muttered a curse. "This isn't good for you. You're probably going to start bleeding again. I'm not going to hurt you."

"That's what Tantona said." She ran faster. "I don't believe you, either. Everyone lies to me. It's all lies."

"If it was lies, I would have spun you a much better story." His hand grasped her shoulder, and he spun her around. "Everything I told you was truth. It would have been much easier to lie to you."

"Would it?" She tried to struggle with him. Strong. Lord, he was strong. "I think you just wanted to scare me."

"That's the last thing I wanted," he said harshly. "This isn't easy for me. You're only a kid. I don't terrorize kids. I wanted to make this as honest and clean as I could."

"Well, you didn't do it." She freed one arm and slapped him. "Let me go." She slapped him again. "Let me *go*, dammit."

"I can't do that, Allie." He grabbed her close and held her immobile in his arms. "Now be still. It will be over in a minute."

"What will be—" Panic was rising within her. "What are you doing, Mandak? I won't let you—"

Dizziness.

Darkness.

SUNLIGHT . . .

Pine trees . . .

Butterflies . . .

Wonderful scents . . .

The wings of the butterflies were moving in slow, beautiful patterns through the forest, she thought dreamily.

Mama was like a butterfly . . .

But somehow the thought of Mama wasn't hurting her right now. She could accept the beauty without the thought of betrayal.

"I'm glad I could at least do that for you," Mandak said ruefully.

She turned to see him leaning against a tree, the sunlight shining on his dark hair. He was beautiful, too, but not like a butterfly.

"Thank God, for that," he said. "I would just have soon skipped the butterfly analogy for your mother, too. I tried to find you a lovely but totally association-free scene from your childhood." He grimaced. "But you had such a lousy childhood that I had to take what I could get."

She looked around her. Beauty. Peace. "You . . . did this?"

"I had to calm you down." His lips twisted. "And anyway, you wanted a demonstration that I could do something besides kill people."

"Just pretty pictures." *She gazed at the butterflies.* "How did you do it?"

"It's one of my talents. I'm not as good at it as some others in my circle, but this came out pretty well."

"You read my memories?"

"I can't actually read your memories. It's not my forte. I can just skim the surface. I'm very good at surfing. I just went dipping for things that made you peaceful and happy."

"Pretty pictures," *she repeated with disgust.*

"*Real pictures. Real scents. Real feelings that you felt at the time. I just brought them back for you. Your own memories.*" He shook his head. "*But there are so many other memories that are tortured. I have to clarify and let you look at them without the hurt.*"

She shook her head.

"*Don't be afraid. We'll start out slow. You can stop me at any time. But if you'll trust me, we can get through this.*"

"*I can't trust you.*"

"*Then just take baby steps, and we'll still make it. I'll show you.*"

"*No. I don't want you to—*"

Serenity.

Sunlight.

Sparkling, glowing beacons in the distance.

Butterflies moving, flying, soaring.

And Mandak.

Gently, carefully, no more intrusion than the butterflies . . .

But he wasn't moving aimlessly as they were doing. He was in her mind, seeking, finding.

Release.

Unchained.

An exquisite burst of freedom.

Then he was there again, soothing, a balm to ease the shock of that sudden release.

"*See?*" His voice was velvet soft in the darkness. "*I'll bring you only good right now. That was only a tiny, ugly scar you needed to be rid of. There is so much worse trauma and ugliness that's paralyzing you. What your father subjected you to was cruel and unusual punishment. It's a wonder you survived it. I'm taking away the scars and unhealed wounds, not giving you new ones. You can feel that, can't you?"*

She could feel it. It was clear and pure as the sunlight. She felt the goodness and the rightness of that release. "Yes." She added belligerently, "But I still don't trust you."

He chuckled. "I didn't expect victory. One step at a time. Sleep. When you wake up, you'll realize that something's changed, something's better. Then we'll take it from there."

"I don't know. You really are weird. Maybe more weird than I am. I have to figure out what just happened. Maybe hypnosis? But I could feel it." It was hard to think now. She was already too drowsy. "But I guess you did prove that you know how to do something besides kill people . . ."

CHAPTER THREE

"YOU SLEPT HARD." MANDAK was sitting in the chair beside her bed when she opened her eyes again. She was in her bedroom at the lodge she realized hazily. "It's been four hours and I was getting a little worried. Though I thought it was probably a mental effort to get away from me that was causing it. The wound looked all right after I rebandaged it."

She looked down at her side and the clean fresh bandage. "It feels okay." She met his gaze. "And I wouldn't try to escape from you that way. I'm not a coward."

"Point taken. Then maybe you were trying to work everything out in your mind." He smiled. "There's something to the old advice about the wisdom of sleeping on it. Did you come up with anything?"

"Was I supposed to wake up and immediately tell you that you were right?" She shook her head. "No way." She wished he would go away. She had to think. She was bewildered and a little scared. But amidst all the fear, something had happened tonight that had made her imagine that maybe . . .

He was silent, his eyes narrowed on her face. "I doubt if you'd ever admit I was right about anything. But what

I did to you, with you, felt right, didn't it? Tell me the truth, Allie."

She hesitated. It was difficult lowering her defenses, but maybe it was time she tried. Then she said awkwardly, "Nothing I've ever felt was as right as those few moments. Afterward, I felt . . . free."

"It will get better. I made you a promise, and I'll keep it."

If she let him keep that promise. The fear was there, but so was that tiny current of excitement. "What . . . would you do?"

"I'd come to you, mostly at night when you're on the verge of sleep, it's easier to access at that time. I'd just sit here, sometimes you'll talk to me."

"I don't like that. It sounds like Dr. Kramer and an analyst's couch."

"Then don't talk to me. Your choice. I can work anyway." He paused. "You want to do it, don't you?"

She did want to do it. He had shown her a brightness at the end of the tunnel. It had only been a single ray of light, but it had held hope. "Maybe." She moistened her lips. "How long will it take? Oh, not all that razzle-dazzle about cleansing my mind. How long before I can function and keep everyone at bay and out of my head?"

"Years."

"What?"

"You said everyone. That's a very big order. It would take years to get even near that goal," he said. "I'm being honest with you. I'm not promising you that you won't be bombarded occasionally. I'm saying that I'll give you immunity about seventy percent of the time."

She tried to judge what that would mean to her. "How long for that seventy percent?"

"About eight weeks. The first five weeks we cleanse and clarify. The last three weeks we concentrate on building."

"Eight weeks is a long time."

"Not for the payoff. Think about it."

She was thinking about it.

Immunity seventy percent of the time. It wasn't perfect, but it could be salvation for her. If she was careful, she would be able to move around almost normally. He hadn't promised that he'd give her everything she wanted, and that honesty made her more prone to believe him.

It might all be a fairy tale. But what if it wasn't? What if there was a chance?

"I still don't trust you."

"That's not the question. In the end, you don't have to trust me," he said softly. "Not if you trust yourself, Allie. Do you?"

His words hit home. He was right, it didn't matter what his intentions were for her. He didn't control her. If she kept her wits sharp and watched him, then she'd be able to detect any sign that could harm her. She was the only person in the world that she did trust.

Then why be afraid or uneasy? She could protect herself. Why not reach out and take what she wanted? "When do we start? Now?"

"Ah, I thought that might be the closing argument." He smiled. "Not tonight. You've already had the first breakthrough. Plus you've had a rough day."

"I feel fine. Stop treating me as if I'm some kind of weakling. I don't want to sit around and wait for you to decide it's the right time. If I'm going to do it, let's do it." She frowned. "I want to get going."

"You won't just be sitting around." He studied her

expression. "But you obviously need to be convinced." He got to his feet. "Since you assure me how strong and fit you are, I won't worry about your wound for tonight. Get up and come with me. I'll show you what happens after you get that wound a little more healed." He helped her out of the bed. "A little puny?"

"No." Her knees were feeling rubbery, but she stepped away from him. She got a funny feeling whenever he touched her. "Where are we going?"

"Just down the hall. To the left." He was across the room, opening the door. "After you."

"What's down the hall?" She went out the door and turned left. "Never mind. I'll find out for myself."

"You don't mind if I trail along?" He was close behind her. "The next door, Allie."

She stopped and hesitated before the door he indicated.

"You're wondering what's behind it," he said, amused. "Like the old story. Will it be something wonderful? Or a tiger who could attack you?"

She reached for the doorknob. "Not a tiger. The tiger's on this side of the door."

He chuckled with genuine amusement. "Very good."

She threw open the door.

Darkness.

He reached around from behind her and turned on the wall switch. Brilliant light illuminated the room. "No tiger."

She stared in bewilderment. "It's just some kind of gym." Her gaze wandered around the room. Mats on the floor. Exercise equipment. Weights.

"Disappointed?" he asked. "It's a very good gym. Exactly what I asked for when I rented the place."

"Why did you want a gym?"

"It's for you. You need to be kept occupied."

"In a gym?"

"Physical release is a good thing." He paused. "And it wouldn't hurt you to learn a few karate moves or maybe more than a few. If you'll let me teach you."

"Karate?"

"Or we could explore a few other martial arts if you prefer."

"Why?" she asked bluntly. "Occupied? You don't care about my being occupied. It's all about learning karate or that other stuff, isn't it? Why should I do that?"

"I like the idea of your being able to take care of yourself."

"Why?"

"I may not be around when you need me to be. I don't want you to have to depend on me."

Shock rippled through her. It shouldn't have surprised her, but it did. She knew in the end that she was alone. She certainly had no intention of ever having to depend on Mandak. Yet she knew his strength and intelligence, and it had been comforting to have someone beside her to fight Camano. "You don't have to worry about that," she said jerkily. "I'll make my own way."

"I'll be there if I can," he said sharply. "But things happen, and I want you to be prepared for them. I want you to be smart and lethal and a finely honed weapon that no one can put down. I think you want that, too."

"I never thought about it."

"No, you were too busy just keeping sane and fighting off the dragons. It's what you're doing at this moment. Think about it now."

Fighting off the dragons.

Yes, that had been her life. But it had always been a defensive battle. She had been the victim. But what if that changed? What if she became the weapon Mandak wanted her to be?

"You like the idea," Mandak said, his gaze on her expression.

"Yes." She added fiercely, "You knew I would. But do you believe I don't know that you're not doing this only for my sake? Maybe you want a weapon of your own, Mandak."

"Maybe I do. But the sword cuts both ways, doesn't it?"

She slowly gazed around the gym again. "What would I have to do?"

"Get well. That won't take long. Get strong. Skill can replace strength in many cases, but it helps. Exercise. You probably didn't ever have a regular exercise regimen."

"I'm stronger than you think. I used to swim for hours in the pool at the compound." She looked at all the exercise machines. "But I can get stronger."

"I'm sure you can."

She turned to look at him, and demanded, "But are you good enough to teach me?"

He smiled. "Yes, I'm good enough."

"And you won't pretend or try to take it easy on me?"

"Not even a little bit." His voice was gentle but still held a hint of steel. "I'll take you down and wipe the floor with you. Fair enough?"

"And you'd enjoy it."

"You'll have to see. I'm torn between thinking of you as a kid and wanting to meet those challenges you throw at me on a purely adult level. That means my every response to you is a crapshoot."

"Whatever." Her brow was furrowed in thought. "But I want more. It's not going to be enough."

"Really?"

"Guns. I want to know how to handle guns. And maybe knives."

"Good God."

"Why are you surprised? You started this. All the martial arts in the world aren't going to do me any good unless I'm close to Camano's men. They'll have guns and knives, and they'll know how to use them. I'm going to know how to use them, too." She added, "I don't think I have to ask if you can teach me about guns. You said you were a mercenary."

"I can teach you."

"This is my life. I'm going to defend myself. I want to be very, very good."

"I can teach you," he repeated.

"Just checking. If you can't, try to find someone who can." She turned away from him. "I'm ready to go back to bed now. I need to rest." She suddenly whirled back to him and took a deep breath. "There's something I have to say to you." She moistened her lips. "Thank you."

His brows rose. "Well, that's a surprise."

"It's hard for me to say because I'm confused, and I don't know why you're doing all this." She shook her head. "But in the end, maybe it doesn't matter. You saved my life. And now you may be going to save my sanity. That's really something, Mandak. You have no idea what it means to me. I can't just turn my back and ignore it."

"Even though I've told you that I'm going to make you pay for it?"

"All my life, people have been doing that. You're no different. I'll work that out later. And, at least, you're giving me something I want more than anything in the world." She started to turn away. "That's all. I don't promise to trust you or not to be suspicious. But I wanted you to know that I value what you're doing for me. Because I probably won't tell you again."

"Once is enough. I believe I'm touched."

"You're making fun of me. That's okay. I expected it."

"No such thing. I meant it."

"Really?" The awkwardness of the moment was back. She headed for the door. "Like I said, I need to go to bed. I'll start exercising early tomorrow morning."

"And probably overdo it."

"I won't hurt myself." She glanced back at him. "And I won't let you hurt me either. You were surprised that I took the initiative just now about the guns, but it wouldn't have been too long before you took another step in the same direction. You're clever and manipulative, and you probably didn't want to shock me."

"Very perceptive."

"Am I right?"

He slowly nodded. "I agree that you need all the tools you can beg, borrow, or steal to get through this."

"I'll get through it. I'll study and learn and fight all the dragons that come my way. But it will be my battle, not yours." She headed for the door. "You want a weapon? I'll give you one, Mandak. But it won't do you one bit of good."

TRENTON, NEW JERSEY

"I've got a license-plate number," Navarro said when Camano picked up.

"It's about time," Camano said.

"We were lucky to get it this soon. It was like working blind. If we hadn't found the blood, we'd still be looking for who took her."

"Blood?"

"Tantona was firing at her. We found traces of blood in the shrubs and at a campsite about thirty miles down the road from where we found Tantona."

"But you didn't find a body?"

"No, but we found a ranger who had spotted a car in the forest that night. He wasn't happy about the campfire. So he took down the license number and was going to talk to the man who had lit it. But they only stayed a couple hours, then took off."

"Man? Description?"

"The ranger was too far away. But it was only one man and, he thought, maybe a woman."

"Bingo. What kind of car?"

"A dark blue Toyota."

"And there was blood at the campsite?"

"Yeah, quite a bit. He might have been trying to bandage her wound."

And it seemed Teresa had survived, Camano thought bitterly. If Tantona had aimed straighter, he wouldn't be having this trouble. "Have you called in the number to our man Vaughn at the precinct?"

"Yeah, it's a rental car. It was rented at Philadelphia Airport. I'm on my way to get a copy of the rental agreement and a photocopy of the guy's driver's license." He paused. "We should have a picture of him within a couple hours."

"Good man," he said. "I should have relied on you

instead of Tantona. Find this son of a bitch, and you'll find me very grateful, Navarro."

"I'll find him," Navarro said eagerly. "You can count on me. I'd never have let her get away to begin with." He hung up.

"Blood?" Gina repeated as she lifted her coffee cup to her lips. "Is that what you said?"

He looked at her across the luncheon table. She was even more gorgeous in the full sunlight of the terrace than she had been last night. Her eyes were fixed intently on him, but he couldn't read her expression. Her beautiful face was smooth and calm and portrayed only curiosity. "It seems Tantona was forced to fire at your little girl when she ran away. I'm sure that it was only a token shot, but he must have hit her. But the blood will probably help us to find her."

She shook her head. "Then that's a good thing. Such a foolish child. I always told Antonio that Teresa must be a little unbalanced because of all that weird stuff in her head. Now look at her running around the country, getting herself hurt. She'll be much better off when she comes home to me."

He smiled mockingly. "They say every child should be with their mother." He took a drink of his coffee. "Only one man in that rental car. I feel better about the possibility she might be in the hands of the police. It's still a possibility, but we may have gotten lucky."

"A pervert?" She tilted her head. "She's a pretty girl. Everyone says she's almost as pretty as I am."

"Nonsense." It was the response Gina wanted, and besides, he had never found Teresa attractive. She always stared at him with those big eyes as if she could see his soul. "I doubt if it's a pervert. He took out three men as if they were nothing. His focus isn't on sex."

"Every man's focus is on sex. It just depends on the time and opportunity." She met his eyes, and her own were wide and clear and totally enigmatic. "And the desirability of the woman. I'm glad you don't find Teresa desirable. It would cause me so many problems."

He chuckled. "I'm sure you would solve them with your usual skill and unique talents." He set down his cup and pushed back his chair. "But Teresa's desirability or lack of it isn't important for you at the moment. When Navarro gets the information I need about the man who took Teresa, we'll be going after her."

"You want me to go?"

"Hell, yes." He started across the terrace. "I don't know what we'll face with that bastard. But I do know you're the one who can lead Teresa back into the fold. Be ready."

HE SHOULD PROBABLY STOP HER, Mandak thought as he stood in the doorway of the gym and watched Allie work out with the weights. Her forehead was creased in concentration and her tee shirt wet with perspiration. But she was smart, and she hadn't overdone her workouts in the past two days. She'd paced the exercise, taken breaks, then started again. He'd been impressed by her sheer determination and deliberately left her on her own to make mental and physical adjustments. It was time for him to step in and start training her at the mental and psychological level, but he could let her physical workouts remain solitary for the time being.

She looked up and saw him. "You're frowning. Go away. I'm not doing anything wrong."

"No you're not. I'm just admiring your stamina."

"Go admire it somewhere else. You bother me."

"Yes, I know. You bother me, too. In a few years, we might have to have a discussion about that." He turned away. "In the meantime, I'll let you have your space. You can have one more day on your own. I start teaching you the fine art of karate tomorrow."

"Why not today?"

"Tomorrow," he said firmly, and started down the hall. If he stayed in the gym, he knew she would persist and gnaw at him like a bulldog. She was nothing if not stubborn.

He'd gone only a few steps when his cell phone rang. He went still when he saw the ID.

N. Praland.

He punched the access. "What do you want, Praland?"

"Why, Mandak. I only want courtesy." Praland's voice was silky smooth. "And to hear that note in your voice that pleases me to my very soul. Are you ready?"

"It wouldn't matter if I was or not. Give it to me."

"Karl Steinam. Age fourteen. Salzburg."

"Fourteen?"

"Ah, that's the note. It always bothers you when I kill the young."

"Because you're a son of a bitch. Why do you always call me? Why not Neal Grady or Renata Wilger?"

"How can you wonder? Our encounters have been so exhilarating. They'd sent many of their people to try to trip me. You came very close, Mandak. And then you made the fatal mistake of stealing that young fool before

I was ready to toss him away. I dearly wanted to cut your throat when you did that. I still do. You're not safe. Look over your shoulder, and I'll be there. I'm going to find you, Mandak."

"Why? When it obviously excites you to make me feel your superiority by killing these kids? Screw you, Praland."

"But I am superior, and you can't do anything about it. I'll let you know when I have something else to report." He hung up.

Cool down. There wasn't anything he could do right now, and getting this angry and upset was exactly what Praland had intended. The son of a bitch knew how to rip him to pieces. He was a consummate sadist and enjoyed every minute of any pain he could inflict. Mandak had dealt with him for years, both in the field and leading raids to try to free the captives he held for profit. He had been marginally successful, but it wasn't enough. His hands had been tied. They were still tied.

And the only one who could cut those ties was Allie Girard.

Allie thought Camano and her father were bad? She had no idea about the depths of the wickedness of which Praland was capable.

But she might learn if Mandak couldn't prepare her to face him when he tossed her in Praland's path. She had to be lethal enough to protect herself while she was doing what Mandak wanted of her. He had started her training, but there was still a long way to go. He was impatient, and he'd been tempted to bring in outside help.

Not yet.

It had to be just Allie and him until the bond was forged.

He pocketed his phone and continued down the hall toward the porch. He had work to do and contacts to be made. He couldn't put his life on hold because he was absorbed with the promise Allie offered. But it was difficult to remember that there was a life outside Allie Girard. She was becoming an obsession.

Another reason to move forward as quickly as possible to push her away from him.

But first, he had to bring her closer . . .

Tonight.

Start tonight . . .

ALLIE TENSED, jerked out of sleep.

Someone was in the room.

Mandak.

She could feel him in the darkness.

"It's all right. You're safe," Mandak said from the chair beside her bed. "Well, as safe as you can be."

"I'm not safe. Not with you." She scrambled to a sitting position. "It's creepy having you come in and stare at me in the dark."

"Then we'll turn on the lamp." He reached forward and flicked on the lamp on the bedside table. "Better?"

She wasn't sure. Now she could see those piercing blue eyes and feel the sheer power of him, which was a mixture of sexuality, charisma, and intelligence. That power was always present, but she could try to ignore it when she was busy. Now she felt vulnerable. "What are you doing here?"

"It's time to start housecleaning in that interesting mind of yours," he said lightly. "I told you how it would be. Though it may not be as easy to access as I thought. You were sleeping very deeply."

"I was tired. I worked hard today."

"I know. You didn't show up for supper."

"I ate later. I robbed the fridge."

"I thought you would. I assumed you just wanted to avoid me."

She nodded, and said bluntly, "You disturb me."

"It's mutual. But it will be easier once we get through a few sessions. Lie back down."

She didn't move. "I think I've changed my mind. Maybe I'll wait a little while to—"

"Coward."

"I'm not a coward." She glared at him. "And I don't have to do anything I don't want to do."

He smiled. "But you do want to do this. Be honest with both of us, Allie."

Honesty could be painful. Honesty could be terrifying. But he was staring at her with that quizzical look, and she wouldn't lie. "You said it wouldn't be anything like Dr. Kramer. I won't put up with that again."

"Nothing like Kramer. Lie down and close your eyes."

She lay back down. "That's like Kramer. Next you'll be attaching wires to me."

"No, I won't. I won't do anything at all for a few minutes. Just go blank. You don't have to talk or think."

"Sneak attack?"

He chuckled. "I guess you might call it that."

"Don't you dare show me any butterflies or any of that kind of stuff."

"I promise."

She closed her eyes. "I feel like an idiot."

He didn't answer.

Her tension was leaving her, she realized. Was she becoming accustomed to him and relaxing? She asked him, "Is the way I feel natural, or are you messing with me?"

"Partly natural," he said. "I have a little to do with it."

"Probably more than a little." But she didn't care. She was committed, and as long as she felt in control and able to back away, it was okay. "Mess away. But I warn you, I'll shut you down if you pull a Kramer on me."

"Shh."

Silence.

No sound.

No sensation.

Nothing.

"Easy. It's coming," Mandak said. "This one isn't bad . . ."

An explosion of release!

She arched as sensation after sensation moved through her.

Relief.

Freedom.

She was panting. "I thought it wasn't working. I didn't know . . . you were doing it."

"Until it happened. That's the ideal procedure." He grimaced. "But removing memory trauma isn't always that simple. That particular memory was a long time ago, before your father brought you in to do his dirty work. Were you aware of any memories while I was doing it?"

"No. Just the release."

"Good. But it won't always be that way. If it gets nasty, it will be like being pulled through a chain saw." He paused. "I'll try to wait until we get toward the end before I put you through that."

"Because you're afraid I won't let you do it any longer."

He nodded. "And because I need to get as far as I can so that you'll recognize the pain is worth it."

"Easy to say when I'm the one with the pain," she said dryly. "Maybe it won't happen. The only thing I was aware of this time was sadness, a little anger, then the release." She shook her head. "I don't know what's happening in my head. But you could be wrong."

"Not likely," he said. "Because I do know what's going on in that mind of yours." He leaned back in the chair. "Are you ready to try again?"

"Yes." She closed her eyes again, and added flippantly, "Go ahead. Vacuum me out."

"I'm not taking anything away. Every memory is still there. I'm just taking out the poison and making you acknowledge them."

"Go ahead." She felt the tension coming again. "What are you waiting for? How many times do we have to go through this again tonight?"

"Only a few more. It won't be bad. And you're beginning to like it."

He was right. The release had felt cleansing and deeply satisfying. "But you just said it won't last."

"For tonight it will. Believe me. Nothing bad will happen tonight."

She wanted to believe him, she realized. Close. She was feeling strangely joined, close to him. That could be dangerous when she couldn't remember feeling close to anyone before. "Prove it."

He chuckled. "I will. Now relax and let me work . . ."

* * *

"HIS NAME IS WILLIAM MONTGOMERY," Navarro said to Camano. "He paid by credit card, and I'm faxing you the slip and the copy of his driver's license."

"Has he turned in the car yet?" Camano asked as he went into his office to wait for the fax.

"Not yet."

"Then he still has her with him, and they're on the road."

"Yeah, maybe."

Camano pulled off the fax. "Brown hair. Blue eyes. He looks like the guy next door. Did you question the clerk? Is this what he really looked like?"

"He said it was probably close."

And no one really glanced at ID if it was in the least close, Camano thought in disgust. The man would have had to have two heads for him to catch that clerk's attention. "I'll send the photos to our man at the precinct and see if they can pull anything up on the database on him."

"The name won't help?"

Stupid. "Would you use your own name?"

"I guess not."

"Stay close to that clerk. He's your best friend. Line his pockets. I want to know the exact moment when he hears that car has been turned in." He hung up the phone.

FOUR WEEKS LATER

"You again?" Allie opened her eyes to see Mandak's shadowy form sitting in his usual chair beside her bed. "You missed last night. I was beginning to feel neglected."

"I thought I'd give you a rest from me. Do you want me to turn on the lamp?"

"Not particularly. I know what you look like." That was an understatement. In the past weeks, she'd practically memorized his features. He'd become the center of her life here at the lodge. In the morning, she got up, exercised on her own for an hour, then met him for breakfast. After breakfast, he disappeared and let her go back to the gym. But a few hours later, he appeared again, and the karate lessons started. Then lunch and gun practice in the woods back of the lodge. More karate, and two days ago, he'd given her a knife and begun tutoring her in its use. Dinner. Then he disappeared again, and she didn't see him again until he appeared in her bedroom sometime in the night. She had only been half joking when she had said she felt neglected when he'd missed coming to her room last night. They had become so attuned to each other, it had seemed wrong for her not to see him then. "You're right, I see enough of you. I just wondered."

"Why didn't you mention it this morning?"

"I felt kind of . . . odd. You know, the day seems broken into compartments. This one is sort of all by itself and doesn't have anything to do with all the other things that we do together."

"No, it's at another end of the scale from karate. By the way, you're doing very well at that particular discipline."

"Oh, sure," she said. "Don't try to flatter me. You kept your promise. You mop the floor with me every day."

"Not quite. You get better every session."

Silence.

Sometimes the silences between them were comfortable, she thought, like the silence between two old friends. It had sometimes surprised her when their relationship usually had a distinct edge. This was not one of those silences. "I don't know if I believe that's the reason why you didn't come last night. What do you do when you're not with me?"

"Work."

"What kind of work?"

He didn't answer.

"I didn't want to know anyway," she said quickly. "I was just making conversation."

"That's good. You'll know when it's time."

"That sounds like a bunch of philosophic crap."

"I've never been exposed to philosophic crap. Would you care to describe it?"

"No."

"Then suppose we get to our work."

"Why not?" She was silent. "Last night, I thought that maybe we were through with all this. We've been doing pretty well."

"Yes."

"But I was wrong? That wasn't true?"

"No. It was true."

"So what's the real reason you didn't show up?"

He didn't answer.

"Did you decide it wasn't doing any good? That you'll never be able to clear enough debris away to teach me to block?"

"It's doing good."

"Dammit, *talk* to me."

"You're doing too well. You've jumped over all kinds of obstacles and left only the final barriers."

"That's what you wanted. That's what I need, right?"

"Right," he said roughly. "But I warned you, it's going to be hell. It's going to blow you apart."

"No, it won't. Is that why you didn't come last night? You thought I needed the time to get ready for it?"

"No, I needed the time for *me* to get ready for it."

She inhaled sharply. "What do you mean?"

"I mean I thought that I was prepared, but I backed away."

"But you came back tonight."

"Yes." His tone bitter. "I'll always come back. That's why you have to be wary of me." His next words were crisp. "Are you ready?"

"Yes." She paused. "But all this nonsense is scaring me."

"We'll get through it together." He reached out, and his hand covered her own on the bed. "You've just got to remember that I'm here for you. I'll not let you be pulled back."

"It can't be that bad. I got through the rest just fine."

"And you'll get through this, too. Go blank. Relax."

"I am relaxing. But it's hard for me to—"

She screamed!

Brains blowing apart.

Jokman falling to the ground.

Her father slapping her.

Blood.

Blood.

Blood.

Guilt.

Shouldn't have told him.

Shouldn't have told him.

Her fault . . .

"It's not your fault," Mandak said. "Stop thinking

that." He was beside her on the bed, holding her, pressing her face into his shoulder. "Let it go. Remember. Accept what happened and let it go."

Let it go?

It was killing her, tearing her apart. All of Jokman's memories, all of her own memories of that hideous night. She clutched blindly at Mandak, taking his warmth to ward off the ice. "Make it go away. Make it go."

"Too late. I can't do it. We have to ride it out."

"Damn you. Damn you." She desperately clutched him closer. "It . . . hurts."

"Then let it go."

"I can't. It's strangling me, smothering me."

He held her tighter. "You'll do it. We'll get through it together."

"No, I'm alone. No one can help me."

"That's a lie. I'm helping you right now. You're not alone."

Was it true? She had always been alone, but somehow she could feel Mandak near her . . .

"I'm here," he said.

In the darkness, in the blood, in the agony.

"There's nothing you can do, nothing that you can feel that will make me go away," Mandak said.

The memories were rushing back to her, attacking.

Jokman's skull was blowing apart.

"Scream. Cry," Mandak said between his teeth. "Let it go."

She was sobbing, clutching him. Because he was the only anchor in this sea of despair.

And, for once, she was not alone.

* * *

IT WAS NEARLY DAWN WHEN Mandak raised himself on one elbow to look down at her. "How do you feel? I think we're through the worst of it."

"How do you expect? I feel like a wrung-out dishrag," she said bitterly. That was the physical reaction to those hours of torment. The emotional response was much more complicated. Somewhere in the center of that upheaval, she had been able to release that hideous memory, but it was as if it had been torn from her. She was still shaking and bleeding from it. "The worst of it? Tell me it won't come back."

"I can't tell you that. It probably will. They were your memories as well as Jokman's." His hand reached out and cupped her cheek. "But it will be sad, not unbearably painful. If you need me, I'll come running."

She should tell him she didn't need him.

She couldn't do that. She did need him. She wasn't sure if she would have survived this horror of a night without him.

"That will be hard for you." It was as if he'd read her thoughts. Perhaps he had, she didn't know what to believe about what he'd told her about what he could do or not do. "But we got along pretty well tonight, didn't we?"

"I guess we did." She wished he'd lie back down and hold her again. She wanted that closeness, that bonding, that feeling that he was holding back the loneliness. She frowned. "But of all the memories, did you have to bring up that night with Jokman?"

"Yes." His hand dropped away from her face, and he got to his feet. "Because it was the worst one. Once we got over that hurdle, it was all downhill."

"You couldn't have started me on something easier?"

"Yes, but it would have always been lurking in the distance threatening both of us."

"Both of us?"

"Both," he repeated. "You don't go through a merging like this without bonding. In sessions like this, there's a joining. Do you think I wasn't feeling pain? The echoes are very strong, Allie."

Bonding. Yes, she had felt that same bonding. She felt it now. She realized she had felt it before when he had been working with her mind. But not like this. Not this strong and powerful. "But it will go away now, right?"

"It will . . . lessen."

"I want it to go *away*."

He shrugged. "In situations like this, you take what you get."

"I'll work on it."

He smiled. "I'm sure you will. But wait until we finish this initial phase. That bond will be a comfort to you."

"But you said this would be as bad as it will get." She moistened her lips. "I won't need you. Isn't that right?"

"You'll have to decide. Yes, nothing will be this bad, but it will still cause you trauma. We have to go over all those cozy little sessions in your father's study. Mega ugliness." He paused. "And then there are a few readings of your mother's memories. Not ugly, just painful for you."

"My . . . mother?"

"You don't want to remember anything she's shown you about herself or how she feels about you. It's necessary, Allie. That could be a few of the worst obstacles we'll have to overcome. Major scarring."

She shook her head.

"We have to do it."

"Oh, very well," she said impatiently. "But I don't see why. As you said, they're not ugly. Nothing about my mother is ugly."

"Except her selfishness. That could be fatal for you."

She knew that was true, but she didn't want to admit it. "I said I'd do it. Go away, Mandak. I need to sleep."

"Yes, you do." He headed for the door. "Don't be late for breakfast. Don't think I'm going to let you ease off on training because of a rough night."

"I know you wouldn't." Though she wasn't sure. He'd been incredibly gentle, impossibly strong, while he'd been holding her tonight. He'd shown her an entirely new aspect of his character. "Just get out of here."

"I'm going." He looked over his shoulder, and his eyes were twinkling. "But you'll find you'll miss me. It's part of that damn bonding."

He was gone.

And she was already missing him, she realized. She felt an emptiness. Her body, where he'd been curved against her own, still felt his imprint. Her mind was searching, trying to find him.

It was all crazy.

She turned off the light and settled back down in bed. Go to sleep. She'd see him soon enough. Her days were filled with Mandak.

And so were her nights.

It wouldn't hurt to put up with this bonding thing until she was done with the mental high jinks Mandak was putting her through. At the end of the path was the beacon of freedom from the prison of memories. She could take it until she'd reached that goal. She could do anything to avoid those constant attacks.

She huddled beneath the covers and closed her eyes.

She just hoped that Mandak was feeling as empty and lonely as she was feeling at this moment. That was only fair, wasn't it? He was the one who had started all of this . . .

CHAPTER FOUR

"THEY'VE FOUND THE CAR," Navarro said. "It was left in the parking garage of a private airport in Louisville, Kentucky. Should I go down and—"

"No, I'll do it myself." It had been weeks since Camano had heard anything. Avis had even reported the car stolen. Damn, he'd been afraid he'd lost the track.

But a parking garage meant video cameras, and an airport had all kinds of ways to trace flights and passengers.

He hung up and called Gina. "I'll pick you up in fifteen minutes. We're going to Louisville."

SIX DAYS LATER

Allie saw the door open and Mandak's silhouette framed against the light of the hall. "You're late."

He came toward her. "What a nag."

"I want this over."

"It will be." He lifted the sheet and slipped into bed. For the last three nights he'd started holding her as the session commenced. He always ended up there anyway within a few minutes of making mental contact. He'd not been lying when he told her that first contact with Jokman might be the worst, but the others were also the stuff of nightmares.

She curled herself around him. "Where were you?"

He shifted back a little away from her. "Busy."

"I was waiting."

"And I was steeling myself. This is becoming increasingly difficult for me."

"Why?"

"Because my focus appears to be shifting. Sixteen. I have to keep reminding myself. Sixteen."

"Oh." He meant sex. She had felt a tingling stirring occasionally when he touched her, but she had been too absorbed in what she was going through to let it affect her. "I guess it might bother you. I've never done it, so I don't know what it's like."

"And I'm trying to keep you in ignorance."

"If it's getting in the way, we could do it. I probably wouldn't mind."

"Allie . . ." He cupped her face in his two hands and kissed her on the nose. "I don't want your first time to be because you don't want it to get in the way. It should mean something."

"Whatever." She shrugged. "Sex was all over the place at the compound, but my father didn't want anyone to touch me, either."

"He probably was afraid sex might destroy that ability he prized so highly."

"That would be silly."

"Yes, but there are stories and legends about the power of virginity and things like that. He wouldn't have wanted to take a chance."

She shook her head doubtfully. "I don't know—"

"Would you mind if we stopped talking about sex and virginity? Both subjects are hot topics for me at the moment."

"You started it."

"So I did. Let's move on."

"That's what I thought we'd—"

"GET OUT, TERESA." MAMA WAS opening the passenger door of the red Corvette convertible. "You'll find everything you need in the cabin. I'll call you to tell you when I'm coming to pick you up." She smiled her brilliant white smile. "You know this is best, don't you, baby? We have to let Mr. Camano become accustomed to the idea of you. It's much better for you to be away from the compound for a while."

Shut out Mama's memories. She didn't want to know.

"If you say so." She got her duffel out of the car. "But not for long. You'll let me come back to you, Mama?"

"Of course." She made a fluttering motion with her beautifully manicured hand, a graceful, butterfly motion. "How I'll miss you." She started the car again. "Take care, baby."

She watched the shiny red car drive down the road.

The dark tunnel.

How happy Mama was to be rid of her. She was remembering Camano and something they had done in bed last night and how he'd told her how pleased he'd be if—

Go blank. Shut out her mother's memories.

Make them go away.

Tantona shouting.

Darkness.

Running.

Betrayal.

Don't remember. Don't remember.

"But you do remember." Mandak was holding her close. "And it's over." He was wiping the tears from her cheeks with his handkerchief. "Accept it. Release."

"Hard . . ."

He muttered a curse. "I knew it would be." He held her closer. "Scars . . ." He rocked her back and forth. "But it's the last one, Allie. Let it go."

"I have." She raised her head, and added shakily, "I don't even know if she feels anything for me. I just don't seem to be there for her. Yet she told me she loved me. Mothers have to love their children, don't they? She kept telling me that she wished she could snatch me away, and we could just be alone together. But that's not what her memories said. I tried and tried not to read those memories, but sometimes they were just there . . ."

"And the truth, Allie."

"Maybe. But it could be that she was trying to love me. She told me that she grew up in the slums and had to fight to survive until my father took her. She probably had to fight him, too. She said that life could be terrible if you were just a weak woman with no weapons. I keep thinking that if we were alone together, she might change."

"Dangerous thinking."

She shook her head. "No. I won't let her stop me."

"I hope not. Your feelings for her are pretty deeply ingrained." He stroked her hair back from her face. "But at least you've faced it." He sat up in bed. "And I'm out of here." He swung his legs to the floor. "First phase finished. Second phase starting. Tomorrow, we start building walls."

She had an instant of panic. "What if it doesn't work?"

"It will work." He got to his feet. "Believe me."

She did believe him. After all she had gone through with him during these weeks, she had no doubt he could do what he promised. But it was difficult to believe in miracles and what he'd promised was a miracle to her.

"How long now?"

"Another three weeks. It will be very different. You'll hardly know it's happening. Now that the road is cleared, it's just concentration and a little help from me." He moved toward the door. "And I believe we'll do that part of the lesson in the library instead of the bedroom . . ."

CAREFUL . . .

Excitement was tingling through Allie as she circled Mandak around the mat. She had never been closer to bringing him down.

Allie swung her foot around and struck Mandak in the neck.

He grunted, grabbed her ankle, flipped her, and followed her down to the gym mat.

His arm held her immobile as he smiled down at her. A lock of dark hair had fallen on his forehead and his blue eyes were glittering down at her. "Beautifully executed. If I hadn't moved an inch, you could have had me."

"Next time." She could feel the flush of excitement in her cheeks. She had the sudden urge to brush that hair away from his face. To touch his chest. To touch *him* . . . "I'll get you next time."

"It just might happen." He got to his feet and pulled her up. "But I doubt it. I'm wary of you now. You've become a force with which to reckon."

"A weapon. It's what you wanted, isn't it?"

"Among other things." He headed for the door. "Now let's move away from the physical to the mental. Go get your jacket. I'll take you to the local Applebee's and buy you a shake."

She stiffened. "That place is full of college students. You know what happened last time. I got torn apart. I couldn't hold them off."

"That doesn't mean you can't do it today. You've had a week longer to build defenses."

"You don't understand. It's like fighting a battering ram. Those kids' memories are damn strong and aggressive."

"And so are you." He glanced back over his shoulder. "I'll bet on you, Allie. Now get your jacket."

RED LEATHER BOOTHS.

All packed with students from the university.

Noise.

Music.

A cacophony of memories surrounding her.

"Block it." Mandak murmured as he seated her in the booth closest to the door. "Block all of it."

"I can't do that."

"Concentrate."

"I'm trying." Her desperate gaze clung to his. "Help me."

He slowly shook his head. "Sink or swim." He turned and started for the door. "I'll be back in an hour."

"Damn you."

"Concentrate."

He walked out the door.

She drew a deep breath.

Concentrate.

Dark tunnel.

Across the aisle, the gangly boy with the long, pink-streaked hair was remembering screwing his roommate the night before.

"Why shouldn't I set up the camera? I want to make you a star. My star. You're beautiful to me. That new tattoo . . ." His forefinger outlined the skull on Ron's hip. "Sexy . . ."

Block it.

Concentrate.

The girl in the corner booth was blank.

But the Asian waitress taking her order was remembering her argument with the cook a few minutes ago.

Dark tunnel.

Anger. Stab the bastard.

"How can I make any tips if you don't move your ass and get the food out. Don't you smirk at me."

Block it.

Concentrate.

Sink or swim.

Fight them off, fight them all off.

Her heart was beating hard.

Please don't let them win.

Block them.

Block them.

Block them.

* * *

"ARE YOU READY TO GO?" Mandak was standing beside the booth, his gaze narrowed on her face. "It's been over an hour. I half expected you to be waiting for me outside."

"Sink or swim," she said jerkily as she got to her feet. "I didn't sink, Mandak. But I didn't swim either. It was more of a dog paddle."

"That's good enough."

"No, it's not." She stalked past him. "Pay the waitress. I want out of here. I'll see you in the car."

She took a deep breath as she walked toward the Camry. She was far enough away from the people in the restaurant not to have to fight and block. But there was a family pulling up in an SUV a few parking spots away.

Dark tunnel.

Not so bad.

The woman driving was remembering her doctor's visit that morning. It had worried her . . .

"Just a few more tests, then we'll know—"

Allie's response was almost automatic.

Block it.

And the memory was gone.

Gone . . .

She froze, her eyes staring blindly straight ahead.

"Something wrong?" Mandak was beside her.

"No, maybe something right." She got into the passenger seat. "Maybe I did swim." Tears were suddenly causing her eyes to sting. "Hey, no dog paddle for me, Mandak."

"And that means?"

"I'm on my way. It's becoming automatic. Give me a little time, and I'll be able to handle it."

"That's what I've been trying to tell you. And I'm giving you time, Allie."

"If you didn't, I'd take it." She swallowed to ease the tightness of her throat. Don't show him how weak she was feeling. Or how gloriously triumphant. "I'm . . . grateful. You kept your promise." She cleared her throat. "Not that I believe you did it for my sake. You keep telling me you have your own agenda. But it means everything to me so I thought I should— Or maybe not. You don't care what I'm feeling."

"Don't I?"

"Oh, maybe a little. It's that bonding thing." She straightened her shoulders. "It doesn't matter. But do you know what I want to do now?"

"I can hardly wait to find out."

"I want to drive through the town and practice."

He chuckled. "Practice blocking?"

"Yes. I know you said that my ability wouldn't be more than seventy percent effective but maybe you're wrong. I could be better than you think."

"You're pretty cocky."

"I want to know. And I want to get better and better." She felt as if she were glowing with excitement. "Okay, so I won't be perfect. I might get very close. That's almost normal, Mandak."

"As opposed to being a freak?"

She made a face. "I'm trying not to say that word. You don't like it."

"Since when did that matter to you?"

"I don't know. It just kind of snuck up on me." She fastened her seat belt. "So take me for a drive. I want to show everyone that I won't be ambushed anymore. I'm going to block the whole world."

"Seventy percent, Allie."

"For now." She looked back at the restaurant as they

pulled out of the parking lot. "I was able to block every single one of the people in the restaurant. It was shaky and messy, and I had to concentrate, but I did it. The woman in the SUV I blocked without thinking, automatic. It was . . . wonderful."

"I can see it was wonderful for you." He smiled at her. "I'll drive very slowly through town and we'll see if you can collect any more scalps to hang on your belt."

"That's not the right metaphor. I don't want to hurt anyone, I just want to keep them from hurting me."

"Correction noted. More like a black belt in karate?"

"Oh, I don't care what you call it. I just want to see if I can *do* it."

THEY HAD DINNER on the road and didn't come back to the lodge for another two hours.

"You've been very quiet." Mandak turned to Allie as he unlocked the door. "No triumphs?"

"Several." She smiled brilliantly. "And some of them automatic."

"Great." He gazed quizzically. "But no exhilaration?"

"Two ambushes. I had to fight them off. One I couldn't get away from until we were over a block away."

"Seventy percent?"

"Not this time. Less. But it sort of pricked the balloon." She looked him in the eye. "But I'll blow that balloon sky-high. I just have to work at it."

"Yes, you will." He turned and moved down the hall. "Go to bed and rest. You deserve it. You've done a good day's work. I'm proud of you."

"You are?"

"Sure." He glanced back at her strange tone. "What?"

"Nothing." She turned and headed for her bedroom. "It's just that no one has ever told me that before. Good night, Mandak."

"Good night." He watched her disappear into her room.

Shit.

He was touched and angry and protective and filled with half a dozen other emotions. They had all come out of nowhere during this singular afternoon. Or maybe it had happened before that, and it had just escaped him. Either way, it was a sign of softness that couldn't be tolerated. She had come too close. He had to distance himself from her.

He was reaching for his phone as he continued to the library.

Lee Walberg answered on the second ring. "You took your time," he said dryly. "You've put me off three times. I assume that you're at last ready to let Natalie and me have a go at taming your little protégée?"

"She doesn't need taming. Well, maybe she does, but I'd defy anyone to do it." He paused. "She needs careful handling. She's vulnerable, dammit."

Lee was silent. "And your attitude is a bit peculiar for you, Mandak."

The softness Mandak was experiencing had clearly evidenced itself in those few words. "I'm just trying to give you a picture of what you'll be facing with her."

"I appreciate the effort." He hesitated. "And I'm wondering if you should have turned her over to us when I last talked to you."

"I couldn't do that. She had too much to learn. She's still not ready, but I've given her a start. She has time to learn the rest while she's with you."

"We're supposed to be her security blanket? Neither Natalie nor I can teach her what you can."

"I'll still be around. Her skills will need constant refreshing. I've just decided it's best that I cut down the personal interaction at present."

"Whatever you say." He paused. "Natalie is looking forward to taking her into our lives. She's been lost since Simon died."

"I know. But there's no comparison between them. Allie's going to be a challenge."

"We're ready for it. Tomorrow?"

"Tomorrow." He hung up.

He looked thoughtfully down at his phone. Tomorrow. Moving to another stage of the game. Lee was probably right, he should have made the move sooner. Had he been fooling himself into thinking he needed additional time? The bonding sometimes had strange and powerful effects.

No, he wouldn't admit that he'd been influenced by emotion. He had only made a judgment and stuck by it.

Perhaps.

But tonight the responsibility for Allie was still his own. She'd had an emotional and exhausting day, and he needed to make sure that she was not suffering from it. He moved down the hall and quietly opened her bedroom door.

Darkness.

The warm, golden light from the hall fell across her bed.

She was sound asleep, and she looked like a weary child.

He could see the streaks of the tears she'd shed on her cheeks. She had been crying, tears she hadn't wanted him to see.

Tears of joy?

Or tears of frustration and pure emotion?

It could be either. Or both.

And it was he who had caused those tears. He'd had the power to sway her and make her do as he wished.

Not that she would admit it, he thought ruefully. She was still all fire and rebellion.

And he would miss that fire. She had belonged to him in a very special way that might never happen again in his lifetime.

She stirred and made a sound.

She must sense that he was there, watching her. She had wonderful instincts.

Okay, I'm leaving. Just checking to see if you're safe and ready to be tossed into the big, bad world out there.

And he was the one who was going to do that tossing, he thought bitterly.

He closed the door softly behind him.

LOUISVILLE, KENTUCKY

"Blank!" Camano violently threw the last security video across the room. "All of them blank for that night the car entered the garage. The son of a bitch had to have erased them."

"What about the flight info?" Gina asked from across the hotel room. "You said the airlines should have records."

"Nothing. I even turned Navarro loose on the guy who schedules the private jets. If he knew anything, he wouldn't talk."

"Then we might as well go home," she said. "We've been in this boring hotel for days. You have to admit I've been very patient." She coaxed. "I've kept you amused, and I've helped you with those security videos. I'm sure that Teresa will turn up soon. She loves me, and she'll want to come home to me."

"You fool, she's not going to go running back to you. She's not alone out there. Whoever took her will keep her."

"I'm not a fool," she said gently. "If you can find another way to find Teresa, then I'll be here for you. But the databases have come up negative and there is no William Montgomery. Now this road is blocked, too. Why not take a deep breath, then go home and try to think of another way?"

"You're not worried about finding her at all, are you?"

"No." She smiled. "I told you, she loves me. I've made sure of that over the years. It was no problem. As soon as I realized that she was special and could be of value, I started paying her extra attention. She was starved for it. Now she comes when I snap my fingers." She stood up and got her suitcase out of the closet. "And there's no way she'd do anything to hurt me." She started packing. "Which means she'll do nothing to hurt you. You have to understand that. As long as you make me happy, and I stay with you, then there's no way she'll be a witness against you."

"That sounds remarkably like blackmail," he said silkily. "And that's a dangerous road, Gina."

"Blackmail? Heavens no. I just wanted to make you feel better." She crossed the room and kissed him. "In every way. It's not as if you won't want me to stay with you. Did you know that Antonio sent me to one of the houses in Quito for six weeks to be taught all kinds of exciting variations? When I came back, I made it so good for both of us." She rubbed against him. "I know so many ways, and I've shown you only a few."

He was getting hard.

Little bitch. She knew it.

She smiled and stepped back. "Anything you want. Teresa? No problem." She returned to her packing. "Just be patient."

She'd almost convinced him. He'd never realized the determination and power she wielded beneath that sexual domination that was her stock in trade. He was beginning to wonder about her influence on Casali.

And that determination could be turned against him as well.

He might do better to get rid of her.

But not now, not when he was so hot for her. Not when she held the key to that freaky kid.

Gina was right, all the ways were blocked. Try to find another way to locate Teresa. "I'm not good at patience. You'll have to show me it's worth it."

"Oh, I will." She smiled at him. "Go make yourself a drink. I'll do your packing for you."

He went over to the window and looked out at the jets taking off from the airport across the street.

Streaks of light.

Booming thunder of sound.

Teresa had probably taken one of those jets, and now she thought she was safe from him.

I'm not giving up, you little freak.

I've got my ace in the hole.

No matter how long it takes I'm going to find you.

* * *

"GET UP ON YOUR FEET, Allie." Mandak was standing in the doorway of the gym. "Exercise is over. Shower and pack a bag. We need to leave in an hour."

"Where are we going?" She jumped up and ran her hand through her short curls. "And what's the hurry?"

"You have people to meet." He turned and started to leave. "It's rude to keep them waiting."

"Don't you leave me hanging like that." She was after him in a heartbeat. "What people? Why?"

"Two people you'll like very much. I'll explain on the way." He smiled. "As to why, you graduated yesterday. I'm cutting you loose. You need to go forth and conquer." He was walking down the hall as he spoke. "Hurry."

She stared after him in bewilderment. Then she slowly turned and went toward her bedroom. His words were swirling in her head. Graduated. Cutting you loose. Go forth and conquer.

He meant that he was leaving her.

Why did that send panic racing through her?

And that strange, hollow loneliness?

It was what she wanted. Independence, to be on her own.

Now that she had a start on blocking and handling the horror of the memories, she surely didn't need him.

But she felt like she needed him. She felt like she'd always need him.

"Hurry," he said again. He had paused to look over his shoulder.

"I'm hurrying." She ran down the hall and threw open her door. Move. Shower. Pack. Get out of here. Worry about her curious reluctance to leave Mandak later.

Forty-five minutes later, she was walking out of the lodge onto the porch.

"Excellent." Mandak took her duffel. "Very quick. But then I knew you'd be eager for a fresh start."

"Of course." She followed him to the car. "That's the lure you held out to me when you picked me up out of that forest in New Jersey. A new start . . ." She didn't look at him as she got into the passenger seat. "But I somehow thought that we'd already started."

"Only the preliminaries. I told you that you'd have to begin college soon." He pressed the accelerator. "But, first, we have to have you tested so that you can be admitted. I don't anticipate any problems since you have that photographic memory. But besides being very young, you may have to have a little coaching."

"Again? What else have we been doing during these weeks?" She snapped her fingers. "Oh that's right. Karate. Guns. Knives. No college would accept that curriculum."

"They should. No subjects would prove more useful."

"Not in your world?"

"Nor in yours, Allie."

"New start. Perhaps someday . . ."

"Perhaps. In the meantime, I'll see that you keep on with your lessons in those subjects."

"You will?"

He nodded. "Two or three times a week. I'll set up sessions with a teacher I trust."

"Why not you?"

"I'll be busy. So will you."

"You said you were cutting me loose." She looked out the window. "I won't see you again?"

"You know better than that. You need reinforcement for the blocking, and I'm the only one who can do that for you. You'll see me every now and then. And I'll be there when you have a special need." He added quietly, "And remember, I have an agenda. That's never changed. That's why we came together. That's why I'll always be there in the background until you're ready for me."

"I'll never be ready for you," she said jerkily. "I'm going to work at making it all about me now, Mandak."

"Then enjoy every minute of it." He smiled. "And the people you're going to be living with from now on will help you to do that. Lee and Natalie Walberg are great people who know how to live life to the fullest."

"I'm going to be living with them? Why?"

"It's part of your cover. Dantlow approves whole-heartedly. Check with him. You're supposed to be their niece, who will be staying with them while you go to the university. Lee and Natalie both taught at the university before they retired. Now they do a little tutoring but principally are involved with their hobbies. Lee collects rare books and Natalie is an artist."

"They won't like me." She frowned. "I don't know anything about either one of those things."

"They'll teach you. Their house is just down this block." He cruised to a stop at the curb. "The red brick with the ivy."

The house was a small, elegant Tudor with beautifully crafted paned windows and a rich oak brown door. Allie had never seen a house that spoke more of home. "It's . . . lovely."

"They like it." His gaze shifted to her face. "And so will you."

"I used to dream of living in a house like that. It's . . . welcoming."

"Yes, and so are Lee and Natalie. Give them a chance, Allie." He paused. "You can't read them. I made sure that your relationship would be perfectly normal and free of tension. I thought you'd want that."

"Yes, but it's scary."

"No more than it would be for the rest of us."

"You said to give them a chance. Why should I? Have you got them under your thumb like you do Dantlow?"

"When you get to know them, you'll realize that Lee and Natalie only do exactly what they want to do. At present, they want to help you. But don't believe me. You're a smart girl." He grimaced. "And very suspicious. I'm sure you'll find out for yourself."

"I'm sure I will, too." But she desperately wanted to believe that the Walbergs would be everything Mandak said they were. It would be almost too good to be true.

He glanced at the house. "There are Lee and Natalie coming out the front door. They must have seen us and gotten impatient." He started to get out of the car. "Come on, I'll introduce you."

"No." She put her hand on his knee. "Stay here. I'll go alone." She jumped out of the car and smiled recklessly at him. "New start, Mandak."

He nodded and leaned back in his seat.

But it was a frightening new start, she thought, as she forced herself to go up the flagstone walk toward the man and woman waiting at the front door. They were a handsome couple in their early sixties. They looked their age but appeared very fit, and Natalie Walberg's shining white hair was cut stylishly and she was fashionably dressed in slacks and a scarlet tunic.

Allie stopped a few yards from them. For an instant, she wished she'd let Mandak come with her.

What should she say?

What could she say? Go for it. "Hello, I'm Allie." She took a deep breath. "What do we do now?"

Lee Walberg laughed. "Hell if I know."

"Pay no attention to him. He's feeling a bit awkward." Natalie's face lit with a smile so kind and loving it took Allie's breath away. "What do we do? You come into the house and we give you a soft drink and we start to talk." She threw the front door open wide. "And I say welcome home, Allie."

Home.

The dream of a lifetime.

And it was Mandak who had made this fragile, tentative dream come true.

She instinctively looked back over her shoulder at him.

But Mandak was gone.

CHAPTER FIVE

"I'M HOME," ALLIE CALLED OUT as she slammed the front door behind her. "I took the damn test, and I didn't do anything that would embarrass you and Natalie. I wrote what Simpson wanted me to write. But you do know that history professor is a fake and an idiot?" She came into the library and threw her briefcase on the couch. "I was so tempted . . ." She brushed a kiss on the top of Lee Walberg's thinning gray hair. "Particularly when he started talking about how the new academic blood at the university was so much sharper than the fuddy-duddies he'd replaced. He was talking about you, Lee. Stupid ass. You're brilliant. Everyone on the staff knows that. I wanted to sock him."

"So what's new?" His grin lit his thin face with warmth. "You're always ready to sock someone in my defense. You've got to realize that I'm no longer respected except in certain circles. I'm not liberal enough. That's why I retired before you came to us. So just ignore idiots like

Simpson." He squeezed her hand. "We both know that you could run rings around him, but you need that course for your master's."

"He'll try every way he can to make sure I don't get it." She made a face. "He made me jump through hoops when I aced his quizzes. He accused me of cheating until I could prove it was just this damn photographic memory."

"He's jealous. But you'd fare better if you'd keep your thoughts to yourself." He chuckled. "And didn't always want to sock him. He's not that stupid, Allie."

"Almost. Where's Natalie?"

"In her studio. Why don't you go see if you can talk her into stopping work and going out to lunch with us? I want to celebrate the immense strides you've made in self-discipline."

"Sarcasm? Today took a hell of a lot of self-discipline, Lee." She turned and headed for the staircase. "And Natalie will think so, too. She can't stand Simpson. Let's do Mexican."

"Whatever."

His tone was absent, she realized. She looked back over her shoulder at him. He was no longer smiling, and he looked older than his seventy years. "You okay?"

"Wonderful." His smile came again. "Why shouldn't I, with a tiger like you to defend me? I was just wondering if my stomach is going to tolerate that hot sauce at your favorite Mexican restaurant. I decided that I'll survive it. Go get Natalie."

She nodded but still hesitated. She was uneasy. Lee was always so fit and full of wit and humor that she wasn't accustomed to thinking about his age. But she supposed she should. He had been in his sixties when he and

Natalie had taken her into their home and lives seven years ago. She had never known anyone like them, and it had taken almost a year before she realized that they were as genuinely good as they appeared on the surface. "I didn't know you had stomach trouble. Why didn't you tell me? We can go somewhere else. Have you been to a doctor and had it checked—"

"Allie, I'm fine. It's not unusual to have indigestion with hot food."

"Then why did you scare me?" She flew back to him and gave him a quick hug. "First, Simpson, then you. This has not been a great day for me, Lee."

"Then we'll have to see that it gets better." His arms closed around her. "How about going to the movies after lunch? There's a new Sorkin film in town. You said that you thought he was always intelligent."

"Sure." She stepped back and turned again toward the stairs. "Why not? I need intelligence at the moment." She ran up the stairs. "Give me thirty minutes, Lee. It will take me at least that long to pry Natalie away from that painting . . ."

"And for you to brag how restrained you were at class today."

"Yeah." She grinned back at him. "She'll want to sock him, too." She ran up the next landing and down the hall. She had been joking, but she could always count on support from both of them. These last seven years had been wonderful, not without problems, but for the most part problems that other young people her age had to face. She had been awkward about interacting with the other students, and she could tell they were sometimes uneasy with her. At first, she'd had to concentrate so hard on not reading them or the effort to totally block those memories that she must have seemed slow on the uptake. But she'd gotten better and eventually was able to have a seminormal relationship with a few of them. She'd even reached out and experimented with sex, which had been stimulating physically but offered its own problems. It was hard to block a partner's past memories when you were sexually aroused. Her solution was just to make the act so exciting that he lived totally in the present. It seemed to work, and she checked another normal accomplishment off the list.

But at the end of all the experiments and challenges, she had come home to Lee and Natalie, and that alone had made those years stellar. The love that had grown between her and Lee and Natalie Walberg had made that happiness complete. "I'm home, Natalie," she called. "We're going out to lunch."

She stopped in the open doorway of Natalie's studio. Natalie always left the door open when she was working. She said that she didn't want to close out the world when she was painting. "Life enriches everything we touch," she'd told Allie. "If I absorb enough life, someday my daubs will become masterpieces. Or not. But anyway I won't miss being with you and Lee because I'm being pretentious."

There was nothing in the least pretentious about Natalie at this moment, Allie thought. She wore sandals and jeans, and her white hair was tied back out of her face. She was frowning absently at the canvas in front of her. "Lunch?"

"Lunch," Allie repeated. "Mexican."

"That's nice." Natalie added a little ochre to the paint

of the bowl of bananas on the canvas. "How did your test go?"

"As expected." She came into the room and climbed on the stool next to the easel. "He's an ass, but I was very good."

Natalie looked up with a grin. "Now that's not what I expected at all."

"Lee would have been upset. I can always stomp on that arrogant bastard after I get my grade."

"True." She stepped back and tilted her head. "What do you think about the background colors I'm using?"

"Honestly? Those streaks look like a cross between a sunset in hell and a cotton-candy contest at a county fair."

"I think so, too." She sighed. "I was going for different and unique. I hate these boring still lifes."

"Then why are you doing it?"

"Because I wanted a challenge. Challenges are important. If you keep doing what you want and what's easy for you, then you never grow." She looked at Allie perched on the stool. "For instance, it would be easy for me to paint you again. Lord, I'm tempted. You've changed since I did that portrait two years ago."

"No." Allie held up her hand. "You made me sit for hours on end for you. I nearly went crazy."

"But Lee loved his birthday present." Her eyes lit with mischief. "He has another birthday coming up in three months. Just enough time to—"

"No," Allie repeated firmly. "That still life is looking better to me all the time. Just tone down the streaks."

"Hmm." She looked back at the canvas. "I'll hurry and get this done, so I can start your sketch. I know you won't want to disappoint Lee."

Allie shook her head. "And you're not going to give up, are you?"

"Why should I? You're soft as butter."

"Could be." About Lee. About Natalie. She couldn't deny it. "We'll talk about it later. Finish up that bowl. I told Lee I'd make you break in thirty minutes."

"Forty-five. I've got to change. Mexican, you said?"

"That's the initial plan." Her brow wrinkled. "But Lee said something about having to watch out for an upset stomach. I didn't know he had problems."

"As far as I know, he doesn't." Natalie looked at her in surprise. "I'll have to ask him about it."

"Do that. He'll tell you and not just pat you on the head."

"He does that with you?"

"You know he does. You both do."

"And do you resent it?"

"It frustrates me sometimes." She smiled. "But, no, I don't resent it. I kind of like it. It shows that you care about whether or not I'm worrying."

"That's what families do, Allie," Natalie said softly. "Care."

"I've found that out." Allie met her eyes, then looked back at the painting. "Forty-five minutes, Natalie. I'm sitting here until you put down that brush."

LEE COULD HEAR ALLIE AND Natalie talking and laughing only a few minutes after Allie disappeared around the bend of the staircase. It was a familiar, endearing sound, and his own lips curved in response.

"She loves you."

Lee turned to look at Andre Mandak, who had just

opened the French doors leading from the garden. "What's not to love?" he asked flippantly. "I'm a grand and wonderful person, and she's a very perceptive woman." He paused. "And I'd just as soon that you don't insist on seeing her unless you have a good reason. She's always disturbed when you leave."

"Is that why you pushed me out into the garden?" Mandak smiled. "How protective you are, Lee. It's not as if I've been dogging her footsteps during these last years. I haven't come here more than ten or twelve times a year. Just when she seemed to be having difficulties adjusting and needed a little streamlining with the blocking."

"But you've been coming more frequently lately. Six times in the last two months."

"Yes."

"Why?"

"Because I wanted to do it. I told you that I was in charge when I delivered Allie to you. You agreed to it."

"That was seven years ago. Things have . . . changed."

"Yes, they have. But some things haven't changed. You and Natalie gave Allie the security and normal life I wished for her." He paused. "But she also needed me. I arranged for you to be her emotional support, and you've done a good job. But I was able to give her something you couldn't."

"Do you think I don't know that?" Lee said roughly. "I could see her beginning to heal the more you worked with her. After every session, she was more confident and eager to face the world. Allie was walking wounded in more ways than one when you and Josh Dantlow brought her to us. But she's almost normal now. You've taught her how to control accepting that damn memory bleed from everyone around her."

"Not entirely. It needs constant reinforcement." He paused. "And that's not the only thing she needs from me. What about all of her own memories of the ugliness that she was forced to tap? Sometimes, it's still overpowering for her. I can go in and neutralize it."

"Those bastards," Lee said harshly. "Doing that to a helpless kid."

"The problem was that she's never been helpless. She's always had weapons that could turn lethal."

"And you've been there to make sure those weapons are honed and ready." Lee was silent a moment. "Back off, Mandak. She's been punished enough. Let her live as good a life as she can."

Mandak smiled. "You didn't say that when I suggested bringing Allie to you. You didn't accept her entirely out of the generosity of your heart. You remembered your son, Simon, and looked at her and saw only revenge. Have you forgotten, Lee?"

"You know better than that. But it was a mistake. We can find another way."

"Perhaps. But I'm not willing to wait," he said without expression. "I went out and searched and found my weapon, and I'm going to use her. I once told Allie that she wasn't unique, but she's very close to it."

"Damn you."

"Seven years ago, you thought I was the answer to your prayers." He studied his face. "But you're soft; I was afraid this would happen. You love Allie. Natalie, too?"

"Yes." He said in a rush, "Dammit, she's worth loving. She's smart and giving and only wants a chance."

"And I gave it to her."

"And now you're getting ready to take it back. Do you

think I don't know why you've been coming so often lately?"

"She's ready for me."

"The hell she is. If you leave her alone, she could finish her education and have a career. Maybe get married and have children."

"She might still be able to have all that afterward."

"If she's not dead or crazy." He urged, "Leave her alone. Natalie and I don't want her sacrificed on Simon's altar. He wouldn't want it either."

"Simon wasn't the only one," Mandak said. "He was just the only one who mattered to you. I have a long list."

Lee started to curse beneath his breath.

Mandak shook his head. "I have to take her." He suddenly smiled. "But not quite yet. You'll have some time with her. I haven't set up the details."

"You may be surprised," Lee said grimly. "Allie has changed from the kid you knew years ago. You've only had short encounters with her. She's a woman who runs her own life now. She may not be willing to be 'taken.'"

"Then that will only make it more interesting." Mandak shrugged. "And I knew she would be difficult from the beginning. All fire and stubbornness . . ." He turned and opened the French doors. "I won't stay and see her now. That would only upset you that I disturbed your gentle little tigress. I'll come tomorrow. Enjoy your day."

The next moment, he was gone.

Lee's hands clenched into fists as he gazed after Mandak. He couldn't make the bastard listen to him. Mandak was a law unto himself, and this project had been on his agenda for a long time. Lee had admired the obsessive determination that had driven Mandak all these years. It had matched his own passion for revenge.

Before Allie had come into their lives. Before they realized that they might have to trade her life for that revenge.

No! He wouldn't let that happen. He and Natalie would find a way to keep Allie safe. He would talk to Natalie tonight, and they would discuss ways and means. They had been married forty-two years, and they had never been beaten yet. Except once.

Except when they had lost their son, Simon, to that butcher, Praland.

He closed his eyes as a rush of pain surged through him. *If you knew her, you wouldn't want her hurt, son. Help us to save her.*

There has to be another way.

LEE MIGHT BECOME A PROBLEM, Mandak thought as he got into his Mercedes rental car. He supposed he should have foreseen that problem. But he'd been so absorbed in the main issues that he'd only been aware that everything appeared to be going along efficiently and left it to Lee and Natalie. In general, he'd chosen well in bringing Allie to them. They'd been so heartbroken about Simon's death and he had taken into account that they were kind, sympathetic people, and Allie was a victim who would appeal to them.

She had even appealed to him that night in the forest and the weeks at the lodge afterward.

He had found himself caught, held, torn between that fire and emotional storm that had shaken him as he interacted with her and the anger that he'd feel this way. It had not been in his plan to have Allie have an effect on him. His duty as a Searcher called on him to seek out and help those who had troubling gifts such as Allie possessed. Yet he was always careful to distance himself when he was dealing with a victim. But he hadn't been able to distance himself that night with Allie. She had touched him with a wild multitude of emotions. A few times he had felt as if he was getting too close . . .

But he'd managed to take control and move forward with the plan. Everything had been in place, and he'd insinuated Allie faultlessly into the life he'd chosen for her. A small university far from Camano's stomping grounds. Two very respected retired teachers to pretend that Allie was a distant relative they'd allowed to come to live with them while she finished her education. Throw in a relatively small student body to give Allie her best chance to keep from going crazy by being bombarded by her fellow students' memories, and the groundwork was there for her to survive. The weeks of intensive working with her when she'd arrived at Flagstaff had been enough to keep her steady and start her on the right path. He'd deliberately kept himself away from her for the next six months and let her adjust to Lee and Natalie after he'd turned her over to them. He'd noticed big progress in those months though Allie was resentfully aware that she still needed him. That resentment had persisted through the years. The bonding had lessened but never left them, and when he had to reinforce her early training, it slipped effortlessly into place. Allie didn't want to rely on anyone or anything, and she was still as suspicious of him as the night they met.

And so she should be, he thought. He had never lied to her nor would he. But he had never told her anything close to the entire truth.

But that time was coming.

Yet his talk with Lee Walberg had made him uneasy. Lee would not tell her anything unless it actually came down to trying to save her from Mandak. He was too grateful for Mandak's help in finding Simon, and loyalty was ingrained in him. But he'd added an element of uncertainty, and it might mean he'd have to escalate the plan.

His cell phone rang. Josh Dantlow. He hadn't been expecting him. He hoped to hell Lee Walberg hadn't called him and tried to— "What is it, Dantlow?"

"A little courtesy would be nice," Dantlow said dryly. "Considering the cooperation I've been giving you all these years, Mandak, I think I deserve it."

"You gave me cooperation because you thought Allie Girard would someday be able to give you information that would bring Camano and the other crime bosses down in one glorious trash heap."

"But she hasn't done it. Seven years is a long time. When can I expect something, anything, from her? It's not as if I can justify budget expenditures for protective surveillance involving her when you wouldn't even let me keep her record on file. It wasn't reasonable that you—"

"Why are you suddenly so concerned?" He didn't like this. Dantlow was not usually on edge. "You agreed that it was worth the wait. I promised you that you'd get what you needed eventually."

Dantlow was silent. "I may need it now. I don't like the way things are shaping up in Allie's case. There are . . . problems."

"Spit it out," Mandak said harshly. "What the hell do you mean?"

"Budget. We have a new administration, and they're

making us cross t's and dot i's. I couldn't just bury the Allie Girard file completely."

Mandak muttered a curse. "Dammit, I took care of all the living expenses for the Walbergs and Allie."

"But I still had to make sure that there was protection for such a valuable witness. It was part of my job." He paused. "And I had to justify that protection."

Mandak asked slowly and precisely, "And just how did you justify it, Dantlow?"

"I didn't enter it into the computer. It was a one-page file that had only the scantiest information. Just enough to—"

"Satisfy the bureaucrats and possibly put Allie in jeopardy. What was in that file?"

"I'll send it to you," Dantlow said. "Seven years, Mandak. I didn't think there was a chance in hell that anyone would still be interested in that kid. I thought we were safe."

"But someone was interested, weren't they? That file was compromised?"

"I can't be sure that it was her file, but the record room showed an intrusion, and the file drawers on that side of the room had been opened and examined."

"And photographed."

"More than likely."

"I could break your neck."

"It might be okay. They might not have been after info about Allie. My witness files could be invaluable to any number of crime figures. I'm just pissed off someone managed to breach my security. They were experts, and they could have been wanting to sell the information to the highest bidder. And we can't be sure that anyone will even recognize her as the same girl. She's changed. I made no mention of Teresa Casali."

"She's not changed that much." But he had to hope that Dantlow was right and the theft was a random hit and that he'd have time to explore the situation.

And get Allie away before all hell broke loose.

"You've seen her more often than I have during these years. Last year when I checked in on her, I was pleasantly surprised. Gorgeous and not at all like the uncivilized urchin you turned over to me that night in Kentucky."

"She must have been on her best behavior," he said dryly. "She's not shown me that side of her character lately."

"Because she didn't trust you?"

"Maybe. At least I wouldn't have put her file in a cabinet for anyone to grab."

"Computer files can be hacked, too. In fact, it's more likely. She may still be safe."

"And she may not. You wouldn't be putting pressure on me to get her to perform and lasso your bad guys if you didn't think that there's a chance that she might be a target."

Silence. "It's possible."

"When were your files compromised?"

"Two nights ago."

"And you didn't call me right away?"

"I was investigating the situation. I sent out feelers to our informants in the Camano organization to see if there were any ripples."

"And?"

"Indeterminate."

"But you were uneasy enough to call me and try to prod me into saving your ass."

"Bullshit. I don't play that way. My ass has been on the line before. I wanted to do my job and complete what we started out to do."

He was probably being honest. Mandak wouldn't have dealt with him if he didn't know he had integrity. But the anger was still flaring and he had to control it. "And still not have trouble with your damn budget."

"Okay, I made a mistake. Can you wrap Allie Girard up?"

"I was on my way to doing that. It will just take a little more time. Do I have it?"

"I told you that the status was indeterminate. I can let you know if I hear anything from Camano's camp."

"I want Allie's security doubled until we're certain one way or the other."

"I've already taken care of that. Joseph Gillen and Bill Pontlin are reporting to me every two hours. Nothing unusual so far." He paused. "This isn't only about Allie. Can't you persuade her to come in and give us a statement? It would take guts, but I'd judge that she might do it."

"And then I'd have to start all over, and it would be a miracle if she lived to go to court. Let me handle it. You just keep her safe until I juggle some priorities and work this out." He hung up.

Son of a *bitch*.

Just when Mandak had been planning to make his move, Camano might be raising his cobra head to complicate issues.

Complicate, hell.

He'd have a tough time just keeping Allie alive, much less moving her toward his agenda.

He heard the ping from his phone and he accessed the Allie report Dantlow had sent him.

It was as scanty as Dantlow had said. Lots of double-talk and not giving specific addresses or true names.

Except for the name of the university.

And the name Allie Girard.

And that might be enough, dammit.

He looked at Allie's photo. It was hard to be objective when that face had been in his mind for the last seven years. There were some changes. As a sixteen-year-old, she'd had a thin, pale face and her enormous brown eyes had seemed to dominate it and given her a waiflike quality. Her short, curly, dark hair had added to the urchin look.

The face of the woman in this photo had the same huge brown eyes, but her features had matured. Her lips were beautifully formed and her high cheekbones interesting and no longer waiflike. He'd told her to grow out her hair, and it hung below her shoulders now and shone with auburn highlights. She kept her skin bronze the year long with a self-tanner to add to the contrast with that elfin appeal. Dantlow was right. She was gorgeous, and a casual glance would not identify her as that kid running through the woods so long ago.

If that report was casual.

But it was Allie's expression that he was most worried about. The features might have matured, but the expression was the same. Bold, challenging, ready to take on the world. Why couldn't Dantlow see it? Mandak had been so aware of that spirit that he'd not allowed himself to notice the cosmetic changes.

But there were people in Allie's past who had faced that expression every day of her young life. Her mother, teachers, the goons Casali had kept around him during her childhood.

If they had cared enough to notice.

He could only hope that they had not cared and that the hunt had not been specifically for Allie.

And that he had enough time to set up a new scenario to keep her from getting killed.

CHAPTER SIX

"OKAY, I'M DONE. I'M GOING to bed." Allie yawned as she threw down her cards. "You two cardsharps can fight it out between you. I've got an early class."

"Excuses. Excuses," Natalie murmured. "We keep giving you our very best instruction in this fine art, and you never quite get it." She looked at Lee. "And Lee would be so easy for you to beat if you concentrated. You wouldn't even have to bluff. He's much too soft where you're concerned."

"True." Lee smiled. "But I'd rather watch your expressions when you're conniving than spoil it by going for the jugular." He glanced at Allie. "Your class isn't with our revered history professor?"

"Hell, no. I wouldn't even have to prepare if it was him."

"I've been thinking about that." He looked back down at his cards. "Perhaps it's time you continued your studies somewhere else."

She froze. "What are you talking about?' "

"You need more of a challenge. I could arrange for you to go to a university in Utah or Colorado that would be more interesting for you."

Her eyes widened. "You want me to go away?"

"No," Natalie said quickly. "Lee is being very clumsy about this. We love having you with us. But that's the point, Allie. You're with us most of the time. As long as you're here, you're not out with people your own age and reaching out for the brass rings."

"Screw the brass rings."

"You haven't had more than a half dozen dates in the last four years. You're a wonderful, loving woman. We want you to have normal relationships."

"So you're sending me away?"

"God, no," Lee said. He glanced at Natalie with disgust. "You didn't do any better than I did. Now she thinks that we believe she's not normal." He said to Allie, "We thought you'd like a complete change of scene. Natalie and I could scratch together enough to hire your own security and get rid of Dantlow. You'd be on your own and free. It was only a suggestion. I just wanted to get your take on it."

"It's a lousy suggestion," Allie said. "That's my take. I don't want to go away from you." She paused. "Unless you're finding me a bother. If that's true, I'll go wherever you want me to go." Her gaze searched Lee's face. "But I don't think you do feel that way. I believe I'd sense it. I'm far too insecure as far as relationships go to ever take it for granted." She moistened her lips. "I don't give a damn about dating and brass rings and hobnobbing with people my own age. For the first time in my life, I feel as if I have a family. We started off kind of shaky, but as time passed, I knew that you felt something for me. And I was sure I felt something for you." She made a face. "See how clumsy I am? I'm afraid to say the word." She was silent, then said awkwardly, "I love you guys. I love and respect you, and I'm grateful you've let me come into your lives. I'll do anything you say if you'll just let me stick around."

"Of course you can stick around," Natalie said crisply. Her hazel eyes were glittering with moisture belying that brusqueness. "But you have to promise us that you'll think about going to another university. Being selfish is a privilege of old age, and Lee and I are too young to have earned that privilege." She made a sweepingly dismissive gesture. "Now go to bed. Though all this emotional nonsense will probably keep you awake anyway."

Allie hesitated, gazing at them uncertainly. It had been a difficult and uneasy few minutes, and she wasn't sure what was expected of her. Then she came forward and gave Natalie a kiss on the forehead. "It wasn't nonsense," she said quietly. "Loving you and Lee is the most intelligent thing I've ever done in my life. The rest of it has been a crazy jumble of incoherency and mistakes, but that shines out bright and true." She gave Lee a quick kiss on the tip of his nose and headed for the stairs. "So finish playing cards and have your discussion about what's good for me. But unless you take a sudden dislike to me, you're going to have to kick me out."

"No danger," Lee said gruffly. "But just do what Natalie suggests. Think about it. Okay?"

"Okay." It wasn't okay. She had hoped the subject had been dropped. This sounded like she might have to face this conversation again. She started up the steps. "Good night."

She paused on the landing to look back at them. They had not started the next game of cards. They were sitting before the fire, gazing at each other. Troubled. She knew that expression, she knew all their expressions. When she had found that she had stumbled on that wonderful bonanza lode of affection, she had wanted to experience every facet of it.

And Lee and Natalie were definitely troubled about her. Why? For God's sake, just because she didn't want to go out on dates? She had experimented with sex and found it exciting. But sex wasn't love, and she had found genuine affection with Lee and Natalie. Affection and safety and the knowledge that she was as important to them as they were to her.

Okay, maybe that wasn't normal. But it was *her* normal. She'd thought Lee and Natalie had understood. Evidently not. Perhaps she'd better make the effort to go out more. Maybe bring some guy home to dinner or spend the night at a motel to prove to them they weren't cramping her style.

She started up the second landing.

As if she had a style yet. She was still stretching, learning, putting bandages on old wounds. She was doing pretty damn well for a cripple, and Lee and Natalie had helped enormously. But there was still a long way to go.

She opened the door to her room. She would just have to work her way around this sudden concern of Lee and Natalie's and give them what they—

"Good evening, Allie. I had no idea you were such an enthusiastic cardplayer. I've been waiting a long time."

Mandak.

She froze as she saw him lounging with legs outstretched before him in the big chair by the window. The sight of him struck her with that tingling awareness, as it always did. The piercing blue eyes that seemed to know and understand everything about her. The sensual mouth that was half-parted in a mocking smile. The muscular body that she had touched, felt the power, challenged, and yet been held and comforted by. Her own body was instinctively readying to meet that challenge.

"Hello, Mandak." She hadn't seen him for a few weeks and that had been for only one short hour. It wasn't like the past sessions, where he'd actually probed, soothed, held her when the confusion and pain was too much. Those last couple visits it was as if he was making a duty call. He'd asked her about blocking problems, inquired about her karate training with Milt Nolan, the martial arts instructor to whom he'd assigned her, talked casually about Natalie and Lee. Then he'd gone as quickly as he'd come.

And left her on edge and feeling that maddening sense of loss and resentment that he could make her respond that way.

"I'm not enthusiastic about cards. Ask Lee and Natalie." She slammed the door behind her. "And you wouldn't have had to wait if you'd called me and asked if I was available instead of creeping up here like a cat burglar." She looked at the open window. "Don't tell me you actually did come in that way? I can't believe it."

"It seemed the best entry under the circumstances. I wanted to talk to you as soon as possible, and I didn't want to run into Lee and Natalie." He smiled. "And, besides, it brought back memories of the old days, when life was a little more exciting than it's been lately."

"The old days? I was joking about the cat burglar." She gazed at him with narrowed eyes. "Should I have been?"

"Let's just say I developed some similar skills in that direction."

"It doesn't surprise me. Cat burglary is minor in comparison to your true potential. Nothing surprises me about you. You killed three men in the first ten minutes after I met you."

"And?"

"Okay." He was waiting for honesty, and she gave it to him. "I would probably have been dead if you hadn't done it."

"But you still resent that I killed them."

"No, I resent that you did it so easily and efficiently. Death should be difficult and hard. It's the difference between good and evil. I grew up with a father and the people around him who had no trouble with killing." She met his eyes. "I felt as if I were back with them when you stepped in and killed Tantona and the others. I was afraid of you."

"You didn't show it."

"It didn't last long. There were too many things happening to me. And I was too worried about the fact that your memories were blank to me." She added, "But it comes back now and then." She braced herself. "Like right now. And I don't like to be afraid. It makes me want to strike out."

"I know."

"So, unless you want to get socked, why don't you tell me why the hell you're here tonight."

He chuckled. "You do amuse me, Allie. There's no one like you. You don't have to be afraid of me."

"I didn't say I was afraid of you," she said quickly. "Well, maybe I did. But I should have said I'm afraid of what you might bring to me, what . . . surrounds you."

"Surrounds me?"

What was she doing speaking to him so bluntly? She had been avoiding that frankness since the moment he had turned her over to Josh Dantlow. No, that wasn't true. Those weeks at the lodge had been honest in their own strange way. Afterward, she had deliberately walked carefully whenever she was with him. She had known in this new life that she could only let him enter tentatively and even then held at a distance. She couldn't read his memories, but she'd always been aware that what lay beneath was violent and forceful and a power like nothing she'd ever encountered.

A power that drew her, fascinated her, as it was doing right now. When she was younger, that power revolved around the mental aura of danger that she had immediately recognized. But as she grew older and matured, it was sometimes overshadowed by the sexual response she had whenever she was near him. At the lodge, she had been too absorbed to let herself feel anything but the emotional response of that weird bonding and the obsession with what she was learning. That changed once he was no longer with her. The first time he'd come back to see her, it had hit her with solid, bewildering force. After that she had explored sex with a number of good-looking, virile men she'd met at the university, but she had never felt anything like the searing sexuality that she felt for Mandak. Dangerous sexuality. Sex could make you weak and pliable. It was one of the principal reasons why she had worked so hard to keep that coolness in place when he had visited her.

"Interesting observation." His brows lifted. "I didn't realize that you were that . . . sensitive. I wonder what else I've missed. I think it's time I found out." He added softly, "Come sit down, Allie. Your hands are clenched. But I doubt if you're going to go on the attack until you hear what I have to say."

She opened the hands she hadn't realized she'd

clenched. "Why didn't you want Lee and Natalie to know that you were here?" She made a motion with her hand. "Never mind, I think I know. You're going to try to persuade me to leave here, aren't you? Well, I won't go. Why should I? I don't owe you anything, Mandak." Only her life and sanity and the only loving family relationship she'd had since the day she was born. "Okay, maybe I do. But what you did for me was done for your own purpose."

"That's true," Mandak said. "But I'm afraid persuasion wasn't going to enter into it. Considering how bullheaded you are, I doubted whether arguments or wiles would work. But there are other methods." He paused. "However, there are complications that have to be addressed before I delve into that. I *am* going to move you from the university, and this time I won't involve Lee and Natalie."

"Bullshit." She stiffened. "I'm not going with you. I'm not leaving here, Mandak."

"Camano may know where you are," he said bluntly. "Your file was compromised."

Shock. No, it couldn't be true. Not after all this time. She'd even had dreams of actually being free. "How convenient. You're lying."

"No."

She searched his expression. How would she even know if he was lying or not? He'd always been an enigma to her.

"It's true, Allie. Call Josh Dantlow."

"You told me that you could control him."

"But you've gotten to know something about him. He's an honest man."

"Yes." Her knees felt weak. She sank down on the bed. The nightmare had returned. She had almost felt as if the threat had disappeared over the horizon, but here was the ugliness staring her in the face. "How much chance is there that they'll find me?"

"I can't give you a percentage. I don't like any odds that involve you and Camano. That's why I'm taking you out of here."

"Does Lee know?"

He shook his head. "I just found out myself."

"Are you sure? Tonight he and Natalie were . . ."

"What?"

"They wanted me to go away."

"I was expecting that to happen. No, that was about me, not Camano."

"You?" She shook her head. "And I thought it was about me. I thought I wasn't behaving normally enough for them." She made a face. "Not surprising since I don't know what normal really is. I was planning on how I could make them think I'd changed."

"It wasn't about you," Mandak said. "They care about you. They were willing to give up a plan that we'd worked on for years to protect you."

"What plan?" When he didn't answer, she said slowly, "They were going to let you use me? I tried to believe they were just an innocent couple who were supposed to furnish credibility to my presence here. They were actually in on it?"

"They didn't know you. All they knew was that you could help me, and they desperately wanted me to get what I needed."

"Why?"

"Ask them. Personal reasons. Intensely personal."

"It would have to be. I know them, and they wouldn't betray anyone for money."

"But you're suspecting I would?"

"I'm suspecting you're totally ruthless and would do anything necessary to move your damn agenda." She added with sudden fierceness, "But you shouldn't have involved Lee and Natalie. You're right, they do care about me. They would have been torn apart by these games you're playing."

"You're not angry with them?"

"We were all tiptoeing around when I came here, trying to find a way to live comfortably together. But then we found that way, and it became damn wonderful." She paused, trying to probe her own feelings as well as explain. "Am I a little hurt? Yes. I wish they hadn't had a reason for being kind to me, but that's life. *My* life. No one is perfect. But they come pretty close. They gave me something very special. They love me. I *know* it. When you weigh that in the balance of the nothing I had before, I don't have the right to be angry."

He was silent. "That's a remarkably mature way of dealing with the issue."

"I am mature." Her lips twisted. "In case you didn't notice, I'm not that kid you picked up and stuffed away in this house seven years ago."

"Oh, I noticed," he said softly.

Sensuality.

Heat.

She lost her breath.

Her breasts were becoming taut.

Back off. Back off. Back off.

"I mean mentally and emotionally," she said quickly. "I've had time to think, to sort things out, and get my feelings straight on a good many subjects."

"I regret I haven't been around you enough to see that come to pass. I was principally concerned with getting you ready to face the world without having to be shredded to pieces by having to deal with the memory albatross." He paused. "And I did a good job, didn't I? During those first few months, I believe you were even grateful."

"I *was* grateful." She was remembering those first three months of intense therapy after she had arrived at the university. Recalling how he had talked to her, made her talk to him, she even suspected that there had been some kind of subtle hypnosis involved. Then he had started making her work, showed her how to build walls and fight off intruders. She hadn't been sure any of it would work. Her mind had been shattered by chaos for so long. Then, she saw that it was clearing, becoming clean and tight and bright with no intrusions bombarding her. It wasn't a total block, there were still attacks that caught her off guard. But he had made it possible for her to function. The last night, after Mandak had left her, she had broken down and wept. "It was the difference between day and night for me."

"I know. You told me. I was surprised you admitted it."

She hadn't wanted to admit it. Because that gift he'd given her showed he wielded too much power, and she hadn't wanted him to know the dependence on him she felt. "Why not? You seemed to know everything else about me."

"Enough to keep you comfortable and give you a chance

to open your mind to something besides other people's memories," he said. "Lee tells me you've had a good life here with a good deal of progress in all areas."

"He gave you reports?"

"Nothing so formal. He just kept me informed."

"But informed regarding personal and educational?"

"I had to know how your therapy was holding."

"That's a report." She shook her head. "I'm not going to dwell on it. It's over. Now I have to decide on what Lee, Natalie, and I are going to do."

"You're going with me. I'm going to move Lee and Natalie to a location in South Carolina. I've set up a safe house for them, and I'll have Dantlow arrange immediate security to protect them."

"You said that you don't even know for sure if I'm in danger. It might suit you to send me on the run from Camano, so that I'd run toward you."

"I thought about that." He shook his head. "But that's not why I'm doing it. As I said, this is a complication."

"And I have to be the one to work out that complication. After all, it's my life."

"And I have no intention of your losing it after I've done so much to preserve it," he said grimly. "I want to move you tonight, now. I'll call Lee and explain once we're on the road."

"You're taking me out the window and down the drainpipe?" she asked sarcastically.

"No drainpipe. There's a roof over the bay window five feet below. You won't have a problem."

"You bet I won't. I have no intention of crawling out there tonight. I'll go down and talk to Lee and Natalie and decide what we're going to do." She frowned, thinking. "I imagine we'll pack up and leave right away, wherever we decide to go. Though I'd like to go on ahead and have them join me. If I'm not here, there won't be any threat to Lee and Natalie." She grimaced. "But I'll have to see if they'll agree."

"I doubt if they'll want to let you out of their sight." He got to his feet. "Once you've left, I gather you're not going to contact me and let me know your plans?"

"I didn't say that. I'll let Dantlow know where we end up. He'll tell you." She paused. "And I may call you. You have an interest in keeping all of us alive. I'd be stupid to sacrifice your help because I can't trust you to let me do things my way."

"Yes, you would." He smiled. "And you're not stupid. Stubborn, not stupid." He moved toward the window. "I'd prefer you come with me now. We could argue out the details and ramifications once we're out of here."

"We could, but I've never noticed that you argue. You take, Mandak."

"But usually in a civilized way." He stopped to look at her as he slid his leg over the sill. "And I almost always find a way to make it palatable. You won't change your mind?"

She shook her head. "I don't think that what you want from me is in the least palatable. Or you wouldn't be so evasive about telling me about it." She met his gaze. "And I've never found you civilized."

His smile faded. "No, that doesn't appear to be working in our relationship. I think I tried it when you were that scared kid in the forest. It should have been easy then. Big brother and all that . . . But I never felt that way about you. Afterward . . . forget it." He paused. "One question. Have you ever contacted your mother since you've been here?"

"No. Have I wanted to do it? Yes. But I knew that she wasn't strong enough to fight Camano. I couldn't risk putting Natalie and Lee in danger." She moistened her lips. "Is she still with him?"

He nodded. "This is the first time you've asked me."

"That life seems very remote. I've tried to forget it."

"Very smart." His body slid out the window and was lost to view.

She heard nothing. Quiet. He was so very quiet as he moved down the side of the house.

Had he really been a cat burglar?

Probably not. She could imagine the wildness and reckless disregard of the law, but he was too intelligent to do that for any length of time.

She went to the window and looked out.

No Mandak.

She hadn't expected to see him, but she was disappointed. She felt somehow that Mandak was the pulse that was driving all of them, and she had to keep tabs on him.

As he had kept tabs on her all these years.

And this time, he had let her go too easily.

He would be out there somewhere, making his own plans, trying to manipulate them all as he had always done.

She shivered. Why did that worry her? That part of her life was over. She was an adult now. She was going forward under her own volition and rules.

She turned away from the window. She would go down and talk to Lee and Natalie, then come back and start packing.

Another new start, a new life, but she would not be alone this time. She would have two people who loved her to ward off that loneliness. She felt her spirits lift at the thought.

But she paused as she opened the door to look back at the darkness beyond that open window through which Mandak had disappeared.

Darkness that was filled with promises and threats.

Yet darkness that was inviting, beckoning . . .

TWO HOURS LATER, THE TEMPORARY plans had been made for Natalie, Lee, and Allie's departure at five the following morning. They'd decided their first stop would be a hotel in Colorado that Lee and Natalie had always loved. From there, they would go up to a cabin in the mountains. Now that the decision was made, there was only the task of packing up necessities, photos, and other treasures before catching a few hours' sleep.

"I'm sorry, Allie." Natalie stopped and turned to Allie as she started up the stairs. "It's not that we really meant to use you. Oh, I guess we did. Why else would we have listened to Mandak? It was just that we were so hurt and angry that our son had been so brutally taken from us that we had a gigantic hope that somehow it would work out that you'd be willing to help us. Mandak thought you might. Believe me. We never meant to hurt you."

"I know that." Allie smiled at her. "And in the end, you told Mandak to go jump in the proverbial lake."

"No, we owe him too much. But we couldn't go on with it." She hesitated. "You didn't ask us why we agreed to take care of you all these years. Why Mandak was able to persuade us to do it."

"And I won't, until you're ready to tell me."

"It's a long, nightmare story," Natalie said. "But you have a right to know." She drew a shaky breath. "Give me a minute. It's hard for me to talk about it."

"Then don't do it." She gave Natalie an impulsive hug. "I don't want to hurt you in any way. I can wait. Maybe when we're up in the mountains would be a good time. We've lived a great life together without me prying into your past. We can keep on doing that."

Natalie looked her in the eyes, and her own hazel eyes were glittering with moisture. "I never had a daughter, Allie. Only my son, Simon, who was a wonderful child, a loving and idealistic young man, who filled our lives and made having another child seem unimportant. Then he was gone, and I thought all the good things had gone with him. But when you came, you enriched every day and healed us. Sometimes I've wondered if Simon hadn't found some way to send you to us. I learned how wrong I'd been to let all the ugliness dominate our lives." She reached up and gently cupped Allie's cheek in her hand. "You know about ugliness, you've lived with it. Do you know what I want for you more than anything in the world? I want you to live every minute with joy and love. I want you to fight the poison and not let it rob you of that joy. That's the only true way of fighting all the ugliness. Will you try to do that for me?"

Allie was so touched, she could barely speak. "Natalie . . ."

"Hey, I didn't mean to make you all weepy." Natalie's voice was throaty as her hand dropped away from Allie's cheek. "I have only one more thing to say." She paused. "I want you to know I look upon you as my daughter."

She put two fingers over Allie's mouth when she opened it to speak. "Now we have to stop this sentimental talk and get busy." She started up the stairs. "I have to go up to my studio and choose two paintings to take with me. Lee won't allow me to take any more than that. He says we'll break the van down if I try to pack up all my work." She made a face. "Philistine. But he won't leave all his precious first editions behind. He's in the garage now, packing them in boxes."

"Natalie."

"It's fine. Stop frowning." Natalie's radiant smile lit her face. "We'll have each other, and that's all that's important."

"I told you that I should probably go on ahead. I still think it's a good idea."

"Just try to do it." She didn't look back at Allie as she mounted the stairs. "We're a family now. We don't leave anyone behind. Now get packed so that we can get on the road."

"Right." Allie didn't move, watching Natalie go up the stairs. She had to get control. My God, she loved her. She hadn't expected those words Natalie had spoken. Daughter? She should have said something. She should have told Natalie how much she— But Natalie always knew what she was feeling.

"Allie," Natalie called down. "Stop dithering and get to bed."

And Natalie had known Allie was down here staring after her and regretting the words she hadn't been allowed to say. "Just a few minutes more."

Allie gave one last lingering look around the cozy foyer and living room that had been her home these last seven years. It was the only place she'd considered home during her entire life. She went across to the fireplace and put out the fire. Then she moved toward the stairs. She could hear Lee moving around in the garage, and she was tempted to go to him and talk a little longer.

No, they all had to say good-bye to this place in their own way.

Time enough to talk before they left in the morning.

MANDAK SAT IN HIS CAR, watching the lights glow, then go out from different windows of the Walberg house. It was clear Lee, Natalie, and Allie were moving from room to room. That meant Allie had stirred them into action, and they would be on the move.

Not without me, Allie.

He had already bugged all the vehicles, and he'd be able to monitor them at some distance, but somehow he hadn't wanted to leave Allie tonight. She had been her usual explosive, independent self, but he'd thought he'd detected a hint of vulnerability. Not that she would admit it. He had thrown Camano's threat at her, and she'd accepted it.

But then she accepted everything that life dealt her.

Even him, he thought bitterly. And he might turn out to be the worst thing ever to come her way.

Maybe.

But maybe not. At any rate, he could keep her alive, dammit.

He reached for his phone and dialed Dantlow. "Things are blown to hell. Has Allie called you yet?"

"No, what do you mean blown to hell?"

"She and the Walbergs are taking it on the lam and not trusting either of us to keep them safe. She said she might call you and tell you their destination."

Dantlow muttered a curse. "I see your fine hand in

this. You shouldn't have told them there was any threat. It's not as if it was confirmed."

"It's not as if it wasn't. I'm not willing to risk her life on the chance that Camano isn't breathing down her neck. Have you heard anything from Trenton PD?"

He was silent a moment. "Nothing. They've been checking on various members of Camano's immediate circle who would likely be sent after Allie, and most of them are accounted for."

He went still. "Most?"

"Sal Navarro and Ben Ledko haven't been seen in their usual haunts recently, but that doesn't mean anything. There's no proof that—"

"Screw proof. Can you send me photos of them?"

"No problem. I just sent them to Allie's security surveillance, Gillen and Pontlin." He paused. "Just in case. I'm not as complacent as you think me, Mandak."

"Where are Gillen and Pontlin stationed?"

"Gillen is in his gray Toyota on Ebenezer Street. Pontlin is on foot near the backyard of the Walberg place. I've told them that you might be on-site and sent them your photo, too." He paused. "You are on-site?"

"You're damn right. And I'll be here until Allie and the Walbergs are on the road."

"And after that, you'll be on their trail. Gillen and Pontlin are good men, Mandak. You could trust them."

"But I won't. Let me know if you hear anything more." He hung up.

Navarro and Ledko. He accessed the photos Dantlow had just sent him of Camano's men. Navarro was small, thin-faced, receding dark hair. Ledko was heavier with plump, rosy cheeks, squinting, dark eyes, and sandy white hair.

Mandak would know them if he saw them now. He clicked off his phone.

Now to go find Gillen and Pontlin and make sure they were on the job. He'd identify himself and tell them he'd be calling to check on them throughout the night. They'd probably be pissed off at the interference, but too bad. They were Dantlow's men, and Dantlow had already screwed up once. He wasn't going to assume it wasn't going to happen again. He got out of his car and headed down the block toward Ebenezer Street.

CHAPTER SEVEN

TWO HOURS LATER

SLEEP.

Easy to tell herself but hard to comply, Allie thought ruefully as she restlessly turned in her bed.

She could still hear Natalie down the hall in her studio, trying to choose which of her precious paintings to take. Lee was probably doing the same with his first editions. Treasures . . .

As Allie grew older, would she start to cling to things as they were doing? She couldn't imagine it. She had dumped only the bare necessities in her brown duffel by the door. There was nothing material she possessed that couldn't be replaced.

But she hoped that Natalie and Lee would not have to leave anything they treasured behind. She wanted them to have everything that they wished for in this world.

Wait, they weren't the only ones who had clung to a treasure.

Allie had tossed something in that duffel that was not at all practical. The small brown leather photo album she had put together since she had come here. Photos were memories, and who should know better than she how precious memories could be?

Nor how terrible.

But the photos in her album were good memories. Remembrances to raise the heart and warm the soul.

But were Lee and Natalie's memories as rich and wonderful of Allie and their time together, she wondered with sudden uncertainty. For the first time, she wished she could read their memories and find out.

No. She skidded away from the thought. The very fact that she couldn't read those memories had made their relationship all the more wonderful. She was grateful to Mandak that he had made it impossible for her to read them so that they could have an entirely normal relationship. She could approach them with all the fallacies of a normal person. She knew only what they wished to confide. Mandak might have given her that mental block for his own purposes, but she had regarded it as merciful when she discovered how successfully he had done it.

She still did. She didn't want to question Natalie's and Lee's motives or draw conclusions from what they held in their memories. She only wanted to hold them close and judge from actions alone. That would be enough for her.

But would it be enough for them? Before Natalie had spoken about him tonight, Allie had known they had a son, Simon, who had died. Though they had barely mentioned him through the years. Yet his death now appeared to have had something to do with their acceptance of her into their home. This home they loved and were now giving up. They were making a sacrifice and battling Mandak for her sake.

She didn't want anyone to make a sacrifice for her,

dammit. And she could not tolerate that sacrifice coming from Lee and Natalie. There had to be some way that
she could make it right for them.

*It will be okay, I won't let it hurt you. We'll work it
out together. I promise I'll make it right.*

Tomorrow. She would start tomorrow.

She closed her eyes.

Tomorrow. Problems to solve. A new life, with no
Mandak.

How strange that would be . . .

DAMMIT.

Mandak's hand clenched on his cell phone.

Gillen wasn't answering. He had answered thirty minutes ago when Mandak had called but not now.

Mandak tried Gillen's partner, Pontlin, in the backyard of the Walberg house. It went immediately to voice
mail.

Shit.

He was out of his car in seconds and tearing across
the front yard toward the sidewalk leading to the Walberg
backyard.

He almost stumbled over Pontlin as he rounded the
corner.

Blood.

Pontlin was crumpled on the brick walk leading
toward the kitchen door. Blood had poured from his
mouth, his eyes were wide open.

Dead.

A sandy-haired man in black trousers and shirt was
standing near the kitchen door, his gaze lifted to the
second floor windows. Mandak recognized him from

the photos of Camano's men e-mailed to him by Josh
Dantlow.

Ledko.

Take him out.

He reached the door in a heartbeat.

Ledko turned, his knife gleaming in his right hand.
His eyes widened as he saw him. "Mandak. What the—"

Mandak kicked him in the groin, then grabbed his
wrist and turned his own weapon on him.

The knife entered Ledko's heart a second later.

Ledko grunted, his eyes bulging.

His knees buckled, and he fell to the ground.

Mandak pushed him aside.

One down.

But Ledko had been looking up at the windows of the
second floor. Looking for what?

Camano's other man, Navarro?

Where the hell was Navarro?

He moved closer to the kitchen door.

The lock had been broken, and the door was cracked
open.

Mandak carefully, silently, opened the door.

"ALLIE."

She was being shaken.

"Wake up, we've got to get out of here."

Mandak. She knew that touch. Knew that voice.

She opened her eyes.

Blood!

Blood on his shirt. Blood on the hand shaking her.

She sat bolt upright in bed. "Mandak, I don't—"

"Just get up. Don't dress, just slip on your shoes. We've got to get out of here."

"Why?" She jumped out of bed and thrust her feet into her strollers. "Camano? You're bleeding. Are you hurt?"

"No." He grabbed her duffel, zipped it, and tossed it to her. "You carry this." He headed for the hall. "I need my hands free."

"Why?" She ran after him. "What happened? Did you wake Natalie and Lee yet?"

He didn't answer.

She stopped short. "Mandak?"

"Come on, Allie. I don't know how much time we have."

"Natalie." She turned and saw the door to Natalie's studio down the hall was thrown wide. "It doesn't make sense. Why wouldn't you wake her?" Her heart was pounding, and the world was whirling, darkening, around her.

Blood. All that blood on him . . .

No!

She ran toward the studio. "Natalie!"

She heard Mandak cursing behind her.

A man's body was lying just inside the studio door. His neck was twisted at an odd angle. His eyes were wide open, staring into nothingness.

Dead.

"Allie." Mandak was behind her. "Come away."

"He's dead. What—"

And then she saw Natalie.

She was crumpled beside her easel. Blood, everywhere. Her head was lying in a pool that streaked and dampened her white chignon with dark red. The front of her russet tunic was covered with blood.

"No!" She ran across the room and fell to her knees beside Natalie. "It's okay." She gathered her thin body close. "You'll be fine. I'll take care of you. You'll be—"

"She's dead, Allie," Mandak said gently. "She was still alive when I came, and I thought I might— But it was too late. Navarro stabbed her in the chest, then cut her throat. I couldn't do anything. She died in my arms."

"She's not dead," she said fiercely, clutching Natalie closer. "I won't let her be—"

But Natalie was so still, too still.

And all that blood . . .

"Natalie . . ." She rocked Natalie's slight body back and forth. "Do something, Mandak. Call 911. *Do* something."

"There's nothing to do, dammit. Except get you out of here to safety. I managed to get rid of Navarro and Ledko, but I can't be sure that there aren't more of Camano's men hovering close enough to—"

"Nothing to do . . ." Her eyes widened in sudden horror. "Lee. Where's Lee? Why isn't he here?" She numbly laid Natalie gently down. "He'd be here if Natalie was hurt. He'd be—"

"If he could," Mandak said. "It wasn't possible this time."

"He wouldn't let her be alone. Not if she was hurt. I know it. He wouldn't—"

She was on her feet and running from the room.

If he could.

Of course, Lee could help. Nothing would keep him from Natalie.

She ran down the stairs.

It wasn't possible this time.

Don't think of those words.

Garage.

Lee had been in the garage packing up his books.

She threw open the hall door leading to the garage. "Lee?"

She stopped short.

Lee was lying by an open cardboard box half-filled with his precious old books.

The back of his skull was crushed and bloody.

"Lee!" She started dazedly toward him.

"No." Mandak was suddenly between her and Lee. "You've had enough. I won't let you go through any more."

"Get out of my way," she said shakily. "I've got to go to him."

"He's dead. Natalie's dead. There's nothing you can do for either one of them. They'd want you to go with me."

"Get out of my way."

"Change your mind. I'm doing what's best for you, Allie."

"The hell you are," she said fiercely. "You're keeping me from helping Lee."

His gaze searched her face. "You're not thinking. And who can blame you?" Then he stepped aside. "Okay. Have it your way."

She started toward Lee.

Mandak's thumb pressed on the side of her neck.

Darkness.

BLOOD.

Natalie . . .

Lee . . .

Blood!

No! Go away. Back to the darkness. None of it was true. It was all a nightmare. She'd wake up and run down the stairs, and Natalie and Lee would be at the breakfast table. Lee would be teasing Natalie and ask Allie to settle the—

"It's time to face it, Allie," Mandak said quietly. "I've let you have healing time, but any longer would be harmful. You have to come back."

Searing anger tore through her.

"That's right, be angry with me. I don't care. It will burn away the darkness."

The darkness was already fading, she thought with panic. Bring it back.

Don't make her see Natalie lying so still that Allie knew she would never—

But the darkness was gone now, and she knew that Mandak wouldn't let it return.

She opened her eyes. "Damn you."

He smiled slightly. "Now that's the Allie I know." He was sitting on a gray, velvet-cushioned chair beside her bed. "But I believe that you might be a little more tolerant if you allow yourself. After all, I gave you time for actions and reactions to sink in." He paused. "Now tell me what happened to Natalie."

She couldn't tell him. She was starting to shake.

"Tell me."

She didn't answer.

"Tell me, Allie."

If she answered, it would mean that it was true.

"You know it's true," Mandak said. "Tell me."

She shied away from the truth he claimed was real. "She was . . . hurt."

He waited.

"Blood."

"And?"

"Dead."

"Say the words."

She didn't want to say the words. "She was dead," she said stiltedly. "That man . . . killed her."

"And Lee?"

"Dead." The word was tearing her apart. "His head . . . it was crushed." She curled up in the bed to ward off the pain. "But I don't know who . . . killed him. Was it the same man who killed Natalie?"

"Either him or Ledko, another one of Camano's men. Ledko was standing watch outside the back door when I got there. Your security guards had already been killed. After I dispatched Ledko, I went inside and found Lee in the garage. My guess is that Ledko killed Lee, then went back out to stand guard. Navarro probably had headed straight upstairs to get to you . . . and Natalie."

He sounded calm and precise. Ugly words, ugly actions. How could he sound so calm when her whole world was falling apart?

"He had to pass my door to get to Natalie's studio," she said numbly. "Why didn't he come into my room instead of attacking her?"

"The door to her studio was wide open when I ran up the stairs. Navarro may have heard her moving around and decided to take out a possible threat before he went after the prime objective."

Blood staining Natalie's beautiful white hair.

"He should have come after me." Allie's voice was shaking. "Lee and Natalie were only trying to help me. They had nothing to do with any of this." She closed her eyes. "I should have left the house as soon as you told me that Camano might be a threat. I should have run away and never contacted them again."

"It was too late even then," Mandak said quietly. "Plans evidently were already in place, and the house was being watched. Navarro and Ledko knew you lived in that house and would have gone after you regardless. When they didn't find you, they would have tortured Lee and Natalie to find out where you were." His lips twisted. "I'd like to tell you that if you'd gone with me, everything would have been different, but I can't do that."

Her eyes opened, and she said fiercely, "There should have been a way to save them. It's my fault. I should have been able to keep them alive."

"Bullshit," he said roughly. "Stop it. I've been fighting that guilt complex you've been carrying for two days, and I thought I'd beaten it down. But here it is raising its head again. Look, it happened. It wasn't your fault. It was Camano's. We all tried to keep it from happening, and we failed. So the only thing we can do is mourn them and take revenge where we can."

"It's not bullshit," she said. "It should never—" She stopped as his words hit home. "Two days?"

He nodded. "I decided to keep you under until you could work through the first shock and trauma. I thought I'd managed to stabilize you, and I couldn't let you stay under much longer. You were harder for me to bring back every time I let you slip away." He paused. "Natalie and Lee meant too much to you. You had to play out all the agony and regret while I was still there to help you filter it."

"I don't remember any of that."

"You might not ever remember it. My presence wasn't really important to you during these days. I was just something to hold on to. Or it might gradually come back to you over time."

"It was very important if you were manipulating what I was thinking." She met his eyes. "You said you were trying to stop me from feeling guilty."

"I was suggesting, arguing. I never tried to force the issue."

"How do I know that?"

He shrugged. "You don't. You don't trust me, and I have no concrete proof." His lips twisted. "But I believe you know that I wish your mind to be clear and strong and healthy. You're no good to me otherwise."

"I don't know anything about what you want from me."

"The same thing that Lee and Natalie wanted from you," he said softly.

"Don't you *dare* use them to get what you want," she said fiercely.

"I'm not going to do that. You'll decide for yourself. And I assure you, I didn't do anything to influence you. I was only concerned with keeping you from going around the bend. You came pretty close a couple times. Now that you're safe, we can take the next step." He leaned back in his chair. "But you'll want to ask questions. I'm at your disposal."

Questions. She supposed she should ask questions, but it was difficult to recognize that anything was important but Natalie and Lee. Her gaze traveled around the luxurious room. Gray and silver and crystal. Rich fabrics and sleek furnishings. "Where the hell am I?"

"Las Vegas. You're at Sean Donavel's apartment on the Strip. He's a friend of mine."

"He must be a very good friend. Do you often drop in with guests who remain unconscious for two days?"

"No, it's a first." He smiled. "But Sean and I go way back, and I knew he wouldn't object. I could have picked someone else, but I thought you'd feel safer to wake in a place that was fairly close to the university. At least you're in the same general area. I didn't want to whisk you away from your comfort zone right away."

"Comfort zone?" Her lips twisted. "Do you actually believe that I'd ever think of that place as home again?"

"No, but you had happy memories as well as that horror there." He stared her in the eye. "Didn't you, Allie?"

"You know I did."

"But I'm not part of those happy memories. I'm the threat, the darkness hovering and blocking out the sun. I thought you might need to know I hadn't kidnapped you and taken you away from everything you'd known. You're not that far from that house in Flagstaff."

"And I'm not to consider this Sean Donavel a threat, too?"

"You'll have to make your own decision about him." He shrugged. "But you will anyway. You're nothing if not opinionated. It goes with the territory with your particular gift. But you'll have to judge him at face value. I've blocked your ability to read his memories."

"What?"

"I've decided to block your ability entirely while you're going through this healing process."

She stared at him, shocked. "You can do that?" She shook her head in disbelief. "I know that you managed to block it entirely with Lee and Natalie, but I was still bombarded by some of the students at the university. That damn seventy percent."

"But it wasn't overwhelming. It wasn't so bad once we did some work on it."

"No." Her lips tightened. "But, dammit, it sounds as if you could have blocked all of those attacks. I didn't have to be constantly on guard and fight off that terrible, overpowering . . ." She drew a deep breath. "You made me go through it when I didn't have to? I could have been totally normal?"

"You'll never be normal. You have to live with it. I can do a total block for short periods but not forever."

"Am I supposed to believe that? Why should I? I've never known whether you were lying to me at any given time. You've never been honest. All I know is that you want to use me."

"Did it occur to you that my telling you that was the height of honesty? I could have deceived you, Allie."

"And wasn't that cozy charade you built with me and Lee and Natalie deceit?"

"It wasn't a charade. It started out that way, but you changed it. You managed to make Lee and Natalie love you."

And she had loved them. How she had loved them . . . A wave of pain washed over her, and she had to steady her voice. "But you don't deny trying to—"

"I don't deny anything," he said harshly. "It wouldn't do me any good, would it? You know me too well. Or at least you think you do."

"How can you say that? I don't know anything about you." She drew a shaky breath. "And I hate that. I *hate* being this dependent on a man who thinks he can pull the strings. I want you out of my life."

"I know."

"I almost got away from you. If Lee and Natalie hadn't been killed, I—" She couldn't finish. "We might have had a good, peaceful life together that wouldn't have had anything to do with you."

He shook his head. "I had a history with Natalie and Lee. In the end, they would have come back to me." He grimaced. "They might not have brought you back into the fold, but they couldn't have left the situation the way it was." He got to his feet. "I'll leave you now. You've had enough of me for the time being." He gestured across the room. "Bathroom. Your suitcase with clothes is beside the door. I grabbed the duffel in your room that you'd packed. Take some time, and I'll send Sean in to talk to you in about an hour. It will be easier for you to deal with him for the time being. There's too much between us that's high-octane. Feel free to ask him any questions about me you wish. I have a few preparations to make." He smiled crookedly. "I know you won't miss me."

"No." She got to her feet and started toward the bathroom. Then she stopped, looking down at herself. She was naked beneath a huge, white terry robe. "I wasn't wearing this. How did I—"

"Blood," he said succinctly. "You were covered with it. I bathed you, washed your hair, and got rid of your clothes."

Natalie's blood. She had held her and rocked her . . .

"Move." He motioned to the bathroom. "Don't slip back."

"I'm not slipping back. I was remembering her . . ." She stiffened. "And don't tell me what to do." She swallowed. "Besides, I have something I have to ask you. You say I've been here for two days. Something has to have

been done with Lee and Natalie. What burial arrangements have been made? I need to go and—"

"Be plucked up by Camano the minute you show your
face. No way."

"I'm not an idiot. But I've got to pay my respects and
say my last good-byes." She smiled bitterly. "I'll even let
you find a way to get me there. Pull your strings. Just
don't try to pull mine."

"I wouldn't presume."

"Bullshit. That night you told me that it was time for
me to pay the piper. That means that all restraints are out
the window." She paused. "And I don't want Dantlow to
try to scoop me up and stuff me away again. I'm done
with him. He was supposed to keep Lee and Natalie safe.
He didn't do it." She glared at him. "And neither did you.
All I want is to be done with all of you. I'll run my own
life. I can't do any worse."

"You may be right," he said wearily. "Natalie and Lee
were my friends. Do you think I'm not feeling a few guilt
pangs myself?" He was moving toward the door. "And I
agree that we won't use Dantlow unless absolutely necessary. He could get in the way." He paused and looked
over his shoulder. "But he was helpful about their final
arrangements. He managed to clean up the crime scene
and remove both of them to the crematorium."

She stared, shocked. "Crematorium?"

"That was their wish," he said quietly. "They wanted
to be cremated and their ashes flown to Tanzania and
scattered where their son had been killed. They wanted to
be with him."

"Cremated. I never thought—" She moistened her lips.
"Has it . . . already been done?"

"Yes. Their ashes are on their way to Africa now. I had a friend take them. I would have done it myself, but I was busy with you." He paused. "But if you wish to be present at the final ceremony, that will be no problem. I think they'd want you there."

"And you want me there. You were able to persuade Lee and Natalie to go along with your plans because of something to do with their son. It's the only thing that would have moved them. Right?"

He nodded.

"And you would have wanted me to leave the U.S. and go there anyway."

"It has certain advantages for me."

"It's all so pat, everything fitting together," she said hoarsely. "How do I know they were even cremated? How do I know their ashes were taken to Tanzania? Manipulation, again?"

"I'll give Sean the telephone number of the crematorium. And their ashes were being turned over to the U.S. embassy in Tanzania. You can call them tomorrow and verify the arrival and the arrangements for the service." He smiled dryly. "Unless you also think I can bulldoze the U.S. diplomatic service."

"I don't know what you're capable of." She stopped at the bathroom door and looked over her shoulder. "Dantlow would have taken your word about Lee's and Natalie's wishes regarding their final arrangements."

"And you believe I'd lie for my own convenience, that I'd use their last rites to get you to do what I want you to do."

"Would you?"

He was silent. "God help me, I probably would. If I couldn't do it any other way."

"You bastard."

"Yes, and neither of them would have condemned me for it before they decided they couldn't risk you. They would have regarded the matter of rites as unimportant." He paused. "But I didn't have to do it. I just had to facilitate and present the choice to you." His lips twisted. "Choose. Say good-bye as you wish to the two people you love. Or run away and hide and try to survive Camano as you've been doing all these years." He opened the door. "But while you're deciding, you might remember that Lee and Natalie only went along with me because they thought you could give them what they wanted most in the world. You can still give them that gift. I'll show you how." His tone suddenly sharpened to steel. "But now you have another debt to pay. Camano. It's no longer self-preservation, is it? It's revenge." His light eyes were glittering in his taut face. "And I'll help you find the way to destroy him. Camano was never my target. Lee, Natalie, and I were up against someone who makes Camano look almost good by comparison. But that's changed. I promise you, Allie. Give me what I need, and you'll have your freedom *and* revenge."

He slammed the door behind him.

She stared after him for an instant before she entered the bathroom and closed the door behind her. Her knees felt weak, and her emotions were in shreds.

Cremation.

A handful of ashes.

She could feel the tears sting her eyes.

Alone.

So terribly alone.

She fell to her knees on the cold white tiles and curled up in a fetal position as waves of pain rocked her.

I miss you. Dear God, I miss you.

Sobs were shaking her body, and she couldn't seem to stop them.

She didn't know how long she lay there on the floor until she could think again.

Fight it. Don't let Camano make her into this weakling.

But it was another ten minutes before she was able to get to her feet and stumble to the shower.

The next moment, she was beneath the warm spray.

She felt the taste of salt on her lips but didn't bother to wipe the tears away.

She vaguely remembered other tears, other agonies, during the last two days, but this was different. No Mandak to protect her.

I didn't need you. I could have handled it, Mandak.

Or could she? Somewhere in the subconscious depths of her mind, she remembered those two days of searing torturous sorrow, mixed with guilt and regret. It had been close to madness.

Well, it was time she stopped relying on Mandak. When she had learned Camano had found her, she had been full of defiance and independence. Yet she hadn't pushed Mandak totally away. He had become a way of life to her. She hadn't turned her back and walked away.

Perhaps if she had, Lee and Natalie would still be alive.

No, she wouldn't go down that path again. She had to come to terms with what had happened.

And start planning how to punish Camano for killing the only two people she loved in the world.

But Gina . . . Her mother wasn't dead.

But Gina wasn't real, she had no substance beside Lee

and Natalie. She was a dream from the past and still held by Camano.

Freedom and revenge.

It was the gift Mandak had offered her, a gift he'd known she'd want above anything else.

"I'll help you find a way to destroy him."

"Freedom and revenge."

Tempting. So tempting.

But Mandak was a master of luring her into doing as he wished. She had to think for herself and decide what she needed to do to survive.

Enough tears. There would be plenty of weeping when she said her final good-byes to Natalie and Lee.

She got out of the shower, dried off, and quickly dressed in jeans and a blue tunic shirt she pulled out of the duffel. She used a blow-dryer to tame down her hair and let it go at that.

She looked terrible. She must have lost ten pounds in the last few days, and there were dark circles beneath her eyes.

Too bad. As if it mattered.

She opened the bathroom door to go back into the bedroom.

"Ah, you're dressed, that's a relief." A red-haired, thirtyish man with brown eyes and a broad smile was sitting in the easy chair across the room. "Mandak told me I had to be on hand to talk to you right away, so I let myself in. But I've suddenly been having images of your wandering back into the bedroom naked." His eyes were twinkling. "Not that I'm averse to seeing beautiful women in their altogether. I just thought it would be awkward to start a new relationship. I'm Sean Donavel."

"You could have waited and politely knocked." She came forward. "What's so urgent? Or do you always obey Mandak?"

"Not always." He leaned back in his chair. "But if it's not too much trouble, I try to be accommodating. I always want Mandak to owe me."

"Is that why you took us into your apartment?"

"One reason." He shrugged. "And Mandak said that you needed a safe place. Now there's no more safe place than here with a strong, handsome Irishman like myself." His Irish accent became definitely more pronounced on the last sentence. "It aroused all my protective instincts." He leaned forward and uncovered a tray on the hassock in front of him. "And part of that caretaking is to heal and provide. Come and sit down and have a bite. I know you must be hungry."

"Do you?" She came toward him. "How? What do you know about Mandak and me?"

"I know you went through hell while you were lying in that bed over there," he said gently. "And I know that Mandak brought you safe to the other side."

"For his own purposes."

"Perhaps. Sometimes I'm not certain what makes him tick. I'd bet that sometimes he doesn't know himself."

"And you're a gambler?" She shook her head. "You'd lose. Mandak knows exactly where he's going and what he's after." Her lips twisted. "I'm the one who is in the dark. I've never known what Mandak wanted from me. He's never seen fit to discuss it. He's been sitting and watching me and waiting to pounce. Whatever it is, it can't be good, Mr. Donavel."

"Sean," he said. "I can't argue that Mandak may prove dangerous for you." He paused. "But have you wondered why he's been waiting? He told me that you've been with him for seven years."

"Not with him," she said quickly.

"Think about it." He poured her a cup of coffee. "Could it be that Mandak knew that he had to let you grow and mature to give you a chance of being able to survive? If he'd taken you all those years ago, he might have gotten what he wanted, but it might have broken you."

Her gaze narrowed on his face. "You know what Mandak wants, don't you? What is it?"

He shook his head. "Ask him. I'm here because he knows your relationship is extremely tentative. He thought you might wish to ask me a few questions about what I know about him."

"And I'm supposed to believe you'd tell me the truth?" she asked skeptically.

"That's entirely up to you." He smiled. "But I never lie about Mandak. It gets too complicated. Unless it means my life or his. We've been together too long." He tilted his head. "And I don't believe you're a threat to either one of us."

"You can never tell."

He chuckled. "That's true." He gestured to the sandwiches on the tray and coaxed, "But you'll need strength to be a worthy antagonist. Come and have a bite."

She hesitated. He was warm and charismatic, and she shouldn't trust him. But she still found herself sitting down across from Sean. Why not? She'd already determined that she had to know more about Mandak if she was going to fight him. She slowly took the cup of coffee Sean handed her. "Tentative is a kind way to describe my relationship with Mandak. He's never been hesitant about letting me know I couldn't trust him."

"Isn't that honesty of a kind?"

"Maybe." She sipped the coffee. "Why did you let Mandak bring me here? I'm not buying that bull about Irish gallantry."

"I'm hurt." He laughed. "But I forgive you since you're not familiar with my sterling character." His smiled faded. "Mandak and I sort of belong to the same club. He's a charter member, and I've chosen to stay out on the edge and opt into the business every now and then."

"Charter member?"

"Which means that Mandak's vastly more talented and valuable than I'll ever be. I just have a wonderful memory and a few other small gifts. Which makes me able to make a very good living at the tables as long as I'm careful not to reveal just how good that memory really is. On the other hand, Mandak is able to go into minds and manipulate and do fairly incredible things when he's called upon."

"Gifts," she repeated bluntly. "That means you're a freak like me, like Mandak."

He flinched. "I don't like that word. I had to fight it for most of my life before Mandak came along."

"It doesn't matter whether you like it or not. It's what we are. You just have to survive it."

"No, you don't." He leaned back in his chair. "You have to twist it to suit yourself and enjoy it."

"Enjoy it?"

"Your circumstances are a bit different, but work at it." He paused. "Mandak could help you. I believe he's already helped you, hasn't he?"

"As long as I pay the price." She asked, "Club? What the hell kind of club?"

"Not club." He hesitated. "Actually, I didn't want to

say 'family.' " He watched her stiffen. "I thought you'd be a bit sensitive to that. But Mandak and I are both linked by ancient ties to the Devanez family. It's a noble family founded in Spain in the fourteenth century. The Devanez clan were reputed to have certain psychic talents that got them in trouble at the time of the Spanish Inquisition. It appears they passed on those gifts to their descendants. They fled Spain, and naturally, over the centuries, the family became splintered and moved from country to country. Most of them have no knowledge of the family origins." He shrugged. "Which can be bewildering when you have a weird talent and no background and no one to teach you what to do with it. I speak from experience. I would have ended up in prison or dead if they hadn't sent Mandak to find me."

"Who is they?"

"The core Devanez family kept to ancient tradition and made it their obligation to seek out those individuals and try to save or stabilize them. It's become a rule and custom that can't be broken."

"Family," Allie repeated distastefully.

"I knew that would bother you." He held up his hand. "Nothing criminal." He thought about it. "Well, sometimes there have been cases of criminality, but usually they can be straightened out by a Searcher like Mandak. I was pretty close to the edge when Mandak found me."

She was now completely bewildered. "Searcher? What the hell are you talking about? Searching for what?"

He grimaced. "The lost ones. You'd call them freaks. I'd call them members of the Devanez family who have certain unusual gifts and don't know how to handle them. Many of them don't even know they're members of the Devanez family. It's Mandak's job to find them, stabilize, and civilize them. He's able to adjust their attitudes and heal psychic disorders."

"This is crazy," she said harshly. "I'm supposed to believe all this?"

"It's up to you." He tilted his head. "But if you can believe in freaks, I'd think you'd be able to take it one step farther."

"It's a damn big step. You're telling me about a whole world dotted with freaks and an equally weird family trying to take care of all of them."

"Hey, you read memories. That's pretty damn strange in itself. May I suggest you just ride with it?"

She was thinking. "Searcher. Was Mandak looking . . . Am I supposed to be a member of this Devanez family?"

"You'll have to ask him. I don't believe you are, but he's never told me one way or the other." He paused. "He may have heard about you and decided he needed you whether or not you were family. I know that he had a problem that he had to solve."

"What kind of—" She stopped as he shook his head. He wasn't going to answer that question. "You said that I wasn't the first or the last. Mandak has brought other people to this place?"

He nodded. "Mandak is a Searcher. You've been tops on his agenda, but it's been seven years, and he wouldn't just wait around and twiddle his thumbs. He's kept himself very busy during those years." He wrinkled his nose. "And it wasn't easy. Some of those people were half-mad, some bitter against the world. Some only victims but having to be taught."

"And you helped him?"

"I gave him a place and a little protection. After that, it was up to him. I wanted to enjoy my life."

"Why do anything at all?"

He smiled. "Because during the time when Mandak was bringing me through my own personal hell, I developed a bond with him." He nodded as he saw her stiffen. "You, too? It's not uncommon. Especially when he has to go deep. It took me a while to accept it. Sometimes I resented him, sometimes I liked him." He met her eyes. "Sometimes I worshipped him."

"You?"

"It's a shock to me, too. You're right, my entire easygoing personality flinches at the idea." He added, "But it's easier to try to work it out than to do without Mandak."

"I don't agree."

"That's your privilege. I'm only sharing my experiences." He got to his feet. "Now if you're through questioning me, I'll leave you alone to absorb my words of wisdom." He gazed at her inquiringly. "I'm dismissed?"

She nodded slowly. "Since you won't tell me anything else I need to know. When can I see Mandak again?"

"Whenever you wish. He said he had arrangements to make. But I know he'll come when you call him. I could send him to you now."

She thought about it. No, her mind was whirling, and she was trying to weigh truth against fairy tale. She needed time to come to terms with what Sean had told her. "I'll call him."

"I'll let him know." He hesitated. "I know all this has been rough on you. If you need me, I'll be in my study. I know you and Mandak have issues. If you just want to talk or have someone to hold on to, I'm volunteering."

She was surprised. She could tell the offer was genuine. "Thank you. I don't believe that was part of your instructions from Mandak."

"Nah, that was all me. I just get a little soft now and then." He turned toward the door. "Good luck, Allie." The door shut behind him.

Good luck.

She might need that good luck. The Earth was spinning and turning upside down. She had lost the only two people in the world who she loved. Mandak was looming, lurking, in the darkness ahead.

Close him out. The only things that were important were the deaths of Lee and Natalie and deciding what to do about them. She leaned back in her chair as she felt the tears sting her eyes again. She'd stay here and let the agony come, then pass. Perhaps in the midst of that terrible sadness, she'd find the answer.

CHAPTER EIGHT

"YOU'VE BEEN CRYING AGAIN," Mandak said as soon as she opened the door for him four hours later.

"So what?" Allie said as she stepped aside for him to enter. "I'm sorry if you're disappointed that your two days of 'handling' my sorrow didn't quite do the job. It still hurts. It will always hurt."

"I knew that. I was only trying to keep you from falling apart. You've actually done better than I hoped."

"Yes, I'm sure you'd think it a terrible waste if I fell apart."

"That it would," he said bluntly. "For you, for me, and for Lee and Natalie. You sent for me. Why am I here?"

"To fill in the blanks. You put a muzzle on Sean Donavel." She moved toward the window and drew back the drapes to look down at the strip. "And everything he did tell me was crazy and absurd and hard to fathom."

"But true."

"You'll have to convince me."

"I'm not sure I can. You have a built-in resistance. You may have to learn as you go."

"But I have no intention of going anywhere." She let the drapes fall and turned back to face him. "Yet."

"But you've left the possibility open." His gaze was narrowed on her face. "I thought you might."

"You've been playing this game with me for years. Guiding me like your puppet, never telling me anything. That ends right now, Mandak." Her tone was hard. "I'm not going to stumble around blind any longer. You've offered me revenge for Lee and Natalie. Do I want it? You bet I do. But I don't know if they'd want me to serve it up the way you've planned."

"Probably not. Because they wouldn't want revenge for themselves. They want it for Simon and the children." He paused. "But I want it for them. And I can have Camano, and I can have Praland. I just have to work it right."

"Praland?"

"Nelson Praland. Scumbag, monster, and your particular target."

"Bullshit. I have no target. And I won't be handed one by you." She paused. "But I could be handed one by Lee and Natalie. Simon. Tell me about Simon. How did he die?"

"He was butchered by Nelson Praland. Simon was a social worker who was sent over to Tanzania by the State Department to help try to track down children who had been kidnapped and sold into slavery by a band of criminals. Praland was second-in-command to Molino, a scumbag who dealt with local bandits as well as Mafia families in Europe and the U.S. Everything was on the table with them, vice, assassinations, and the kidnapping and selling of children. The latter was particularly profitable in Africa since many men there believed breaking a virgin could cure AIDS."

"Filth."

"Without a doubt."

"So did Simon find the children?"

"A few. But the buyers hid most of them away in small tribal villages in the jungle. Only Praland knew where they could be found."

"What about this Molino? You said Praland was his second-in-command."

"We managed to take Molino out. We found some documents and records on his property that we thought would help in finding the children." He shook his head. "But Praland had already taken over the operation, and they didn't do us any good. We've been searching for those children for years. The biggest percentage of them were little girls. A good many have probably grown into their teens and been married off or sold into whorehouses by now." His lips twisted. "But they've been replaced by an entire flood of new kidnapped children during these last years. Praland has been very busy."

"How did Praland catch Simon Walberg?"

"Simon was obsessed with locating the children. He wouldn't give up. He got too close, and Praland pounced." He added grimly, "He was an easy target. Simon was no fighter. He was in the Peace Corps after he graduated from college, then worked with UNESCO. Lee and Natalie were very proud of him."

Allie remembered that last night when Natalie had spoken to her of her son. "I know they loved him very much."

"He was everything to them." He paused, then said bluntly, "Praland tortured Simon, then cut him into pieces. He called Simon's parents and told him that he laughed, then walked away after he'd done it. It nearly destroyed them."

"Couldn't the government do anything about Praland? Simon was a U.S. citizen."

"Praland had money, contacts, and corruption was rampant in Africa. Very difficult to fight. I watched the Walbergs battle against the system, but I knew it would be futile. They even tried to go after Praland themselves, but the CIA scooped them up and sent them home."

"You let the CIA do it? Couldn't you help them?"

"Not at the time. I was occupied with something else."

"And Lee and Natalie weren't important enough for you to bother."

"Not fair," he said sharply. "I just couldn't put them first on the list."

"Why not?"

"Because I'd just found out that Praland had managed to steal something that made everything else he'd done pale in comparison." He held up his hand as she opened her lips to speak. "I'll tell you. Give me a chance." He pushed her down in the chair. "I told Sean to tell you about the Devanez family. Did you believe him?"

"No. Yes. I'm not certain. The entire story is crazy."

"But then so is a woman who can read memories and a man who has his own particular brand of strangeness."

"Sean said something like that."

"I hate to be repetitive, so I'll skip trying to convince you. He told you about the ledger?"

"No. What ledger?"

"When Jose Devanez sent all of the members of the family to the four corners of the Earth, he still wanted to keep tight rein on them for their protection. That meant keeping records of births, deaths, marriages, and the cities to where they'd moved. He sent his brother with a ledger to travel the world and keep those records. It became his lifework, and when he died, the job was given to another member of the family. As centuries passed the family became disconnected except for the core Devanez group. But the tradition and the duty of maintaining that ledger was ingrained and active in the family. It's considered absolutely necessary to prevent chaos and harm to those members who don't even know why it's happening to them."

"And what does all this have to do with Praland?"

"Praland's boss, Molino, hated what he called freaks because he blamed them for his son's death. He wanted to destroy all of them. When he learned about the ledger, he began searching frantically for it. Before he was killed, he almost had it in his hands. We thought that we'd fooled him with a duplicate."

"Thought?"

"Molino had pulled Praland into the plan to work behind the scenes. Praland managed to pull a sleight-of-hand gambit and snatched the true ledger."

"And that was so important? You said Molino was dead."

"It was the most important event imaginable to the Devanez family. Not only were all those families listed in the ledger in danger, but they were vulnerable to a man who had absolutely no scruples. Praland wasn't as obsessed with psychics as Molino, but he was clever, vicious, and ready to become king of his particular world." He paused. "And there were also account codes of the economic activities of the families that would be worth billions if deciphered. The entire family core was in an uproar."

"That's only money. Simon Walberg was dead and his parents in agony."

"The money was the smallest part of the picture." His lips thinned. "You have no idea how helpless some of those people are who have no idea how to control their gifts. Some of them go mad. Suicides are common if we don't find them in time. We knew they'd be sitting ducks for a man like Praland."

"And some of the people in your family are far from helpless if you're any example."

"True. But it's a fragile balance."

"Then why not send some of your high-powered psychic wizards after him to get the ledger back? Someone who could perhaps read his mind and just go after it?"

"We tried. Everything from special forces who tore through his residences trying to find the ledger, to sending some of our best mental 'wizards' as you call them. Praland has a natural mind block. Very strong."

"And he's evidently hidden the ledger very well."

"We haven't been able to find it in nine years."

She was silent. "And am I supposed to be next on your list of 'wizards'?"

"You could *do* it."

"How do you know?"

"I was one of the first on the list sent to probe and try to find out where he'd hidden the ledger. I couldn't get anywhere reading his mind, but I could see movement and vulnerability in the memory area."

"And you want me to dip into that cesspool he calls a memory and pull out your ledger."

He nodded. "What you're able to do is unusual and almost unique. If there are any others capable of reading Praland, I haven't found them."

"Even if I could find out what you want to know, I'd

have to get close enough to read him. And sometimes people live in the present and seldom think about the past."

"I know all that. But I'll get you to him; and then we'll worry about the rest. It's worth it, Allie."

"In your opinion."

"Dammit, it's worth it." He paused. "Because Praland is playing games with that ledger. He told us he was using that ledger to list all the children that his organization kidnapped together with their purchasers. He's been teasing us with that damn list. Also, in the last nine years, he's killed seventeen family members. He's taking his time and plucking them one by one. Seven of those people didn't even know they belonged to the Devanez family. One day, they were living their lives, and the next, they were dead."

"Why is he taking his time? Seventeen lives are a terrible price, but there could be many more. Right?"

"Right." He shrugged. "Blackmail."

"What?"

"Praland is blackmailing the family. Not money. I'm not sure he knows about those economic codes yet. But he wants to continue with his rotten little empire, and he's forcing the Devanez family to pull back from exerting even a minimum of political or police interference on Praland's turf. As long as we play along and give him protection, he'll keep the killing to a minimum. If we fail to do it, he'll turn loose the bloodhounds. If he thinks that he's in danger, he's given orders that those children he's sold to his clients are to die. If we get too close to the ledger for his comfort, he'll either burn it or throw it to the crocodiles."

"Ugly. But what you're doing isn't clean either."

"Because we're protecting ourselves? You're right, we're playing a dirty game, and we hate it. We try to walk a double line. We send people in to rescue his captives whenever we can do it. I've been trying for years to find ways to get to Praland that would keep the ledger safe." He looked her in the eyes. "So far, you're the only hope we have."

"And you were ready to force me to give up everything I wanted to do with my life to give you that hope."

"Yes."

"No shame?"

"I did what was necessary. You were the solution. I'll try to help you survive."

"You're not answering."

"Guilt, yes. But I made the decision, and I have to stand by it."

She shook her head. "The decision's in my court now."

"Not entirely. There are things that I could do to alter circumstances." He paused. "But I prefer not to do them."

"And now that I know what game you're playing, you might have a hard time leading me down the garden path."

"When was it ever easy between us? I'm not asking you to embrace me or the Devanez family. That would be completely ridiculous and unrealistic. I believe what we're doing is the only possibility under the circumstances, but you seldom agree with me. All I'm asking is that you remember what I offered you. Freedom from Camano. Revenge for the killing of your friends." He added, "And one more thing. The justice for Simon that Lee and Natalie wanted above everything."

"God, you're clever." She could feel the tears sting

again, and she didn't want him to see them. "Get out of here, Mandak. I'll call you when I've made up my mind."

He nodded as he headed for the door. "I'll be waiting."

But not long, she thought. He'd be moving and shaking and subtly pushing. She leaned her head back against the cushioned chair and closed her eyes. But she wouldn't be pushed. She had to have time, and she had to be clear about what she needed to do. What Natalie and Lee would want her to do.

"Help me, guys," she murmured. "You thought it was worthwhile when you let Mandak talk you into it. You're both so smart. You must have thought it was right."

But she was alone now, and she was the one to decide right and wrong . . .

SIX HOURS LATER, SHE CALLED Mandak.

"I'll do it," she said curtly. "But you were too vague about what you were offering me in return. I'm going to spell out exactly the terms you have to offer me. Revenge. I want Camano dead and his crime organization broken up. Freedom. I want out of the Witness Protection Program. I'm tired of being a prisoner. Camano's death could help with that, but Dantlow might want me to testify against other crime figures. You see that I'm not held hostage to the program."

"Done. Anything else?"

She hesitated. "I don't want my mother hurt or killed. She couldn't have been involved in this atrocity. She's only entertainment for Camano. I want her free of him to make a new life."

Silence. "With you?"

"I don't know." But the thought of starting a new life

with someone who had told her that she loved her and wanted to be with her was comforting in this vacuum of loneliness. "I'll have to see. I'm confused and hurting right now."

"And that's very dangerous for you."

"I'll handle it. Is it strange that I want my mother to survive?"

"Done," he said tersely. "And what do you give me in return?"

"I go after your bogeyman, Praland, and find out where he's hidden your ledger. I won't stop until you have the damn thing. Fair?"

"More than fair."

"But first I'll go to Tanzania for the funeral service for Lee and Natalie. After it's over, I'll take a look around and see where I'm going next. And so help me, if everything isn't exactly what you've told me, I'll be out of there so quickly it will make your head swim." She paused. "And, if I go along, I'm holding you to your word on every single thing you promised me."

"You'll get it. I'll deliver." He paused. "Even if you're not able to find out what I want from Praland. After all my time with you, I know you'll keep your word to do everything you possibly can. If you make the attempt and fail, I'll accept it as done."

She was silent, shocked. "That's unexpected . . . and remarkably generous."

"I'm the one who is rolling the dice on you. I found you, I convinced everyone in the Devanez core group that you could do it. If I'm wrong, then I'm the one to shoulder the blame." He added dryly, "I'm sure that you'll agree to that logic."

"If you're telling me the truth."

"You'll have to decide that for yourself. But it will be better for you and our chances of taking Praland down if you can bring yourself to trust me. After all, you're tentatively committed now. I've told you what I want, and you've agreed that, for your own reasons, you want it, too. You'll find me a capable and reliable ally."

And a dangerous and lethal one, she thought. She'd had experience with Mandak's deadly intelligence and skill all those years ago. "Capable and reliable don't seem the words to describe you. I'll have to become used to the thought of them."

"By all means. We're about to open new doors. I'm sure that we'll both have a few surprises." He went on quickly, "I've had Sean arrange a private jet to pick us up at the airport here. You'll have an hour or so to rest before we have to leave the apartment. Is that okay?"

"I'm ready now."

"You always were." Suddenly, his voice was filled with humor. "You never wanted to wait for anything. I always had to gauge my actions to your lack of patience."

"Did you?" She hadn't known that about him. She wondered how many other things there were about him of which she hadn't been aware during those years. Everything had been perceived from her defensive point of view and the feeling that Mandak was both a savior and a threat. "Well, then, you should have realized that I wouldn't want to rest and twiddle my thumbs waiting for your jet. When can you pick me up?"

"Fifteen minutes. I'll take you to the airport and buy you a new wardrobe in the shops there until we get the call for the plane. They have anything from haute couture to Frederick's of Hollywood."

"I don't need any new clothes."

"It won't hurt. You only have the things in your duffel, and I don't know what circumstances we'll be facing. We'll be tracking Praland, and he travels in very high-income circles these days." He hung up before she could protest again.

It was done. The decision had been made and the action taken.

And Mandak had already started to plan and move her in the way he wanted her to go. He had taken an element of her character and used it as an excuse to do that.

Clever.

If she thought about it objectively, she could admire that subtle shifting and prodding.

But there was no way she was objective about Mandak at any time. So she would accept this move but let him know that she was aware of the manipulation. Perhaps if he realized he couldn't deceive her, he would back off.

Perhaps.

Right now, she was too tired and raw and broken to put up a decent fight. All she could think about were the funeral services waiting for her in Tanzania. After that, she would worry about her promise to Mandak.

And ponder that strange, generous promise he had just made to her.

"I CERTAINLY DIDN'T NEED ALL those outfits." Allie was frowning as she climbed the steps of the private plane. "You went overboard, Mandak. It's a total waste of money."

"But not a waste of time. I agree that you may not need them. There's a chance that you might be able to get close enough to Praland in a casino or nightclub to read him.

He likes beautiful women, and you're exceptional. However, the chance is slim. We're more likely to have to move onto his turf."

"Then it was a waste of time."

He shook his head. "You weren't interested, but you were distracted. That was important. It delayed my being bombarded by more questions I'm sure you've been thinking since I left you at Sean's apartment." He entered the plane and gestured to a seat. "Buckle up. I'm going to the cockpit to talk to the pilot."

"How long will it take us to get to Tanzania?"

"Twenty hours or so. We'll be stopping over in London. It will take us at least ten hours to get there."

"Why do we have to stop over in London?"

"We have to meet someone. Don't worry, it will only be for one night." He disappeared into the cockpit.

Someone? He had been entirely too vague. He was right, she was beginning to have more questions now that she was away from Sean's apartment and stepping into this new life. She felt helpless, and she needed to take control. But how could she do that if she had no direction?

She took her computer out of her duffel and Googled Tanzania. Lord, it was far away, literally the other side of the world. Dodoma appeared to be the capital. Was that their destination?

"I thought you'd be busily checking everything out," Mandak said as he came out of the cockpit. He dropped down in the seat across from her. "Well?"

"You have to have a clue before you can check something out." She whirled her computer to show him the map of Tanzania. "Dodoma?"

"No, that's the capital, but the U.S. Embassy is in

Dar es Salaam. That's where we start. That's where Lee's and Natalie's remains were sent." He pointed to a green area southeast of the city. "But that's our target. That's where Praland has his grand palace. It's in the jungle, not too far from the principal mining area."

"Palace?"

He nodded. "Sandek Palace. He forced a mine owner to 'sell' it to him. Unfortunately, the owner had an accident before he reached the capital, and the money was never found. The palace had been in his family for a couple centuries, and it was complete with dungeons and harems. Just what Praland wanted. Since he fancies himself as a sort of modern-day Genghis Khan."

"More like Attila the Hun."

"There are similarities in his methods. But he's very rich, and he lives large. The last I heard he had five or six women he kept as concubines. He has enough men guarding his palace to constitute a small army. He sends them out on bandit raids within the country, and over the borders and they have trucks, missiles, and various other sophisticated weaponry."

"Good God, it sounds like he runs the country."

"Sometimes it comes close. I guarantee that the government wants him out as much as we do. They just don't have the resources or the influence to pull it off. Money is everything. And if the man who is wielding it is also a murderer willing to take any revenge necessary, it stops them in their tracks." He shrugged. "But the Devanez family has agents all over the country, and we're able to strike a balance sometimes. Not often enough. Not with his holding the ledger over our heads."

"And you think that he keeps the ledger at the palace?"

"I have no idea. We've infiltrated the palace and haven't found it yet." He met her eyes. "You'll have to tell us."

"If you can get me into that place."

"I'll get you there." He shrugged. "But it may not be necessary. Praland moves around a lot. He also operates out of Madagascar and Morocco. He has an extensive prostitution operation in Madagascar." His lips thinned. "That's where we managed to find several of the little girls he kidnapped in Italy and Switzerland. We staged a raid on two of the bordellos and got them out."

"Thank God."

"But it took almost a year to cure them of drug addiction."

She gazed at him, shocked. She felt sick at the thought. "He must be a total son of a bitch."

"In practically every way. No, take out the 'practically.'" He tapped the name Dar es Salaam on the map. "But this is your first area of concern. We can think about Praland later. I just called Phillip Stanley, the man who delivered Lee's and Natalie's ashes to the embassy in Tanzania. He's arranging for the service now. James McKeller, a young clerk, has the job of smuggling the canisters out of the embassy." He paused. "I told him that I want it kept absolutely private. No one is to know that we're in the country."

"Is that possible?"

"We have a chance. As I said, corruption is rife, and Praland has informants everywhere. But then, so does the Devanez family. For years, we've been keeping our eye on Praland and hoping to make a move."

"And who's the head of this Devanez family? Sean seemed to think that you were important to them."

He shook his head. "I'm regarded as something of a loose cannon. But you could say I have the ear of the core group. It's a structure that's mobile in nature and right now is headed by the keeper of the ledger. Very efficiently, I would add. The agents are slick, well trained, and completely loyal." He tapped Dar es Salaam on the map again. "Stanley will call on the local agents to make a smoke screen of misinformation to give us our chance to say good-bye to the Walbergs."

"Smoke screen? It shouldn't be that way."

"No, they deserve dignity and respect and anything else the world can give them. But that's not going to happen. Not right now. Maybe later."

"Why would you think that it would matter to Praland if they arranged to be buried in Tanzania? You said the reason they wanted to do it was only because their son's remains were there."

"And are you still skeptical that was the truth?"

She was silent. "No. I think that even you would have a problem being that callous. I was hurting and struck out."

"Even me," he repeated. "I suppose I should be grateful that I was included." He added, "Did it occur to you that I was hurting, too? They were both my friends, Allie."

"It occurred to me. I tried to look at all sides when I was trying to decide what to do. I don't want to make any mistakes. It's too important I give them what they wanted," she said. "I remembered the night you brought me to them. There was genuine feeling and liking in your expression. Whatever there has been between us, I don't believe pretense was one of them." She stopped, thinking about it. "And Lee and Natalie were grateful to you.

Natalie told me that she couldn't resent you because they owed you." She stared him in the eye. "Why were they grateful to you, Mandak? It was something to do with Simon."

"Yes."

"What was it?"

"I shot him."

Her eyes widened with shock. "What?"

"Simon was Praland's prisoner. I was friends with Lee and Natalie at the time, and they asked me to help him. The CIA was pressuring me, too. Because I was familiar with the territory and Praland's operation, there was a slim chance I could get Simon out. The CIA dropped me in the jungle near the palace, and I went after Simon to try to get him away from that bastard." His face was hard, shadowed. "I could hear Simon screaming as I made my way through the jungle to the palace. Praland had him staked out in the courtyard and was torturing him. He and his men were laughing every time Simon screamed."

"My God."

"I'm not going to tell you what they'd done to him. I was too late. He'd been torn to pieces. Simon was hanging on by a thread. He couldn't live. All he could do was suffer." His jaw clenched. "And I wasn't going to let that bastard, Praland, make him suffer one more second. I'd managed to climb up to the top of the wall above the compound. I'm a very good shot. I took careful aim. I killed him."

She was silent. She could see that scene that he had painted for her, and the sheer horror of it stunned her. "I don't know if I could have done that. It must have been a terrible decision."

"It was no decision at all. I couldn't let the torment go on. I knew that Praland had too many men for me to have a hope of doing anything else. It was the only way Simon would be free and have peace." His lips twisted. "And I still failed. My second shot was for Praland but he dodged out of the way after I killed Simon. His men were pouring toward the wall, and I had to get the hell out of there. As it was, I spent two weeks in the jungle dodging Praland and his men with a bullet wound in my arm."

"Did he know it was you who had killed Simon?"

"Not at the time. But it wasn't long before he found out. He wanted to know, and he dug and mutilated until he found out my name. He was furious at the thought I'd managed to rob him of the pleasure of torturing Simon. He was even more angry at the thought that I'd humiliated him by getting that close, then thumbed my nose at him. He's never forgotten in the last eight years. I hear from him every time he thinks he's scored by killing another of the family."

"I'm beginning to believe I know this Praland very well," she said shakily. "He's like a mirror image of the people I grew up with. Though I never actually saw the true violence until the night my father killed Jokman." She shook her head. "What . . . did you tell Lee and Natalie?"

"The truth. They'd already heard what happened to Simon from the CIA and Praland by the time I managed to get back to the city. Praland made a point of looking them up to brag about all the atrocities they'd done to Simon. He thought it was one way he could get back at me for his humiliation. I went to them and told them I'd killed their son." He shrugged. "And braced myself for the storm. They didn't say anything to me. I think they were in shock."

"Who could blame them?"

"Not me. They came to see me two months later and thanked me. I could see it was hard for them. But they genuinely meant it. It let me see what special people they were." He paused. "And it gave me a peace I didn't know I needed. From that time on, we were allies as well as friends."

"Against Praland."

He nodded. "The thought of what he'd done filled their lives. They couldn't stand the thought of the torture he'd inflicted on Simon or the thought of what he was doing to those children Simon was trying to save."

"So you drew them in to help prepare me to take down Praland."

"It was a great plan until it all went wrong. Emotion can ruin the most intelligent schemes."

"You were annoyed with them?"

"Yes. And frustrated." He smiled. "And a little envious."

"No way."

"I won't try to convince you. You've been more tolerant than I would have thought. It might be too much to expect you to accept that I occasionally have mixed and human feelings."

"It might. You didn't give any indications that night you were trying to whisk me out that bedroom window."

"The destination was in sight after eight years. I had to try to close the deal." He paused. "But I didn't close it," he said bitterly. "Just as I failed the night I had my shot at Praland, and I didn't kill him."

She stared at him with mixed emotions. Frustration,

surprise, even sympathy. "For God's sake, just listen to you. So you're not perfect. You did what you could. It sounds to me as if you risked your neck that night to try to save Simon. You're always telling me not to blame myself. What the hell are you doing?"

He gazed at her for an instant, then chuckled. "I'm glad you believe I did what I could. I thought I was high up on the blame list."

"Camano heads that list. It took a little while, but that's clear to me now." She shook her head. "And, for the rest, Praland is looming right beside him." She shook her head. "And I've never even seen him. I don't know what he looks like."

"Allow me." He took his phone back and accessed another site. "The tall man with straw-colored hair is Praland. The man sitting next to him is Hans Bruker, his lieutenant." He lifted his shoulder in a half shrug as he handed it back to her. "Or maybe I should call him 'cobra in training.' He's almost as vicious as Praland."

The two men were sitting on a tiled veranda dressed in boots and dark pants and shirts. Praland was lean and sinewy with a long face and pale gray eyes. He was smiling but without humor, his thin lips pulled back from large, white teeth. Straw hair? It looked more platinum-colored and was long and coarse. Bruker was smaller, chunky, with a plump face and uptilted, dark eyes.

"I didn't know Bruker existed either," Allie said. "Praland, Bruker . . . Lee and Natalie wouldn't have even been with me if it hadn't been for Praland. It's like a complicated chain with all spiked links. The links have nothing do with each other, yet the chain exists."

"How very deep."

"Bullshit," she said wearily. "I'm just trying to work out why this happened. There has to be a reason."

"Evil."

"Yes, it's probably as simple as that. But Lee and Natalie always told me that I should look at both sides of the coin." Her lips twisted. "Even when it came to a certain Professor Simpson, who was driving me crazy. Funny I should think of him now. He's so unimportant in the scheme of things."

"Evidently he was important to you at the time. That's one of the reasons why I turned you over to Lee and Natalie. I knew they'd furnish you with the kind of normal background training I never could."

"No, you gave me karate lessons. You would probably have told me to go after Simpson and take him down."

"Possibly." He smiled. "If it didn't interfere."

"But it would have interfered with the life I was planning for myself." She paused. "They wanted to keep those plans safe and intact. I didn't appreciate what they were giving up to let me have my chance."

"They cared about you."

"I know that. They said we were a family. Do you know what that meant to me? I'd never had a family. Not really. You may have persuaded them to take me into their home, but they did much more." She drew a ragged breath. "And now it's payback time. I have to give back. They wanted the man who killed their son to be given his just punishment? Okay, I'll do it. I don't care about your ledger or your fine Devanez family. As far as I'm concerned, it's all about Lee and Natalie. How convenient that I suddenly have a reason to give you what you want from me."

"Not fair, Allie."

"I guess not." She looked down at the computer. "I'm trying, but I'm not going to be able to shed the suspicion and wariness overnight. I know I'm going to have to work with you now. But my only protection against you seemed to be Lee and Natalie and the defensiveness that I'd developed." She pointed to the jungle area outside Dar es Salaam. "I don't know anything about jungles. I'll need to know about them, won't I? Why didn't you teach me?"

"I couldn't teach you everything." He smiled faintly. "As you pointed out to me, you had a life to live. You did very well with what I did throw at you."

"I haven't done any physical training for two months. I need to do that."

"My last report said that you were very competent."

"I want to be more than competent. I can't fail because I'm not prepared for Praland."

"It may not come down to that kind of battle, Allie."

"And it might. You need to work with me every day while we have the chance," she said fiercely. "I don't know anything about this bastard you're throwing at me. I'm feeling *helpless*. I'm not going to stay that way. I thought I was preparing myself for Camano. Now this Praland has to come first."

"And you made the decision."

"No, I didn't. Lee and Natalie made the decision. They wanted to have him brought down. It's the last gift I can give them. But I have to be ready."

"Easy. I'll work with you. We just may not have much time."

"It will have to be enough." Her gaze shifted to look

out the window. "And who are we supposed to be meeting in London? You were entirely too vague."

"Sorry. It's a habit I've had to cultivate over the years. Most of the family prefer not to be identified or even placed at a given location. I generally try to accommodate them."

"Family? Devanez?"

"Yes. *My* family," he said quietly. "And they mean as much to me as Lee and Natalie did to you."

"Do they?" She frowned thoughtfully. "I've been thinking of the Devanez clan as some kind of extensive . . ." She didn't know what words to use. "It sounds as if they're pulling strings and trying to manipulate the world to suit themselves. That's not how I think of family."

"A family is made up of individuals. They are what they are. The Devanezes just have a different set of challenges."

"And which Devanez member am I going to have to meet in London?" she asked warily.

"A very important one. Renata Wilger is booked at the Windsor Hotel. She's been very anxious to meet you for a number of years. I've been holding her at bay from coming to Flagstaff and trying to take you away from me."

"Why?"

"Because she's the Keeper of the Ledger. I told you there's always a family member in charge of the gathering of information and keeping records. In this case, she pretty well runs both the operation and the family. Renata Wilger was chosen when she was only a teenager, and she was in charge of it when Praland stole it. She's been frantic to get it back. She feels that everything Praland has done since he took it is her responsibility."

"The Keeper of the Ledger. It sounds like some kind of fantasy movie like *Lord of the Rings*." She made a face. "And I'm not liking the idea of this Renata Wilger wanting to hijack me. I can see why you'd claim the Devanezes as your family. The family traits are beginning to emerge."

"Give us a chance. We might grow on you."

"I doubt that. But I have to give you a chance. I've been backed into a corner. I have no choice."

"No, you don't." His lips tightened. "But I'll make it up to you. I'll keep my promise, Allie."

She didn't reply.

He muttered a curse. "And I'll find a way to keep you safe." The words were vibrating with power, and his entire body was taut, every muscle corded and sparking with intensity. She could feel that vibration in her wrists, in the palms of her hands, in the swelling of her breasts. She had to force herself to look away from him.

He sounded as if he meant what he said, but she couldn't count on anyone but herself. He'd made it clear he was loyal to the Devanez family, and his whole concentration and effort had been to bring her to this point to help them. She was as alone as she'd always been before Lee and Natalie.

Her gaze returned to the map. "Do you have a floor plan for this palace?"

"Yes." He took out his phone. "I'll send it to your e-mail. I bribed a servant to get it for me when I was trying to free Simon. I'd even had him dig a tunnel from the outer wall to the dungeon." He added bitterly, "But I never got a chance to use it. Praland had Simon on display in the courtyard when I heard his screams." He was sending the e-mail. "It should still be pretty much the same."

"Good. We have a long time before we get to London. I want to memorize it." She opened the document and studied the palace. "It's pretty spread out, isn't it? That's okay. I'll still be able to do it. Concentration. Isn't that what you always told me when you were teaching me to block? You've got to concentrate, Allie."

"That's what I told you." He leaned back in his chair, his gaze on her face. "And you always gave me what I wanted. Well, maybe not what I wanted. But what was good for you at the time."

She had a fleeting memory of those hours of emotion, sensuality, and desperation. She quickly veered away. Don't think of the way she'd felt about him during those months. He had meant too much to her at the time, but she had managed to walk away to a new life.

Now that life, too, was over. She had to do what was needed, then walk away again.

She could feel his gaze on her face.

Ignore him. Ignore what she was feeling. Think of this palace on the screen before her and the monster who inhabited it.

Or that woman, Renata Wilger, who was waiting for her in London to try to force her to give the Devanez family what it needed.

She could imagine the toughness and hardness of a woman who had been chosen as Keeper of the Ledger. But she wouldn't be intimidated by her. She had only one focus, and that was the funeral. After that, she'd worry about the ledger and what it meant to Praland's targets and those poor children he was holding captive.

Screw Renata Wilger.

CHAPTER NINE

"OH, FOR GOD'S SAKE, MANDAK. She's not much more than a child," Renata Wilger said in disgust, as her gaze raked Allie's face. "And she's pale and fragile as a ghost. You told me you'd been training her."

"Back off, Renata," Mandak said quietly. "She's no child, and she's had a hell of a lot to deal with lately."

"Including rudeness from a woman I don't know and have no intention of getting to know," Allie said coldly. In spite of Renata's rudeness, her appearance didn't reflect the hardness Allie had expected. Renata Wilger was small, red-haired, slim, and in her late twenties or early thirties. She seemed to radiate passion and force that was sweeping in intensity. Allie found herself having to brace against that intensity. "And I don't give a damn about your precious ledger. I have my own agenda. I'll do what Lee and Natalie would want me to do, then I'm gone."

Renata Wilger's brows rose. "She might do after all," she said slowly. "At least, she's not a wimp. But I still think you should have turned her over to me in the beginning, Mandak."

"I would have cut my throat," Allie said with precision. "It was bad enough having Mandak hovering over me." She turned to leave the hotel room. "Now I'll wait in the lobby and let you talk about me."

"Wait." Renata Wilger hesitated. "Okay, I was rude. I suppose I should apologize. But I've been waiting for a long time, and you're not what I expected. You look . . . soft. Praland is probably going to be able to chew you up and spit you out." Her lips thinned. "And that means the killing goes on, and so will the kidnapping of those kids."

The hideous thought of the condition of those children rescued from the bordellos that Mandak had told her about caused Allie's anger to ebb. "I'm not soft. And no one is going to chew me up and spit me out."

"I'll vouch for that," Mandak said dryly.

"Maybe not." Renata gestured to a chair. "Sit down, Allie. We have to talk."

"No, we don't."

"Did I shoot myself in the foot, Mandak?" Renata asked ruefully.

"Probably. But she'll listen if you can convince her that it's to her advantage."

"It is to your advantage," she said to Allie. "I originally set up this meeting because I wanted to have a look at you, but we seem to have another problem." She glanced at Mandak. "I just got a report from Paris. We think Praland managed to break the tracking code on your phone sometime within the last two months."

Mandak went still. *"Shit."*

"You know he's been trying for years, but our techs say they think he was able to hit the right tower last month. He may have been able to track you to Flagstaff."

Mandak muttered a curse. "Then why the hell didn't he come after me? It's what he's been wanting for years.

He's been threatening me every time he's phoned me with one of his damn updates."

"That's what we've been wanting to know," Renata said grimly. "Why wait? Why not send in one of his death squads?"

"I can't figure it out," Mandak said slowly. "Of course, he wouldn't find it as easy operating in the U.S. as it is on his home turf. He avoids it whenever he can. But Praland is nothing if not determined, and he can be tricky as hell. So the question is, how did he plan on taking me out?"

Allie was gazing at both of them in frustration. "What is this all about?"

"Didn't Mandak tell you?" Renata asked. "Praland wasn't pleased about Mandak's getting close enough to do that mercy killing on Simon. He believed he'd been humiliated. He put a bounty on Mandak's head. And every year that Mandak survived, the bounty has gone up. How high is it now, Mandak?"

He shrugged. "That's not important. It hasn't gotten in the way of my work."

"No, he didn't tell me," Allie said. "But he did say that he wanted our presence in Tanzania to be kept quiet. I didn't realize what the urgency was about."

"It would have been urgent regardless," Mandak said. "But I thought that if I was spotted in Dar es Salaam, the fact that I had you with me would send up a red flag. Praland would start asking questions about you." He met her eyes. "And he moves in the kinds of circles where he would get the answers."

"You mean he'd find out that I'm a possible threat to him?" she asked curtly. "But then that was only a matter of time, right?"

"I was hoping for the element of surprise."

"But not expecting it. You always thought I might be a target."

"Do you expect me to deny it? Yes, I always thought that might happen." He turned to Renata. "So have you been searching for answers? You've obviously been privy to this information longer than I have."

"Not much longer," Renata said. "I got word right after you left Las Vegas. I wish I'd heard before everything blew up, and the Walbergs were killed." She turned to Allie. "I'm sorry for your loss. They were fine people."

"Yes, they were. Exceptional people. And they didn't deserve to die."

"We're all agreed on that." Renata turned back to Mandak. "I have another coded phone ready for you. Get rid of the one you have. When was the last time you used it?"

"Only a few local calls that last day in Las Vegas. And a call to Dantlow. Sean set up the transport of the ashes and our own flight, so that shouldn't have been traced. I was in Las Vegas for days, and no one tried to hit me. Again, why not?" His voice was tense. "And those days probably put Sean Donavel in major jeopardy."

"I've already pulled him out of Las Vegas," Renata said. "The moment I got confirmation that your phone had been accessed, I called him personally and told him that he was to leave Las Vegas and go to Monte Carlo." She made a face. "He had no quarrel with that reassignment."

"I imagine that's true," Mandak said dryly. "As long as he was kept in his comfort zone. Anything else?"

She shook her head. "I've just been trying to put all the pieces together and fill in some very intriguing blanks." She looked him directly in the eye. "But you're very, very

smart, Mandak. Perhaps the most intelligent and innovative man in the Devanez group. I'm sure you're going
to try to do the same thing as I am once I leave you to
it. Suppose we meet here for dinner and discuss what
we've come up with?" She opened the door for them and
handed a key to Mandak. "I've taken a room for you two
doors down. I'll order dinner for seven. That should give
us a chance to explore a few possibilities." She turned to
Allie. "I probably handled you all wrong, but this new
threat to Mandak has me ready to explode. Do you know
what kind of risk he runs whenever he goes out on one
of his searches? If the family member he's trying to help
is a name in that book, there's every chance that Praland's
men might be there, too. Praland has *owned* that book
for the past eight years."

Allie's gaze was on the other woman's face. "And it's
driving you crazy. Mandak tried to explain that to me.
But I didn't realize how extensive your involvement went."

"Everything that happens to do with that book is my
responsibility. And Mandak has been like a brother to
me all these years. It *kills* me to think of Praland going
after him. What Praland did to Simon would be child's
play compared to the torture he'd hand out to Mandak if
he ever caught him."

"That's not going to happen, Renata," Mandak said
quietly.

"No, it's not. Because we're not going to let it." She
gestured impatiently with her hand. "And you don't
understand any of it, Allie. All you know is that you've
been caught in the middle and can't get out."

"I can get out," Allie said. "All I have to do is walk
away. Lee and Natalie might have wanted me to do that.
But that's not an option for me any longer. I have to give

them what they wanted for their Simon." She went past Renata and out into the hall. "That's all I can concentrate on right now. You do what you have to do to protect each other and your wonderful ledger. All I ask is that you get me in a position where I can try to read Praland, then get me out. After that, it's up to Mandak." She glanced at him. "Knowing you, I don't believe Praland will last long once he doesn't have the protection of that book."

"Only a heartbeat," Renata called grimly as she closed the door. "Count on it."

"Less." Mandak had caught up with Allie and was unlocking the hotel-room door. "I've been waiting a long time." He pushed open the door and stepped aside for Allie to enter. "And I have a long, bloody list with Praland's name on it."

"And one of them is Simon Walberg. That name belongs to me, too." She went to the window and looked down at the street below. It was a gray day, but there was bustle and life on those streets. London. She hadn't paid much attention on the drive from the airport, but she was remotely aware that the city had a distinct flavor. "Lee used to get some of his first editions at a bookstore on Hanover Street. He'd get so excited when they came by UPS. I remember the stamps . . ." She looked over her shoulder as she heard him pick up the house phone. "What are you doing?"

"Just calling room service to send up coffee and sandwiches. You didn't eat anything on the plane." He spoke briefly into the phone, then hung up. "Why don't you go into the bedroom and rest? The coffee should be here soon."

"I'll just go to the bathroom and splash some water on my face." She moved toward the bathroom door. "I feel gritty. And I need to clear my head after dealing with your Renata Wilger."

"She's not mine. She's purely her own person. What did you think of her?"

"At first, I wanted to sock her."

"And then?"

"And then I began to see that she was very human. I still wanted to sock her, but I could see where she was coming from." She paused at the bathroom door. "She appears to be a cross between a high-powered CEO and an FBI special agent."

He smiled. "Funny you should say that. Renata's cousin, Marc, raised her and trained her as Keeper and he was a special agent with Israeli intelligence."

"It shows." She paused. "I expected her to be tough, and she is. I didn't expect her to be so . . . intense. She really cares about you."

"We're family," he said simply as he dropped down in the chair beside the desk. "It's goes with the territory. I believe you've come to realize that. Now go and splash your face and try to get Renata out of your mind. It probably won't be possible. She tends to dominate."

"She doesn't dominate you."

He smiled. "Sure she does. Didn't you hear her tell me to put my thinking cap on and figure out what Praland's up to? I have every intention of doing just that while I'm waiting for room service to come knocking."

"Really?" Her brows lifted. "I know Renata seems to have a good deal of faith in you, but you're not allowing yourself much time."

"I've already started." His smile faded. "In fact, I'm halfway there. I've just got to get the possibilities in line."

And the possibilities evidently were not pleasant.

Allie could sense the edge, the sharpness, beneath that expression. "Whatever. That's between you and Renata. I've told you my focus." She went into the bathroom and closed the door.

She leaned against it for a moment and closed her eyes. She was tired and sad and a little bewildered. She could accept the first two, but she had to keep her mind clear and focused. The interchange with Renata had confused her. She'd come close to liking the woman, and she did understand her. Under the same circumstances, she might have had the same intensity as Renata had shown. As Mandak had said, in these last years, Allie, too, had discovered that love of family was everything. Not only had she begun to understand Renata's viewpoint, but as she'd watched Renata and Mandak together, she had begun to question her judgment of Mandak. Throughout her entire relationship with Mandak, she had thought of him as totally invulnerable. She'd been the one who'd had to fight for her independence against his intelligence and strength.

But Renata had not seen him as invulnerable. She had seen him as threatened and a friend to protect. It had been an eye-opener. But it was a vision Allie couldn't accept. Mandak was already too much in her thoughts and emotions. Both the disturbing sensuality and that bonding that had never left her in all those years. He struck sparks whenever he was around her. She certainly didn't need to believe he might actually need her at some point.

No way.

Her eyes flicked open, she took a step closer to the vanity, and turned on the water.

I'm out of it, she told her reflection in the mirror as

she splashed her face with cold water. I won't be drawn into the net.

Let Renata worry about you, Mandak . . .

"COFFEE." MANDAK WAS POURING the dark brew into her cup as she came out of the bathroom ten minutes later. "You take it black, right?"

She felt foolish as she stared at him. What had she been thinking? No one could look less like they needed anyone to worry about them. Mandak had taken off his black leather jacket and rolled up the sleeves of his blue shirt. He looked tough and virile and totally able to handle anything.

"You know I take it black." She came toward him. "How many times did you fix it for me when we were at the lodge?"

"That was a long time ago. You were only a kid. Tastes change. I wouldn't insult you by assuming that you're the same person as when I turned you over to Lee and Natalie." He handed her the cup and saucer. "You've clearly matured."

Was there a hint of sensuality in his tone? She felt a tingle of heat. It surprised her. She'd thought she was too numb to feel anything but sorrow. It was the first time she had experienced that sexuality since that night he had come to her room at the house in Flagstaff. She supposed some responses were mindless and could never be controlled.

Then, if it couldn't be controlled, ignore it.

"Yes, I have." She sat down in the chair across from him. "In many, many ways. I'm sure Lee must have given you a report on my personal life as well as the other items on the list."

"You mean sex? Only in general terms. I just wanted to be assured that you weren't becoming serious enough about anyone for it to become a problem for us."

"Heaven forbid," she said sarcastically.

He smiled faintly. "And besides, I've always regretted having to be so damn noble and saying no when I wanted desperately to accept. I didn't want to hear any details."

The heat was there again and so was the tension and lack of breath. She remembered lying against him in that bed and feeling the hardness of his muscles against her softness. She could almost smell the musk and lemon scent of him. She was smelling it. He was using the same aftershave as he had when she was sixteen. He even looked the same, the flat stomach, the dark hair on his muscular forearms and his chest. And she knew how they felt against her . . . so familiar. But she wasn't the same, every sense was tuned to a dizzying sexual arousal. She had felt something then but nothing compared to what she was feeling now.

And he must have sensed it. His eyes narrowed. "Allie?"

She quickly looked away from him. "And I wouldn't have forgiven Lee if he'd given you any details."

He shook his head. "Wrong. You would have forgiven Lee anything. You would have just blamed it on me."

"You're probably right." She could feel her eyes sting. "Because he would have had a good reason for doing it. Not that he would ask me. All they ever wanted was for me to be safe and not be hurt."

"If you'll recall, I said something like that at the time."

"You did, didn't you? I'd forgotten."

"Curses." He dramatically struck his forehead with his palm. "Forgot? My one attempt at being the good guy, and you obviously weren't impressed."

She had never seen him like this. "You can hardly blame me." The corners of her lips turned up. "It was so rare that I must have missed it."

"There's always that possibility." He took a sip of his coffee before he gazed down into the depths of his cup. "But believe me, that was a difficult week. We've had a lot of difficult times." He looked up to meet her eyes. "And there are going to be more coming. I was sitting here trying to put two and two together as Renata told me to do. I came up with a double bull's-eye."

She stiffened. Any hint of humor had vanished in those last sentences. Mandak's expression was grim. "What?"

"I was hoping for separate targets, but that might not be possible."

"I don't know what you're talking about, Mandak."

"I'm talking about the fact that Praland should have acted against me and didn't do it. He's practically salivating to get his hands on me. Yet when he had his chance, he didn't follow through. He's crafty as hell, and there had to be a reason why."

"And what reason would that be?"

"He found someone to do his dirty work for him."

"Who?"

"Camano."

She froze, stunned. "You're crazy. That doesn't make sense."

"I wish it didn't. Do you want to hear the scenario?" He didn't wait for her answer. "Praland managed to get a general location on me, but I move around a lot, and he

wouldn't have been able to get a precise target area. But
the signal must have constantly returned to Flagstaff. So
he started looking for a reason, a connection."

"Lee and Natalie," she whispered. "Simon's parents."

"Two senior citizens who had retired at their old college town. But what did he find besides Lee and Natalie?
A young girl who was supposed to be their niece. But
under investigation and intense scrutiny, that proved untrue. She was *not* their niece. So who was she, and why
would the Walbergs and I both be interested in her?"

"They couldn't know it was Witness Protection."

"You have a security detail. Praland could have traced
him to Dantlow. There are the usual school photos that
have been taken of you during the last seven years. You
were memorable when you were sixteen, you're even
more unforgettable now. Praland probably started to cir-
culate those pictures among the underbelly of society
and suddenly came up with an interested party. Camano."
He nodded. "And a reason I might also be interested in
you. We hadn't been able to touch Praland or find a trace
of where he'd hidden the ledger because of his natural
block. But you might prove to be a threat if what Camano
told him about you was true. So it was to Praland's advantage to rid himself of you and anyone else who stood
in the way. He started to deal with Camano to have him
take care of the problem for him, so that he could avoid
risking his empire in Africa by going up against the Feds
in the U.S." His lips twisted. "And I'm sure my head on
a platter was a major part of the deal Praland insisted
upon."

"And the break-in at Dantlow's office was by Praland's
men and not Camano's?"

"No, I believe that was Camano. But he was verifying,

not searching. He wanted to make sure that the deal he was making with Praland was the real thing. Praland would have been more cautious about a break-in. He would have been afraid that Dantlow would warn me of a possible problem."

"Which he did," Allie said numbly. "I wonder how much Praland was willing to pay to Camano to create his bloodbath. It might have been very cheap for him. After all, they really wanted the same thing." She moved her shoulders as if shrugging off a burden. "But this is all supposition. You're guessing, Mandak."

"Yes. I'm guessing," he said grimly. "And the only thing that might substantiate it is the fact that Camano's goon, Ledko, said my name before I killed him. He recognized me. He was probably furnished a photo of me by Praland. I didn't think anything of it at the time. I was too involved with getting you and the Walbergs out of the house."

"Guesswork," she repeated.

"That I'm going to accept until I know it's not true," Mandak said. "Because I want to know if we've got battles on two different fronts or if we have to face a combined enemy. I'm going to assume it's the latter."

And Allie was beginning to believe he could be right. Her mind was in a whirl, and yet the scenario Mandak had depicted could well be true. Had her enemy, Camano, and the monster who had poisoned Lee's and Natalie's lives come together to attack and destroy them that night?

"It's okay." Mandak was reading her expression. "We'll get through it."

"That's what you said when you were trying to keep me from going crazy and pull me through one of those damn memory sessions," she said shakily. "This is a little more than that, Mandak."

"You didn't think so at the time." He reached out and gently touched her cheek. "But this *is* more, and that may be a good thing. No fighting against phantoms. We'll be able to go for the jugular. We just have to figure out how to do it."

"Oh, is that all?"

He smiled. "I know. I know. But we'll do it." His hand moved down to cup her throat. "Your pulse just jumped. I can feel it pounding." He was suddenly still, his hand tightening. Then he took a breath and pulled his hand away from her. "Sorry. Not a good idea."

"No." She nodded jerkily as she stepped back from his touch. She was liking it too much. It was giving her comfort as well as that fiery, tingling warmth. "We have no choice but to figure out how to get some sort of plan together. So where do we go from here?"

"I go to see Renata, and we compare notes. She's probably coming up with something on similar lines."

"Because you think alike?"

"Because we have similar experiences, and we generally think out of the box. I'll ask her to send someone to Camano's camp to try to verify." He moved toward the door. "Drink your coffee and have a bite to eat. Not much. We'll have dinner with Renata at seven, then we'll be leaving from the airport at eleven tonight. I should be back soon. I won't—" He stopped as he saw her expression. "What?"

"I'll do as you suggest because I can't contribute right now, and you may come up with something valuable if I leave you to it." She met his gaze across the room. "But don't expect me to let you pat me on the head and do whatever you tell me to do. I'm going to be part of every aspect of getting Praland. I have a very personal interest now that I realize that his hands are as stained and bloody as Camano's."

He smiled. "I know you too well to expect you to be that meek. I remember having to chase you through the forest that first night, so that you could be sure that I'd put down those three men of Camano's. I'm just grateful you're not chasing after me to Renata's room. She's very wary of antagonism from any quarter."

"I'm not antagonistic. Not anymore. I'll take help wherever I can get it." She lifted her cup to her lips. "Particularly from you, Mandak. It appears we're both targets, and we may need each other to survive." She added, "So by all means, go and have your chat with Renata. But while you're talking strategy, start planning how to get me to that service for Lee and Natalie. Nothing you've told me just now has changed that priority. Nothing is more important to me."

He nodded soberly. "I'll get you there." He opened the door. "And, what's more important, I'll get you out."

HEATHROW AIRPORT
LONDON

"Just do what Mandak tells you to do." Renata watched Mandak head for the cockpit. "He's smart and lethal and everything I'd want in someone in my corner." She turned to face Allie. "He'll do whatever is—" She stopped as she saw Allie's expression. "Okay, you're not going to do that. Good advice but not realistic for you." She made a face. "Or for me, for that matter."

"I'll try to go along with what seems sensible to me."

"From what Mandak has told me about you, that's quite a concession."

"I'm trying to do what Lee and Natalie would want me to do." She shrugged. "Sometimes it's not easy. But there has to be a middle road somewhere, and I'll find it."

"I'm sure Mandak will be grateful," Renata said dryly. She was silent a moment. "Good luck. I'm sorry I started out wrong with you. You have every right to resent me."

"I don't resent you." She realized she was telling the truth. That first moment in Renata's suite seemed a long time ago. During the last hours she had spent with the woman, Allie had realized how intensely Renata not only cared about all the individuals she called family but also those children who had been Praland's victims. "You were worried about Mandak and being protective." She smiled slightly. "I do find that idea a bit bizarre."

"Sometimes I do, too. What can I say? He's family." Renata reached out and took Allie's hand to shake. "But I want you to know I regard you as family now, too. I'll protect you as much as I can."

"Thank you. But I'm sure both you and Mandak regard me as expendable."

Renata flinched. "Sometimes I don't have a choice. But Mandak doesn't consider you expendable. It would be a hell of a lot safer for him if he did. In case you haven't noticed, he goes the extra mile even when everyone else considers it a suicide mission."

"Like the night he went after Simon Walberg?"

Renata nodded. "I told him not to go. It was my duty. I knew it was probably a lost cause."

"And you were right."

"It doesn't make me sleep any better at night. And who's to say who was right. I had logic on my side, but Mandak had hope. And because of that hope, he was able to spare Simon unbearable suffering."

"And put himself on Praland's hit list."

"He knew that was going to happen the minute he pulled the trigger and put Simon out of his misery. He's never regretted it." Her smile ebbed. "But I've regretted it for him. Every time he doesn't check in for a little while, I make an excuse to call him. He pretends not to know why I'm doing it." Her gaze moved to the cockpit door. "But he knows." She shrugged and turned back to Allie. "This memory reading that you do. How does it work? Is it a sure thing?"

"How do I know? When I was reading the memories of those men for my father, I was able to do it every time. But I've never run across anyone who has a natural mind block. Mandak says he believes I'll be able to do it. He detected a weakness in Praland's memory area."

"That's what he told me, too."

"But you have to realize I haven't tried to read anyone's memory in the last seven years. On the contrary, I've been shoving them away."

"Understandable. That's what Mandak wanted from you."

"What?"

She shrugged. "I asked him why not concentrate on making that gift itself stronger? But he said that you were already so strong that it would be taking coals to Newcastle. It wasn't strength you needed. It was control, to keep you sane and balanced. He wouldn't let any of us push you or try to take over your training. We all thought it was taking far too long. But he said you needed to heal and grow strong." She made a face. "Seven years? It was an eternity, with everything that was going on with Pra-land. We have to hope Mandak was right."

"I'm always right." Mandak was smiling as he came out of the cockpit. "I won't even ask what you were discussing. It's immaterial. Get out of here, Renata. We're taking off in a few minutes."

"I'm going." She reached forward and kissed his cheek. "Take care. I called Marc and told him to set a watch on Camano to monitor his moves. After you killed his men in Flagstaff, he appears to have crawled into a hole and disappeared. But the minute he sticks his head out of the ground, we'll be there. Maybe we'll be able to give you warning if we find out he's heading this way."

"That would be helpful," Mandak said dryly. "That's not a surprise I'd welcome. And I've just made the arrangements we discussed. Have that helicopter on the ground waiting."

"I will." Renata reached into her bag as she turned to Allie. "I brought you a present." She pulled out a Luger revolver and handed it to her butt first. "Mandak may have furnished you with one, but this one is better. I've used it many times. It's a fine weapon, and the balance is just right. But it shoots a little to the left. Remember that."

"Thank you." Allie's hand closed on the pistol. The weapon looked cold and lethal, but it felt oddly warm to the touch. "I'll remember. And Mandak hasn't seen fit to give me such a useful gift. However, he did give me a designer wardrobe."

"What?" Renata glanced at Mandak.

"It was a distraction," Mandak said.

"And a gun would have been a shock to my delicate nervous system," Allie said. "Even though he taught me to use one years ago."

"Your nerves *are* delicate right now," Mandak said bluntly. "But I would have gotten you a weapon before we got to Tanzania. Praland won't give a damn about your sensitive soul."

"Well, now you won't have to bother." She tucked the gun in her jacket pocket. "And what plans have you and Renata made that you haven't told me about?"

"I'm out of here." Renata turned toward the door. "You'll let me know when it's over, Mandak?"

"As soon as I get the chance."

"I can wait. Don't take any risks." The next moment, she was running down the steps of the plane.

"When what's over?" Allie asked.

"Buckle up." He sat down and fastened his seat belt. "I'll tell you once we're airborne. I'm not trying to keep anything from you."

"You could have fooled me." She buckled her seat belt.

"Earlier today you told me that I should go see Renata and make my plans." He smiled. "I took that as permission. Now you're complaining?"

She had told him that, she thought, annoyed. She hadn't realized that she would feel so isolated and out of the loop when it happened. "Yes."

"Well, at least you're not denying or making excuses." He leaned back in his seat as the plane started rolling down the runway. "And that very contrary attitude makes me think that you're beginning to come back to normal."

"I don't know what normal is anymore. My normal was never like anyone else's." She glanced sideways at him as the plane began to lift off the ground. "And neither was yours, according to Renata. It appears you were a bad boy and didn't obey the family rules."

"Guilty. But I always tried to do what was best for the family." He met her gaze. "And I never risked anyone's life but my own."

"Until now."

His lips tightened. "Until now."

She could feel the force and tension in that brief reply. It caused a ripple of disturbance to run through her. She had learned a good deal about him tonight from Renata. She wasn't sure that she wished to know this much. She hurriedly glanced away from him to the wisp of clouds drifting by the window. "What helicopter were you talking about?"

"We're not going directly to Dar es Salaam. I'm having the pilot land in the hills about a hundred miles south of the city. We're going to be met by a helicopter flown by Dirk Thorne, one of Renata's agents. He'll take us to Talboa." He made a face. "Renata knows I could fly the damn helicopter, but she wants Thorne as a backup in case of trouble."

And another indication of Renata's protectiveness about Mandak, Allie thought. "What's in Talboa?"

"It's the area where Simon's ashes were scattered after Lee and Natalie had him cremated. That's why they wanted their ashes returned here to Tanzania, so that they could be with him."

"Ashes? Simon was cremated, too?"

"There wasn't much left to bury." He added grimly, "And if they'd seen fit to do anything else, Lee and Natalie couldn't have been sure that Praland wouldn't have dug up the remains and desecrated them. He was absolutely furious about everything connected to that night I took away his toy. He was foaming at the mouth and making wild threats when he heard about Simon's final arrangements. He tried to bribe the crematorium to tell him where they'd taken the ashes."

"Sick," Allie said. More than sick. Praland's behavior bordered on being unhinged. "Simon wasn't safe from him even in death."

"Lee and Natalie made sure that their son was safe. They knew what a monster Praland was, and they took precautions."

"And are we taking precautions? You said that no one could know about the funeral."

"That's why we're avoiding Dar es Salaam. As I told you, I've arranged for Lee's and Natalie's ashes to be smuggled out of the embassy by James McKeller, one of the clerks. He'll be taking them to Talboa. We'll be there to meet him when he arrives."

"It seems . . . obscene having to sneak around like this. It's a funeral, for God's sake."

"And Praland has nothing to do with God. He's strictly at the other end of the spectrum."

"I know," she said wearily. "And we'll make it right for Lee and Natalie. Where is this place?"

"It's a very beautiful little cove on a large lake," he said gently. He handed her his phone and pointed to the tiny mark on the map. "Talboa."

CHAPTER TEN

"TALBOA, PRALAND," AMAN KOBU said as he checked his GPS. "It looks as if McKeller is heading for Lake Talboa. There's nothing else on this stretch of road."

"And you're certain that McKeller took the ashes?"

"Of course I'm certain." Kobu realized his mistake when Praland fell silent. The son of a bitch didn't tolerate any sign of arrogance or disrespect. He went on hurriedly, "I've had a man watching the embassy for the past twenty-four hours. The two stainless-steel containers that were in the storeroom of the embassy are now in McKeller's car. Father Elwyn, the chaplain, left the embassy at noon today without saying where he was going."

"But no sign of Mandak or the woman?"

"Not yet. But I'm sure that we'll have Mandak in our sights soon."

"I don't want him in your sights," Praland said with soft venom. "I want him brought to me so that I can tear his testicles out of his body. You can kill the woman, but I want Mandak."

"And you'll have him. Are you sending me more men to help bring—"

"You'll have to make do with your own men. You have

weapons, even missiles. What more do you need? I'll send you reinforcements when you tell me that Talboa is McKeller's definite destination. Mandak has fooled us before. I won't be tricked again." He added mockingly, "You're not afraid of facing Mandak by yourself, are you? He's such a gentle soul."

"More like a tiger."

"It's odd that you should mention that glorious beast. You know I have a great fondness for tigers. You've seen the tiger I acquired from that poacher in India?"

Kobu tensed. "You know I have."

"Yes, I thought you were present during his last feeding. I'm planning on using him in many more interesting and innovative ways. For instance, I've not been pleased with the performance of a little whore I took out of one of our houses in Madagascar. True, she's only thirteen, but she should be able to do what I wish without weeping and screaming. Don't you think that's true, Kobu?"

"Whatever you say."

"So I thought that I'd put the tiger cage next to the bed and tell her if she didn't please me that she'd join him." He chuckled. "I believe that should arouse her enthusiasm. Though I don't know if I can resist giving her to that striped beauty even if she does please me. Can you imagine the carnage, the exquisite agony?"

Kobu swallowed. "Why are you telling me this, Praland?"

"Why, you mentioned a tiger. I thought you'd be interested." He paused. "Just as I'm interested that we may have gotten close to Mandak after all these years. I just wanted you to know that if you screw up and let him get away, you'll have an intimate meeting with my tiger. I'll let you watch him toy with the whore the first night.

The second night, I'll have you be his evening meal. Do you understand?"

"We're not certain Mandak will be—" He inhaled sharply. "Yes, I understand, Praland." He hung up.

Shit!

He wished he'd never told Praland that McKeller could be on his way to meet Mandak with those canisters. Let someone else take the pressure.

His palms were moist on the steering wheel as he guided the SUV over the bumpy dirt road.

He reached for his phone to get his men moving from their encampment a good thirty miles away. He wouldn't wait for Praland to send any more men. He couldn't take that chance if they got here too late. He'd also see if he could pick up a few men in the village on the way to Talboa. He knew of at least four bandits who operated out of this area. He could round up more if he dangled enough money at them. That was the smart thing to do.

It was the only thing to do to be certain of survival. He had to kill the woman and serve Mandak up to Praland.

Then he could relax and watch Mandak be the meal for Praland's tiger.

"THERE IT IS." MANDAK WAS looking out the window of the helicopter as it banked over the lake. "But I don't see McKeller."

"There he is." Thorne, the pilot, was staring down at the crisscross of paths and the twisting dirt road that branched off from the larger two-lane rock road. "I think he's coming up the road toward the lake."

Mandak nodded. "And he told Renata he'd be driving

an SUV." He turned to Allie. "What do you think? It's a beautiful place, isn't it?"

She nodded jerkily. She could see that it was lovely, but she was too tense to fully appreciate it.

"We'll be down in two minutes," the pilot said. "And I shouldn't give you more than thirty minutes before I need to take off again. This isn't Praland territory, but he has eyes and ears everywhere. One phone call, and he'd have men streaming down here toward the town."

"Thirty should be enough." Mandak shook his head as Allie opened her lips to protest. "I told you that I'd get you to their funeral service. I didn't tell you how long you could stay. I'm not risking your neck. We'll make those minutes count." He looked down at the ground again. "I can see someone getting out of another car parked down by the lake. I think it's Father Elwyn. He conducted the service for Simon. I told McKeller to make arrangements with him to come and bless the ashes. Lee and Natalie always liked him."

Allie had known Lee and Natalie were Catholic, but they had seldom attended church in Flagstaff. She had thought that they just didn't want to arouse interest or questions about her arrival in town. "Then I'm glad you were able to make the arrangements with him. It will make everything seem more normal." As if anything could have any semblance of normalcy with this hideous game of hide-and-seek going on. "I see a canoe down there on the bank. What is it doing there?"

"We'll be going out on the lake to scatter the ashes. That's what they did with Simon's remains."

"So Praland had no chance of recovering them?" she asked grimly.

"That's right."

"Ugly. So terribly ugly." The helicopter had reached the ground, and Father Elwyn was walking toward them. Allie reached for the handle of the door. "I want to at least have a word with the priest."

Mandak nodded. "I'm going to scout around a little to make sure it's safe. Then I'll go talk to McKeller and help him take out the canisters and put them in the canoe."

"Thirty minutes," Thorne repeated. "No more, Mandak."

"Right. But I won't cheat them."

"No, we can't do that." The air was sticky and warm, and Allie shrugged out of her jacket and left it on her seat as she opened the door to jump out of the helicopter.

"I hope everything goes well, ma'am." Thorne was there to help her, his hazel eyes shining with sympathy. "God bless."

"Thank you. You're very kind."

But she closed both Mandak and the pilot out as she walked toward Father Elwyn. He was a man in his sixties, with gray hair and a tanned face that showed deep crow's-feet around brown eyes that held only gentleness and sympathy. "I'm Allie Girard, Lee and Natalie Walberg were family to me. Thank you for coming, Father. I know there must be an element of risk for you."

"If I were afraid of risk, I would have left this country a long time ago." He took her hand and shook it. "But the need is here, and so is the satisfaction of supplying that need. Lee and Natalie were good people, and I'm sorry for your loss, Miss Girard. But you must remember, it's only the loss of the ones left behind. They're now in the hands of the angels with their son, Simon."

"I'm trying to remember." Her eyes were stinging with

tears as she looked up at him. "But there's so much evil. It's very difficult, Father."

"Do as I do, serve the need. Forgive those who trespass against you."

She shook her head. "I'm sorry. I'm not that generous. And I can't forgive those who trespassed against Lee and Natalie."

"Then I'll pray for you as well as the Walbergs." He took her arm. "Now let's go to the boat. I see Mr. Mandak frowning at us." He was leading her toward the canoe. "He also has trouble with forgiveness. But he's an extraordinary man, and you'll be safe with him. Just cling to him as you would Lee and Natalie."

"Cling to him? I don't think so, Father." She smiled shakily. "But thank you for talking to me. I don't know much about religion. My only experience is once a year having my mother dress me up in fancy clothes and take me to Easter Mass. It was more like a show than a service. But I wanted to feel that death wasn't the end for Lee and Natalie."

"It's not the end. After we say good-bye to them, let's arrange to meet and have a long talk."

"I'd like that, Father. But I may be very busy for the next couple weeks." Survival. Revenge. Killing. Very busy. "Let me get in touch with you." She gazed out over the crystal blue water, the verdant trees hanging low, the flamboyant blossoms exploding with pink and orchid color. "It's so beautiful here."

"The Gates of Heaven."

"What?"

"Natalie Walberg told me she wanted Simon's ashes to be scattered at a place as close to the Gates of Heaven as I could find. I'd done missionary work in this area and remembered it."

"The Gates of Heaven," she repeated. "I like that."

"It seems a particularly holy place to me. We'll row through those waters and I'll say a prayer and we'll stream the ashes into that beautiful crystal water. Perhaps they'll join with their Simon's."

"Perhaps. I hope so."

"But it doesn't matter," he repeated, as they reached the canoe. "This is only the Gates of Heaven. They're already inside and together."

"Get in the canoe," Mandak said curtly. "Sorry, Father. I have to get Miss Girard out of here as soon as possible. I've checked out the area as much as I can, and it seems safe, but everything could change in minutes." He swung Allie into the canoe and turned to the sandy-haired young man standing beside him. "McKeller, you've done your job. Get back in your SUV and get out of here."

McKeller nodded. "Right." He turned to Allie, and said gently, "My condolences, ma'am." He looked to be only in his middle twenties, and his brown eyes were warm and kind. "I wish I could stay. I'll pray for them."

"Thank you."

"And I'll also pray for you." Then he was moving toward the SUV. "I'll report in to Renata on the way back to the embassy and tell her so far, so good, Mandak."

"Fine." Mandak jumped into the canoe and took a paddle. "Father?"

"Coming." Father Elwyn was already in the canoe and settling himself beside the two shiny stainless-steel canisters. "Good to see you, Mr. Mandak. We always seem to meet at these regrettable occasions."

"But you say they're not really sad occasions."
Mandak was dipping the oar into the water. "I'm afraid
you've never been able to convince me."

"Give me time." The priest smiled. "Miss Girard is
also a skeptic, but she's more open than you."

"Because she desperately wants to believe. You've
caught her at a vulnerable moment."

"All our moments on this Earth are vulnerable. It's
just a matter of degree." He unscrewed first one canister,
then the other. Then he bowed his head. "Now shall we
pray for the eternal souls of these two fine people?"

ALLIE WATCHED THE MIST OF ash drift into the clear water,
lie on the surface for an instant, then disappear. The
priest's words came back to her.

*Maybe their ashes will merge with those of their son,
Simon.*

I hope it's true. I hope you're with him now. I know
you're with each other. God would make sure you stayed
together.

I'm feeling a little lost now. I know you're going to
be happy with him, but will it be all right if I talk to
you now and then?

Peace. Serenity. Love.

Maybe that's an answer? I don't think that's wishful
thinking. Okay, then that's what I'll do. I promise I won't
bother you too often.

The ashes were gone now, vanished beneath the clear
lake waters.

"Allie." Father Elwyn was smiling at her. "Remember.
It's only their bodies at the Gates of Heaven. Their souls
have gone ahead." His face was lit with loving kindness.

"It's true. Believe it. They're together and you can be sure that those souls will see—"

His head exploded!

She screamed as brain matter flew in all directions.

"Down!" Mandak threw down his oar and pushed her to the bottom of the canoe.

A bullet struck the side of the boat.

The priest had slumped to the side and was lying over the edge of the canoe.

It wasn't happening.

It couldn't be happening.

His head exploding.

Just like the night her father had shot Jokman in the head.

Gates of Heaven. Gates of Heaven.

A barrage of shots were being rained on them from the bank. She could see nine or ten men firing rifles and handguns.

"We've got to get off this canoe. We're sitting targets." Mandak began to rock the boat. "When I tilt it, slide into the water and head for the far shore. I'll be with you."

But the priest would not be with them.

Dead.

Gates of Heaven.

"Now!"

She slid into the icy water.

A bullet struck the water next to her.

She went beneath the water and began swimming.

Mandak! Where was he?

There he was just to the side.

He was surfacing, heading for the far shore as he'd told her to do.

He shouldn't have surfaced. She could see the bullets striking on all sides of him.

But then he was underwater, beside her, gesturing in the opposite direction.

He wanted her to go toward the bank from where their attackers had been firing.

Why?

Because he'd been leading those men in a false direction and wanted to double back to escape them?

Would it work?

No way of knowing.

Keep swimming. Take as few breaths as possible. She'd always been a strong swimmer.

Keep going.

Gates of Heaven.

Head exploding. Brain matter flying.

Father Elwyn smiling at her with loving kindness.

Keep swimming.

She could see the bank up ahead.

Mandak had already reached the bank and was waiting, treading water.

She warily surfaced beside him.

No shooters on this bank. They must have been drawn to the far shore.

"What's happening?" she gasped. "Who are they?"

Noise, and crashing brush on the far shore.

"The tall man in the camouflage uniform is Aman Kobu, one of Praland's officers. I don't know the rest." Mandak's hands were on her waist, preparing to lift her. "Get out and run into the brush," Mandak said. "Fast. Keep low. I'll be behind you. We'll circle around toward the helicopter."

She nodded, and the next instant, she was on the bank

and heading for the brush. It was only seconds until she was out of sight in the thick shrubbery.

"Run," Mandak said curtly. "Low and fast. I'll be covering you."

She knew he had a gun, but he'd been in the water. Would it still fire?

She wasn't going to question him.

Run.

Brush was scraping her face and arms.

Her shoes were wet and muddy before she'd gone a hundred yards.

She couldn't hear Mandak behind her.

Keep running.

She was almost there.

A bullet splintered the wood of the tree next to her.

But the bullet came from in front of her, not behind, not from the far shore where there were screams and shouts.

Why would it—

"Down, Allie!" It was Mandak but he'd somehow managed to circle and get in front of her. He was only yards from the helicopter. "Down!"

She fell to the ground.

Another bullet whistled by her shoulder. She rolled to one side into the shrubs as she saw the shooter.

He was a brown-skinned man in loose jeans with a bare, tattooed chest. He was standing beside the helicopter, his white teeth gleaming as he let off another round of shots.

Mandak was dodging bullets himself as he weaved in and out to avoid them.

Then he was on top of the shooter, his knife slicing at the man's throat.

But there was another man in a yellow shirt coming out from the other side of the copter toward the struggling figures with a pistol in his hand.

"No!" She instinctively jumped to her feet. She couldn't stay here hiding. Gun. She had to have a gun. Where was—

She had slipped Renata's gun into her jacket pocket.

And that jacket was in the helicopter. She ran through the brush and around the other side of the helicopter.

More bullets.

She glanced over her shoulder to see that Mandak had pulled the body of the man he'd knifed over his body to protect his body from the bullets of the new threat.

God, let her get to her jacket. Don't let there be any more of Kobu's men blocking her way.

She almost stumbled over the body of Thorne, the pilot, who was huddled beside the door. His eyes were staring straight ahead. He had a bullet in his forehead.

Don't look at him. Don't feel anger or sadness. Get the gun.

The next instant, she had the Luger in her hand.

She moved around the helicopter.

The shooter's back was to her, and he was moving forward, toward Mandak, his gun still spitting bullets.

Stop him from firing at Mandak.

Don't think about anything else but keeping Mandak alive.

No, now was also the time to think about Thorne, the pilot who had been murdered by that shooter.

Now was the time to remember the priest's kind smile before they'd shot his head off.

She started firing.

She saw blood blossom, spread, on the back of the man's yellow shirt.

The man whirled, his gun aimed at her.

She kept firing.

She blew off the hand holding his pistol.

He screamed.

She took another step forward.

Gates of Heaven. Gates of Heaven.

She aimed carefully.

She could see the fear in his eyes.

Gates of Heaven.

She shot him in the heart.

She watched him fall to the ground.

"Allie." Mandak was on his feet. The next moment he was beside her, grabbing her arm. "Come on. We have to get out of here."

"Thorne is dead," she said numbly as he pulled her toward the door of the helicopter. "They killed him."

"I was afraid they had. Kobu would have had to plug that exit." He opened the door and lifted her inside the copter. "But it was safer to chance it than risk being run down on foot." He started the engine, and the rotors whirled. "It was lucky they only assigned two men to guard—"

A bullet splintered the helicopter windshield!

"Shit!"

Allie could see Kobu and the other men pouring back around the edge of the lake toward them.

The helicopter lifted jerkily.

Another bullet struck the door.

"Let's hope they don't hit the gas tank," Mandak said grimly, as they climbed through the torrent of bullets.

"Stop him!" Kobu was screaming frantically as he ran

toward the helicopter. "Do you know what you're doing to me? You fools, stop him!"

But it was too late. They were over the trees and out of range.

Mandak waited until he'd gained more altitude before he turned to Allie. "Are you okay?"

"No," she said jerkily. "But I've not been shot if that's what you mean." She looked at him. "You have blood on your chin."

"Not my blood." He wiped his chin with his shirt-sleeve. "It happens when you cut someone's throat."

"Does it?" She glanced away from him. " I wouldn't know. I've never done that."

"I know." He muttered a curse as he banked the heli-copter. "And you've never killed a man until today."

"No. I've never done that either," she said dully. "I thought he was going to kill you. I had to stop him."

"And you did." He said roughly, "And just look at you. It's nearly made a basket case of you."

"No, it hasn't." She reached up and rubbed her temple. "I can't let that happen. That would destroy me. They killed that priest, they killed Thorne. They tried to turn something beautiful and sacred into pure ugliness. They tried to kill you, Mandak. It had to stop. I had to stop it."

"And you did," Mandak said quietly. "And, if you think it was the right thing to do, then give yourself a little time to answer all the whys. I wish to hell it hadn't happened, but it did." He took her hand and gently squeezed it. "And I'm grateful you think that my neck was worth saving."

"It had to stop," she whispered. She pulled her hand away and looked out the window. "We've lost altitude. Why are we flying so low? What's that road down there?"

"It's the road that leads to Dar es Salaam." His lips thinned. "I sent McKeller back to the embassy. I'm just checking to make sure he wasn't on Kobu's hit list."

She tensed. She felt suddenly cold. Not again. Her eyes were straining on the snakelike road below them. "Phone him."

"I will. But I'd feel better if I saw—"

"Smoke!" She saw the gray cloud of smoke before she saw the fire. "Around that next turn. Is it the SUV?"

"I can't tell." The vehicle was completely engulfed in flames. "But it would be too much of a coincidence if it wasn't."

"Land," she said. "He might still be alive."

"I can't risk you. Kobu's men could still be down there. I'll phone Renata to have one of her people in the area go check and see—"

"No. That might not be in time. Cruise low and see if you can see any threat." Her hands clenched. "But regardless, we're going to go down there and see if we can save him. No more deaths, Mandak."

"Allie, the chances are that he's already—"

"Did you hear me? No more deaths." Her eyes were blazing into his. "You wouldn't even think twice if I wasn't with you. You know you wouldn't. But because you think I'm so important because of that damn ledger, you won't do it."

His lips tightened. "Would it be too much to believe that it's not all because of the ledger?" Then he was suddenly smiling recklessly. "I guess it would, considering what I've put you through today. So what the hell." He banked the helicopter. "I feel lucky. Something has to go right today. Let's go see if McKeller survived that bonfire."

* * *

MANDAK DID TWO TURNS OVER the wreckage before he landed several yards up the road from the burning SUV.

"Stay close," Mandak said. "I want you within an arm's distance from me."

Thick smoke.

Heat.

Acrid chemicals.

Smothering.

Allie's eyes were stinging as she got closer to the pile of burning metal. The gas tank had already blown, and the heat was almost overpowering.

Dear God, how could anyone survive this?

"The SUV was taken out by a short-range missile." Mandak was examining the wreckage. "Kobu must have wanted to make a clean sweep of everything connected with the funeral service. He's always been desperate to please Praland." He stared thoughtfully at the flames. "That missile might have been be a good thing."

"How?"

"If the SUV exploded immediately, Kobu's men wouldn't be likely to attack the vehicle or McKeller after the missile hit. They'd assume their job was done."

"And they'd be right."

"Not if McKeller caught sight of them before they loosed their missile." He was kneeling on the road examining the swerving tracks on the dirt road. "Not if he jumped out on one of those curves. It looks like no one in the SUV was in control for several yards along this stretch."

Hope. Please let it be true.

"Then where is he?"

"I've no idea. But, judging by the distance McKeller traveled on the road before the explosion, Kobu must have sent a team of men to follow McKeller even before we went out on the lake. We've just got to hope that Kobu believed the report he received that McKeller was dead and didn't try to take him captive." He added bitterly, "Kobu knows how much Praland loves to toy with prisoners. He might think that he'd be excused for not bringing him bigger game."

She remembered Kobu's frantic expression as he'd been running toward them. "He seemed desperate."

"I'm sure he is." He was moving toward the side of the road. "Stay close. I'll cover this side of the road and— Allie!"

"It's quicker if we split up." She was already moving to the other side of the steep incline on the opposite side of the road. "Even if he didn't die in that explosion, we don't how badly he could be hurt. Maybe they shot him before . . ." She trailed off as she slipped and slid down the incline. "I'll call out if I see him."

She could almost feel Mandak's impatience and exasperation. Too bad.

Couldn't he see that she had to do it?

If there was the slightest chance McKeller was alive, she had to move fast, they had to find him.

No more deaths.

But she could see no sign of life. No crumpled body, no McKeller struggling to crawl up the incline. She moved toward the edge of the jungle.

Nothing there either.

"Allie!"

"Here!" she answered Mandak. "Did you find him?"

"No, get up here, dammit."

"I'm going back to where the road curves. There's so much deep shrubbery and palms down here, he could be anywhere."

Not in the inferno in that SUV, she prayed. Let him have had his chance. Let her find him.

But even if he was hurt, he might be able to hear her.

"McKeller!"

Nothing.

No sound.

"I'm on my way down," Mandak called. "I've checked out the other side of the road and incline. He has to be on this side or nowhere."

She paid no attention, as she tore through the palms. "McKeller!"

No answer.

Or was there?

She stopped to listen.

Nothing.

But there had been a sound, she *knew* it.

And it came again.

Low, more like a grunt than a call for help.

Where . . .

To the left, up closer to the road, where the grass was high and thick.

"McKeller!" She tore up the incline, pushing through the tall grass. "We're here. We're coming. Let me—"

Then she saw him.

Blood. McKeller's face was bruised and bloody. His clothes were almost torn from his body from the sharpness of the rocks and the edge of the high grasses. His shoulder was twisted at an odd angle. His eyes were closed and they didn't open as she ran forward to drop to her knees beside him.

"No," she said fiercely. "Open your eyes, McKeller. I heard you. I know I heard you. You're not going to die. Do you hear me? It's not going to happen."

"Allie." Mandak was suddenly there, dropping down beside her. "Easy. Let me take a look at him."

"I heard him, Mandak. That's what brought me here. He's going to be—"

McKeller's eyes were slowly opening. They focused on Mandak. "Missile . . ."

"I know." He was examining the wound on McKeller's temple. "You jumped?"

"It seemed to be the thing to do." McKeller's gaze went to Allie. "I . . . heard you calling. I don't think I was even conscious. But you seemed to want so badly . . . for me to answer."

She nodded. "I had to find you." She turned to Mandak. "We have to get him out of here. What if Kobu's men come back? Can we move him to the helicopter?"

"It appears we're going to do it whether we should or not." He looked at McKeller. "I'm going to try to cause you as little pain as possible. I think your arm is broken and it may be out of the socket. You probably have a concussion. We'll take care of all of that when we can. But we've got to get you out of here." His hand went to McKeller's neck. "It'll just be a little twinge . . ."

"I don't know what—" McKeller's head slumped to one side. He was unconscious.

"I'll need you to help, Allie." Mandak was already levering, lifting McKeller's limp body. "I want to damage him as little as possible, so I have to bear most of the weight of this broken arm and shoulder on this side of his body. Get on the other side and support him. It's going to be a hell of a job getting him up this incline."

She was already on McKeller's other side, draping his arm over her shoulders. Limp. Very heavy. And Mandak was bearing most of his weight. "I can help more. Let me do it."

"Too late." He was dragging McKeller up the incline. "I don't want to readjust. Just keep up with me."

And that was more than enough challenge, she found. She had to keep her footing and try to bear what weight Mandak would allow her. It took fifteen minutes to get up to the level road and another twenty to reach the helicopter.

She was panting as she helped him arrange McKeller in the rear seat and fasten the seat belt. She shuddered as she looked at that crooked, broken shoulder. "That's going to be agonizing. How long will he be out?"

"Probably not long enough." He was getting into the pilot's seat. "I can't take him back to the embassy. He's a target now. We just have to keep Praland thinking that Kobu managed to take him out."

She fastened her seat belt. "So where do we take him?"

"Sargol, it's a village on the coast where Renata has set up a clinic."

"Safe?"

"Yes. It's handled entirely by the family. We had to have a place in this country that would be safe from Praland." His lips thinned. "There's been a need in the last nine years. That's where we took those children we rescued."

"But McKeller will wake up before we get there?"

"Yes. At least thirty or forty minutes before we get to the village." He lifted off. "Nothing I can do about it. I couldn't take a chance on putting him out any longer. I can't be certain he doesn't have a concussion."

"You did what you could." She leaned back in the seat, trying to ward off the sudden exhaustion. "They didn't kill him. That's all that's important. He's alive. We'll make sure he stays alive."

"And you did more than your part to guarantee that, Allie." He asked quietly, "Can you rest and trust me to make sure of that from now on? You know I can make all this go away for you."

"No, don't you dare do that!" He didn't understand. Death was all around them. She couldn't let go until at least McKeller was safe.

Or maybe he did understand. Because he turned away and looked straight ahead. "I'm familiar with every corner of that mind of yours. It's going to be very painful for you when you see how much McKeller is going to suffer. If you change your mind, let me know."

"I won't change my mind."

"I know," he said grimly as he turned east toward the coast. "That would be too much to expect. And that only means I'll have to watch both of you going through hell."

CHAPTER ELEVEN

WHEN THEY LANDED AT SARGOL, four techs with a gurney ran out to the helicopter pad the minute it touched down.

"Get him to surgery." Mandak jumped out of the helicopter and ran around to where they were trying to gently get McKeller out of the seat. "Is Megan here?"

"She's on her way. She's in surgery," one of the techs said. "She had a gunshot wound to—"

McKeller screamed.

"You're hurting him." Allie was out of the helicopter, her eyes blazing. "Be careful. Can't you see that his shoulder is—"

"They see," Mandak said. "He's safe now, Allie. They know what they're doing. You can let him go."

"They *hurt* him." He was in such terrible pain. He'd been moaning and gasping for the last thirty minutes. And every minute had been a burning wound for Allie. And now he was still in agony. "How can I be sure that they know what they're doing?"

"Because I say they do." A woman in surgical blues was walking toward her. "I chose every one of these techs and watched their training." She turned and motioned for the techs to take McKeller into the clinic. "Take X-rays, then get him ready for surgery. Give him a shot of morphine for the pain." She turned back to Allie. "I'm Dr. Megan Blair; I'll be taking care of the patient." She looked at Mandak. "How was he injured, Mandak?"

"He jumped out of a speeding SUV and rolled down a steep incline. He was out when Allie found him. I thought maybe a concussion beside the obvious injury. I had to transport him immediately, and I couldn't be careful."

"That's par for the course with most of the patients I get here," she said wearily. She turned back to Allie. "He was unconscious?"

"No, I heard him. I know I heard him."

Mandak shrugged. "Possible. I didn't hear him. Or it could have been something else. She wanted to find him very much." He smiled faintly. "Even McKeller said he felt as if he had to answer her."

"What difference does it make?" Allie asked. "He's here, and you have to make him better. He has to live, Dr. Blair."

"Megan." Her eyes narrowed on Allie's face. "Both you and Mandak look as if you've gone through a war. How do you feel, Allie?"

"I'm fine. Just fine. It's McKeller you have to worry about."

Megan smiled gently. "Then I'd better go do my job, hadn't I? I'm a very good doctor, Allie. You can trust me. I'll let you know as soon as I make my examination. He means a great deal to you?"

"He can't die. I won't have him die, too."

Megan's expression changed to thoughtfulness as she

studied Allie. She glanced at Mandak. "I'll be busy with your friend McKeller. I believe I'll have to leave everything else in your hands."

He nodded. "I'll need ammunition. Get that examination to me right away."

She nodded. "You can wait in my office. I won't be needing it while I'm in surgery." She turned and hurried across the grounds after the techs.

"I think she'll help him." Allie's gaze followed Megan until she disappeared into the clinic. "She seems . . . kind." She rubbed her temple. "But I guess that doesn't matter. How good is she, Mandak?"

"Very good. A fine surgeon, and she never gives up. She could practice anywhere in the world, but Renata convinced her to stay here."

"Is she one of the Devanez family?"

"Yes, though she didn't realize it until she was already a practicing MD." He took her elbow and guided her toward the clinic. "Come on. We'll go to Megan's office to wait."

"She said she'd be quick."

"And she will."

"He was hurting so terribly."

"He'll have had his pain shot by now. She wouldn't allow the X-rays without it."

He opened the door of the clinic, then an oak door immediately to the left. "Sit down." He pushed her into a brown leather chair against the wall. "I'll get you a cup of coffee. Megan always keeps a pot brewing."

She shook her head.

"Okay." He sat down beside her. "Then we'll just wait."

She sat very straight, her spine rigid.

Don't let go.

Five minutes passed.

Ten.

Fifteen.

Megan suddenly popped her head into the office. "No serious damage. Minor concussion. Broken arm and shoulder. But I can put him back together, and he'll only have a few aches when it rains." She looked meaningfully at Mandak. "Now I have to get into surgery. Do your job. I don't want to face another problem when I come out." She smiled at Allie. "McKeller will be fine. I promise." The door closed behind her.

Allie breathed a profound sigh of relief. "Thank God."

"Yes," he answered. "And Allie Girard." He smiled. "And Megan, who has just sternly reminded me of my duty."

"What duty?" She looked at him in alarm. "She said that McKeller is going to be fine. Wasn't that—"

"My job isn't McKeller," he interrupted. "She'll take care of him. She's worried about you."

"She shouldn't be worried about me. I'm fine. I told her I was fine."

"But she's a good doctor and excellent at seeing through bullshit." His lips thinned. "You're sitting there so straight, you look as if you have a poker in your back. You're exhausted. You're torn apart. And you killed your first man today. But you won't let go."

"I'm fine."

"Let go, Allie."

"Shut up, Mandak." She crossed her arms over her chest and stared at the landscape print on the wall over his shoulder. Natalie had painted a landscape something like that a few years ago. Only her painting was much better.

Gates of Heaven.

The priest's brains exploding, his body slumping to the side of the canoe.

"I'm not going to shut up."

"Then I won't listen to you." Her breath was coming in short pants. Control it. She mustn't lose control. If she did, she didn't know if she'd ever be able to get it back. "I'm just going to sit here and wait until Megan gets McKeller out of surgery."

"I can't let you do that," he said quietly. "I have to help you let go. Doctor's orders."

"Stop interfering." Her gaze swung back to his face. "And don't you play any of your tricks on me."

"No tricks." He reached out and pulled her to her feet. "I'm just going to help you give yourself permission to let yourself do what you won't let me do. Talk to me." He pulled her close, and his hand cupped the back of her neck. "For God's sake," he said roughly. "You feel as if you're made of crystal that could break in a million pieces."

"I won't break."

"No, you won't. But you're afraid that you will. That's why you won't let go." His lips were pressed to her ear, and his words came with soft force. "But I watched you today, and I know what you are. You went through hell at Talboa, and God knows what hideous memories Kobu managed to stir in you. But you never quit. You kept with me all the way." His lips brushed her temple. "No, you went past me."

"Death. The priest, Thorne. So many deaths. Death all around us."

"And you killed a man who might have killed me."

"Yes, I thought I'd hate it. I didn't. I just wanted to make sure there would be no more deaths."

"I'm grateful that it was my neck you saved to demonstrate that belief. But you may feel differently later."

"I don't think so. I told the priest that I didn't know if I could forgive the people who trespassed against Lee and Natalie." She was beginning to shiver, and she instinctively slid her arms around him to embrace his warmth. "Trespass? They *killed* them. No one has the right to kill someone else. Not if they're good and kind like Lee and Natalie. Not if they're like Father Elwyn, who only wanted to help, not hurt. And it goes on and on, doesn't it?"

"Yes, until you stop it."

"And that's killing, too." She looked up into his face. "Why?" She was starting to shake, waves and waves of violent trembling. She had to hold on to him to keep from falling. "It goes on and on. Not only the killing but the ugliness, the desecration. I can't let it happen anymore."

"You saved McKeller. Hell, you saved me. That's enough for today. We'll work on the rest of the world tomorrow." He lifted her in his arms and carried her into the adjoining examination room. "Now you're going to lie here and pretend today was a bad memory you have to block."

"I'll never be able to block it. I don't want to block it. People died, and I have to do something . . ."

He moved down to lie beside her. "Just for an hour. You need to heal. I don't want to do it for you." He held her so tight that she felt as if she were being absorbed into his body. "Go blank. You can't do anything while you're shaking like this. Doesn't that make sense?"

"Yes." She nestled closer, so that she could feel that strength. "But I don't know if I can—"

"You can do anything. I told you, I watched you today."

"Liar. Everything was moving too fast for you to—"

"Then I felt you. Every movement you made seemed part of me." His fingers were tangled in her hair. "Just as it is right now." His lips brushed her temple. "Can't you feel it, too?"

She did feel it. The shaking was beginning to subside, and she was only aware of the bonding, the sensation of being part of his body, part of his mind. It was so much stronger than it had been years ago . . .

But she had to be sure that she still had control through this comfort that was close to salvation. "No tricks?"

He pulled her even closer. He whispered, "Absolutely no tricks, Allie."

MANDAK HEARD MEGAN COME into the outer office over two hours later.

He carefully shifted away from Allie and got off the table. She had been sleeping for over an hour, but she needed more. He covered her with the blanket draped over the chair and moved quietly toward the door.

Megan was at the desk writing up her notes and glanced up as he came into the office. "Mission accomplished?"

"It's not that simple. McKeller?"

"My job wasn't that simple either, but I did what I set out to do." She glanced at the door. "Rough day for her?"

"The roughest."

"I thought so." She got up from the desk and went to

the coffee bar. "Shell-shocked." She poured two cups of coffee and brought them back and handed him one. "Renata told me that all our hopes are riding on Allie."

"Not all." He took a drink of coffee. "But a hell of a lot."

"She's not going to be much good to us if she goes into a tailspin. Praland will eat her alive."

"No he won't," Mandak said harshly. "I'd let Praland keep that ledger another ten years before I'd let anything happen to her."

Megan gave a low whistle. "Renata said that she thought you should have given Allie to her. Are you getting a little too involved? Judging by today, she may be—"

"Judging by today, she was magnificent," Mandak said curtly. "I couldn't have asked for anything else from her. If you'd been there, you would have thought the same thing."

"If you say so." She sat down and lifted her cup to her lips. "I'm just tired of patching up people like McKeller. Those kids I had to treat nearly broke my heart. Praland has to be stopped."

"That's what Allie said. The killing has to stop." His lips twisted. "She went through a trial by fire today. It made everything much clearer to her."

"The fire touched you, too," Megan said. "You're hurting, Mandak."

He shrugged. "I knew it was coming from the beginning. But I put the play into motion, and now I can't stop it even if I wanted to." He met Megan's eyes. "I did all I could with Allie, but she could use someone to talk to whom she can trust."

"And that isn't you?"

"We have a history. But it's complicated."

"I can see how it would be." She nodded. "I'll be there when she wakes up. We'll see how it goes." She sat down at her desk again. "Now get out of here. Go to the bunkhouse and get a shower and a few hours sleep yourself. You look like hell. Allie doesn't need any reminders of what the two of you went through."

"As you command." He moved toward the examination room. "I'll just check to make sure she's okay and still sleeping."

Megan nodded. "How very protective. Not at all like the hard-ass we know and love." She was already absorbed in her paperwork. "By all means, make certain that your charge is well and in the arms of Morpheus."

He quietly opened the door and moved to stand beside the table. Allie was curled up, sound asleep, her lips slightly parted, her breathing deep and steady.

He wanted to reach out and touch her, make contact in some way.

Protective? Hell, yes. It had nearly killed him to watch the horror that she had gone through today. It had even been worse to know that he had to stand by and not take over. She had been so fragilely balanced that he had known that he had to be careful not to disturb that balance.

Are you getting a little too involved?

Megan's question was almost ironic. How could he help but be involved? Allie had been his main concern and passion for seven years. And these last days had shown him a different Allie from the one he'd grown to know.

Dangerous.

He had told Megan he would delay the mission he had

worked so hard to complete to save Allie. It had come impulsively out of his lips, but he had known that it was true.

Back off.

There were too many lives at stake. Praland had to be killed. The ledger had to be found.

And he had to find a way to keep Allie alive through all of it.

"HI, ALLIE." MEGAN SMILED AS Allie drowsily opened her eyes. "Remember me? I thought I'd be here to give you good news when you woke. McKeller is doing fine and having a snack even as we speak."

"That's wonderful." But she was feeling terribly alone and suddenly anxious. She looked around the room. "Where's Mandak?"

"I sent him to get some rest." She made a face. "And a shower. You need one, too. You can use the shower adjoining my office." She got to her feet. "But, first, I'll get you a cup of coffee to wake you up. How do you take it?"

"Black."

"Right." Megan disappeared into the office.

Allie slowly sat up and swung her legs off the table. That feeling of anxiety at Mandak's absence she had experienced was making her uneasy. She had to stand on her own feet. She couldn't depend on Mandak to—

"Here we are." Megan came into the room and handed her the cup of coffee. "Drink it. The caffeine will do you good." She sat back down in the chair she'd vacated. "I wanted you to sleep but I knew that you were too on edge to really relax. That's why I had to count on Mandak."

She smiled. "But no problem. I've found I can always do that."

"Can you?" She sipped the hot coffee. "Have you known him a long time?"

"Yes. He's been in and out of Tanzania all the time I've run this clinic. When Renata needed him, he was there for her. He's the one who rescued those children from Praland's bordello in Madagascar."

"I didn't know that. He only mentioned there was a rescue." She studied Megan. "That sounds like you've been working here for some time. Why? Because you're part of this Devanez family?"

"I've never really thought of myself in that light. I only found out that I was descended from the Devanezes after I was an adult and out of medical school. By then I had other issues connected to what I discovered about myself that seemed more important to me."

Allie asked bluntly, "You mean you found out you were a freak like me?"

"No, I found out that I wasn't like everyone else. Which is a different thing entirely," Megan said quietly. "Though I had a few problems adjusting, and I admit that word jumped up in my mind several times. But since I married Neal Grady, a man who is also what you call a freak and works closely with Renata, I guess I'm pretty close to that adjustment." She shook her head. "And I'm definitely not like you, Allie. You have a gift that Renata and Mandak and all the rest of the clan are counting on to help save lives." She smiled. "I would have given anything to be able to do that. I'm a doctor. I couldn't understand if I had to have some kind of bizarre gift, I couldn't be a healer."

She asked skeptically, "Are there really healers?"

"Oh, yes. I know of at least two. One helps out at St. Jude's in Memphis."

Allie was silent a moment. "If you're not a healer, what kind of weird gift do—"

"You might say I'm a facilitator. They call me a Pandora."

"And what is that?"

"Under certain circumstances, I'm able to touch people and bring out whatever psychic talents they possess." She shrugged. "Which causes a multitude of problems. I don't discuss it. We all have our own crosses to bear. I've been trying to find out how to get control for years. I've had moderate success, but I have a long way to go." She smiled. "So you're not the only one with problems, and Mandak has been there helping, training you, for a long time."

"I never asked him to do it."

"No," Megan said. "And it's not fair to you, but that's the way it is. What's happening to those people Praland is targeting isn't fair, either." Her expression became shadowed. "I originally came to Tanzania to see if I could help find some of the victims targeted by Molino and Praland. My mother was one of those victims. She was murdered."

"I'm sorry. And did you find the other victims?"

"A few of them. But by then Praland had taken over the operation of the gang, and everything was getting worse. What started out as a quick job became . . ." She made a motion with one hand to indicate the exam room. "Became this clinic to try to do what I could to keep some of the pain and violence in check."

"It seems you did it. You might have saved McKeller."

"He wasn't that bad. But I have saved others." She

met Allie's eyes. "But those are temporary fixes. We have to get rid of Praland to make sure that none of it happens again."

Allie's lips twisted. "I've just had a terrible lesson to that effect. I know what Mandak expects. I know what Renata wants from me. You don't have to lecture me, Megan."

"I wasn't lecturing." She got to her feet. "I just wanted you to see the problem from my point of view. And have you know that I'll help you in any way I can." She moved toward the door. "Now I'll go check on McKeller and stop by the bunkhouse to tell Mandak you're awake. Your duffel is in the office bathroom. You'll probably want to throw those clothes you're wearing in the trash."

Allie looked down at her torn and filthy shirt and pants. "What there is left of them."

"Exactly."

She jumped off the table and followed Megan into the outer office. "And I want to stop in and see McKeller if that's okay."

"For a few minutes. He'll be glad to see you. He was asking about you."

"I don't see how he could even remember me. He was in such pain yesterday."

"People have a habit of remembering kindness . . . and caring. In the end, we have to forget the horrors and cling to the love."

"Who is this?" Allie had stopped beside the bulletin board beside the bathroom door. She was looking at a photo of a fair-haired child of about ten or eleven. The little girl was smiling, her face brimming with happiness. "She's beautiful. Your daughter?"

"No, Neal and I have no children. It didn't seem the time." She came over to the bulletin board and gently touched the photo with one finger. "Her name is Elizabeth Delft. I asked her parents to send me a photo of her. Not that I wouldn't remember her. I just wanted to remind myself why I was here when the times got bad." She turned away. "She was one of the children Mandak brought to me. We were able to save the rest, but she died of complications from a drug overdose. It was not a merciful death."

She left the office.

Allie stood there, frozen, staring at the photo after the door had closed behind Megan.

She had always been touched and angry about the stories about those children who had been victimized, but this hit home in an entirely personal way. That beautiful child . . .

She reached out and gently touched the photo as Megan had done.

Hello, Elizabeth. I'll say a prayer for you to Lee and Natalie. Maybe they'll be able to find you and help you as they did me.

Then she turned away and went into the bathroom. Her muscles were stiff and sore, not surprising considering what she had been through.

She avoided looking in the mirror except for one brief glance before she got into the shower. Dark circles beneath her eyes. Her jaw firm and set. She looked . . . harder.

And that was how she felt. Stark and bare. As if all the softness had been trimmed away.

Leaving what behind?

God only knew.

* * *

"IT'S NOT MY FAULT, PRALAND," Aman Kobu said desperately. "I told you that I thought they were heading for Talboa. I used my men as you told me. We even managed to take out McKeller going back to the embassy. But the men I picked up in the village weren't adequate. You should have sent me—"

"Mandak and the woman got away?" Praland asked softly. "Now how did that happen, Kobu? You killed a priest, a pilot, and the clerk from the embassy. All people I did not give a damn about. Yet Mandak flew away as if you didn't exist." He paused. "Which is what I'm beginning to wish would happen."

"Everything was happening too quickly. We thought he was at one end of the lake, then we saw him by the helicopter." He said quickly, "But I'll find him, Praland. I've been searching for someone who can tell me anything. You know I have contacts all over the country. I've been questioning the people in the village for hours and seeing—"

"You're wasting your time. You won't be able to locate him now. Those ashes were an opportunity, and you failed me. But there will be another opportunity. He has this Allie Girard, and the fool actually must believe he can use her. If he does, he'll come knocking on my door." He paused and said thoughtfully, "It may be amusing to see if my tiger likes the taste of Mandak's little friend as much as he did the whore I gave him for company a few hours ago."

The tiger.

Kobu broke into a sweat. "It wasn't my fault," he repeated.

"I believe you need to come back to the palace and explain to me how it wasn't your fault, Kobu. I'm having trouble understanding."

"I'll come back soon. Right now, I'm still searching. You know that I'll do everything I can to—"

"You sound a little breathless. You must be searching very hard. I'll allow you another day to bring me Mandak and that woman. After that, I'll send Hans Bruker to escort you back here. Have a nice hunt, Kobu." He hung up.

One more day, Kobu thought.

His heart was beating hard as he jammed the phone in his jacket.

He had to find Mandak and Allie Girard, or he was a dead man. He might not even make it back to the palace. Bruker could be almost as vicious as Praland, and he'd never liked Kobu.

No, he'd survive somehow. He'd always been able to wriggle his way out of every tight corner.

But this time he didn't see how he was going to do it.

And the tiger was waiting.

"KOBU SCREWED UP," PRALAND said as he turned to Hans Bruker. "He's history. And you may get the privilege of taking care of it."

Bruker smiled. "I'll enjoy it. He's an arrogant little prick. But you gave him another day."

"Desperation can accomplish miracles. He may actually come up with Mandak."

Bruker's eyes narrowed on his face. "You're not as upset as I thought you'd be."

"I thought there was a chance Mandak would slip

away from Kobu. As I told him, there's another way of springing a trap." He started to dial his phone. "But first one must prepare that trap with suitable bait." The phone rang three times before it was answered. "Ah, Camano, I've decided to forgive you for making such an outrageous mess of the opportunity I gave you to rid ourselves of a common problem. I'm going to give you another chance."

MANDAK WAS SITTING ON THE wooden bench outside the clinic when Allie came out of the building. He was dressed in jeans and a casual black shirt, and his dark hair shone in the sunlight. His legs were stretched out before him and he looked lazy and sensual and yet she could sense wariness. Strange, she was always the one who was wary. Wary of what to expect from him, wary of what she felt when she was with him. But she wasn't wary now. Too much had happened. She felt the usual tension, the tingling awareness, but it didn't intimidate her.

He smiled. "Hey, amazing what can be done with a little soap and water. We both look almost civilized." He got to his feet. "How are you doing?"

"I don't know." She shrugged. "I guess as good as can be expected. I'm pretty raw inside. I'm confused and angry and sad. I stopped by and saw McKeller. It made me feel happy to see how much better he's doing. What's going to happen to him now?"

"When he's well enough to travel, we'll send him out of the country to someplace safe."

"That's good." She paused. "And Father Elwyn and Thorne? Who is taking care of—"

"Renata sent her people in to retrieve them and begin

arrangements according to any wishes that they'd expressed."

"More arrangements. More deaths. I'm glad Renata was so quick. I felt as if we'd abandoned them." She looked around the neat, clean little village that seemed to be occupied principally by uniformed hospital personnel. "When we were flying in, I couldn't even tell this place was here. It's very well camouflaged."

"I told you, the clinic has to be secure. We made damn sure that it was safe." He walked with her toward the rocks sheltered by the overhanging cliff that overlooked the Indian Ocean. "We even have a twenty-four-hour watch to spot any boats that come too close to the area." He dropped down on the rocks. "Sit down. Relax. Watching the surf can be soothing."

"And you think I need soothing?" She sat down beside him. "Maybe I do." She looked out at the sea. "But I don't think that this is going to do it for me."

"I don't either. It's long past that, isn't it?" His gaze searched her face. "You look . . . frozen."

"That's the way I feel." Her gaze shifted to his face. "When I told you that I'd made my decision to help you get Praland, I didn't really know what that meant. I thought I did. Lee and Natalie wanted their son avenged. I wanted to give them what they wanted." She moistened her lips. "But yesterday it all came home to me."

"And you want to back away?"

"I didn't say that." She stared him in the eye. "He's a monster. He kills innocent people. He made *me* kill. I'll never back away until you have your ledger and Praland can't use it to kill any longer. I won't back away until Praland is dead." She smiled bitterly. "So I guess you have what you've always wanted, Mandak."

"It appears that I have," he said harshly. "Lucky me."

"Not pleased? You can't have it all ways."

"The hell I can't. I'm going to do my damnedest." He got to his feet and started back down the path. "Come on. We'll go to the commissary and get something to eat. You look as if you're ready to blow away. I have to keep you fit, don't I? I have a few ideas that might help move us along at a faster pace. I'll go over them with you. Then we'll see about getting out of here."

She had to almost run to catch up with him. "You're suddenly in a great hurry."

"I've always been in a hurry, but I wanted to do it right. Now I have to take advantage of the fact that you're being so damn accommodating. I can't waste a minute." He looked over his shoulder and his eyes were cold and fierce and yet something else that could be hurt. "After all, it's all I ever wanted."

"I CAN'T EAT ANY MORE." Allie pushed the plate of chicken away from her. "Stop trying to force-feed me." She looked around the pristine-clean cafeteria. "Though both the food and the place are appetizing."

"Megan's work again. Not only is the staff kept happy, but we get fighters and specialists who use the clinic as a base while they're on their missions. A good hot meal is appreciated by all and sundry. You didn't eat as much as I wished, but it will have to do."

"To keep me fit?" she asked sarcastically.

"Absolutely. Why else?" He took a notebook out of his jacket pocket. "You may need every bit of that strength if things don't work out the way I want them to. I think we may have found a way to get you to Praland." He flipped open the cover. "Aman Kobu."

She stiffened. She had a sudden memory of Kobu's wild, furious face as he ran toward the helicopter. "You told me that he was one of Praland's officers. For God's sake, he was giving the orders to those men. He probably gave the order to kill the priest and Thorne."

"It's more than likely."

"And you think you can use that homicidal bastard?" She shook her head emphatically. "No way. I can't forget his eyes when he was screaming and running toward us. He looked like a crazy man."

"He's not too sane." Mandak shrugged. "But you can say the same thing about any of the men who work for Praland. They all have a generous amount of sadism in their makeup. Praland chooses them for that very reason. It makes his army feared by the people in the countryside. Besides, they know that they can earn decent money and occasionally get their thrill."

"Like when Kobu killed Father Elwyn."

"That's a good example."

"It's a terrible example."

"We're talking about Kobu's psychological makeup. I looked up his history with Praland today after I woke from my nap. I already knew quite a bit about him because I'd dealt with him over the years. But I have to make a judgment, so I went in depth." He met her eyes. "Because, if I guess wrong, one or both of us will end up dead."

She wanted to protest, but Mandak was no fool. He must have reasons. She had to listen to him. "So tell me about that maniac."

"Kobu grew up in Tanzania and was recruited by

Praland when he was a boy. He was a bandit by the time he was twelve and did his first kill at thirteen. He fit right in with Praland's men. He's an efficient soldier most of the time. He obeys orders and rose in the ranks. He likes to think of himself as superior to all of Praland's other officers." He grimaced. "Which doesn't sit well with Hans Bruker, who cherishes his power as second-in-command. Bruker is always undercutting Kobu to Praland." He paused. "And that may be our wild card."

"What do you mean?"

"Praland isn't tolerant of fools or inefficiency. With Bruker constantly rubbing salt in the wounds, Praland has probably been making Kobu feel very insecure." He tilted his head. "Remember, you said that Kobu looked desperate when he was chasing us? It was your first impression of him. Desperation."

"Of course. He was losing. We were getting away."

"Praland wants my head. I'm very high on his hit list. He's been dreaming about getting his hands on me for years." He lightly tapped her chest. "And Camano had to have told him that you'd be a threat to him. I'm sure Kobu had orders to bring us to him for fun and games."

"Like Simon."

"Oh, much worse than Simon. I humiliated Praland, and that was an unthinkable sin." He smiled. "And that leaves Kobu in a terrible position. Praland will be bringing him back to the palace for punishment. Kobu has been a participant at too many of Praland's torture sessions, and he has to know what to expect." He nodded at his phone. "I just checked with one of Renata's agents assigned to watch Kobu, and he's been frantically questioning villagers and trying to track down any of the Devanez agents who might be forced to talk. He's even been trying to find out the registration number on the helicopter. Praland evidently is allowing him enough rope to hang himself. But that won't last long. We've got to move fast."

"And do what?" she asked warily.

"Why, we've got to go rescue Kobu. We can't let him be savaged when he can be so helpful to us."

"No way," she said flatly.

"Bitterness." He nodded. "I'm bitter, too. But I prefer to make Kobu work his fanny off for us." He smiled brilliantly. "And kill him later."

"And how do you intend to do that?"

"You need to be within thirty feet of Praland to be able to have a chance at reading his memories. Not an easy thing to arrange without getting yourself killed."

"I can see the problem," she said dryly.

"We need someone who knows the palace and the areas where Praland can be found with a degree of privacy. I'm familiar with the general layout of the place but not Praland's most frequent haunts. But Kobu is both a sneaky son of a bitch and is familiar with Praland, the palace, and the gate codes."

"And we're supposed to be able to persuade him to guide me to Praland?"

He nodded. "Not we. That's really my job. You told me that all I had to do was give you access to Praland." He added, "So I do the prep work, then let you handle the rest."

"How . . . simple." She looked down at the notebook. "What kind of prep work?"

"I go to Kobu's camp tonight, and we have a little chat. Then he agrees to do anything I want him to do."

She gazed at him in disbelief. "You're going into his camp alone? His men will tear you apart."

"Not if I handle the situation right. I don't believe I'll have a problem getting into Kobu's tent. After that, it's just a question of overcoming mental resistance."

"What do you mean?"

"It's what I do. It's part of my particular talent." He lifted one shoulder in a half shrug. "Sometimes, if I choose, I can go into a mind and scan character traits and personal feelings that make up a subject's personality. Then I can bend and whittle at those traits to mold them the way I want them to go."

"What?" She stared at him in horror. "Is that what you did to me when you were supposedly helping me get rid of those memories blocking me?"

"No. Hell, no," he said with emphasis. "I knew you'd jump in that direction. I said 'if I choose.' I did exactly what I told you I was doing. I eased the ugliness and pain and made it break and release. I did *not* interfere in any other way. I'm not even sure I could have changed anything in that mind of yours if I'd tried. Your personality is very strong." He stared her in the eye. "And even if the opportunity was there, I would never do that. Not to you. Not ever."

She believed him. She couldn't take her eyes away from him. She felt chained, held. In all the years she had known Mandak, she had never seen him this intense, this sincere. "And you weren't tempted to try?"

He shook his head. "I have a code. I stick to it. God knows, it took me a lot of mistakes to develop it. When I was experimenting when I was a wild kid, it was a heady power to have. It was like being a surgeon or a sculptor."

"Or a Frankenstein."

He inclined his head. "There are elements of that, too.

But Renata and the family were able to use me in that way every now and then. It can be tremendously valuable to influence and change the way the bad guys look at any given subject. I could even sometimes turn them against each other. They sent me after some very bad scum. Why not? Those minds were pure filth, and who cared? Anything I did could only make them better." He grimaced. "But it wasn't making me any better. I was beginning to like the power too much. I didn't like the man I was turning into. I told Renata that something had to change."

"And she immediately cut out those missions."

He nodded. "Good guess."

"No guess. She cares about you. And anyone can see she's protective. She'd want you to stop if it was going to hurt you in any way."

"But she knew she had to keep me busy, so she found something else for me to do that would give me enough of a challenge and still be useful." His lips twisted. "And might possibly let me keep my soul intact."

"A Searcher."

"Yes. It was a noble and worthwhile job and not as boring as I thought it would be. Renata was smart enough to throw in an occasional violent and bloody mission against Praland and his men that was pure pleasure." He smiled. "So you see, I'm fully qualified to go after Kobu in that way."

"I don't know any such thing. All I know is that you're looking forward to being Frankenstein again."

He chuckled. "I admit that it will be intriguing."

"Bullshit. How do you know it will work? You said that you weren't sure it would work with me."

"Kobu has a very simple mind. I'll do a little fine-tuning, then intimidate him enough to give me a chance to influence him."

"Can you do that? Is it a sure thing?"

"I told you, I'm very good, and Kobu has no block."

"You're not answering me."

"I have an excellent chance."

"Then, dammit, have Renata get someone who is a sure thing. You told me that you have whiz-bang people in the Devanez family who can read minds and do all kinds of crap. You don't have to risk your life doing this."

"But those whiz-bang people can't do what I do. They can't reshape Kobu and make it stick so that you'll be as safe as I can make it for you. They don't have the same qualifications in military and special-forces skills. They don't have my knowledge of Praland's palace and the surrounding countryside. I know that area like the back of my hand." He smiled. "And they have no bond with you, Allie. I can feel you, sense you, from several hundred yards away. That bond could make the difference."

"Not enough." She gazed at him helplessly. "And I thought Kobu was crazy."

"He is, that's why I have to appeal to his self-preservation instead of his good sense."

He was going to do it.

Allie felt a chill run down her spine. She was staring at him, seeing the strength, the vital aliveness of him. Life was so fragile. All those lives that had been taken yesterday. None of those people had thought they would not live to see another day. Panic was suddenly racing through her. "Don't do this."

"It's an opportunity, Allie," he said quietly. "If we

work it right, it could be safer than any other way to get to Praland."

"If you even survive Kobu," she said unsteadily. "You said he's an expert killer. You know the minute he sees you, he's going to try to capture you and turn you over to Praland. Nothing else would make sense."

"I'll try to give him an offer that he can't refuse." He flipped the notebook closed. "You may not have much trust in me, but I think you should know that I'm capable of defending myself against a scumbag like Kobu."

Her hand reached out and grasped his wrist. "Find another way."

He looked down at her hand. "You have a strong grip. There's so much about you that's strong. And I feel your heart beating in your palm. That's strong, too."

He was also strong. The corded muscles, the veins of his wrist. She was once again aware of that warmth and vitality, and she didn't want to let him go. She wanted to keep on touching him. Keep him with her. Keep him alive. "Stop avoiding the subject."

"I'm not avoiding it. I'm just pointing out that I love that strength in you." He lifted her hand to his lips. "I helped create that strength. But I'm not going to step aside and let you have everything your own way." He let go of her hand and stood up. "And now it's time we got going. I want to be at Kobu's camp by nightfall. We'll take the helicopter, but we have to leave it some miles away, so that it won't be heard from Kobu's camp."

She looked at him in helpless frustration and anger. "Oh, you're allowing me to go with you? How kind."

"I've arranged to have one of Renata's agents take care of you outside the encampment area while I deal with Kobu." He smiled. "I'm sure you'll get along with him."

"I don't want a babysitter. Let me go with you. We're supposed to be doing this together."

"We are." He moved toward the door. "As far as I can let it happen that way. How do you think I'll feel when I have to watch you go into that palace by yourself? Remember when I set up your karate lessons, I told you that there would be some times when I couldn't be with you?"

And she had felt terribly alone at the thought that he wasn't going to be there. She felt the same way now. But not about her danger. Too many deaths. And he could die, too. Tonight. Tomorrow. Next week. If she didn't reach out to him, if she didn't stop him . . .

"But it shouldn't be like this." She moved after him out the door of the commissary. "You're being foolish."

"And you're being emotional," he said softly. "But I like that far better than the way you were when I first saw you today. You were an ice woman. I'm not used to that in you. You're all firecrackers and Roman candles. Now I'm watching the ice begin to break up. I'm glad it was only temporary. That bodes well for the future."

"If you have a future. Which you won't if you do stupid things like going after Kobu."

"I stand corrected." He slanted her a glance as he moved toward the helicopter. "Then we might have to live for the moment and not the future. I've been thinking on those lines anyway lately . . ."

CHAPTER TWELVE

THE SUN WAS SETTING WHEN Mandak set down the helicopter on a plateau bordered by lush jungle.

"Right on time." He jumped out of the pilot's seat and ran around to open her door. "We should reach Kobu's camp in an hour by jeep. Then you can drop me off and go a safe distance away and—"

"What jeep?" she interrupted.

"The one coming up the road. Don't you hear it? He's a bit late." He took her arm and nudged her across the plateau and into the forest. "Would I make you walk all those miles? You'd make them very unpleasant for me. Particularly since you're not good company at the moment anyway. You've scarcely said a word since we left the clinic."

"Because I had nothing to say," she said through her teeth. "Because you shouldn't do this. It's an insane risk. Let's think of another way to—" She stopped as she saw the headlights of the jeep he'd spoken about spear the darkness as it pulled around the curve up ahead.

"You're late," Mandak called to the driver. "I should have known. I told Renata to send someone reliable."

"I *am* reliable." Sean Donavel pulled up beside them.

"Only five minutes late," he said indignantly. "I had to dodge some of Praland's men. And I'm not accustomed to these crummy roads. To think I gave up Monte Carlo to face this barbarian country." He mournfully shook his head. "And no gratitude." He turned to Allie and smiled. "Hi, how are you doing?" he asked gently. "Renata tells me that you've had it rough lately."

She nodded. "And it's not getting any better." She got into the passenger seat of the jeep. "Mandak is being an idiot."

Sean gave a low whistle. "Harsh."

"True," she said. She glanced at Mandak, who had climbed into the rear seat. "You know his 'brilliant' plan?"

He nodded. "Renata told me. I've seen him pull off worse." He pressed the accelerator, and the jeep jumped forward. "She also said he'd requested help to take care of you and get you out if necessary. I volunteered."

"You're a gambler. I thought you were on your way to Monte Carlo."

"Which would be much better for all concerned," Mandak said.

Sean ignored him, and said to Allie, "I told you I jumped in occasionally on family business when I was needed. This appeared to be a situation where I was needed. Mandak seemed to be calling me."

Mandak grunted.

"Don't be rude." Sean grinned. "Renata wouldn't have sent me if she hadn't known I'd come through for you. And you know it, too. I've been on missions with you before." He turned back to Allie. "We'll drop Mandak off to do his excruciatingly boring tasks, and I'll take you up to the mountain to the cave from which Renata's agent has been spying on Kobu. We'll have to find a way to amuse ourselves. Do you play poker?"

"Yes." She experienced a sharp pang as she remembered that last night by the fire playing with Lee and Natalie. "I'm terrible at it."

"Good. I've no objection to dealing out humiliating defeats."

"I don't think so," she said.

"Whatever." He paused before saying quietly, "I'm sorry that the Walbergs' service was such a disaster."

"The killings were a disaster. The priest . . . It was ugly and horrible," she said unevenly. "But the service itself wasn't a disaster. We got Lee and Natalie home to their son. I won't let myself think Praland ruined that for them. That was the only victory we could take away." Her hands clenched. "But we can't let Praland have any other victories." She glanced back at Mandak. "He can't have you, Mandak. I won't *have* it."

"Neither will I," Mandak said. "But I'm glad you're so passionate about it."

Passionate. Yes, she guessed that was how she felt. If passion meant intensity verging on desperation. If passion meant anger. If passion meant the fear she might have to live without Mandak.

But she could see that he wasn't going to pay any attention to her. She'd have to knock him out and tie him up. Lord, and she was tempted to do it. "Why should I care?" she said fiercely. "You're an idiot."

"I believe you called me that before."

"Because it's true." She drew a deep breath. Don't speak to him. She was becoming too upset. Just sit here and think of a way to avoid the inevitable. Be silent. Think.

Forty-five minutes later, they arrived at the edge of the forest where Kobu had set up camp. "It will take you another fifteen minutes to hike to the camp itself, Mandak," Sean said as he turned off the engine. "I'll take Allie up the mountain, and you can call me when you want us to pick you up. Be safe."

Mandak nodded as he got out of the jeep. "Take care of her. You let anything happen to Allie, and I'll come after you."

"If Kobu doesn't cut your throat," Allie said coldly. "That would seriously get in the way."

He gave a mock shiver. "The ice is back. I think I'd better get about my business, so that I can prove that I do know what I'm doing. It may be my only safety net." He turned and moved away from the jeep. "I'll see you soon, Allie."

The next instant, he'd disappeared into the trees.

She felt instant panic. He was gone. She should have stopped him.

Or if she couldn't stop him, she shouldn't have let him go like that. She had been cold and sharp. Life was too short. Just because she was angry and afraid was no reason to risk eternal regret if he didn't come back.

Eternal? Where had that come from, she wondered, shocked.

And he might not come back.

The panic was growing. She wanted to run after him and tell him all the things that were sealed inside her. All the words she wouldn't admit, speak, even to herself.

"Allie?" Sean was looking at her. "He'll be fine. He's a tough bastard. We have to get moving. Okay?"

"No, it's not okay." She jumped out of the jeep and strode toward the forest. "It's not at all okay."

"Oh, shit." He jumped out of the jeep and ran after her. "This is not cool, Allie. You cause a ruckus, and you could get Mandak killed."

"Don't be ridiculous." She moved into the trees. "Do you think I'd do anything that stupid? I'm not going to burst into that camp and spoil whatever plan Mandak is trying to pull off. Even if it is insane." She stared fiercely at him. "But I'm not going to be taken up to some mountain and be coddled until it's safe for me to come down and play. You know where Kobu's camp is located?"

"Yes," he said warily.

"Then take me there. I want to be within striking distance if I'm needed."

"That's exactly what Mandak didn't want."

"He ignored everything I wanted. He can't have everything his own way. I told him that I wouldn't let them have him." She drew a deep breath. "Now you take me to a place close enough to Kobu so that I can see if Mandak needs me. If you don't, I'll go by myself."

He muttered a curse. "Okay, but you let me go ahead and check out the sentries. I don't want to stumble over one of them and rouse the camp."

"Be my guest." Her brows rose. "That didn't sound like a man who spends his nights in casinos."

"I told you that Renata wouldn't have sent me unless she could trust me. I asked Mandak to train me during one of my weaker moments, when I was all sentimental about the family." He glided ahead of her. "Stay here. Five minutes."

She stopped, listening. She could hear voices somewhere ahead. Not close.

Night sounds.

Birds.

Crickets.

She could feel her palms perspiring.

Was Mandak already in the camp?

"Come on," Sean whispered. "Quiet."

She hadn't even heard him return. Evidently Mandak had trained him well.

She faded into step behind him.

The sounds of voices were closer.

She could see the glare of a campfire in the distance.

Bedrolls.

One camouflage tent at the edge of the clearing.

"Is this close enough?" Sean whispered.

She shook her head.

He grimaced and started forward again.

"No closer," he said firmly a few minutes later. They were about forty feet from Kobu's tent. "For God's sake, we're right on top of him." He fell to the ground beside a huge tree and pulled her down with him. "And Mandak is going to murder me."

"Hush." Her gaze was searching the surrounding shrubs and trees. Where was Mandak? He had to be somewhere close. He had started out before she had dragged Sean into the woods.

The bonding . . .

Mandak had said he could locate her within a few hundred yards because of the bonding. Shouldn't it work the same for her? She had never tried to concentrate on locating Mandak. For most of those seven years, she had wanted to push him aside, to be her own person.

So do it now.

Concentrate.

She shut her eyes.

The closeness, the bonding, the feeling of being one . . .

Mandak!

She couldn't see him. He was on the other side of the tent. But she could feel him. He was sliding forward, moving toward the tent, a knife in his hand. He was going to slit the canvas and slide inside.

But did Kobu know he was there?

Could he hear him?

She could feel her heart beat harder at the thought.

Try to find out.

She started crawling forward.

Sean was crawling frantically after her. "No," he mouthed.

She ignored him. Thirty feet. She had to be at least within thirty feet.

She stopped and drew a deep breath.

Mandak was very close to the tent now.

Kobu.

She focused. If he was thinking and alert, it might mean he was aware of Mandak's presence. She wouldn't be able to read him, but she'd know that there—

He wasn't thinking.

The tunnel was dark and smooth, whisking her inside.

Tiger.

He was thinking about a tiger, remembering how he'd felt when Praland had been taunting him.

Son of a bitch Praland.

He'd throw me to that tiger and laugh.

Throw me with that little whore and let him eat both of us.

Have to get Mandak and the woman.

Throw them to the tiger instead.

All Mandak's fault, like the time he'd taken the children and made Kobu look foolish in front of Praland.

Kill the bastard. He should have done it then, and—
Tunnel closed. Tunnel closed.

Fear. Death.

Mandak!

Allie's body stiffened, her spine arching with shock. She couldn't breathe.

Mandak was in that tent with Kobu.

And Kobu was afraid for his life.

"BE VERY STILL." MANDAK'S knife pressed deep enough to bring blood to Kobu's throat. "I get nervous when I'm surrounded by scum, and you wouldn't want my hand to shake."

"Bastard." Kobu was breathing hard. "I'll kill you."

"You're not in a position to hurl threats around. I'm very angry about what you did at Talboa. You need to be quiet and let me try to save your life."

"Save my life? Do you think I'm a fool?"

"No. Well, maybe. I'd have to think about it. But I do know you have a certain natural cunning that might save your life. But I have to make sure that you'll be trustworthy." He said, "Now, we're going to sit here, and I'm going to find out."

"Filthy freak. Don't you touch me."

Mandak made a clucking noise. "Don't be rude." He drew a little more blood. "And I've no desire to touch you, particularly in that sewer of a brain. But I've no choice."

He dove deep and clean. That was the only thing clean, he thought as he sorted out Kobu's thinking processes. He reacted to the usual stimulus. No particular ogre of whom he was afraid. Praland came close, but Kobu was so arrogant he thought he could find a way to beat Praland and grow in his army.

That was something he'd have to change. He spent a few minutes altering that arrogance and creating a terrifying conviction that Praland would destroy him if he didn't run.

He also had a hatred of Mandak because of past humiliations. Leave the dislike, eliminate the hatred. Add the belief that Mandak was often right.

Kobu's ambitions were aimed solely on a local level and gaining favor with Praland. Give him a desire to spread his wings and maybe join up with a terrorist group in Iran.

Anything else?

He had a basic hatred of women.

That was dangerous for Allie. He couldn't change a deep-seated prejudice without more time, but he could temper it. He could make Kobu have a contempt that would make him wish to demonstrate his superiority. Allie could play on that characteristic.

Enough?

Enough.

In this short time, Mandak wouldn't be able to do a permanent fix. But it should last a week, possibly a month, and that should give them time to use Kobu to the fullest extent.

Now to bring him back around and start the manipulation.

Kobu opened his eyes. "You son of a bitch. What did you do to me?"

Dislike. Not hatred. Good.

He smiled. "I just did a little exploratory investigation. I told you, I have to make sure I can trust you. You don't feel any different, do you?"

He frowned. "No."

"Of course, you don't. Now listen to me. I'm here to do us both a favor."

"That's crap."

"No. I could have sliced your throat. I still could do that." He took the knife away from Kobu's throat. "But you have a better chance with me than you do with Praland. He doesn't like failures. Has he been a little threatening?"

Stark fear. Panic.

Kobu moistened his lips. "Maybe."

"I thought so. Bruker wants you out. You're a dead man, Kobu."

"Not if I bring Praland your head," Kobu said viciously.

"But you won't be able to do that. You've tried before." He smiled. "And what if you somehow managed to kill me? You're still walking a tightrope. The next time you fail Praland would be your last." He paused. "Think about another scenario. The Devanez family deposits a hefty sum in your bank account, and you go off to some other organization that will appreciate you."

A flicker of interest crossed his face. "Money?"

"Iran has use for men of your experience. I'm sure you've thought about it."

"Yes," he said slowly.

The implants were working with slick precision, Mandak thought.

"You could rise to the top in a place where you weren't being smothered by Bruker. In a year, you might have a palace like Praland's."

"This is all lies and bullshit."

But that wasn't what he was thinking. Kobu was seeing himself with the power and the riches.

Yes.

It would take a considerable time to seal the deal, but he was on his way. Persuasion, bribery, a minimum of threats, making the desirable seem absolutely possible.

Go another step.

"You know a lot about Praland's operation, and with the right backing, you might be able to walk in and take over. Have you thought of that?" He watched the excitement begin to stir. "You want the world, Kobu?" he asked softly. "I can give it to you. Let me tell you how I'm going to do it . . ."

"WHY HASN'T HE COME OUT of there?" Allie's hands clenched so hard, her nails bit into her palms. "It's been over an hour. Maybe I should—"

"No," Sean whispered. "Do nothing, Allie. Or so help me, I'll knock you out and carry you back to the jeep. You said you weren't going to take any action unless necessary."

But that was before she'd had to lie here in the grass for over an hour with her nerves stretched to the breaking point.

Easy. There hadn't been any noise. Surely, that was a good sign.

How the hell did she know what was a good sign? Kobu could have stabbed Mandak and was watching him bleed to death.

Not likely. Calm down. Mandak was smart, and he

thought he knew what he was doing. She was praying he was right.

Dammit, she should have forced him to let her go with him. This was tearing her apart, and she couldn't bear it one more—

The bonding.

He was moving!

He was out of the tent and moving into the forest.

"Out." She nudged Sean, then started wriggling backward until they reached the thicker trees. Then she jumped to her feet and started running in the direction where they'd left the jeep. They moved at top speed until they were almost halfway to the road.

She stopped. "Wait."

She listened.

No sound from the camp behind them. No alert from Kobu from his tent.

Good? Bad?

She didn't care what Mandak had left behind him in that tent. He was out of there. He was alive. That was all that mattered. "Mandak's supposed to call you, Sean. But he probably won't do it until he's away from the camp."

"Why should I call him?" Mandak was suddenly beside them, and his voice had a distinct edge. "When the two of you were practically on top of me. I was too busy with Kobu to sense Allie was close while I was in the tent, but it hit me in the face when I left him. I may break your neck, Sean."

"Go ahead." He sighed. "I expected it. But I might point out that she's not very malleable, and since you're the one who had control of her for all these years, it's more your fault than mine."

"Let's get out of here before you start arguing," Allie said. She glanced back over her shoulder. Just the glare of the campfire. Still no movement. "It's very quiet. Either what you did worked, or you killed him or tied him up."

"I didn't kill him. I didn't tie him up. We'll see if it worked. He could still turn his men loose to hunt us down. If he doesn't, we have a chance that I managed to pull it off." He grabbed Allie's wrist and was running toward the jeep. "There's always a possibility of a back-lash. Though I do believe I got him." He nudged Allie toward the backseat. "Keep low." He jumped in the pas-senger seat. "Get us out of here, Sean."

"Where am I supposed to go?"

"Where you should have gone to begin with," he said grimly. "That cave in the mountains. I gave Kobu his options. Now I have to keep an eye on what Kobu is going to do in the next day or so."

THE CAVE WAS ONLY SEVEN to eight miles up the winding road of the mountain, and they reached it within an hour.

Allie got out of the jeep and walked to the edge of the cliff to look down at the jungle below. "Still no sign of activity in the camp. This was a good spot to spy on Kobu's men. I can see Kobu's campfire from here."

"You could see it a lot closer from where you decided to perch next to Kobu's tent," Mandak said curtly. He took her duffel out of the jeep. "You were almost on his lap."

"Uh-oh." Sean looked from Mandak to Allie, then moved toward the cave. "I think I'll get out of the line of fire and build a fire of our own inside."

"By all means," Mandak said. "Maybe you'll do that right."

He was still angry. He hadn't spoken more than the bare minimum since they'd left Kobu's camp. She turned to look at him. Even in the dim moonlight, she could see the tautness of his jaw. Too bad. She was angry, too. "I wasn't as close to Kobu as you were," she said defiantly. "And then you blame me for not going meekly up the mountain and letting you do whatever you wanted to do."

"Yes, I do." His eyes were glittering. "Because it's important you stay alive. I set it up so that you wouldn't be at risk."

"Because Renata and your precious family say that I have to be protected, so I'm able to give my all for your ledger? That's hogwash."

He was suddenly next to her, gripping her shoulders. "Renata and the family have nothing to do with it. I won't let you—" His lips were covering hers, hard, hot. He lifted them, then his lips were on the side of her throat. "This is what it's all about. Maybe it should be because of the family, but it's not." His tongue was in the hollow of her throat. "It's you, dammit. I think it's always been you."

She couldn't breathe. The muscles of her stomach were tightening, her breasts hardening. What was happening to her? She wanted to flow into him, melt into him. She was panting as she looked up at him. "No." It was more of a gasp than a word. "Not true . . ."

"The hell it's not." His hands were tangled in her hair. "Everything else may be screwed up and crazy, but that's clear as crystal to me."

"Well, it's not clear to me." She tried to back away but immediately wanted to go back to him. "Nothing about the way we are together is clear. It's probably about that damn bonding or the way you—"

"I've never wanted to go to bed with anyone I've bonded with before. Okay, so we've been intimate in ways that couples seldom reach. But that doesn't mean that there's anything wrong with it."

"It doesn't mean there's anything right."

"There's only one way to find out." His tongue moved delicately across her lips. "You wouldn't be sorry, Allie. I'd make it good for you."

Her lips were tingling, throbbing at that touch of his tongue. Her hair held taut in his fingers was strangely erotic. Everything about him was erotic, she thought dazedly. His touch, the musk-lemon smell of him, the heat, the hardness. All so familiar and yet dizzyingly exotic and different. She could feel her breasts firm, swell, push against him. She wanted to tear open her shirt, put his hands on them, let his mouth and tongue bite and toy and suck.

Then his hands fell away from her hair, and he started to unbutton her shirt. "Say yes," his voice was thick. His hands dropped and went behind her to cup her bottom and draw her closer to him. "You want it. I can feel how much you want it. How much *I* want it. It's always been there burning in the background for us."

"That's not all that's been between us," she said unsteadily. "But right now, I'm so confused that I can't tell what's right or wrong for me."

"I'm right for you. Let me show you how right." His voice was soft, persuasive, sensual. His blue eyes glittered with intensity. "I'll come inside you, and I'll make your body—" He stopped, his eyes shutting tight. "Son of a bitch." His eyes flicked open. "Dammit to hell." His hands dropped away from her, and he said roughly, "Button up your shirt."

She stood there, unmoving, staring at him in bewilderment.

He muttered a curse. His fingers were buttoning her shirt himself.

Her nipples were still stinging, exquisitely sensitive, as they brushed against the cotton of the shirt. "Mandak?"

"Give me a minute." He took a step back. His chest was moving back and forth with the harshness of his breathing. "I can't believe I'm being this idiotic. It's not as if I'd hurt you. You'd like it, dammit. No, you'd love it. I could make you go crazy. There are things I can do to you that would make you never want to stop." He paused. "And I would use them. I've never wanted a woman the way I want you. And I just realized I was going to do anything and everything to get what I wanted. I could see that you were uncertain. Good God, why shouldn't you be?" His lips tightened. "I wanted you too much to care."

Shock.

She felt as if she'd been punched in the stomach.

"How very honest of you." She drew a shaky breath. "But then you changed your mind?"

"I must have some vestige of conscience somewhere. It's amazing considering my track record," he said roughly. "After all, I bring you to this country in harm's way. I nearly got you killed at Talboa. I fully intend to let you risk your life at Praland's palace to get the ledger for me. Why shouldn't I seduce you, too? Icing on the cake."

"There wasn't much seduction connected to it." It had been all heat and sexuality and that powerful magnetism that had united them from the beginning. Even now, when she had been jarred out of that erotic haze, she was having trouble not wanting to step closer to him, touch him.

"There would have been seduction. I'd want to give you everything, Allie."

"Would you?" She turned away. She couldn't take any more. "You'll forgive me if I don't believe you."

"I'd be surprised if you did," he said hoarsely. "But it's true. Because I'm beginning to think that the reason I stopped was something more complicated than guilt. I can't stand the thought of your being hurt. Not by me."

"Bullshit." She suddenly whirled on him, her eyes blazing. "You flatter yourself. I'm the only one who can hurt me. All that crap about what you've put me through and risking me at the palace? I made the decision, not you. If I was going to screw you, that would be my decision, too. Yes, I'm uncertain. I've always been uncertain about you. Lately, I've been thinking that maybe I do have a clue to what makes you tick." She took a step toward him and punched her index finger at his chest. "And you're not what I always thought you were, and that's confusing, too. But I'm the one who has to work that out in my head. I'm in control of me. I can say yes. I can say no. I won't have you thinking you can stop and start and set the pace. Do you understand, Mandak?"

He didn't speak for a moment. Then a faint smile touched his lips. "Do you know how much I love to see you spark? Even when it's against me?" He inclined his head. "My apologies. What could I have been thinking?"

"Nothing intelligent. Maybe the sexual positions of the Kama Sutra." She turned and strode toward the cave. "Now stay out of my way for a while. I've spent most of the evening worrying about whether you were going to get killed, then you spring this on me."

"It kind of sprung itself," he called after her. "You have to admit you were the impetus. How could you not expect me to—"

"Stay out of my way," she repeated.

"Right. Whatever you say."

Yeah, sure. She stopped just inside the cave. She was shaking, but she didn't know whether it was from anger or the lingering sexual tension that was still gripping her.

"You okay?" Sean was kneeling beside a small fire and looked up to study her face. "You look upset. Mandak must have really been pissed off."

"It was mutual." She came toward the fire and dropped down across from Sean. "And it became . . . complicated."

"When isn't it complicated with Mandak?" He handed her a metal cup containing steaming coffee. "But this seemed pretty straightforward for him. It wasn't about having his own way. He was scared."

"Not Mandak. I've never seen him scared."

"I have." He stared into the flames. "Those two days at the apartment when he was trying to keep you from going off the deep end after Lee and Natalie had been killed. He was scared he was going to lose you. Mandak's a pretty cool customer. I didn't expect that reaction from him." He looked up at her. "I'd thought you were only a job to him."

"So did I," she said dryly.

"But you didn't see him during those two days." He smiled. "And I believe you might have changed your opinion lately. Or you wouldn't have been so hell-bent on trying to save him tonight."

"He wasn't being reasonable. Someone had to be there for him."

"And you were." He finished his coffee. "And the rest is history." He poured another cup of coffee and got to his feet. "I think I'll go take this cup out to Mandak, and we'll decide who's going to take the first watch. He doesn't appear to be eager to join us. You must have been most discouraging."

She didn't answer. Nothing about her early response to Mandak had been discouraging. She could still remember the sensation of searing sensuality when he had touched her. She felt as if she could still feel it. When the hell would it go away?

"No?" Sean had stopped at the cave opening and his gaze was narrowed on her face. "Interesting . . ."

The next moment, he was gone.

Sean was more shrewd than she had realized, she thought ruefully. Not only in his observations but in his instincts. She was glad that he had gone. She didn't need those bright, warm eyes trying to decipher what she was feeling. She was having enough trouble trying to figure it out herself.

She moved back from the fire, grabbed a blanket, and curled up against the stone wall of the cave.

Try to sleep.

Try to forget Mandak.

Try to forget the way her body seemed to tingle and sing when he touched her.

Sex. It was only sex.

Or was it? It hadn't been sex when she had been frantic to get to Mandak in case he needed her. She had felt that she would lose a part of herself if Mandak was taken from her. She had claimed it could be the bonding, but her feeling toward Mandak had been there from the beginning. Beneath suspicion and fear, there had always been this closeness, this deep-seated wish to be with him. That night he had taken her to live with Lee and Natalie, she had felt a wrenching loneliness that she'd hidden from him.

No, it wasn't only sex.

But now the sex was here, and she would have to contend with it. It was part of her obsession with Mandak. She could no more walk away from it than she could dismiss all the rest of her feelings for him.

She was too tired to deal with this right now.

I'm not going to think about you any more tonight, Mandak.

Concentrate. Block him, the way he'd taught her to block those attacking memories.

It was much harder because Mandak was not only in her memory but her body. He seemed to possess all of her.

Even when she thought she had cast him out and was drifting off to sleep, he insinuated himself like a persistent melody.

I think it's always been you.

MANDAK WAS NEAR HER, she thought drowsily.

She could feel the warmth and the substance of him even though he wasn't touching her.

"Mandak . . ."

"Shh." He was tucking her blanket closer around her. "Go back to sleep. I just wanted to make sure you were okay."

She forced her eyes open to look at him. "Why wouldn't I be okay?"

"No reason." He smiled. "But you've already told me how stupid and unreasonable I am."

"And you are. Sometimes."

"And you can be pigheaded and stubborn. Sometimes." His hand stroked back her hair from her temple. "I didn't mean to wake you. You told me to give you space, and I thought I had a better chance of checking on you if you were asleep."

"Did you expect me to be in tears because you were displeased with me? That time is long gone, Mandak."

"If it ever existed. I hope I never caused you tears. You were such a tough kid, I thought I did pretty well to just keep up with you."

"I didn't feel tough. I was always fighting to survive."

"Survive me?"

It felt strange lying here, with the fire casting leaping shadows on the stone wall and telling him things that she had never thought she would tell him. Why not? He had been an integral part of her life for years. They had gone through too much together not to be honest with each other.

"At first, then you became an ally. Even when I knew I had to fight you, too, I knew that you were like a big wolfhound who would keep me safe from the rest of the world."

"Wolfhound? What a comparison. Should I be offended?"

"Whatever. But I like dogs. Wolfhounds are beautiful. They're lean and powerful, and their eyes seem to mesmerize you." She yawned. "Though your eyes are blue, not dark . . ."

"And you need to go back to sleep." He got to his feet. "I'm glad you knew that I'd keep you safe, Allie. I've told you that, but I was never sure you believed me."

"I believed you." Her eyes were closing. "Why did you really come in here? You had to know I was all right."

He chuckled. "I was still having problems not wanting to have sex with you. I wanted to look at you and try to remember there were a hell of a lot of other facets to what we are together."

"And did you?"

"Yeah, I remembered." He started to turn away. "It may be a fix that will last a little while."

She wasn't sure that it would last that long for her. But maybe it would. She wasn't sure at the moment whether she wanted him to make love to her or just to hold her and let her feel his strength.

"Mandak."

"Yes."

"Kobu is going to do what you wanted, isn't he? There's no sign that he's on the hunt for you?"

"No sign. Tomorrow I'll wire half the money I promised into his bank account. I'll hold the other half as an automatic deposit until the job's completed." He paused. "There could still be a double cross."

"I don't know how you did it. His memories were so vicious, and he hates you."

"Memories? You went in and scanned him? You didn't tell me."

"You didn't give me a chance. I thought I'd be able to tell if Kobu was alert and knew you were outside the tent."

"You avoid scanning like the plague. You hate it."

"It is a plague to me. And Kobu's memories were every bit as ugly and full of poison as those men my father had me read. But it would have been worse to not do it and be unable to keep something terrible from happening."

He nodded. "You've taken a big step tonight."

"Have I? It doesn't feel like it. I just did what I had to do." She closed her eyes. "The tiger . . . Kobu was afraid of a tiger. He wanted to throw you and me to the tiger. Do you know anything about it?"

"Yes, I'll tell you about it later. Not now. It's the stuff of nightmares."

Nightmares . . . She wanted to tell him that their lives had been nothing else since the night Lee and Natalie had been killed.

But Mandak was gone.

And she had to try to sleep and not dwell on Kobu and his frantic terror of the tiger . . .

"A TIGER? A REAL TIGER?" GINA smiled at Camano as her gaze traveled around the silk and ivory wall hangings of the palace to the gilt-embossed doorway the servant had pointed out to them on the way to showing them to their quarters. "I can't believe Praland has a special fancy chamber where he keeps his pet tiger. How amusing. Though it's in keeping with all this exotic luxury, isn't it? Praland must have good taste." She frowned. "Or perhaps not. He didn't pay very much attention to me when you introduced us."

"He's accustomed to using women and not catering to their whims." He glanced at her, then inserted a jab.

"And his concubines are far younger and more lush than you, Gina."

"Younger only means less experienced, and that can be the kiss of death in a relationship. Lush is a matter of taste, and I can change any man's taste." She smiled. "Isn't that true, Camano? Have you ever been disappointed?"

"No."

"Then stop trying to make me unhappy." Her gaze was wandering over the marble floors, the gold- and jewel-studded insets in the rosewood tables. "I like this. It suits my style."

"If your style is Taj Mahal," he said sourly.

"But of course it is. What does everyone say when they meet me? I'm queen to your king, my darling. But this is much more grand than what we have at home."

"Don't get used to it. I've brought you here for one purpose. Praland wants your daughter as much as I do. When you find a way to lure her into a trap, then your job is done, and we're on the next plane out."

"Perhaps."

"Gina." His hand grasped her wrist. "Teresa is more of a threat to me now than she was before. You *will* do it."

"Of course." She reached up and kissed him. "I meant that perhaps we'd stay awhile and have a few weeks here. You said that Praland doesn't like the idea of taking care of difficulties within the U.S. borders. I thought it might be an opportunity for you to give him what he needs as you did in Flagstaff. He appears to have the funds to make it worth your while."

"And the funds to make it worth your while?" he asked dryly. "Don't make the mistake of trying to manipulate Praland."

"Only for you," she said.

"Yeah, sure."

"Well, you've learned that if I'm happy, I make you happy."

"And if you're not happy, you try to make my life hell. I don't know why I don't just kick you out."

"Because you've found you need me in all kinds of ways. Why else did you bring me here?"

"Because Praland offered to supply the trap if I'd bring you to spring it."

"And a gorgeous trap it is," she murmured. She looked over her shoulder at the gilt door that led to the tiger cage. "I saw a movie once where a Roman empress had a pet panther and led him around on an emerald-studded collar. She looked pretty, but she wasn't as pretty as I am. But I thought how exciting it must be to control a big cat with only a slender leash. The sheer power of it . . ."

"I can see you getting off on the idea."

"But a tiger would be much more impressive than a panther. I wonder if Praland has had him trained."

"Why don't you ask him?" He paused at the door of their suite, which the servant had just opened. "You could offer to do it yourself."

"Don't be sarcastic." She smiled faintly. "There is always a man available to take the risks if I want something. And I think Praland might be amused at the idea of my putting his tiger on a leash. It would set me apart from his other women."

"Other?" Camano repeated softly. "Are you thinking of trying to lure Praland into your web? Forget it, Gina. No woman walks out on me. You're mine until I decide to get rid of you."

"Why would I want any other man than you? You give

me everything I want. I just wanted to impress Praland so that he'd let me influence him about the deal I mentioned." She sailed past him into the suite. "I'm flattered you're still jealous about me after all these years."

"Jealous? No. Just wary. For some reason, I still have a yen for you I can't shake. But I won't be made a fool, Gina. Walk the line, or you'll be sorry."

"Threats?" Her brows rose. "Did it occur to you that when I'm threatened, I set out to protect myself? It's what they call self-preservation." She went to her suitcase the servant had placed on the luggage rack. "Now let's forget all this nonsense. I'm here to do what you and Praland want me to do. If I manage to amuse myself while I'm here, what's the harm?" She smiled. "All this fuss because of that silly tiger."

CHAPTER THIRTEEN

"GOOD MORNING." SEAN DONAVEL grinned at Allie as she sat up and pushed aside her blanket. "You slept hard. After I came in from my watch and started making coffee, I thought that I'd wake you, but you didn't stir."

"I still feel drugged." She shook her head to clear it. "I guess it's a delayed reaction. Where's Mandak?"

"Outside. He's been on the phone with the Devanez family bank arranging a transfer to Kobu's account. Breakfast? I have bacon and a couple eggs."

"Not right now." She got to her knees and opened her duffel. "I feel dirty, and I need to brush my teeth. Do we have any water source around here?"

"Take some of that bottled water. And there's a small pond about five hundred yards down the mountain on the eastern slope. It's not uber clean, but I used it earlier. Beggars can't be choosers."

"They can, but not when they feel as gritty as I do." She got to her feet and strode out of the cave. Mandak was standing on the edge of the cliff, still talking on the phone. She moved past him and headed toward the east slope.

Ten minutes later, she was bending over the pond that

Sean had described as not uber clean and washing her
face and neck. She had considered immersing herself,
then thought better of it. Sean had seriously overesti-
mated the pond in his description. The waters were a
thick, brownish yellow, and she was wary about what
could be swimming beneath them.

"You didn't tell me where you were going."

She looked back to see Mandak standing on the trail
watching her. "Sean knew."

"But I didn't. And Sean is a gambler and likes to play
the odds." His lips tightened. "Tell me, okay?"

She shrugged. "It seemed pretty safe. Sean told me
the watches were just precautions." She nodded at her
jacket on the ground beside her. "And I took my gun."

"Which was good." He came toward her. "But you can't
go off on your own from now on. It could be dangerous
for all of us."

"Because you felt you had to come after me." She
nodded. "I can see that could become a problem." She
made a face. "I just wanted to get clean. It's not going to
happen in this pond." She started to button up her blouse.
"I brushed my teeth in the bottled water, but I'll just
have to comb my hair and tie it up out of my face."

"We might run across a decent lake or pond on the
way to the palace." He picked up her jacket and handed it
to her. "We'll see what we can do." He paused. "But that
won't be until tomorrow. I have a couple things I have to
check out before we get on the road."

She tensed. "What things?"

"I'm having Renata's guys monitor Kobu's calls to
make sure that he isn't planning a surprise party with
Praland as the host."

"That was my first thought," she said. "But I don't

understand how all that sculpting and stuff works. You said I'd have to trust you."

"Which is damn hard for you."

"Yes." She looked him in the eye. "No. I do trust you, Mandak."

He went still. "How unusual. I believe that's a break-through."

She nodded slowly. "It feels like that to me, too. I don't know how you pulled it off, but I know you wouldn't let me go with Kobu if you weren't almost certain that I'd survive."

" 'Almost' is the key word," he said. "You *will* survive. I just have to determine what steps I'm going to have to take to assure that." He turned and started up the trail. "I'll call the bank later to see if Kobu has verified that the money has been transferred. That would indicate a healthy greed and an interest in the deal. If he doesn't contact Praland, then we'll set off for the palace tomorrow morning."

"He's terrified of Praland." She added, "And that tiger."

"He's not alone. From the reports I've had, all of Praland's men are scared of that tiger."

"Why? You said you'd tell me."

He stopped and looked back at her. "Praland keeps his tiger in a huge cage in a luxurious room near the rear of the palace. Outside the cage, there are velvet couches and tables and hookahs and various other amusements. He likes his comforts because he spends a good deal of time there." He paused. "You can imagine what the main attraction is."

"Throw Mandak and the woman to the tiger," she whispered. "Kobu was remembering what he'd thought when Praland was threatening him about the tiger. Praland punishes his men by putting them in the cage with that tiger?"

"And invites his officers and anyone he suspects might be less than loyal to watch the show. Not only his men, anyone who displeases him. He keeps the tiger hungry."

She shuddered. "No wonder Kobu was frightened. It's hard to fight against fear like that."

"But I was able to use it to lure him away. No one likes a threat hanging over him."

"You hope."

"I spent a lot of time reinforcing that part of his adjustment," he said grimly. "I got it right, Allie."

She nodded. "Kobu was just so damned determined that the two of us had to be thrown to the tiger."

"It's not going to happen."

She smiled faintly. "Do you remember when we were at the lodge all those years ago, and you took me to see the gym? You were joking about that legend about the lady having to choose what was behind a particular door."

"And you said that the 'tiger'"—he tapped his chest—"was on this side of the door."

"You do remember."

"I remember everything that's ever happened between us, Allie." He met her eyes. "Every single thing."

She couldn't breathe. She couldn't look away from him. Heat, sexuality, and something deeper, stronger, brighter, was vibrating in that sudden silence.

He nodded jerkily. "Yeah, here it is again. Kind of difficult to keep it down. You have no idea." He started to turn away, then whirled back to face her. "But here's a little something to distract us both. Renata called early this morning. I was going to wait until I had an additional report before I filled you in on the picture. But I've decided that not telling you was hypocritical after I'd just told you it was dangerous not to keep me informed."

"Tell me what?"

"Renata said that the agents she'd had searching for Camano and your mother reported that they'd surfaced. Briefly. They boarded a private jet out of Kennedy yesterday. Their flight plan listed Rome as their destination."

"Rome?"

"Yes, but that doesn't mean that's where they ended up."

"No." She swallowed. "And it's an odd coincidence that they left the U.S. so soon after we did. You think that they could be coming here?"

"Or that they're already here."

She was silent. "Then Camano is joining with Praland to hunt me down."

"That's the way I see it."

She shook her head. "It's crazy. Camano and Praland coming together here."

"I thought it might happen," he said. "But, then, I believe in fate."

"Do you? I'd think you'd want to mold it to suit yourself."

"I didn't say I didn't fight it, just that it exists."

"And my mother, too?"

He nodded.

Allie was still having trouble picturing Gina here in this wild, savage country. The idea was bizarre. Rome. Paris. Not here. "I can see why Camano would still be on the hunt for me. But why would he bring my mother with him?"

"Why indeed?" He shrugged as he turned away. "I want

like hell to answer you, but I'm not going to do it. It's time you asked yourself that question. You've been hiding your head in the sand for too long." He moved up the hill and disappeared around a curve in the trail.

And she wanted to keep hiding her head, she thought with panic. Don't look at it, and it might go away.

Don't look at it, and maybe it was all a mistake, and Gina hadn't known what Camano planned.

Don't look at it, and her mother might love her.

But how long could she turn her eyes away? From the time she was a small child, she had been on the run in one way or the other. She was no longer that child crying for someone to care about her. She'd been given the gift of Lee's and Natalie's love, and she had all the confidence that love had brought with it.

Mandak was right, she had to ask herself questions. Not only about Gina but about Lee and Natalie and Mandak. About what was true and false, what was important to her and where she wanted it to lead her.

Lord, it was going to be hard, but somehow she'd do it.

If she could just manage to pull her head out of the sand before it smothered her.

"HE'S QUITE BEAUTIFUL, PRALAND." Gina took a sip of her wine, her gaze on the tiger pacing in the huge cage. "Does he have a name?"

"No, that would give him importance," Praland said. "He's not a pet, he's a servant."

"But very exciting. I love that fancy cage. All that gilt trim . . ."

"I'm surprised you like it. Camano says you prefer the

real thing." Praland's lips twisted. "But at the price of gold these days, I'm not about to waste it on a cage for an animal." His gaze traveled over her, lingering on her breasts. "Though I might be persuaded to buy a bauble or two for you. If you prove that you're worth it."

He was responding just as she had anticipated he would, she thought. He would not be easy, but he could be had. "I have safety boxes full of baubles." She chuckled. "You'd have to do better than that. But then I'm sure you could. You're obviously a man who is able to set his own rules. This palace, that army that takes your orders." Her gaze went across the room, to where Camano was sitting on a low couch sniffing coke. "I thought I'd found a man who had that kind of power. These days, Rico's only interested in his damn drugs . . . and me, of course. I try to tell him that he shouldn't be that complacent, that he should reach out and grab for the same kind of life that you're living. But he doesn't have the guts." She took another sip of wine. "Too bad."

"If I heard one of my women talking like that about me, I'd cut her throat." His eyes shifted to the tiger. "If there was anything left of her."

"But you wouldn't have to worry about those bimbos insulting you. They shake when you raise an eyebrow. Don't you get bored with all that bowing and scraping?"

"On occasion." He looked at her. "Why did you ask me to bring you in here tonight, Gina?"

"I was curious about the tiger, of course."

"Liar. You were curious about me."

"Well, there are similarities," she said. "You're definitely king of your jungle. Or is that supposed to be the lion?"

"Why?" he repeated.

"I'm fascinated. I think that we could be an unbeatable team." She met his eyes. "And you'd find me completely stimulating. You've never met a woman like me. You'd send those stupid concubines packing after a day in my bed."

"Really? Intriguing."

He was interested. Sex always interested men, but she'd never seen colder eyes than Praland's. She had to offer him something else until she actually had him in bed. "And I can be useful to you in any number of ways. Let me prove it. Ask me anything."

"Oh, I will. Why else are you here?" He lifted his wineglass to her. "I was thinking that Camano might have to persuade you to be accommodating where your daughter is concerned, but I can see that it's in my court."

"Teresa has caused us so much trouble. She has to be made to realize that it can't go on. Now she's worrying you with her nonsense." She smiled into his eyes. "I won't let that continue. You want this Mandak? I'll see that Teresa tells me where he is as soon as I have a chance to talk to her."

"Teresa . . . They call her Allie now."

"Such an ugly name. 'Teresa' is much prettier."

"I'm just pointing out that things have changed with your daughter. I was skeptical when Camano assured me that you were the key to getting me Mandak. But I've had experience with the child-mother relationship when I was interrogating prisoners. I've seen tough men break when I've barely started to put their mothers to torture. I found it very strange. Just be sure that your influence is still strong enough to give me what I need."

"Some things never change." She leaned toward him,

not too close, not too obvious, just enough so that he could feel her warmth and smell her perfume. She said softly, "I promise I'll give you whatever you need, Praland."

ALLIE COULD FEEL her muscles tense as she pulled the blanket closer about her.

Mandak would be here soon.

Sean had left the cave only a few minutes ago to relieve Mandak at watch.

Relax. It wasn't as if she had to do this. She could back out. It was her choice.

And that would be the wrong choice. No more backing out. No more looking away.

Mandak was in the cave.

She could see his shadow on the cave wall as he moved silently toward his blankets.

He went still. "What's wrong? You're drawn as tight as a violin string."

That damn bonding. She should have known that he would be able to read her tension. She sat up and threw her blanket aside. "So I'm a little edgy." She moistened her lips. "I've been waiting for you."

"Have you?" he asked warily. "Why am I so honored?"

"Because you gave me one hell of a day, and I had to tell you that I—" She stopped.

"Tell me what?" He came toward her. "What am I to blame for now?"

"A terrible sin," she said haltingly. "You made me look at myself and the world around me. It's much more comfortable with my head in the sand."

"You had a right to want to hide yourself away. You

had wounds. I'm sorry you had a bad day. I'm not sorry that I made you examine why you were hiding." He fell to his knees in front of her. "Your mother?"

She nodded jerkily. "I know she's not a good person. I want to believe in her, but I'm not blind or stupid." She swallowed to ease the tightness of her throat. "I wanted it so badly. I still want it. She was the only one that I loved for so long that I can't seem to stop. I don't want to think she knew about what Camano was planning. I tried to run away from reading her memories, but sometimes they were just there. I got little glimpses . . ." She shook her head. "And I do think that she might have known, Mandak. And before Lee and Natalie, I would have wondered if I wasn't worthy of having my own mother love me."

He muttered a curse.

She held up her hand. "No, I know I'm worthy, or Lee and Natalie wouldn't have loved me. So the fault has to lie with her."

"You're damn right it does."

"And yet I still hope I'm wrong about her. Isn't that crazy?"

"No, just very human."

"Oh, I'm definitely human." She took a deep breath. "So that's one lie I'd been telling myself out of the way."

"There are more?"

"Since Lee and Natalie died, I've been very bitter. I've been telling myself that revenge was all that was left. It seemed as if the world was filled with ugliness and pain."

"A good portion of your world was pretty ugly. I couldn't seem to keep it away from you."

"You tried. It's just something we have to work through. Ugliness and evil exist and have to be fought. But we can't lose our humanity doing it." She blinked to keep back the tears. "Natalie said something like that on the night she died. She said that I knew about ugliness because I'd lived with it. She said that the thing she wanted for me more than anything in the world was for me to live every minute with joy and love. To fight the poison and not let it rob me of the joy. Isn't that wonderful? *She* was wonderful." She smiled unsteadily. "But I forgot all that when they were killed. I was so angry that I couldn't remember anything but the pain." She cleared her throat. "But I remember now, and I won't forget again. I'm not going to let anyone cheat me, not Camano, not Praland." She paused. "Not my mother."

"You left me out. Haven't I always been the bane of your existence?"

"Another lie. What have you done to me, Mandak? Saved my life, saved my sanity, gave me the only family I've ever had. You saw that I had an education and protection against the bad guys."

"I had a motive."

"Yes, and it scared me, but your motive was remarkably selfless. So you're not exactly the bogeyman I'd blown up to throw darts at."

"No, I'm the man who drew a target on your back, then brought you to the hunting ground," he said bitterly.

"Yes, you did. But I could have said no, and I didn't."

"That doesn't absolve me."

"No, everyone has to bear their own share of the burden in this nightmare." Her hands clenched into fists at her sides. "But now it doesn't matter any longer because we're in it together. I found that out when I was waiting outside Kobu's tent and wondering if you'd come out alive. I was so angry with you for risking yourself with that maniac. Then I realized that it wasn't anger but panic." She paused. "Because I knew I couldn't bear the thought of losing you. I couldn't stand the thought of your not being in my life."

He stiffened, and a muscle jerked in his cheek. "Oh, shit. What's that supposed to mean?"

"What do you think it means? This isn't easy for me, Mandak. You could help me a little." She reached out, and her palm touched his chest. She could feel his warmth beneath the cotton shirt. "Somewhere along the way, you became the most important thing in my life. Even when you'd faded into the background, you were always there. That's why I couldn't let you come too close. You meant too much to me. I don't know where it's going, but it's here, and I have to deal with it. I won't ignore it." This next was harder. "I . . . want you. All ways, every way. I don't want to miss anything. Natalie said that I should reach out for the joy. That's what I'm doing." She went on in a rush, "I'm not trying to put you in a corner. I know you feel something for me, too, but it might not be—" She stopped as his fingers touched her lips.

"I don't know where it's going, either." His eyes were glittering with moisture. "Hell, I shouldn't be listening to you. After all you've gone through, you probably aren't thinking straight." His hand moved down to touch her throat. "But my first reaction is to reach out and grab. I'm scared shitless that you're going to change your mind."

Her skin was tingling, burning beneath his fingers. She could feel the pulse leap in the hollow of her throat. She reached up and started to unbutton her blouse. "I'm not going to do that. I couldn't. But you probably know more about this than I do, so maybe you should—" She broke off and inhaled sharply.

He had brushed her hands aside and pushed her bra straps down, then off.

Then his mouth was on her nipples, his teeth teasing, sucking as he pushed her down on her back. She gasped as his fingers moved between her legs and slipped inside. "Mandak!" Her back arched helplessly as the rhythm started.

Not enough.

Not enough.

She had to have him . . .

Her hands were running, blindly, frantically over his body, stripping him, pulling him over her.

"Shh. Not yet." His face was flushed, his lips purely sensual as he looked down at her, trying to hold her still. "I'm going crazy. I want it to be good for you."

"Not yet?" She stared up at him in dazed disbelief. Every nerve in her body was alive and in need. Her breasts were taut, full. The muscles of her stomach were flexing, clenching. She was throbbing, hot, empty. "No way, Mandak." She wrapped her legs around his hips, rubbing against him. "I've changed my mind about your knowing more than I do. Not if you're going to be so damn noble. What was I thinking?"

He cried out and arched against her as she squeezed. "Allie, this isn't what— Oh, what the hell. Later." He was inside her, deep, fast, lifting her to every thrust. "Is this what you want? Take it. Take *me*."

She was taking him, all of him. He was filling her, every movement burning, hungry.

"More." She gasped.

He was giving her more.

Her head was thrashing back and forth on the blanket. She was squeezing, rubbing against him.

"Allie . . ." His face was flushed, his eyes . . . "Give me a break. I can't—"

Neither could she.

Her arms tightened around him.

Deeper.

A torrent of fire.

Deeper.

Faster.

Madness.

He lifted her, his breath coming in harsh sobs. "Allie . . ."

She nodded desperately. She couldn't speak.

He cried out, his muscles convulsing, his back arching.

Wildness. Completion.

Joy.

His face was buried in her shoulder. "I warned you, dammit. I tried to—"

"Hush." She was trying to get her breath. He was still inside her and he felt good, part of her. But then he'd always been part of her from that first night in the forest. She just hadn't realized it. "You did exactly what I wanted you to do."

He leaned down and kissed her nipple. "You gave me no choice. Why doesn't it surprise me? You always wanted to run the show." He got off her but moved only inches away. "But it came out pretty well, considering."

She made a rude sound. "Pretty well? It was great. Just because you didn't get to exercise your fantastic sexual control to impress me is no sign you were right and I was wrong."

"Heaven forbid." His hand touched her hair. "And, you're correct, it was fantastic."

"Fantastic?" She was silent, savoring the word. "It was more than that. It was joy. Just like Natalie said. We reached out and closed out all the poison and let in the joy." She rubbed her cheek against his shoulder. "But I want more, Mandak."

He chuckled. "I'm at your beck and call. All I have to do is touch you, and I'm—"

"No, I don't mean sex. Not right now. I want you to hold me like this for a little while. That's joy, too."

"Yes, it is." His arms enfolded her, and his voice was husky. "Whatever you want, Allie."

"I want it all." She cuddled closer. "Sex and this beautiful feeling of belonging. I've always wanted to belong to someone . . ."

"You never let it show. You're the most independent woman I know."

"But you knew . . . You always knew what I was feeling."

His lips brushed her temple. "Yes, I knew."

She was silent, thinking. "But you couldn't let me belong to you, could you? I had to be strong and stand alone. You gave me Lee and Natalie, but that was different. That didn't interfere with what I had to do."

"You were already strong when I met you." He paused. "And you're right about the rest. I gave you what I thought I could." His voice was suddenly violent. "It wasn't enough. Not then. Not now. And I can't let it go on. I can't let you go into that palace with Kobu. I'll try something else."

She raised her head and looked him in the eye. "You will take me to that palace. You said it could work."

"I also said there's a margin of error."

"You wouldn't have done all this prep and planning if the chances weren't good. I told you that I trust you. Don't tell me you're walking away. There's too much at stake. Those children Megan told me about, the Devanez family members on Praland's kill list. Maybe revenge could wait, but they can't. I'm not going to hide out until you find a safer plan. I've been doing nothing but hiding for the last seven years. This is what you've been preparing me for since the day I came to you. But it's not your battle any longer, it's *mine*. I'll find that ledger. Dammit, I'm committed, Mandak."

"I can see that you are," he said between clenched teeth. "And it's killing me."

"Well, get over it." She deliberately moved closer to him. "I'm not going to give up what we have tonight worrying about tomorrow."

His body was stiff and resisting. Then his naked muscular thigh was suddenly between both of her own. "That's right, you want it all. Well, why not?" His eyes were glittering, reckless. "So do I. But I'm feeling a little frustrated and barbaric at the moment." He was parting her thighs and moving over her. "Let's deal with that before we go on to gentler pastures . . ."

"YOUR TIME'S UP, KOBU." PRALAND'S words were clipped and harsh. "You promised me that you'd give me Mandak within three days. You failed me. I believe I'm going to have to send Bruker to escort you back here."

Panic iced through Kobu. "I'm close. I swear I'm close. I've found a source who knows where Mandak is. You have to give me another day."

"You're stalling."

"No, you're too smart to fall for that shit. It's true. One more day."

Silence. "And the woman, Allie Girard?"

"She's with him. I'll give them both to you."

"Why not now, today?"

"Mandak is tricky. I have to set him up before I can take him down." He moistened his dry lips. "You should know that, Praland. You haven't been able to touch him in almost ten years."

"Are you insulting me, Kobu?" Praland asked softly.

"No, no," he said quickly. "I just wanted to remind you how hard it is to trap Mandak. But I'll do it. Give me a little more time."

Another silence. "One more day. If you don't deliver, I'll go another route." He paused. "And you will no longer be necessary to me. Do you understand?"

"I won't disappoint you. I'll hand him to you on a silver platter. Mandak and the woman, too."

"See that you do." He hung up.

Kobu's hand was shaking. Son of a bitch. Praland had no right to talk to him like that. He hated feeling this humiliation and fear. He'd served him better than Bruker, but he was given no respect. Praland would be sorry. Once he left the country, other people would realize that Kobu was the one who had kept Praland on top.

But that would be chancy, too. If he betrayed him, Praland would put a price on his head. He'd be dessert for that big cat.

If he betrayed him.

He could still back out and hand Mandak and Allie Girard over to Praland when they reached the palace.

But there was that mountain of cash in his bank account and more to come.

A new life.

New lives could be scary. He could stay here and whittle at Bruker's influence on Praland.

But if Praland caught Allie Girard and not Mandak, then Mandak would be after Kobu. He had made it clear in bloody detail exactly what he would do to Kobu if he betrayed him. He was not certain who he feared most, Praland or Mandak.

There was a good chance that he could kill Allie Girard once they entered the palace. She was just a woman and only worthy of contempt. Praland might accept her death as a sacrifice that would keep Kobu out of the tiger's cage. Then he could sound the alarm on Mandak and, if he was lucky, Praland would eliminate him and his danger to Kobu.

Yes, that might work.

He had options. He just had to decide where the danger was greatest and the rewards most plentiful . . .

"WAKE UP, ALLIE. IT'S ALMOST dawn. We don't want Sean wandering in here to get a cup of coffee and have to scramble."

She wasn't sleeping. She was just lying here, feeling flushed and sleek and totally sexual. She opened her eyes to see Mandak pulling on his clothes. Too bad, she thought regretfully. He was beautiful naked. Why did people think naked women were all that lovely when men had such clean, powerful lines?

"Move." He leaned over and cupped her left breast in his hand. "You feel delightfully full and swollen." He bent over and outlined her nipple with his tongue. "And mine." He lifted his head. "I didn't hurt you?"

"Maybe. I don't think I noticed." The play had been wild and erotic, then gentle, then once again searingly, basically sexual.

Sean . . .

She forced herself to sit up and begin to dress. "You promised me you'd find me a pond or lake that didn't look like a cesspool on the way to the palace. I'm holding you to that, Mandak." She wrinkled her nose. "I need it."

He smiled as he headed for the cave entrance. "Pity. I kind of like my smell on you." His smile faded. "I'll check to make sure that Kobu hasn't made any calls to Praland. He might be getting nervous."

He wasn't the only one. But the last thing she wanted was to show apprehension to Mandak. "You said that he was sure that he could lead me through the palace and locate Praland with no trouble. How?"

"Because he wouldn't have to take you inside the palace. You could go through the garden to the terrace outside the room Praland enjoys most in the world. He goes to visit his demon tiger friend almost every evening. The wing is fairly isolated, and Kobu thinks he can position you on the terrace or nearby."

"The tiger again." She shook her head. "And it's not fair to call the tiger a demon. Praland is the demon. He keeps the tiger locked up instead of letting him roam his natural habitat. He starves him, then uses him to do his killing."

"You're feeling sorry for a man-eating tiger."

"Who knows if he would have been man-eating if he hadn't been taught. As I said, Praland is the demon."

"I won't argue that description. I'll make those calls and see if Kobu is leaning in Praland's direction. Then we'll have breakfast and set out." He looked at her. "Or say screw it and let me work on another plan."

She shook her head.

"I didn't think so." He turned and walked out of the cave.

It had been hard to say no. Last night had been extraordinary, both sexually and emotionally. She wanted to be safe and cling to that fragile happiness.

Admit it. She wanted to cling to Mandak.

But Mandak was one of the people most in danger if she didn't locate that ledger.

So finish getting dressed. Get on the road.

By dusk, they should have reached the palace.

And her meeting with Aman Kobu.

CHAPTER FOURTEEN

MANDAK WAS HANGING UP THE phone when she came out of the cave. "Kobu talked to Praland during the night."

She tensed. "And?"

"High-level threats from Praland. Panicky reassurances from Kobu. But he didn't set up any traps or tell Praland we had an arrangement. So there's a good chance that he'll go through with it."

"Comforting."

"That's all I can give you."

His phone rang and he answered it. "It's Renata." He held out the phone to Allie. "She wants to talk to you."

Renata started talking the moment Allie answered, "I don't like this. I think my job is to give you some inspiring bullshit, but that's not me. This is so damn important to us that I have to let you go for it. All I can say is that I'm scared for you. I'm grateful to you. I thank you for myself and for my family. I think you've got a hell of a lot of guts, and I respect you. If you get out of this alive, I'll owe you big-time. Now let me talk to Mandak."

She raised her brows as she handed the phone back to Mandak. "That was an interesting conversation. I hope she lets you say something."

He smiled and turned away. "She'll just want to make sure she gives me orders to take care of you. As if I wouldn't. But Renata thinks she has to run the world."

Allie heard him talking as she turned back toward the cave. It seemed to run in the family, she wanted to tell him. But that dominant trait could be comforting when everything seemed to be attacking from all sides. And honesty was a quality that was above price.

Renata's call had not made Allie feel less afraid, but there was now a warmth that had not been there before to fight the chill.

"Ready for breakfast?" Sean asked.

She wasn't hungry, but she had to have strength. "Sure. Why not?"

TEN MILES FROM SANDEK PALACE
5:15 P.M.

"You look a hell of a lot better," Sean said, as Allie came out of the forest, braiding her wet hair into a single braid. "Where's Mandak?"

"Coming. He's taking a quick dip. He insisted on standing guard while I took my bath." She smiled. "I told him that he should trust you more."

"Not with you," Sean said. "I've noticed that he doesn't think anyone else can take care of you." He shrugged. "I understand. He's on edge . . . and scared."

"Who isn't?" She did feel better after taking that dip, but her nerves were stretched raw. She was only hours away from going into that palace, trying to get the information, and still survive. "I just hope it's not all for nothing. I've never tried to read anyone with a mind block. What if it extends to memory?"

"Mandak didn't think it did."

"But no one knows for sure."

"True." Mandak walked out of the forest toward them. "But if you can't do it, that's the end of it. I told you that I'd think of something else."

"It's a little late," she said dryly. "After you've wasted seven years on me."

"Not wasted." He stopped in front of her. "Never wasted, Allie." He tugged gently at her braid. "Those seven years created an extraordinary human being."

She had the impulse to take a step closer to him. He smelled of the fresh earthiness of the forest. His dark hair was wet from the pond and shining in the sunlight. The sleeves of his shirt were rolled up to the elbow, and she could see the sleek flex of the muscles of his forearms. She wanted to reach out and touch—

She drew a deep breath and took a step back. "It would be a waste as far as stopping Praland in his tracks. We've got to hope you were right about my being able to read him. Sometimes memories are random."

"I'm going to try to give you a little insurance. I'll call his cell as soon as I gauge you in position and start talking to him about the ledger. With any luck, it should trigger memories."

"Logical." She felt relieved. She didn't know about luck, but she'd take any break she could get. She turned away. "Should we get on our way? We wouldn't want to keep Kobu waiting."

"Not quite yet. I want to go over the route that Kobu will take you through the gardens." He took out his computer and pulled up the palace schematic. "He'll bring you in the east gate, take you west and down the garden and pergola to the wing closest to the house. There's an ornate flagstone terrace here." His finger punched a window in the schematic. "And that's the Tiger Room. Window number fifteen. If Kobu tries to take you in any other direction, be on the alert. He might be betraying you."

She nodded. "Oh, I'll be watching him." She looked down at the schematic. "Where will you be?"

"Not close enough," he said grimly. "I want to go with you, but I can't do it. If Kobu runs into a guard, he might be able to talk himself out of it. But not if I'm along. Praland has made sure that every one of his men knows what I look like." He pointed to the east gate. "So I have to take out the sentry who guards this gate. After that I have to make the phone call to Praland. Then I have to take out another two guards on the route back into the jungle to clear a path for us to the jeep. Sean will meet you at the gate after you're finished and bring you back to the jeep."

"And we'll get the hell out of there," Allie said. "Those jungles will be crawling with Praland's men once they find those sentries."

"I know these jungles. I spent two weeks dodging and hiding in them after I shot Simon. I told Renata to have a pilot and helicopter waiting about five miles north of here."

"If we get that far," Sean said.

"We'll get there. Once Allie's out of the palace grounds, it will be my show. And it will be about time," he said bitterly. "I'll take over. I guarantee I won't let her be caught."

"I've got to get into the palace before we worry about

that," Allie said as she turned and got into the jeep. "And we're still making Kobu wait and get edgier by the minute. I don't like that idea."

"I didn't mean to make you uneasy, just cautious." He got into the jeep. "He may think about betraying you but I'm ninety percent sure he won't do it."

"And I'll watch out for the last ten percent," Allie said. "You can bet on it."

IT WAS DUSK WHEN THEY left the jeep in the jungle three miles away from Sandek Palace and moved warily toward the high white stone walls Allie could see in the distance.

"It's beautiful," she murmured. "I was expecting something more like a fortress. This reminds me of a palace in an Arabian Nights tale."

"Praland would like that idea," Mandak said. "It brings power to mind, and he's into that big-time."

"Hence the tiger."

"Yeah," he said curtly. "That's a good example." He stopped. "Kobu should be meeting us about five hundred yards ahead. Slow down. I'm going to check out the surrounding area to make sure that we don't have any other visitors."

"So much for ninety percent," Allie murmured.

"It still goes. I'm just not going to have much of a chance to keep you safe. I'm taking advantage of every opportunity. Take care of her, Sean." He disappeared into the brush.

"You heard him." Sean moved in front of Allie. "I'm to display all my superpowers to keep the bad guys from making toast of you."

"By all means, but your superpowers have to do with odds and gambling."

"And bravery and keen intelligence. Don't leave those out."

"I wouldn't think of it." Her gaze was wandering around the palms in front of them, and she was trying to keep the tension from her voice. The walls of the palace seemed overpoweringly close. Where was Kobu? They were close enough now. He should be here.

And where was Mandak?

"Stop!" Kobu was suddenly on the trail in front of them, a rifle in his hands. She remembered that face, the mustache, those dark, gleaming eyes. "You are the Girard woman. But where is Mandak?"

"He's here." Her hand slipped down to the gun in her jacket pocket. "I think he's looking for you."

"Stupid woman. Why don't you know? You wander through the jungle, and you have no—"

"She's not stupid." Mandak was behind Kobu. "It would be a great mistake for you to assume that she is." He looked at Allie and Sean. "It's clear up ahead. It appears Kobu is going to do the smart thing and make himself a rich man."

"You thought I would betray you?" Kobu's smile was forced. "Why would I do that? We made a deal."

"We won't discuss our deal now." He put his hand on Kobu's shoulder and pushed him away from Allie and toward the trees ahead. "We'll just execute it. Give me ten minutes to take out the sentry at the east gate. Then you can come and bypass the lock on the gate, Kobu." He disappeared into the jungle. "I'll see you there."

"After you." Sean gestured to Kobu. "I'll just amble

along behind you with Allie. I'd like to keep an eye on you."

Kobu shrugged. "It may all be a waste of time. Mandak is overconfident. Those sentries are very good, and they know what would happen to them if they failed Praland."

"It won't be a waste of time," Sean said. "I'll give you odds. I've gone on missions with Mandak before. He's not only good, this time he's highly motivated. He'll take that sentry out."

THERE WAS NO sign of the sentry when they reached the east gate.

"Inside." Mandak stepped out of the shadows, his expression tense. "Bypass that lock, Kobu. Get moving, Allie. I turned off the guard's phone when I dragged him into the shrubs, but there's no telling if someone will get curious if he doesn't answer. I don't know how much time we have." He turned to Allie. "Last chance. I'll scrub it if you say the word."

She shook her head.

"Then take care of yourself, dammit." He turned on Kobu. "Listen very well." His voice was deadly cold. "Betray her, and anything that Praland would do to you will pale by comparison to what I have in mind. I'd hunt you down and never quit."

Kobu flinched. "She dies, and I don't get the rest of my money. That wouldn't make sense." He hurried down the path. "But if the woman is clumsy and gets nervous, it wouldn't be my fault."

"From this moment on, I'm looking at everything as

being your fault." He turned back to Allie. "I'll make the call to Praland in ten minutes. You should be in position and ready by that time." His hand reached out and gently touched her cheek. "I *hate* this. Don't take any chances you don't have to take." He strode away, with Sean following.

Did he think she didn't hate it? She was scared and worried about him and Sean. Not to mention what this slimy scumbag Kobu might decide to do before they got out of that garden.

Kobu was looking over his shoulder at her with a sneer on his face. "Coming?"

She smothered her anger and walked quickly after him. He gestured to the west and set out at a fast pace.

Right direction at least. Mandak had said west, then the fifteenth window.

The tiger window.

MANDAK STOPPED AFTER GOING several hundred yards into the forest. He checked his watch. "Five minutes to go."

Sean nodded, his gaze on the palace walls. "So far, so good."

"Not good," Mandak said tightly. "There's nothing good about this situation. She's in there, and I'm out here."

"You gave her a choice. She said it was her job."

"After I railroaded her into a position where she thought it was her duty."

"I think that she'd be hard to railroad."

"But I'm so good at it."

"And so hard on yourself."

Mandak checked his watch again. "Three more minutes."

FOURTEEN.

The next window was fifteen.

It was a large, multipaned window, set back into the stone facade and trimmed with surrounding open-worked exotic metal designs.

"There it is," Kobu whispered. "I leave you now. I've done what Mandak wished."

She stiffened. "You're not going anywhere. That wasn't in the plan." She slipped her gun out of her pocket of her jacket. "You leave when I leave."

"You fire that gun, and you'll have every guard in the palace on top of you," he snarled.

"But I'm only a stupid woman. Isn't that what you said? What difference will it make if I rouse the palace when that may be your plan when you leave me?" Her gaze narrowed on his face. "Either way, Mandak will blame you." She could see that shook him. That last threat Mandak had made had been both fierce and terrifying. "Now I'm going to go sit behind those oleander shrubs beneath the window. You're going to sit down four or five feet away from me, where I can clearly see you. Do you understand?"

"Bitch."

She kept the gun pointed at him as she moved toward the window. "I can't talk to you any longer. Someone from inside may be able to hear because of that open metalwork on the window. Do as I say, Kobu."

He hesitated, glaring at her. Then he shrugged and slowly sat down where she'd indicated.

She felt a rush of relief. She didn't know if he'd actually been planning to betray her or just to remove himself from potential danger. Either way, it was safer to keep him with her until she was back with Mandak.

Damn, she hadn't needed this, she thought as she insinuated herself closer to the window. She had to concentrate on Praland, not worry about a move from Kobu. She kept her gun propped and ready in her hand as she turned her attention to what was going on in the room.

The first thing she saw was the tiger. Striped, magnificent, and deadly in his scarlet-and-gilt cage.

The next thing she saw was Praland, sitting on the couch in front of the cage.

The third thing she saw was her mother, moving from the bar across the room to hand Praland a drink.

Shock.

The breath left Allie's body.

She'd accepted the possibility of her mother's being here, not the reality.

Accept it now. Clear your head. Do your job.

But her gaze was glued on Gina in her sunburst orange gown. Gina who was staring down at Praland with a smiling intimacy that Allie had seen on her face when she had spoken to her father and Camano. It was all there, willing, alluring temptation incarnate. Along with confidence and power. All her life, Gina had tried to make Allie believe that she was helpless, molded by the men in her life. But there was nothing helpless about the woman standing beside Praland. Allie could hear her low laugh as she lifted her drink to her lips.

Allie tried to focus. Don't look at Gina. Don't think about the lies of a lifetime. Concentrate.

Praland was only a scant twenty-five feet away from her. If it was possible that his memory would be open to her, then the distance was right. That was a big if. She tried to probe.

Nothing.

But that might mean his memory was not engaged. He was looking at Gina, and she could hear her mother laugh again and say something in a low voice. Praland was occupied with her mother and what was happening now. She'd have to wait until Mandak made his call.

She gave a quick glance at Kobu. Still glaring at her, tense, frightened, but not moving.

Call, Mandak, she silently urged.

Talk to Praland. I can't get near him.

"TIME," MANDAK SAID.

He pressed the button on his cell. There would be no ID, but Praland would be both curious and wary about anyone having his private number.

He was right. It rang only twice before Praland picked up. "Hello."

"Mandak. You've called me so many times in the last eight years that I thought that I'd return the favor."

"But I always had a reason for calling you," Praland said. "I was always delighted to see you sweat." He chuckled. "After all, you stole from me. I wasn't finished with toying with Simon Walberg. You made me look a fool in front of my men. But I've paid you back since then. How many of your precious family have I killed?"

"Seventeen."

"I'm so glad you've kept a tally. There will be more. Besides, the taking of the children that seems to bother you so much. I've got plans to expand my operations in that direction. They are so very profitable."

"We'll shut you down. The reason I'm calling is that you've crossed the line when you had Camano kill Lee and Natalie Walberg. I don't want you to sleep well again. We're getting close to you. The minute we find the ledger, you're a dead man."

"Ah, but you've got to find the ledger."

"Tell me, Praland, how does your vicious little mind work? Do you take out the ledger and go through it and just pick a name? Did you make out a death list?"

"Oh, no. When it's time, I take out the ledger and savor the moment. There's no stronger sense of power. It gives me a great deal of pleasure to select just the right victim, who will cause you the most upset. Of course, I try to pick the youngest and strongest. The ones who have the most to lose. It's the best sensation to . . ."

DARK TUNNEL.

It was happening, Allie thought.

Dark tunnel. Dark tunnel. Dark tunnel.

Suddenly she was there.

So much ugliness. The monstrous things Praland had done. Block it. Don't think of it. Just let his memories ignited by Mandak flow over her.

GET HIM BACK, YOU FOOL. Do you want to get me killed? Praland took the ancient leather book in his hands and drew it out of the compartment. Satisfaction surged through him. Time to give Mandak and those other fools another lesson in who was the one in control. He'd added the new children taken from Ukraine in the book last month, but now it was time to play his game with Mandak...

HE WAS FADING, ALLIE REALIZED with panic.

Talk to him, Mandak. I almost had it.

"YOU CAN SHUT UP about what you did with those young kids," Mandak broke into Praland's dialogue. "I know what kind of monster you are."

"Well, you did ask a question. I thought you were curious. I'm always willing to elaborate." Praland added slowly, "Much as I'm enjoying our conversation, I'm wondering why you're calling me. You issued a few threats, but I don't believe you would go to the trouble of contacting me only for that."

Mandak was silent. "The Devanez family resources have been stretched to the max dealing with all your brutalities and the protection we're having to give our people."

"Which in most cases proves to be futile."

"As you say, we've been thinking about asking for a compromise."

Praland burst out laughing. "Compromise? My how the mighty have fallen. Why should I deal with you? I hold all the power."

"We'd be willing to deposit an extraordinarily large amount in your accounts that would make you richer and more powerful than you could imagine."

"Really? And what in return?"

"Only the ledger."

"How single-minded. But I've developed a great affection for that ledger."

"Still, it must be a burden possessing it, caring for it, moving it from place to place to keep us from finding it. You know we'll never give up trying to take you down while you still have the ledger."

"And if I gave you the ledger, it would be the signal for you to go after me with all guns blazing. I know you, Mandak. Even with your hands tied these last years, you've caused me trouble."

"You'll regret it if you refuse me. That ledger is an albatross around your neck. You can't hide it forever. We'll locate it eventually."

Praland chuckled. "You know, sometimes I look forward to your doing that. It would be the most exquisite pleasure that you could . . ."

GOT IT!

Allie's heart was pounding with excitement.

Her palms damp with perspiration.

Now get out and break the connection. Would Mandak know that she'd gotten what they needed?

She never knew to what extent Mandak could know what she was thinking. That bonding was evidently stronger on his side.

I'm out of here, Mandak. I think I—

The thought vanished as her eyes met Kobu's. She had made an effort and kept her attention partially on the bastard.

But not enough during this last moment. He was on his feet and coming toward her.

* * *

SON OF A bitch. Kobu!

Mandak felt a bolt of panic

Get off the phone with Praland.

Get to her.

He started running toward the palace.

"If that's your answer, I'm done talking to you," he said curtly to Praland. "I just thought I'd give you the chance to be reasonable."

"I'm being reasonable. I've got all the cards, Mandak. Your calling me just confirms that fact. I almost had you a few days ago at Talboa. Next time, you'll be mine. I'm going to have you to play with as I did Simon. Do you think I don't know what's going on? You thought you'd try to bring in one of your freaky kids to help you find the ledger. I doubt if it would work, but I'm blocking it just in case. Do you know who just fixed me a drink? Beautiful Gina, who wants to give me everything I want in the world." He chuckled. "Including her daughter. She assures me that's entirely possible. What do you think?"

Mandak had reached the east gate. Allie was not there. He'd known she would not be. He still sensed her alarm and panic. "I'm hanging up, Praland, call me if you change your mind."

KOBU SMILED AS HE RECOGNIZED the panic Allie hadn't been able to hide. He moved toward her, his words soft and venomous. "I decided you were bluffing, bitch. You're not going to fire that gun. You're scared shitless of the noise. So am I. So I'm going to take it away from you and get the hell out of here. I'm done with you and Mandak."

Get him away from that window. She couldn't risk any noise.

She got to her feet and backed away from him and onto the path.

No sound.

He was right, it had been a bluff. She couldn't fire that gun.

And she didn't trust Kobu once she had no weapon. He was a bully and killer, and he didn't like it that she'd had him at gunpoint for almost a quarter of an hour.

Okay, fake it. Make him believe that she was terrified of what he'd do to her. It wouldn't take much. She was scared and had to control her shaking.

She backed farther down the path, her hand outstretched pleadingly.

She could see Kobu's expression change to contemptuous satisfaction as he followed her. He held out his hand for the gun.

Did he think it would be that easy?

Evidently he did.

She stopped and extended the gun butt first to him.

He reached for the gun.

She threw the gun aside, kicked his wrist, then whirled, and her foot jerked his head backward as she kicked him in the throat.

She was diving for the gun as he fell to the ground.

She grabbed the gun and was straddling Kobu the next moment.

She hit him in the head with the butt of the gun. Then hit him again. She raised her gun to hit him again.

"Enough." It was Mandak standing beside her, jerking her to her feet. He pushed her toward the east gate. "Run.

I'll take care of him. Get the hell out of here. I'll be right behind you."

She ran!

She was halfway to the gate when she looked back. Mandak was straightening away from dragging Kobu's body into the bushes.

Then he was running after her.

He overtook her as she reached the gate. "Stay behind me. I didn't have time to clear the way to the jeep. We may have to wing it."

Her heart was beating hard as she flew after him through the forest. "Where's Sean?"

"Right here." Sean stepped out of the bushes ahead of them. "Mandak sent me ahead to get rid of the sentries when he decided that you might need a little help." He looked at Mandak. "Only one, Mandak. I took him out."

"Good. Move!"

It took them only a few more minutes to reach the jeep. They piled into the vehicle, and Sean jumped into the driver's seat and started the engine.

Allie was looking back at the palace. No uproar. No pursuit. She couldn't believe it. "We got away?"

"Not clean," Mandak said. "They're going to find those sentries soon. Then they'll find Kobu. But we have time to get to the helicopter."

"That's clean enough," Sean said. "You always were a perfectionist."

Allie gave a shaky sigh of relief as she leaned back in her seat. It was over. After all the nervous anticipation and fear, the years of dread culminating in this night, she had managed to get through it.

"Okay?" Mandak's gaze was on her face.

"Better than okay." A smile illuminated her face. "I *got* it, Mandak."

He went still. "What?"

"You heard me. I got it. At first, I didn't think it was going to work. I was getting only bits and pieces, but then it all came clear, and it was right there in front of me."

"The ledger?" He grasped her shoulders. "You know where it is?"

"I saw it. Praland was very proud of finding a fool-proof hiding place, almost smirking. Every time you said something that had to do with you finding the ledger, it sent him spiraling back to the time when he ordered it built or when he was taking the ledger out of the compartment."

"Compartment? Where the hell is it?"

"Inside the tiger's cage. He had a false roof put inside the cage. Every time he wanted to access the ledger, he'd have the tiger removed, and he'd climb in the cage and open the compartment."

"Son of a bitch," Sean murmured. "Talk about a built-in booby trap. No one would be eager to search that cage."

"Particularly since it had the reputation of being Praland's private butcher store," Mandak said grimly. "You're certain, Allie?"

"I'm certain." She couldn't keep from grinning. She felt as if a gigantic burden had been lifted from her shoulders. "I *saw* it. Why are you doubting me? You always told me that I'd be able to do it. That's what all this has been about."

"Because it's too good to be true." His eyes were glittering with excitement. "We have our chance now."

She nodded. "The code for opening the compartment is 1485."

"The year that the Devanez fled the Inquisition," Mandak said.

She nodded. "He was remembering something about having the Devanez family on the run."

"The hell he has."

She looked back at the palace, which was now almost lost to view. Her smile faded. She said haltingly, "My mother was with Praland in that room."

"I know." He reached out and grasped her hand. "He told me she was going to be very accommodating. Evidently, she'd promised to help reel you in. He didn't know whether he believed you could be a danger to him, but he thought he'd play it safe."

And her mother was going to help keep him safe. It hurt. It was one thing to admit to herself that Gina could betray her. It was another to see it confirmed. "Camano wasn't there. She and Praland looked . . . intimate."

"It could be that she's in the process of changing allegiance, and Camano is no longer necessary to her."

"Yes, I guess that could be." Smother the hurt. Try not to think about it. Focus on the positive. She had done what she had set out to do.

Or had she?

Her eyes widened, and she went tense as a sudden thought occurred to her. "Kobu. We left Kobu in that garden. When Praland's guards find him, they'll question him, they'll torture him. He'll tell Praland that he brought me to the garden and why. Praland will move the ledger."

Mandak was shaking his head.

"Don't tell me no. You know what he did to Simon. I only left Kobu unconscious. They'll make him—"

"He won't tell them anything," Mandak said. "I told you I'd take care of Kobu. I did what I promised."

She had a memory of Mandak's dragging Kobu into the bushes. "You killed him?" she whispered.

"I couldn't take the chance. I had to make it as clean as I could." He shrugged. "And I was mad as hell when I thought that he was on the attack with you. But it would only have been a matter of time anyway. I never intended to let him live. He killed Thorne, he killed Father Elwyn and God knows how many others of our people over the years. It just happened sooner than later."

"I'm not arguing he deserved it. I'm just . . . surprised."

"And I was surprised to see him lying there unconscious." He made a face. "I thought I was going to rescue you."

"You shouldn't have been surprised. You taught me, didn't you?"

"And very well, evidently." Sean grinned over his shoulder. "But not well enough to keep him from freaking out when he thought you were in danger." His smile faded. "But is there still a possibility of Praland's moving that ledger?"

"Yes. But not if we move fast enough. There will be confusion . . . and suspicion. Let's hope the confusion is stronger. I broke Kobu's neck. Praland will probably suspect a man, not a woman. I planted one of Kobu's guns in his hand. Kobu had the gate codes. He knew the sentry schedules. Everyone knew he was terrified of what Praland was planning for him. Who's to say he didn't try to find a way to assassinate Praland?"

"Except for the fact that he turns up with a broken neck," Allie said.

"That's where the suspicion comes into play. Maybe he turned traitor, then got chicken? Praland will be trying to work out scenarios."

"He won't want to move the ledger," Allie said slowly. "He thought it was a stroke of genius."

"And there's no reason he should have to do it if he doesn't think you were in that garden tonight. I rubbed out your footprints on the dirt near the window. And, as I said, he's not entirely sure you could do what Camano and your mother said you could do. An element of doubt may help." He was frowning. "But he may have second thoughts. We have to act before he does." He reached for his cell and pressed the speakerphone. "Renata, we know where the ledger is hidden. It's in the palace."

"Thank God." She immediately pounced. "How do we get it? Do you need men?"

"Not to get the ledger. We have to be lean and mean. Too much could go wrong if we blunder through that palace with a full attack team." He paused. "That being said, I think it's time we erased Praland from the face of the Earth."

Silence. "So do I. I could set up the attack on the palace for as early as nine tomorrow night. Will you promise me that the ledger will be safe? The first thing Praland will do is keep his word that he'll destroy it and those children."

"I guarantee that the ledger will be safe and in our hands by the time you launch."

"I'm trusting you, Mandak." She paused. "You were right about her? Allie was able to do it?"

"Smooth as glass. But not without risk."

"I didn't think it would be. Is she safe?"

"Yes, she's right here. She can hear you. I'm on the way to put her on the helicopter. I'm going to need a few items flown back here right away."

"You'll get them." Another silence. "Good job, Allie." She hung up the phone.

Crazy. Allie was feeling a rush of pride, as if she'd received a medal. "Renata can throw a major assault together that quickly?" Allie asked. "I'm impressed."

"It's been planned and on standby for a long time. We knew that once we took the ledger, we'd have to move fast so that none of Praland's confederates had an opportunity to move the children. She just has to coordinate and give the word."

"And trust you to get the ledger."

"I'll get it."

"How? You told Renata that you didn't want additional help before the assault tomorrow night. But Praland's bound to have the palace on alert after tonight."

"I have a few ideas."

"Share them."

"Not quite jelled."

"And you don't want me involved."

"You were involved up to your eyebrows tonight. You've done your part. Leave the rest to me."

"And me," Sean said. "I'm feeling a little cheated that I had so little to do tonight. One sentry does not a mission make. Now I'm a true animal lover, but I'm not sure I'd get along with that tiger. What do you think, Mandak?"

"I think we'll both have an opportunity to find out."

They were joking, Allie realized, frustrated. She wanted to strangle them both. She had seen that tiger and heard what Mandak said about him. They were going to have to get into that cage without being mauled. Before that, they had to negotiate the twists and turns of the palace and avoid Praland and his men. "It's nothing to joke about. You have to see that damn—" She broke off as they turned a corner of the road, and she saw the beige-and-gold helicopter sitting in the clearing. A gray-haired man stepped out of the aircraft as the jeep came to a stop.

Sean got out of the jeep and strode forward to greet the pilot.

"Out," Mandak told Allie as he jumped out of the jeep. "I have to give the pilot a list of supplies. First on the list will be a dart gun with knockout darts capable of sending that tiger to the Land of Nod. After that, I'll have to improvise. Then you can both get out of here."

"Can I?" She didn't move. "You've always told me what I could do, what I should do. When are you going to learn to ask me what I'm going to do?"

He went still. "What's that supposed to mean?"

"I'm not going to get on that helicopter. I'm not going to let the pilot take me to some cozy safe haven because you believe that's where I should be."

"That's exactly where you should be," he said roughly.

She shook her head.

"You're done here," he said. "What the hell are you thinking?"

"I'm thinking that you're not telling the truth. I'm not done here. I'll decide when I'm done." She looked him in the eye. "Praland, Camano." She hesitated before she said haltingly, "My mother. They're all responsible for what happened to Lee and Natalie. I have to make sure that they're punished for it."

"I'll make sure of it. Get on that helicopter."

She shook her head. "I told you once that I wasn't

going to let you be taken down. There's only you and
Sean here. I can help. You taught me about weapons, to
shoot, to protect myself."

"To protect yourself," he repeated. "Not to do this."

"Not to protect you or Sean? Sorry, I have the skill, I
have the choice."

His hands clenched into fists. "I'm tempted to knock
you out and throw you on that helicopter."

"Go ahead. You're good, but you'd have to hurt me.
I'd fight you."

"Allie."

"Give the pilot your list. I'll wait here." She smiled
faintly. "It should teach you that you can't bank on everything going your way, Mandak. I gave you what you
wanted tonight. Now you have to give me what I want."

He stood looking at her, his face pale in the moonlight.
"Don't do this, Allie."

"Give the pilot your list," she repeated. "I hope it has
a missile or two. We might need it."

He muttered a curse, turned on his heel, and strode
toward the helicopter.

CHAPTER FIFTEEN

"THE SON OF A BITCH." Praland viciously kicked Kobu's body in the ribs. He turned to Bruker. "How long ago did the guards find him?"

"Fifteen minutes. The lock at the east gate had been bypassed. We haven't located the sentry who was on duty."

"Kobu knew the gate codes." Praland's gaze went to the gun in Kobu's hand. "What the hell happened here?"

Bruker shrugged. "I told you that you shouldn't have given him that extra day to catch Mandak. Maybe he panicked and decided that he either had to run or take you out. He knew you'd never stop searching for him." He suddenly chuckled. "Or maybe he decided to take out the tiger."

"I'm glad you find this so amusing," Praland said softly. "Kobu was close enough to that window to have me in his sights."

Bruker's smile disappeared. "I'm having my men question everyone on duty. We'll find out what happened."

"The bastard was trying to assassinate me." Praland looked down at Kobu's twisted neck. "But maybe that's not all. He had to have had company. I got a call from

Mandak tonight. Maybe he was trying to set me up for Kobu and sent one of his men to come along to make sure that Kobu did the job."

"And Kobu panicked and tried to back out?"

"Perhaps. It's possible. I won't know until I get a chance to question Mandak personally." His lips curled. "And in agonizing depth. I thought he was beginning to cave, to back down, but he was trying to make a fool of me." His gaze lifted to the window and the tiger cage in the room beyond it. Gina was still sitting on the couch and looked ravishingly gorgeous and as serene as the tiger was restless. "And Kobu came too close. I'm not letting it happen again." He moved down the path toward the terrace door. "I believe it's time that we showed Mandak that I'm the only one in control. I learned a lesson when Mandak went against all the odds to kill Simon Walberg. It made no sense, and I came within an inch of catching the bastard a dozen times in the following two weeks."

"Stupid."

"No, it could only mean Mandak might have a fatal weakness I can use . . ."

"I JUST TALKED TO RENATA, and she said to tell you the helicopter is loaded and should get under way soon." Sean strolled back from the clearing, where he'd taken the call to Allie and Mandak. "It should arrive in a couple hours."

"Soon enough," Mandak said. "We won't need it before evening."

"But it's going to be a boring few hours," Sean said. "Anyone want to play some blackjack?"

"I'll pass," Mandak said.

"Allie?"

She shook her head.

"What a disappointment you two are. Don't you realize that in times of high stress, you should always keep your mind sharp and alert?" He sighed and moved back to the clearing. "Then I guess I'll just play solitaire and keep an eye on the road."

High stress, Allie thought. She supposed that was a correct term for what she felt but it was more of a zinging, edgy state than really being nervous or in distress.

And she wasn't frightened.

Which was pretty dumb considering what the next hours could bring.

But she could sense the tension gripping Mandak. He'd barely said a word to her since the helicopter had taken off three hours ago.

Well, she wasn't going to let that go on. She got up and strode over to where Mandak was sitting leaning against a tree.

"If we're not making a move until evening, aren't we cutting it close getting the ledger out before the assault?"

"A little." He looked up at her. "I want it close. If we have to go on the run, I want Praland and company to still be at the palace and not scattered around the countryside chasing us during an attack."

"That sounds smart." She dropped down beside him. "But, then, you're always smart. You're planning a diversion?"

He nodded. "A garden party like no other. Lots of fireworks."

She was silent. "And am I invited?"

"No." He suddenly reached out and pulled her close

to him. "But I know it's no good trying to keep you out." His voice was hoarse. "You'd just gate-crash."

"Yes." She cuddled closer to him and tucked her cheek in the hollow of his shoulder. It was so good feeling the warmth, the vitality of him. "I said you were smart. Now that that's settled, be quiet for a little while and just hold me. I don't want to think about what's going to happen tomorrow night."

"Because you're being an idiot about it."

"Because it's something I have to do, but there's no use dwelling on it. I'd rather do what Natalie told me to do. Enjoy the moment. Feel that joy." She brushed her lips against his throat. "And think about what we've had." She was silent. "I told you that I didn't know where this was going, but I believe it's coming to me. So once it clicks, you may have a problem with holding me off."

"No problem." His hand was gently rubbing her nape. "I guarantee that I'll meekly surrender."

"You're never meek. You never surrender."

"You're the exception that proves the rule." He was silent for a minute before he said, "In all ways, Allie. You have to take care. I don't think I could stand it if you—"

"Hush." She nestled closer. "I'm not used to your being this sappy. It's not like you. It makes me uneasy."

"I can see how it would." He chuckled. "Hell, it makes me uneasy, too. Okay, I'll watch it."

"Right. I wouldn't want you to—"

Her cell phone rang.

She stiffened in surprise. "What?" Her phone had not rung since the night Lee and Natalie had been killed. She reached in her jacket pocket and pulled it out. No ID.

It rang again.

She punched the access button.

"Teresa? Thank God, you answered." Gina's voice was shaking. "Praland said that if you didn't answer, it would all be over."

Shock. "Mother?"

Mandak stiffened, then straightened away from her.

"Of course, it's me. It's so good to hear your voice. It's been so long, baby. I've missed you so much. Why did you run away?"

"Ask Camano."

"He didn't mean you any real harm. It was all a mistake, then Mandak stepped in and made it worse. It was all Mandak's fault and his vendetta with that Praland. We were all just caught in the middle." Her voice lowered to velvet sweetness. "I've never stopped searching for you. It broke my heart when I couldn't find you."

Did she expect Allie to believe her? Just say the words that Allie wanted to hear and expect her to suspend logic and reason?

But, God help her, Allie wanted to believe her.

And, yes, Gina probably did still think that she would go along with whatever she said was true. She had an incredible confidence in her power to attract and sway.

"Why are you calling me, Mother?"

"Praland. He's very angry. It's Mandak again. Praland thinks he wants to use you against him in the way your father did. I tried to tell him that you wouldn't do that, but he won't believe me." She said brokenly, "He said he'll hurt me if you don't leave Mandak and come back to me. He means it, Teresa. There's a tiger . . ."

A little truth, a pack of lies, a twist of the knife. "And what's to stop Praland from hurting me, Mother?"

"He wouldn't do that. He thinks that what you did for

your father was very clever. You might be able to do the same thing for him."

Nightmare scenario.

"I couldn't trust him, Mother."

"Then trust me." Gina's voice was full and rich and brimming with affection. "No matter how you feel about anyone else, you know that I love you and would never hurt you."

How many times had Gina said that to Allie when she was a little girl? It had been the magic bullet to get her to do whatever her mother wanted.

Gina didn't like the silence. "Just come back to me. We'll make Praland understand that you're through dealing with Mandak, then we'll go away together. Just as I've always planned to do when I found you, Teresa." She paused. "But you have to come right away. You don't want him to hurt me because that Mandak is causing all this trouble."

Allie didn't answer.

"Teresa?" There was a hint of panic in Gina's voice. "He means it. You have to tell me that you'll come and help me."

Help Gina, help the beautiful butterfly.

"I love you, baby. You wouldn't want anyone to hurt me."

Allie was silent, then said wearily, "No, I don't want anyone to hurt you, Mother."

She felt Mandak's muscles tense.

"Good. Then you'll come right away?"

"Where?" Allie wasn't supposed to know about the palace or anything that had happened there. "Where am I supposed to come, Mother?"

"Praland has a sort of palace in southern Tanzania.

It's quite spectacular. Praland says that Mandak would know."

"And you think I'd come with Mandak? Praland would love to get his hands on him. Mandak will be angry with me for going there at all. He had plans for me."

"Then come alone. I don't care."

No, that was evident beneath all the honey and manipulation. "I'll be there. I won't let anything happen to you, Mother." She drew a deep shaky breath. "But I don't think I'm anywhere near that palace. I'll have to find it, and Mandak won't help. I'll try to be there by tomorrow evening. I'll call you when I'm close." She paused. "But I'm not going to go into that place until I'm sure we can make a deal with Praland to let you leave with me. I'll meet you outside the gates."

"Whatever," Gina said. "I knew you'd never desert me when I needed you." She added softly, "Everything's going to be different from now on. The way I wanted it to be in the beginning. Thank you for giving me a chance to make a good life for both of us." She hung up the phone.

So clever, Allie thought sadly. So able to manipulate and shift emotions in the way Gina wanted them to go.

"Tell me that she didn't take you in." Mandak's eyes were blazing in his taut face. "Because from what I heard, it sounded remarkably like it to me." He grabbed her shoulders and shook her. "I thought you'd gotten over that fixation, dammit. It's a trap. You're not going to be able to make any deal with Praland or Camano."

"I know that." She shrugged away from his grip. "But it's a trap that could go both ways. Could Praland have traced that call?"

"No, it was too short. I'd have disconnected it myself

if he'd had a chance while Gina was giving you all that bullshit."

"It seemed like a long time to me." Long and painful. "Now stop yelling at me. I'm feeling pretty raw and hurting. I need a little time to pull myself together and start thinking. I was just acting on instinct when I was talking to my mother."

"And that could be even worse. I don't like where that instinct is taking you."

"It's the only path that would get Praland and the others outside the gates and a good distance away from that Tiger Room at the time of your choosing," she said. "No diversion tactics necessary in the garden. I'd be the diversion and one that Praland and my mother set up themselves."

"And they'll snap you up like a steel trap."

"Then you think of a way for me to get out of it," she said wearily. "Because I'm going to do it, Mandak. You'd have a better chance of getting the ledger, and it would be safer for you and Sean. I don't have your experience or tactical know-how, so I have to rely on you. Just make it work."

"With your life in the balance. Not again, Allie."

"Then you make sure the balance is on my side." She got to her feet. "You told me once that you believed in fate. I don't think my mother does. She believes she can twist life to suit herself, and everything she's touched has been ugly. Because I loved her, I let her persuade me to do what my father wanted me to do. Which made me ugly, too." Her lips twisted. "But maybe this is the way that we can straighten it all out and use her to do it."

"It's too risky."

"Work it out," she repeated. "Or I'll do it myself. Don't talk to me again until you've done it." She turned and walked away from him.

There wasn't anything more to say. He would just argue, and she couldn't pay attention to arguments. As she had told him, she was hurting and raw and still a little in shock. Somewhere deep inside, there had still been a tendril of hope that Gina would not use her or betray her. It had been ripped out as she had listened to her mother and remembered those words of love and coaxing persuasion from her childhood. All Gina had to do was tell her that she loved her, and she would have done anything for her.

Not this time. The memory of Gina's plying her wiles on Praland tonight was too fresh, too shocking.

Don't think of those past betrayals.

Think of a way that this betrayal could boomerang and do good.

And stay here in the darkness of the night until the hurt faded, and she was strong again.

MANDAK CAME TO FIND HER over an hour later.

She instinctively straightened defensively.

"Don't do that," he said curtly. "I've had my orders. I know I'm not going to be able to persuade you to change your mind." He pulled out his computer and pulled up the palace schematics. "You'll drive the jeep to the west gate, that's the farthest away from the entrance to the Tiger Room. Timing is important. You'll arrive at eight fifteen in the evening. I've told Renata to have one of her agents come here with another vehicle to pick up Sean, me, and the supplies the helicopter is delivering. We'll set out as soon as he gets here and should be back at the palace before dawn."

"Why are you going so early?"

"I have things to do that may take time. Do you remember I told you that when Simon was being held by Praland, I bribed a servant to dig a tunnel from the outer wall to the dungeon?"

She nodded. "But then you weren't able to use it. It was too late for Simon."

"I wasn't able to use it at the time. But Renata's agents used it occasionally to get into the palace to search for the ledger and get information. The tunnel is still there."

"Guards?"

He shook his head. "No prisoners. Not since Praland got his tiger. They go straight to the cage. I'll still have to check out the tunnel, but it won't take me long to get down to that dungeon to wait for my opportunity to get to the Tiger Room." He paused. "But I'll also need the extra time and the dark to prep the area around the west gate for you. I'll find a way to stash a gun for you behind the stones in the wall. Three stones up from the ground. They'll make you give up any weapons the moment they see you." He punched his finger at another stone just above the one he'd indicated. "There will be a bomb behind this stone. Small but very powerful. You don't have to pull this stone out. I'll put mud and gunpowder in the grout lines. Fire into it, and it will explode. Make sure you're a good distance away from it. It will probably take half the wall with it."

"Yes, I'd say that's very powerful," she said dryly.

"I had to give you your best chance." He pointed to the garden. "You see these small windows that are only a few feet aboveground? Those are the dungeon windows. I'll set several explosives in them and around the garden and back terrace. After we've got the ledger, I'll set the bombs off. That should cause Praland, Camano, and any of your other welcoming committee to be distracted and pour back into the garden. You'll be able to get to that gun behind the stone." He added grimly, "Maybe. If they don't decide to shoot you before they go to find out what's happening. I don't believe that's likely. But be ready for anything."

"I will. How much time will you need to get the ledger after I show up at the gate?"

"At least fifteen minutes. We have to make sure Praland isn't anywhere near that Tiger Room. Once we shoot the tiger with the knockout dart, he should be out in five minutes. Then we have to jimmy the lock on the cage and get to the compartment."

"And then get out of there."

"And get to you," Mandak said. "If you're still alive."

"I'll be alive. I want to live, Mandak," she said. "And I want you to live. So be careful with that tiger." She smiled faintly. "Or I may be the one to have to beat down those walls to come and rescue you."

He didn't return her smile. "I can give you a gun, I can give you a bomb. I can't help you stall Praland for those fifteen minutes. That's up to you and it may seem a long fifteen minutes. If he gets suspicious and starts wondering if that's what you're doing, it's all over. Forget giving me my time and play the game his way."

She shook her head. "It has gone his way too long. It has gone my mother's way too long. I'll do what I—" She stopped as she saw the flashing lights in the north sky. "There's your helicopter. Let's hope the pilot didn't forget that knockout dart for the tiger. It's a very strange request."

"He won't. I made that a priority. I was thinking about getting a dart that would kill him, but I was afraid we might have to postpone at the last minute, and that would tell Praland that we knew about the ledger." He started for the clearing. Then he suddenly turned to face her. "I'm not going to waste my breath trying to talk you out of this." His voice was harsh. "But you do everything right. Do you hear me? You don't get emotional because of that bitch of a mother. You think about you and the life you have to live. And maybe you think a little about me and what it would mean to me if you get yourself killed." He turned back and started for the helicopter that was landing. "Do it *right,* Allie."

SANDEK PALACE
8:10 P.M.

Five minutes.

She should be at the palace in five minutes.

Allie's heart was pounding hard.

Dear God, she hoped that Mandak and Sean had managed to get inside and were safe. She hadn't heard from them since early morning, just as they were approaching the palace. Mandak had told her any communication was dangerous.

Assume everything was all right.

Keep to the plan.

Allie drew a deep breath and took out her phone. She pressed the callback for Gina. "I'm about five minutes away from the palace. I told you I'd phone you." She should say something else. "Are you still okay, Mother?"

"I'm fine. But Praland doesn't like the idea of coming outside the walls. You come in, baby."

"No, I told you how it has to be. I have to make sure you'll be safe. According to my map, I seem to be driving toward the west gate. Meet me outside, and we'll talk."

Allie heard her talking to someone in the background. Then Gina was back on the line. "He said he's been having you watched for the past several miles, and you seem to not be trying to cause him a problem. But he still doesn't like it. I'll try to persuade him, but you should really—"

"Outside those walls." Allie hung up.

Praland had been having her watched. Of course he had. Gina could be mesmerizing, but it would be difficult to believe she'd been able to persuade Allie to take this risk for her. He'd think Mandak would be shadowing her.

Instead, she hoped desperately that Mandak was already in the palace and waiting to make his move.

Three more minutes.

TWO MORE MINUTES.

From the dungeon window, Mandak saw Praland and Bruker crossing the garden toward the west gate. Gina was smiling as she came forward to meet them from the guest quarters. No guards in the garden itself.

Yes.

He turned to Sean. "Allie got them outside." But God

knows how long she could keep up the distraction before they closed in on her. He started to wriggle up the narrow tunnel to the window he'd already loosened and unlatched. *"Move."*

ONE MINUTE.

Allie saw her mother come out through the west gate. Praland and Bruker followed closely behind her.

But where was Camano?

Gina was smiling at her, and Allie felt a ripple of shock. Her beauty was no surprise. She had been aware that it had not faded when she'd had that glimpse of her in the Tiger Room. She had expected her to still be beautiful, but if anything, her mother was even more stunning. She looked older, but it was as if maturity had merely enhanced and deepened that glowing beauty. Butterfly. Fairy princess. And her smile had the same warmth and affection it had when she'd been the only caring person in Allie's world. For an instant, Allie felt the same dazzlement she had experienced as a child.

Then she saw Praland step forward to stand beside Gina. Her mother looked up at him and smiled proudly.

Pride that she had delivered what Praland wanted.

Allie's pain was like a dash of ice water, washing away everything but what she had to do.

She slowed the jeep until it finally came to a halt twenty feet from them. "I'm here, Praland."

"So you are." Praland's gaze slowly went over her. "Your photos don't do you justice. You're quite beautiful. Maybe more beautiful than Gina."

"Bullshit."

"No, true. Now throw out any weapons you have on the ground outside the jeep. Bruker, go pick them up."

She had known that would come. She could risk the holster at her calf that held her dagger as long as she didn't get out of the jeep. But she had to give them something. She threw her gun in the dirt, followed by a spray container of mace. Bruker quickly retrieved them and took them back to Praland.

Her hands clenched on the steering wheel. She didn't try to hide it. Showing a few nerves wouldn't hurt. "Now tell me how you and I can come to a deal that will keep you from hurting my mother."

Praland chuckled. "You're either naïve or very cunning. The minute you came within sight of my gates, you lost any bargaining power you might have had. I don't have to give you anything."

Gina laid her hand on Praland's arm. "That may not be true. Don't be unkind to her. You said that she might have value to you because of Mandak. Perhaps you could persuade her to call him and bring him here."

"I don't need your suggestions, Gina. I'm not Camano," he said coldly. "That's exactly what I had in mind. I'm skeptical about the harm you say she could do me with that trick Mandak thought she could pull off. I went through a whole gamut of Devanez so-called mind readers. None of them could touch me. No, that's not the way to get Mandak. He may be angry about having her walk into your trap, but he has a weakness." He smiled at Allie. "He rushed to rescue Simon Walberg. A few phone calls, a body part or two. Let's see how much he'll take before he decides he has to come calling again."

"He won't come. He had only one use for me, and that

ended when I came here." Allie looked at her mother.
"And I'm not naïve. I just want you to let her go. She's my
mother, and I can't seem to stop feeling something for
her. I realize you probably didn't hurt her, but you could."

"Yes, I could," Praland said. "But she's been both
helpful and entertaining. It would be a shame to have
anything happen to her."

"Thank you." Gina smiled at him. "But you wouldn't
do that. I've done everything that I've promised."

"No? I might need a call from her to Mandak. It
depends on whether it would hurt your beautiful daughter to see you in pain."

For an instant, Gina appeared disconcerted. "You're
joking."

"Really?" Praland looked at Allie. "Am I?"

"No, you're not joking. That's why I want her out of
here."

"And I've already refused to discuss any deal." He
took out his gun and pointed it at her. "And I believe it's
time you got out of that jeep and came to join us. I have
a feline friend to whom I'd like to introduce you."

8:22 P.M.

The tiger had fallen unconscious, and his breathing was
steady and rhythmic.

But was his state deep enough? Mandak wondered. It
had taken him longer to go under than it should have.
Almost seven minutes. He had to take a chance. He
couldn't stand here and wait while the clock was ticking,
and Allie was having to hold off Praland.

"I'm going to start jimmying the door of the cage." He

told Sean, who was keeping watch at the window. He started working at the bars. "Any sign of trouble?"

"Not yet. But you may find it inside that cage," Sean said dryly. "It's only been four minutes since the cat went down. He's a strong son of a bitch. He may decide to rouse and—" He stopped and held his breath as the tiger suddenly half lifted his head, then let it fall back. "Go very slowly, Mandak."

Mandak was working quickly, frantically at the lock. "That's no longer an option. Time's running out."

8:23 P.M.

It was too soon, Allie thought in panic. She hadn't been able to stall long enough. She hadn't given Mandak enough time.

Keep calm. Go down another road that might intrigue Praland and keep him occupied for a few minutes more.

Allie looked him in the eye. "I'm not going anywhere with you until we come to an agreement. Put down that gun."

Praland laughed incredulously. "You're not listening."

"I hear you say that my only value to you is as a lure to bring Mandak here. That's a lie."

"We'll see, won't we?"

"Yes. We'll see right now. Because Camano and my mother are right. I can go in and read your memory and almost anyone else's that you tell me to read. My father found that a treasure trove. I don't know how he used that information, but I'm sure you would be able to think of a multitude of uses. We could make a deal. You wouldn't be sorry."

Praland was staring at her curiously. "It might be of interest if it's true."

"It is true, Praland," Gina said quickly. "How many times do I have to tell you?"

He ignored her, his gaze on Allie. "She appears to be certain. I find Gina a little transparent but I'd be interested in just what memories she has in that gorgeous head. Why don't you tell me?"

"Oh, no," Gina said. "I'm different. I'm her mother. She's never been able to read me."

"How unusual." He looked at Allie. "Is that true?"

"I could read her. I've never wanted to do it. I don't want to do it now."

"Then she'd be a perfect case to prove that you're able to do it. Go ahead."

Gina was gazing at her warily.

Go blank. Please don't give me a memory, Mother.

Concentrate.

Nothing.

Dark tunnel . . .

A whooshing, and Allie was there.

Too easy. It had come too easily.

Gina's memories, provoked by that wariness, were clear and without conscience.

Such a pretty black bottle with a gold top.

She'd known she'd have some use for it when she'd seen Camano becoming unmanageable.

White powder mixed with his coke.

Everyone would think it an overdose.

Just a little more, and she'd be through with Camano. He'd become such a bore and no use to her at all. Praland could take his place and give her more than—

Murder.

The shock sent Allie spiraling back out of the tunnel.

"Evidently not pleasant," Praland said. "Would you care to disclose it?"

"No." She looked at Gina. "I was wondering where Camano was."

"He's ill," she said quickly. "We didn't need him."

"No, I can tell you don't."

"Our lovely Gina has actually turned pale." Praland was laughing. "I'm beginning to believe you might actually have read her memories." He shrugged. "But she's your mother. Could be different. That's someone else's memory, not mine."

"You, too," Allie said quietly. "Test me. Pull up a memory you want me to identify and think about it."

"A circus trick?"

"Test me."

He was already testing her, she realized.

His memories were sweeping forward, enveloping her.

Dark tunnel. Dark tunnel.

Screams. Agony.

She almost threw up as she read the memory he'd brought up for her.

Get away. Get away. Get away.

She jerked herself free and leaned her head on the steering wheel.

"Damn you."

"I just wanted you to know what was in store for you if Mandak doesn't cooperate. Tell me about it."

"Simon Walberg. The night you were torturing him."

"Amazing. I'm feeling quite vulnerable."

And that was dangerous for Allie.

Mandak, where are you?

It had been over fifteen minutes.

He'd be here. Distract Praland.

"I wouldn't be fool enough to put you in a vulnerable position. I'd be working for you." She glanced at Bruker. "Would you like me to read his memories? I imagine he has quite a few that he wouldn't want you to know about."

Bruker's eyes widened in alarm. "Kill the bitch. Or let me do it. Can't you see she's a big-time threat to you?"

"Or to you," Praland said softly. "Interesting possibility. I'll have to think which—"

Kaboom.

The explosion from inside the walls rocked the ground.

Another blast immediately followed.

Mandak! Setting off the signal that he had the ledger and to draw Praland away from her.

Thank God.

Praland was cursing, already running for the gate. Gina was right after him. "What the hell's happening? Bruker, get those guards in here!"

Allie dove out of the jeep and rolled under the vehicle.

Get to that fifth stone in the wall, take out the gun, and fire a bullet into that bomb.

But Bruker wasn't following Praland. He was coming toward her, firing under the jeep.

Wait until he got closer, then roll out and grab his legs and bring him down.

"Got too smart, didn't you?" Bruker asked. "Let's see how smart you are after I blow your head off."

She braced herself to launch.

And the wall behind her exploded with a tremendous blast.

It knocked Bruker to the ground.

Go after him.

But Mandak was already on top of Bruker, his hands on his throat.

He must have set off that bomb in the wall that she had been struggling to reach, she realized.

The next instant, Mandak had his knife out, and the blade was sinking into Bruker's chest.

Then he was jumping off him and pulling Allie from beneath the jeep. "Come on, I don't want to leave you here. Praland's men are going to be all over the place. We have to get back to Sean. I left the ledger with him and sent him back down into the dungeon." He was pulling her through the nearly destroyed wall. "But Praland is going to check that Tiger Room for the ledger, then send his men all over the palace. I have to take him out before he gives that order."

Smoke.

Acrid smell of chemicals.

Allie could dimly see armed men in camouflage gear moving around the garden and over the walls. Bombs were exploding at several points near the dungeon windows in the garden, and the smoke was getting thicker.

And so was the confusion and misdirection, she thought gratefully.

They had reached the terrace, and Mandak pulled her over the flagstones toward the Tiger Room.

They heard Praland cursing before they entered the room.

He stood before the door of the gilt cage, which was hanging off its hinges. He was staring down at the tiger, still unconscious on the floor of the cage.

"He's not dead?" Gina was standing close beside him. "He was so pretty. I think he's still breathing. But you can get another one if he is dead, can't you?"

"You fool." Praland lifted his gaze to the empty compartment in the cage ceiling. "Shut up and get away from me. I've got to get it back."

"You don't mean that. I'm here to help you," Gina said. "From now on, everything I do will be to help you, Praland. Didn't I bring Teresa here for you?"

"Yes, you did. And me, too," Mandak said from the doorway as he barreled forward into the room. "Get down, Allie!"

"You son of a bitch." Praland whirled and raised his gun, dodging behind the velvet couch.

Gina screamed and dropped to the floor.

"You think you'll keep that ledger?" Praland shouted. "I'll find it, and I'll burn it in front of you while I cut off your nuts." He got off a shot that splintered the doorjamb beside Allie. "And then I'll start on that freak that you brought here to trip me up."

"No, you won't." Mandak was moving, crawling across the floor. "Because you're a dead man, Praland."

"Crazy. Bruker will be here in a minute with my men." He got off another shot, which thudded against the velvet cushion inches from Mandak's head. "I have an army, and you have nothing."

"Bruker is in hell. He won't be coming to help you." He tilted his head. "And by the sound of the firing and shouting out there in the garden, I think your so-called army is about to join him. Renata decided it was time to take you down. I do believe the troops have arrived."

Allie could hear the sound of helicopter rotors overhead.

But it could be too late for Mandak if Praland got to him. She instinctively started to crawl toward him.

"No," Mandak said sharply. "Allie, let me do it."

She kept crawling and reached into her calf holster for her knife. "I'm only a backup. I won't let him kill you, Mandak."

"You can see how worried she is," Praland said. "She's smarter than you. She realizes that you're nothing compared to me. I'll take you down and cut you into—"

He grunted with pain as Mandak dove over the couch on top of him. His gun discharged, and Allie saw Mandak flinch.

Shot. Mandak was shot, she thought frantically.

But Mandak straightened, and the gun flew out of Praland's hand and across the room.

Praland's fist arced upward, striking Mandak in the jaw. He pushed Mandak off him and went for the gun.

"Here!" Gina had the gun and was pushing it toward Praland. "I told you that I—" She screamed as Allie's dagger entered her hand. She jerked her hand away from the gun and cradled her bloody palm. "You *hurt* me."

"I hope so." Allie picked up Praland's gun. "Don't move, or I'll do it again."

There was no chance for Allie to use the gun.

Praland cursed as Mandak brought him down once more. Praland's eyes were glittering wildly in his contorted face. "Look at you. You're bleeding. I did that. I hope you bleed to death. I'll get out of this, and I'll find that ledger. The killing will go on. It will never stop. I'll call you with name after name, body after body."

"It will stop." Mandak's hands were around Praland's throat. "Now." His grip tightened. "I wish I could drag it out, make it more painful. But I have to get out of here and protect the ledger from that scum you keep around you. So this will have to do."

Praland's eyes were bulging from their sockets as he fought for air. "No!"

"Yes." Mandak's hands twisted, and Praland's neck broke.

Mandak sat back on his heels and drew a deep breath. "Burn in hell, you bastard." The next moment, he was getting off Praland's limp body and turning to Allie. "Come on, we've got to get to Sean and get that ledger out of the palace. All hell's breaking loose out there, and I promised Renata it would be safe."

She was already on her feet, her gaze on his shoulder, which had taken Praland's bullet. "You're bleeding. We should stop and—"

"Later." He moved toward the door. "I promise I won't bleed to death. I wouldn't give Praland the satisfaction."

"Camano? He wasn't out there to meet me."

"I'll have Renata's people pick him up. He won't survive the day."

As Allie started to follow him, she glanced at her mother. "He might not have survived it anyway."

"You're leaving me here, Teresa?" Gina asked incredulously. "I'm hurt. You did this to me. Can't you see I'm bleeding?"

"I can see it," Allie said. "But no one survives better than you do, Mother. I'm not going to worry about you." She asked mockingly, "Why don't you call Camano and tell him to come and take care of you?"

"I may do that," she said defiantly. "You're right, I always survive. I don't need any of you."

Allie nodded. "But we all have to learn to survive you. Good-bye, Mother."

She hurried to catch up with Mandak.

CHAPTER SIXTEEN

GINA COULDN'T BELIEVE IT. How could they do this to her? Her hand was throbbing with pain, and she was bleeding. She would need a doctor, then a plastic surgeon to take away the ugliness. But first she would need help from someone. She glanced at Praland. All his fault. He should have been able to kill Mandak, and this would never have happened to her.

Camano.

He was her only salvation now. She would have to use him until she found someone more powerful to meet her needs. She reached in her pocket, drew out her cell, and dialed Camano. He answered immediately. "What the hell's happening? It looks like a small war is going on in that garden."

"It's terrible. You have to help me. Are you in our suite?"

"Yes, I just woke up. I'm groggy as hell. Where are you?"

"The Tiger Room. Praland's dead. I'm hurt. Come and help me, then we'll get out of here."

"Right." He hung up.

It would be all right. She had handled it.

Camano opened the door of the Tiger Room only a
few minutes later. He glanced at Praland. "Who did it?"

"Mandak." She held out her hand. "And Teresa did
this to me. The bitch. I'm bleeding. Bandage it."

"I don't have time." He walked over to the cage and
looked down at the tiger. "I was afraid he was dead. But
I see he's stirring. He's opening those big yellow eyes . . ."

"You don't have time?" She stared at him in outrage.
"What do you mean? I'm hurt. Take care of me."

He went over to the terrace door, opened it, shot the
outside bolt, and closed it again. "I took care of you for
a number of years, Gina. I might have continued since
you're so entertaining." He went toward the hall door.
"Then you got greedy and decided that you didn't need
me any longer. But you couldn't risk making me angry."
He reached into his pocket and pulled out a small black
bottle with a gold lid. "I'm not a fool, Gina. I know about
drugs. I've been having strong aftereffects from the
coke. Grogginess after waking, dizziness, increased
heartbeat. Today, I decided to go hunting for answers."
He held up the bottle. "I found it in your cosmetic bag. I
tasted it. Very carefully. It was bitter, and if I sent it to a
lab, I'd bet it would come back with a skull and cross-
bones on it."

"You're wrong. You're just guessing." She moistened
her lips. "I'll prove it to you. Just get me out of here, and
we'll talk, and I'll show you—"

He was shaking his head. "You'll show me nothing.
That's over, Gina." He slipped the black bottle back in
his pocket. "But I'll have the lab check this when I get
back to the States. However, it may be too late for you."

"What do you mean?"

"You've always been proud of being a survivor. Let's

see how really good you are." He looked at her hand. "Blood can be so appetizing." His gaze went to the tiger in the cage. "The cage door is broken. It would take only a swipe of his paw, and it would fly open. The tiger is going to wake up any minute."

She started for the hall door. "I'm getting out of here."

"No." He held up the key. "That wouldn't be a test at all. The terrace door is locked. I'm going to lock this one as I leave. We'll see how well you survive, Gina."

"No!" The hall door was closing, and she heard the sound of the key turning in the lock. "Camano, come back here!"

She heard him laughing as he walked down the hall.

She started to jerk at the doorknob. He couldn't do this to her. When she got out of here, she'd kill him. He was a complete—

She froze as she heard a sound behind her.

Soft, but heavy.

Like a tiger getting to his feet.

Silence.

Then she heard him batting at the broken door.

She screamed.

"HE'LL BE ALL RIGHT, ALLIE," Sean said as he sat back from putting the temporary bandage on Mandak's shoulder. "As good as you can be with a bullet in your shoulder." His brows rose. "Very clumsy of you, Mandak. My respect is crumbling into the dust."

"That had better be a decent bandage. I told Allie I wouldn't bleed to death." His gaze went to the walls of the palace a good distance away from the jungle to which they'd run several minutes ago. "I think that the fighting's dying down. We should be hearing from Renata soon. I texted her with our location a few minutes ago."

"When you should have been still, so that he could get that bandage right," Allie said. She looked down at the ledger on the ground beside him. The ledger's brown leather was simple and unembossed, it appeared old but still smooth and rich from the careful handling of centuries of Devanezes. "It's the first time I've seen it. It doesn't look as if it has the power to cause all this trouble and disaster."

"Praland caused the disaster." Mandak's hand gently touched the book. "The ledger has saved thousands of Devanez families and individuals through the centuries. It will save more in the future. It just has to be—"

"You have it?" Renata was hurrying toward them through the jungle. Her eyes fell on the ledger, and she broke into a run. "Thank God." She snatched up the journal. "The children's names and locations?"

"They're in there," Mandak said. "Sean glanced through the last pages when he was waiting for us down in that dungeon. He said Praland was very precise."

"Bastard." Renata was looking for herself, rapidly turning the pages. "I'll send out people right away to retrieve them before they can be moved." Her gaze shifted to Mandak's shoulder. "You said everything was okay in your text. You don't look okay. What have you done to yourself?"

"A bullet," Sean said. "Praland. I've just been telling Mandak how clumsy he was."

"He needs to get that bullet out," Allie said curtly. "So take your ledger and get him out of here, Renata."

Renata's brows lifted. "Orders? I'm not accustomed to taking orders, Allie."

"Bullshit. Do you expect me to kowtow to you because you snap your fingers, and all your people jump? You know I'm right. You'd have said the same thing the minute you got here if you hadn't been dazzled by that damn book."

"True." She chuckled. "Maybe I'm getting a little arrogant. It goes with the territory." She turned to Mandak. "Can you walk? My helicopter is in the clearing. I'll take you to Megan's clinic for treatment."

"He can walk." Sean was already helping Mandak to his feet. "We wouldn't want to pamper him. He's prone to arrogance, too."

"I've noticed." Renata started through the brush toward the clearing. "It's a wonder we get along so well." Then her hand lovingly caressed the journal. "Or maybe not. You give great and wonderful gifts, Mandak. Thank you. You know how much this means to me."

"I know."

"Stop talking." Allie was suddenly beside Mandak, putting his good arm around her shoulders. "Get him to the helicopter. Lean on me, Mandak."

He smiled. "Delighted. I don't mind being pampered. I deserve it. We all deserve it. It was one hell of a—" He stopped, his head lifting. "Smoke?" His gaze went back to the palace. "Renata?"

Allie's gaze followed his, and her eyes widened in surprise.

Fire. Flames were leaping toward the sky. In a few more minutes, the entire palace would be engulfed.

"I told them to torch it," Renata said grimly. "The entire place stinks of corruption and killings and torture. I don't want a stone left standing to remind anyone that Praland was ever here."

"Prisoners?"

"Praland's men were all running for their lives when I left the palace. We'll hunt them down and dispose of them if they survived. I don't want anyone taking over like Praland did when his partner Molino was killed. It stops here."

If they survived.

Allie had told Gina that she had to survive on her own before she had left her.

Was she one of the people fleeing through these jungles? If she was caught, would she manage to manipulate her way to some sort of safety?

"Allie?" Mandak said.

Her gaze shifted to his face. She knew what he was wondering. Renata's words had sparked a response in her that was the pure instinct to reach out to Gina. And Mandak knew Allie so well, her past, her present, every emotion that had guided her through those years. The chains that had held her to Gina.

She slowly shook her head. "She's on her own, Mandak." She tightened her arm around his waist and looked straight ahead. "Let's get you to that helicopter."

"THE OPERATION WENT WELL, no complications. But Mandak will have to stay overnight for observation," Megan said as she came back to her office, where Allie was waiting. "He's in Room 8."

Relief surged through her. "May I go back to see him?"

"I'm surprised you ask." Megan smiled. "You were issuing orders all over the place when you brought him to me."

"Renata complained about that, too."

"Renata would. I understand that it's part of your basic nature. I would have quashed it if it had gotten in my way. Besides, I was feeling very warm and benevolent toward you at the time. Renata told me that you'd helped to get the ledger." She went across the room to gaze at the child's photo on the bulletin board. "We've got them, Elizabeth," she said softly. "They'll all be safe. Rest in peace."

Allie felt her eyes sting. "Yes, rest in peace." She swallowed hard. "So what's next for you, Megan?"

"I'm not sure. Like everyone else in the family, I've been geared to fight Praland and do damage control. It seems strange not to have to worry about that any longer. I guess I'll stay here at the clinic for a while until I'm sure it's in good hands. After that, I have some research to do about my particular talent that I had to put on hold." Her brilliant smile suddenly lit her face. "And I'm going to grab my husband, check into a hotel in the south of France, and make love to him for a month, maybe longer."

"That sounds like a great topping for a plan."

"The best part of it." She shrugged. "All the rest is duty and discovering ways to make life make sense. But Grady *is* my life." She checked her watch. "And I have a date to call him in ten minutes." She made a face. "God, it will be good not to have this long-distance marriage."

"Mandak," Allie reminded her. "You didn't answer me. May I go back to see him?"

"Sure. But he may still be a little woozy from the anesthesia." She grinned. "Or maybe it will make him mellow. Wouldn't that be different?"

"Yes, it would." Allie headed for the door. "And unprecedented."

Two minutes later, she was carefully opening the door to Mandak's room. There was only a dim light illuminating the darkness, but she could see that Mandak had his eyes open, and they instantly focused on her.

"Get me out of here," he said impatiently.

Definitely not woozy. Certainly not mellow.

"Can't do it." She sat down in the chair next to his bed. "She said one night's observation."

"I'm fine, dammit."

"Talk to Megan. But she's on the phone with her husband right now and won't be very cooperative if you interrupt her."

He scowled. "I'll wait."

She smiled. "I'm sure she'll appreciate that." He was entirely sharp, entirely Mandak. Lord, she was glad. "Do you really feel fine? Pain? Do you need medication? Anything?"

He was silent. "I need to look at you. I need you to hold my hand. There are several other needs on my list, but I don't think you'd meet them right now."

She reached over and took his hand. "I need this, too." She felt an instant sense of rightness, bonding. "But you should probably not talk, or Megan will kick out."

"She's busy talking to Grady."

"There's a nurse down the hall."

He lifted her hand to his lips. "I'll risk it."

"Why? Just rest, Mandak."

"If I doze off, I'm afraid you won't be here when I wake up. I can't let that happen. There are things to be settled, and I don't want to have to run halfway across the world to find you."

"What things?"

"You. Me. What else? That's all that's important." His

hand tightened on hers. "You're thinking that it's over, done. That all the years and the bonding will just fade away into the past. I'm not going to let that happen."

She went still. "Why not?"

"Because I can't give you up. It has to go on." His voice was low, intense. "I . . . think I love you. I know you're still wary of me in some ways. But you do feel something pretty close to the way I feel. All I'm asking is that you stay around, give it a chance to grow."

"And where would you be? You're a Searcher, and that's not going to change. Am I supposed to wait around and be at your beck and call?"

"We can work it out. I'll do—"

"No, I've already worked it out," she said firmly. "While I was sitting waiting for Megan to dig that bullet out of you. I have things to do with my life."

He was tense. "I'm not letting you go."

"Be quiet and listen. The first thing I have to do is go back home and contact Dantlow. I'm done with hiding. If Camano is out there, I'll go after him. If not, I have a head full of hideous memories that belong to some of the biggest crime families in the U.S. Dantlow will get what he's always wanted. I'll testify before a grand jury."

"You'll be a target. You'd have to go undercover again with Witness Protection."

She shook her head. "I'll let Dantlow cover for me, but I have a different sort of witness protection in mind."

His eyes narrowed. "And that is?"

"Renata. I'll go to work for her and let her protect me." She smiled. "She'd be far better than Dantlow. She knows all about secrets. After all, she's the Keeper of the Ledger."

He gave a low whistle. "You might make it work."

"I will make it work. Because Renata has all kinds of truly exceptional agents at her disposal." She paused. "And tops on her list is you, Mandak. You should be right at home managing my protection." She tilted her head. "If you choose to accept the assignment."

He tugged at her hand. "Come here."

She stood up and moved to sit on his bed. "Is that a yes?"

"I need the words."

The bonding was there between them, strong and enduring as it would always be. Still, she would say the words. "We're both afraid to commit. But I'll be braver and take the plunge." She looked directly into his eyes. "I don't 'think' I love you. I do love you. But I don't know all the facets or ins and outs of it. So I have to learn it." She smiled. "Megan had a great idea. She's going to take Grady to the south of France and make love to him for a solid month. I don't care where we go, but I'd bet we'll come out of that month knowing what we are together."

"No bet," he said. "And I do love you, Allie Girard."

"See? It's already starting." She kicked off her shoes. "Now try to scoot over without hurting yourself. I'm going to lie down and hold you for a while."

He took her in his arms. "That nurse will be scandalized."

"She'll get over it. I'm not going to have sex with you. I'm not an exhibitionist."

"What a disappointment."

"Or maybe I will." She sighed. "No, that would be totally without conscience considering your delicate state."

"Delicate? Is a demonstration in order?"

She cuddled closer to him. "The only demonstration

I want is the one you're doing now. I feel treasured and loved."

"And you are . . . forever."

Don't cry. Accept the gift. Give it in return.

Live every minute with joy and love, Natalie had said.

Oh, I'm starting, Natalie. Can you tell?

How am I doing?

Read on for an excerpt from the next book by
Iris Johansen and Roy Johansen

THE NAKED EYE

Available in July 2015 in hardcover
from St. Martin's Press!

CHAPTER ONE

GOT ONE FOR YOU.

Kendra Michaels stared at the text message on her phone.

Damn.

She threw her legs over the edge of the bed and studied the message header. It was from Martin Stokes, a San Diego Police Department homicide detective. He'd included an address and a few details.

She took a few minutes to steady her breathing, trying to gain control. She was still trembling from her nightmare, and her face was covered with sweat. And here in her hands a real-life nightmare beckoned. She didn't have to go, of course; a glance at the crime scene photos and a reading of the case file would probably tell her everything she needed to know.

Probably.

Who in the hell was she kidding? She knew she was going.

No matter how horrific the scene was, it couldn't compare with the beast still taunting her in her dreams.

A quick shower and then she'd be out of here. She reached for her jeans and headed for the bathroom.

* * *

"I DIDN'T THINK you were going to show." Detective Stokes lifted the police tape for Kendra to duck under and join him in the driveway of the one-story craftsman home. Four squad cars were parked on the street, flashers pounding the house with out-of-sync strobes of red and blue lights. The scene was crawling with uniformed officers, detectives, and forensics experts.

Kendra shrugged. "What else would I have to do at three-thirty in the morning?"

"I could think of lots of things. Especially since you don't *have* to be here."

What did he know? She felt the familiar chill. "I do have to be here."

She tried to suppress the shudder, but Stokes's narrowed stare told her the effort was unsuccessful. "Sure, but you should be thanking Detective Kael. He's the one who beat it into my brain that I should contact you if I encountered any killings of a serial or ritualistic nature. He thinks you're the real deal."

"Kael is a good man."

"He's a rotten softball player, but other than that . . ." He motioned for her to follow him up the driveway. "I trust him most of the time. But you know I've heard so many incredible things about you that it's hard to separate the truth from the bullshit."

She half-smiled. "Bank on the bullshit."

"I don't think so. Tell me, were you really blind for the first twenty years of your life?"

"Yes."

"Completely blind?"

"Yep. I'd never seen a thing in my life."

"That's amazing. Kael says it was some kind of stem cell surgery."

She nodded. "In England. They did a lot of the early work in corneal regeneration techniques."

"I've always heard that blind people developed their other senses to compensate. And that's how you pick up on stuff most other people don't."

She wished he'd just drop it. Patience. At least he was pleasant enough and she might need him to notify her again if he ran across one of the target murders. "I guess so. But I don't think my senses of hearing, smell, taste, or touch are better than anyone else's. I just had to use them to make my way in the world."

"Let's hold up here for a second." Stokes held up his hand as he looked inside the open front door. "The photographer's doing his thing."

"Sure."

Stokes crossed his arms in front of him. "From what I understand, you're also pretty sharp about things you see."

"Well, I just don't take things for granted. Things I see aren't just details to me. They're *gifts*. They're part of the world that was closed off to me for so long. I guess I just want to take in everything."

He grimaced. "I'm afraid you'll get more than you bargained for in there. It's not a pretty scene."

She just wanted to get to it, dammit. Kendra glanced at the driveway next door, where another detective was talking to a distraught-looking bald man in sweatpants and a Padres T-shirt.

"That's the husband?"

"Yeah. He fell asleep watching TV upstairs in bed. A little before two, he came downstairs and found his wife's body in the kitchen. It's a mess."

"He has no clue who could have done this?"

"No. His wife was an elementary schoolteacher, no enemies that he knows of."

"Maybe *he* has enemies. What does he do?"

"Residential mortgage manager at a bank." Stokes glanced back inside. "All clear."

Kendra followed him through a small living room, carpeted with a thick burnt-orange rug that probably wasn't even in style when laid fifteen years before. She scanned the room. Photographs, vacation souvenirs, and two watercolor prints probably purchased from a cruise ship auction.

Through a doorway on the far wall, she heard at least half a dozen pairs of footsteps. No, she self-corrected, more like eight.

Stokes motioned her through the doorway. Kendra walked through and nodded her greeting at the seven men and one woman working the crime scene. She recognized most of them from other recent investigations. They'd become much more at ease with her now that they knew she wasn't interested in grabbing credit from them.

That's never what this was about.

Two forensics men were crouched in front of the open refrigerator. Upon seeing Kendra, they stood and moved away to reveal what had brought them all there:

Thirty-five-year-old Marissa Kohler, lying in a pool of her own blood.

Kendra had seen many murder victims over the years, many at much more gruesome scenes than this one, but it still hit her like a kick in the stomach. She hoped she'd never become too callous to feel that horror. This woman had probably just gone through the motions on her last day on earth, with nary an idea that it would all soon come to a horrific end.

Detach. Focus.

Time to see if *he* did this. The monster.

Kendra crouched next to the corpse, trying to avoid the splatter trails on the tile floor. Dressed in sleeper shorts and a long T-shirt, the victim was lying in front of the open refrigerator as if attacked while getting a midnight snack. Her hands were near her face, suggesting a defensive position even after falling. A pair of round spectacles rested on the floor about five feet away. Obviously, the victim's glasses, confirmed by the distinctive mark on her nose that matched the spectacles' arched bridge.

Stokes pointed toward the open back door, which was splintered as if kicked open with a fierce kick. "Point of entry over there. No curtains on the back windows, so the killer could have spotted her in here."

"Maybe." Kendra leaned over and examined the victim's wounds. The woman's throat had been opened in five horizontal gashes, plus over a dozen punctures to the torso.

Who did this to you, Marissa? Could it really have been . . . him?

Show me. Give me something. Anything . . .

Her eyes flicked from Marissa's face to the back door. Of course.

Kendra stood up and brushed herself off. "Thank you all. I'm sorry for disturbing you." She turned and walked out of the room.

Stokes ran after her. "Wait. That's it?"

"Yes."

He grabbed her arm. "Are you gonna let me in on the secret?"

She stopped in the living room and looked back through the doorway. "This isn't the work of a serial killer. Certainly not the one I'm looking for."

"Then whose work is it?"

"Her husband's."

Stokes lowered his voice. "What?"

"That scene in the kitchen was staged. Check upstairs. She was killed there."

"How do you figure that?"

"The smell of blood is wafting down that staircase. Sickly sweet and more than a bit metallic. Plus a useless attempt to cover it up with half a can of Lysol Powder Fresh."

He sniffed the air. "I smell the Lysol . . ."

"I'm sure you smell the blood, too. You just don't realize it. Send your forensics team up there with Lumi- nol. The victim also has faint rug burns on the back of her heels. She was dragged down the stairs, posed, and maybe even stabbed a few more times post-mortem. It looks like there are punctures without much bleeding."

"And the door?"

"He knew enough to go outside and kick it in to give the appearance of forced entry. But he obviously didn't go any farther outside than the patio. The ground in the yard is a muddy mess, but there are no footprints out there."

"Are you sure? It's dark."

"The porch lights give at least fifteen feet of visibil- ity. Trust me, no one approached the house from the yard. And I spotted a tiny shard of orange rubber on the splin- tered door frame."

He stared at her. "Orange rubber."

She nodded. "Surely you noticed the obnoxious orange rubber soles of the athletic shoes her husband is wearing?"

"Holy shit," Stokes whispered.

"I'm done," she said wearily. "Good night, Detective. I'm sure you'll have no trouble taking it from here."

Stokes didn't answer as he dashed out the door.

Kendra left the house and walked slowly down the driveway. She was in no hurry to get home. She was disappointed and tired, but there might be only nightmares when she got back to sleep.

She cast a glance back at Stokes as he approached the husband, who was still playing the part of the bereaved widower. The guy was an amateur; he'd undoubtedly left many more clues behind, and the cops would have their case against him sewn up in a matter of hours.

"Finished already?" A familiar voice called out mockingly to her from the street.

She let out an exasperated sigh. "Adam Lynch . . . Seriously?"

"Hey, I don't like your tone. You're hurting my feelings here."

She turned back and saw Lynch leaning against her car. While everyone else on the scene was middle-of-the-night bedraggled, Lynch's every dark hair was in place. Probably just the way he rolled out of bed, the bastard. He wore jeans, a pullover sweater, loafers, and a sexy, high-wattage smile that seemed terribly out of place at a grim murder scene.

"Feelings?" she said. "Why would I think you actually have feelings?"

"You got me there." He checked his watch. "By the way,

you wrapped up this case in about two and a half minutes. That's a new record, isn't it?"

"I didn't come here to wrap up the case."

His smile faded. "I know that, Kendra. I hear you've been visiting a lot of murder scenes lately."

"Not because I enjoy it."

"I know that, too."

She let the silence hang between them. "He'll be back, Lynch. We both know it."

"It's been four months."

"Colby's methodical. He's had years to plan his next move. What's another few months to him?"

Lynch's gaze slid away from her. "You've got a point."

"You don't believe me, do you?"

"I didn't say that."

"You don't need to. It's obvious you don't believe Colby is really still alive."

"If you believe it, I believe it."

She slammed her palms onto her car hood. "That's one of the most patronizing things anyone has ever said to me. And believe me, when I was blind, I heard a lot of patronizing things."

His gaze shifted back to her. "I mean it, Kendra," he said quietly. "I do trust your judgment."

"Even if the California Department of Corrections doesn't."

"Colby was their prisoner, and it was their responsibility to put him to death. For them to admit that they may have botched it and let a convicted serial killer escape, well, that's asking a lot."

"The prison's attending physician and his wife were

found dead less than forty-eight hours later. I can't believe they still think that was a coincidence."

"It appeared to be an accident. And even you couldn't find any evidence to prove otherwise."

Kendra nodded. "Colby and his partner were too smart to leave behind any evidence. The doctor administered a drug to slow Colby's heart and pronounced him dead in front of a roomful of witnesses, and a rented hearse drove him right out of the main gates of San Quentin State Prison."

"If you could offer any proof of this, I guarantee you that a lot of people would listen."

"I tried." Her fists clenched in frustration. "No one cared."

"I cared, Kendra."

"To a point."

"You weren't able to get anywhere with the cremation service?"

"No. A body with the correct paperwork was delivered to them that night. The crematorium didn't fingerprint the body or do anything to confirm the corpse's identity. The system doesn't account for the fact that there are monsters out there that can drive to skid row and easily come out with a dead body no one will miss."

"Again, still no proof."

"Even you have to admit that there was enough to follow up on. Colby's partner, Myatt, had the medication in his possession, and he had the prison physician's name in his notebook. Before he died, he as much as told me Colby was still alive."

"He could have been taunting you. He had a history of that."

"That's what the FBI thinks. I thought you were on my side."

"I am. That's why I'm out here at four in the morning."

"So the FBI sent you to tell me to stop making waves and lay off—"

"No. For God's sake, I'm not the FBI's errand boy."

"Funny you should say that, when you're the go-to errand boy for any government agency that decides to pay your fee. Who is it this week? FBI, CIA, NSA?"

"None. This is all about you, Kendra."

"Is it?" She stared at him for a long moment. She'd gotten to know Lynch fairly well during the course of their two previous cases together. So well that she'd found herself confused about how much was sexual attraction and how much was the stimulation of working with a tough, intelligent partner who managed to strike a rare note in her mind and soul. In this moment she was feeling a little of both but principally she was aware of a new vibe from him. He was . . . truly concerned. Concerned about her. The surge of warmth she felt at the realization made her smile. "You didn't look this worried even when you thought a killer was stalking me."

"This may be worse. Colby has gotten under your skin. In your head. Are you still having the dreams?"

She looked away and didn't answer. He was the only one she'd told about her nightmares.

"You've been having that dream for months . . . He pulls you back to that gully night after night. But it shouldn't be a nightmare. That's the night you caught the bastard. That's where you beat him, Kendra. Literally, I wish you'd killed him with that rock."

"That makes two of us. I thought prison was the best place for him. I was wrong."

"Come back to my house. You'll feel safe there."

"I can't hide out in your suburban fortress for the rest of my life, Lynch. And if you remember, that's where those awful dreams began."

"Maybe that's where they can end."

"Besides, your Asian bikini model girlfriend might not like me hanging around."

"Ashley is almost never in town these days. Her career has taken off. She actually wants to meet you."

"I might say that she just wants to size up the competition, but women that beautiful don't really have competition."

Lynch stepped closer to her. "You're every bit as beautiful as she is, Kendra."

She looked up at him. His sudden closeness was disturbingly intimate.

Too disturbing, she admitted to herself. Damn him.

She made herself look away. "Now I know you're patronizing me. I don't have all that many fashion designers jetting me off to the French Riviera for photo shoots." She smiled. "I've seen her picture in a few magazines lately. Ashley has branched out from swimsuits to cocktail dresses and athletic wear."

"Enough about her," he said roughly. "You're the one I'm worried about."

"Don't be."

"Then stop this."

"Stop what?"

He waved his arm toward the crime scene. "This. Dropping everything and running at the first sign of a bloody corpse. There was a time that the cops and the FBI had to beg you to come help them out on their cases. Now they can't keep you away."

"I assure you that they make me feel very welcome."

"Dammit, you know what I mean."

"You're damn right, I do." She stared him in the eye. "It's because I know Colby will be back. He *needs* to kill. It's part of who he is. He can hide for only so long. When he resurfaces, I need to be there."

"And you will be. But for now, just let the cops and the FBI do their job. They're good at it. They have labs, worldwide databases, and lots of manpower. Trust them."

"How can I? When they don't even believe he's alive? They're not even looking for him."

"He may not even be in the country. You can visit every crime scene in the state, but it won't mean anything if he's killing people in Budapest."

Kendra leaned wearily against her car. "I know. I've been spending a lot of time combing the Web for any sign of him."

Lynch shook his head. "You need to take a step back. Please. This isn't good for you. God, you look tired."

"It's almost four AM. Of course I look tired. You're the freak here for looking so damned chipper."

He slipped his hands into his pockets and shrugged. "Let's go to breakfast. Ever been to Brian's 24?"

She laughed. "I'm going to bed."

"That's even better." His smile was both intimate and mischievous. "Whatever you want, Kendra."

"By myself. In my own place."

"Okay, fine." He nodded toward the detectives, who were putting the husband in the backseat of a squad car. "But the next time you feel compelled to barge in on someone else's murder scene, give me a call."

"Why? So you can stop me?"

"I know better than that. So I can go with you. Which is a hell of a lot better than trailing after you." He turned and moved away. "Think about it. I always thought we made a pretty good team . . ."

THE SKY HAD BEGUN TO lighten by the time Kendra made it back to her condo in the Gaslamp Quarter. She was already wound up by the double-punch of the crime scene and Lynch's unexpected appearance, but the sunlight's psychological effect would soon make it even more difficult for her to get any sleep. The first year she'd had her sight, she'd covered her bedroom windows with aluminum foil to keep the daylight from poking around her curtains and nudging her awake. She had moved beyond that, but once awake, it was still tough for her to go to sleep once it was light outside.

Might be time to invest in blackout curtains, or at least a jumbo roll of aluminum foil.

It would be more difficult to put Lynch out of her mind. How in the hell did he know she'd be there?

Of course he knew. He was Adam Lynch, and he had connections everywhere.

A light flashed on the phone in her living room, indicating a message had been received while she was gone. Between 3:30 and 4:30 in the morning. Probably someone from the crime scene she had just left. Or possibly her mother, who was presently at a conference in Amsterdam and frequently forgot to take into account the time difference.

She picked up the phone and checked the Caller ID: Fresno Police Department.

Another murder scene? Fresno was over two hundred miles away; she hadn't cast her net that wide. She tried to remember if she even knew anyone on the force there.

No, she was sure she didn't.

And if there was an active scene, they had to know there was no way she could get there quickly. So why call in the middle of the night?

Kendra retrieved the voice mail, and there was only a brief message asking her to call Sergeant Hank Filardi at the Fresno PD at her earliest convenience.

She stared at the cordless phone in her hand.

No.

Lynch was right. She needed to step back. Whatever it was, it could wait a few hours while she tried to salvage what was left of this night.

She put down the phone.

TODOS SANTOS, MEXICO

VICTOR CHILDRESS

He stared at the name on the ID card he had just purchased. Victor Childress. Not a name he would have chosen for himself but it would do.

He pocketed the passport and turned toward the pounding surf. He couldn't see the waves crashing on the dark beach, though he could hear them. He took a deep breath. It should have been refreshing, but it wasn't. It was like inhaling salt and dirt.

He couldn't wait to leave this place.

Less than an hour from San Diego, yet a world away. A shit hole to be sure, but it suited his purposes. No one knew him here, and no one would even think of looking

for him. And after all those years in that prison, he needed the time to recharge his batteries and make preparations for his return.

It was time. Years of planning had finally led to this moment.

At his feet, a chunky Mexican man struggled to catch his breath as he rolled in a puddle of his own blood. The man's lungs had collapsed and he would survive only another minute or so.

He pocketed his knife and took another look at the forged California driver's license. The dying man had done magnificent work, but he couldn't be allowed to live. Things had progressed too far to be derailed by an overtalkative tradesman.

He stepped over the dying man and walked across the warm sand. The wind suddenly kicked up, as if heralding the start of his journey.

He felt a surge of exhilaration. It was all coming together.

The waiting was over.

Eric Colby smiled. "This is it, Kendra," he whispered. "Can you feel it? You will soon. This will be our masterpiece . . ."